Rosita's Way

A Novel by John H. Gray

Website: www.johnsnovels.com

ISBN Number: 978-0-995238756

Part 1

Innocent Evil Begins

Chapter 1

Nos Grande Village

It was hot and dusty in the small South American village. Swirls of red dust drifted up the narrow path that climbed to the Old Spanish style church overlooking the little barrio. The sun-dried yellow grass along the border danced as an occasional breath of wind blew down from the surrounding hills. Waves of shimmering heat rose from the large dirt-encrusted boulders that were hidden amongst the mangled and dying shrubs.

Nos Grande was suffering an unusually long heatwave.

Children ran and laughed as they hit a stone back and forth with the sticks they had torn from the dying trees. The heat did not seem to affect them.

The barrio was quiet, except for squeals of laughter from the children and the crowing of the roosters scurrying along the edge of the path. A large pack of dogs of differing sizes and colors roamed the dirt paths and inspected anything representing food scraps.

The late morning air was hot and smelled of the smoke from the burning wood as it drifted from small open fires. The fires were used to roast various meats and heat the women's brick ovens for making their tacos and bread.

The morning sun beat down mercilessly. Women carried baskets of clothes to wash in the narrow river that ran through the center of the little community. While it was poor, the people were happy and loved each other.

A dirt-packed road ran through the center of the barrio. An old decrepit building housed the local cantina. Men sat on the open porch playing dominoes and drinking local liquor. They laughed and joked with each other. In the background, sounds of soft guitar music emanated from a huge old floor standing radio. The music was frequently punctuated by an announcer making staccato bursts of news, and other items of interest. No one paid attention.

It was noon when the radio burst forth with a heart-rendering blast of trumpets and drums, signifying the noon hour and reminding the population of their independence and the importance of the country's national anthem, which had been the cry of the long-ago revolution.

As the anthem tapered off, the bells at the church pealed. They announced the birth of Rosita Valquez.

No one foresaw the impact that Rosita would have on many lives.

The men stopped playing their dominoes and watched as a young girl quickly ran down from the church and toward them. She sprinted up the rickety stairs to the porch.

"Senor Jorge, you are a father. Senora Rosa has given you a beautiful little girl."

The men loudly called to Jorge and some clapped him on his back. This was indeed a new reason to celebrate with more of the special liquor.

Tears poured down Jorge's cheeks. He was ecstatic. He was a simple peasant farmer, but deeply religious. He and his wife Rosa had prayed to God every day since the doctors had told them Rosa would never have a child. God had blessed him.

Bottles of the local corn liquor were rushed from the bar and slammed down on the table where the dominoes had previously been played. The radio was shut off and two of the local men took guitars and the rejoicing began.

 It wasn't long before the women of the barrio passed by the cantina making their way to the little adobe next to the church that served as the medical home for the community.

After they visited Rosa, the women returned to the cantina to join the men. The rejoicing in the barrio started. The men sang as plates of fresh tacos, cornbread, refried beans, and fruit were piled on the table.

Rosita was the last child born in the barrio, and therefore she would always be the youngest and also the happiest child in the barrio.

Chapter 2

In the days after Rosita's birth, the task of selecting godparents before El Bautizo (the Baptism) commenced. Within their religion, the responsibilities of the godparents were taken seriously. The selected godparents were required to be Catholic and active in the church.

Finally, a decision was made. Jorge and Rosa chose friends they had known since childhood. They were happy when Julia and Carlos Rodriguez accepted.

The domineering priest insisted that since it was believed Rosa was infertile, that God had been gracious and answered their prayers. Accordingly, he demanded that both the Valquez and Rodriguez families attend special religious classes and attend a rehearsal of the ceremony. Father Lopez lectured the Rodriguez family on the role of godparents.

"You are not there for the ceremony. You will be the child's friend, advisor, and provide her guidance. Afterward, you and the Valquez family will be compadre…you will each have that special and sacred relationship. If you cannot accept and solemnly agree to this then I will not perform the Baptism."

Carlos spoke. "We accept our responsibilities."

The priest continued.

"I want you to understand that your role going ahead in life is a deeply significant one for both the parents and the child. You will be the other parents to Rosita. I bless you now. Leave and be joyous of this blessed event."

On Saturday afternoon, two weeks after Rosita's birth, the well planned and serious Baptism was performed. Almost the entire village was in attendance.

Rosa glowed, her natural beauty was enhanced by the elegant white lace dress she wore and the small hat tucked back over her long thick dark curly hair. She held Rosita cradled in her folded arms. Jorge stood beside her preening to the other men. He was proud.

The Rodriguez husband and wife stood beside them, dressed in their best formal attire.

The priest, dressed in the traditional long robes, stood beside the baptismal font with a thick prayer book held under his arm. His stern look was never accepted easily by the locals. He was feared.

He turned to the assembled group and extended his arms in a symbolic welcome.

"Welcome to the House of God. We are gathered here today to initiate this child into our faith. Before we proceed, I ask you all to kneel and join in prayer to thank the Lord Almighty for the wonderful blessing he has bestowed on Rosa and Jorge Valquez."

There was a shuffling and murmuring as the gathered souls knelt and followed the priest's recital of prayers.

When the prayers were completed, he commenced the ceremony. Rosa handed the infant to Julia. She cradled Rosita with a firm hand behind the child's head and her other hand supported the baby's back.

The baby was dressed in a traditional and extremely decorative christening gown. It was the same gown that Rosa had been christened in. It had been passed down by Rosa's deceased mother and guarded like a treasure. Rosa hoped that maybe one day Rosita would baptize her baby in the gown.

The priest droned on explaining the use of the holy water to banish original sin and purify the infant.

Men in the congregation were becoming restless. They were

eager to celebrate and party.

Finally, the words were spoken.

"I baptize thee, Rosita Marie Valquez, and welcome you to our faith. I bless you, and the Rodriguez as your godparents, and Jorge and Rosa your loving parents."

The words were barely spoken before the men started to file out of the church. The church bells rang loudly. Small groups gathered to talk and smoke before heading to the cantina for the party.

The mood was festive and could be felt throughout the atmosphere of the village. All the residents seemed happy.

Chapter 3

In the cantina, handmade decorations hung from the walls and rafters. The aroma of freshly baked goods wafted from the kitchen located in the back. At one end of the cantina, a small makeshift stage had been prepared. Various types of musical instruments had been carefully arranged on chairs.

In the packed dirt yard outside the front of the cantina, the fire and coals in old oil drums sputtered as the fat dripped from the roasting meats suspended over the embers on chicken wire. As was the custom, the men in the small communal village had killed and prepared their best animals for a celebratory feast.

Over the grills, there were suckling pigs on wooden spits. A young boy had been tasked with turning the pigs to ensure they cooked correctly. He took great pride in this and in being an important part of the festivities.

The afternoon remained hot. Upon their arrival, the men removed their vests and jackets and their white shirts and trousers were accentuated in the bright sunlight. They were dressed traditionally and wore colorful sashes. This gave them the appearance of a group of performers.

The men remained outside drinking cervezas from dark brown bottles. Laughter and shouts erupted from time to time. All fell silent when Jorge and Rosa walked into the dirt yard carrying their infant, Rosita.

The women of the village rushed forward to see the child and kiss Jorge and Rosa.

The men cheered and called Jorge to join them.

The women went into the cantina while the men
remained to drink and continue their joking. Children
from the village ran in and out of the cantina without
care.

The festivities intensified as the men drank and the
women talked and danced with each other, or their
husbands if they could detach him from the other
men.

Life in Nos Grande was serene. In many ways, it was just one big
family that managed to cooperate and accept others. There were
no fights or hatred. The idea of jail or police was foreign to the
people.

It was in this environment Rosita would grow and learn.

The devout parents and grandparents ensured that the religious
events a child was meant to participate in, were honored.

At the age of three, Rosita had grown into a pretty young girl, and
Jorge and Rosa were proud when they attended La Presentacion
del Niño. They had dressed her in a white dress set off with a pale
blue sash. Rosita was to be presented to God.

During the ceremony, Rosita was aware of Father Lopez staring at
her. She did not understand why.

Chapter 4

Life in the barrio was peaceful. Rosita became a favorite of the residents. She was always ready to help neighbors with their gardens or assist with small jobs on the farms. At the church-run school, she excelled. It seemed that Jorge and Rosa had indeed been blessed with a special child.

Rosita was a fast learner, not only academically, but also in life. Nature fascinated her. She knew the names of plants, trees, flowers, and fruits, and studied the habits of the native birds that nested in the trees on the farms. She consoled the other children when they were hurt by accidents and assisted the elderly of the village by running errands and caring for them during periods of illness. One of her favorite activities was helping the other girls making dolls from corn husks and helping the boys make toys from the discarded cans and bottles. Most in the barrio considered her to be a saint.

All in the barrio liked her with one exception. Father Lopez despised that she drew attention. He sensed that within her was a deep-seated spirit of evil. He tried to discuss this with Jorge and Rosa. They refused to accept the priest's belief and scorned him. He continually watched Rosita and wondered what she would eventually confess. He did not trust her and believed she would bring problems and distress to the barrio.

Rosita sensed this disdain and ensured that she adhered to the strict rules Father Lopez taught at the school. She knew he was right. Some days she sensed the desire to do something wrong. She didn't know why or understand the feelings when this desire arose. It scared her.

When not in school, or playing in the village, the more adventurous children would sneak away and run for miles to an area in the hills. There was a tall chain-link fence around a large area of land. A rusted sign hung on the gates and at intervals around the fence. It read:

PRIVATE PROPERTY

NO TRESPASSING

GUARDED BY ATTACK DOGS AND ARMED GUARDS

YOU WILL BE SHOT OR ATTACKED BY THE DOGS

Buena Azul Mining Company, Canada

The message was repeated in Spanish.

The children would lay in the tall grasses that surrounded the fence and watched as men walked from huts to a large opening that had been drilled into the face of the mountain. They watched and made up wild stories about what was behind the hole and who the men were. As they watched, small steel carts on rails were pulled from the inside of the mountain, and their contents dumped near the river that flowed to the center of the barrio. Some men sorted through what was dumped and discarded some of the stones and mud into the river.

It was all a mystery to the children. In the barrio, the adults never spoke about the happenings or what the place was. This only served to fuel more wild stories in the children's imaginations.

It was too much for Rosita. After an evening meal, she decided to ask.

"Papi, what is that place with the hole in the mountain and all those men? Why do they have those vicious dogs and that big fence?”

“Rosita, it is some crazy gringos. They want to take a useless rock. We have no use for it. It cannot be used for building. It does not make nice jewelry. We cannot cook with it. It is useless. Those men gave the government some money to own that land where the stone is found. They are loco.”

“Why don’t our men go there to help and maybe make money?”

“When the men first came here years ago, they made trouble in our little village. They drank and had fought and one stole another man’s woman during the night. We do not like them or want to be near them. I order you and your friends to stay away from that place.”

Rosita pressed on.

“Papi, the sign says Canada. What is that?”

Jorge was embarrassed. He did not know. He had tried to hide his lack of education from her for years.

“I do not know my little one. I was told he is a rich man. Now it is time for prayers and a night’s sleep.”

Rosita saw his embarrassment and decided not to continue with any more questions. She was determined she would find out. Maybe Father Lopez would know.

“Goodnight Papi. Goodnight Mama.”

Rosita left the kitchen and went to her little room.

She knelt on the rough floor beside her bed and prayed. She then climbed onto the bed and lay awake deciding how she would ask Father Lopez to help her.

As she lay awake, Rosita felt the strange emotion pass through her. She did not want to disobey her parents, nor did she respect them. Ideas filled her head with things she would like to do. She thought of one boy who had teased her. She had already decided to hurt him. Now as she lay in bed, her mind turned to the most painful things she could do to him.

She drifted into sleep with visions of him with his arms cut open and his face smashed with a rock. In her sleep, she had a smile on her lips. The evil was surfacing.

Chapter 5

Life continued with little change or adventure in Nos Grande. On occasion, one of the men from the mine would drive into town to purchase the locally made corn liquor. The villagers were polite but always glad to see him leave. They wanted no trouble.

The children of the barrio were growing older and the boys were getting bored. They wanted more than the barrio could offer. They listened enraptured to the tales of relatives who visited from the faraway city and who brought dresses for the girls and toys for the boys. They often brought magazines and newspapers for the adults, though most could not read and only looked at the pictures.

Rosita was a fast learner and excelled in all academic and sports activities. It wasn't long before she reached the age of eight and again she was to participate in yet another religious ceremony. This one was her first communion and she was excited. It meant yet another new and special dress.

The day arrived and at the church, she joined other children. The boys were smartly clothed in military-style dress and the girls in white gowns. There was a nervousness that buzzed in the little group.

After the ceremony, a small celebration was held at the church. It was not the same as in previous celebrations. While there was happiness it was somewhat reserved. Several families had experienced the loss of their sons to the city in search of interesting work and adventure. Many viewed this as the start of the demise of their happy barrio. There was a great concern. Outside influences were affecting their rural lives.

Rosita continued to help the families with tasks on the farms and look after their young children. She had become an idol for both the adults and the young children who looked up to her. She was clever and kind.

The forces inside Rosita spoke to her. She had realized at her young age that there was a better life away from the rural barrio. She wanted to confide in someone but could not trust anyone. For a short while, she wondered if Father Lopez could counsel her. He was, after all, a man of the church and God. He was smart and had traveled the world. Surely he would help her to be rid of the demons that were playing in her young mind.

Days came and went. Festivals were held, yet it seemed the spirit and joy had gone from them. People in the village were falling ill with an unknown sickness. Some had died. In the history of the barrio, no one had died the way these people had.

In addition to the illnesses, both crops and farm animals were dying off. The simple peasant people believed that they were being punished by God. Father Lopez took advantage and advised them to pray and contribute whatever food and money they had to his church.

For the first time since the barrio had been settled, poverty arrived. Sick and weakened people could not work in the fields and relied on others to help them. As was their custom, the villagers agreed and did their best, but the disease and farming failures were too much for them.

Jorge had never left the barrio or the farming countryside in his life. He pleaded with a neighbor to go with him to seek assistance and bring a doctor from the city. The neighbor had been to the city on several previous occasions and finally agreed. Rosita, in turn, pleaded with Jorge to take her to see what a city was like. Reluctantly he agreed. This drew the wrath of Father Lopez.

"How can you take this innocent young girl to such a place of sin and greed? It will change her forever. I insist you leave her here. She is too young to see the way that people live in a city. You must not take her."

That night Jorge and Rosa spoke of the Father's concern and demand. Rosita sat quietly at the table listening to every word until she spoke.

"Papi. I will be there to look after you. Like I do here. I will not be any trouble. Please let me go with you. The Father is wrong. I know things and the city will not change me. Please let me go with you."

Silence enveloped the room for a long period. It was Rosa who spoke.

"Jorge, she is wise beyond her age. She will be an excellent companion for you. She can read and help you with the doctor. I think she should go with you. I love you both and want to see you find help. I am sure Rosita can assist. She is young but smart."

"If you agree then she can join us."

The next morning, Jorge, Rosita, and Martinez, the neighbor, set off. They had packed meager rations into the side pockets of two donkeys. Marco, one of the local boys had agreed to go with them as far as the bus stop and then return the donkeys to the barrio.

Rosita had special feelings for Marco. He was not like any of the other boys. He did not have an olive complexion and black hair. He was white with blonde hair and blue eyes. He had no father and this made him and his mother the gossip of all the women in the barrio. They speculated on love affairs and where Marco may have come from if he wasn't hers by birth. Much was made of this.

The small contingent plodded along the dirt road on their way to the bus shelter. They passed by the mine and observed that several large trucks and a crane had arrived recently.

As they walked by the gate several large dark-colored German Shepherd dogs attacked at the fence. The dogs snarled and snapped through the wire.

Jorge watched them in their frenzy.

"Martinez, Rosita, that is not the normal behavior of a dog. They have been cruelly trained to attack. I may not be the smartest person, but I know nature and animals. There is something wrong here at this mine. Why do these people stay away from us and need to protect it so fiercely?"

As they continued their walk past the mine, the dogs ran the length of the fence trying to jump its height. The noise attracted the attention of one of the men. He came forward to observe them and then raised a rifle and fired into the air. The dogs immediately fell silent.

"Again, I say there is something wrong and bad at that place. Why do they want those useless rocks?"

They were almost about to lose sight of the mine entrance and buildings when Rosita saw something that shocked her. She tugged Jorge's sleeve and pointed. There, standing in a shadowed area with a fat slovenly man, smoking a cigarette and holding a beer in his other hand was Father Lopez.

Jorge quickly assessed the situation.

"Marco, you must not speak of what you have seen to anyone. When we return we will find out what this is all about. You must promise this."

Marco nodded his head, but in reality, he wanted to tell his friends.

Father Lopez was not from the barrio and not well-liked. Even the women who loved their priests were reserved in their comments on Father Lopez.

They continued to walk on in silence until they reached the bus stop. It was a structure built from bamboo with a roof of thatched palm leaves. Jorge thought how lucky they were that it rained infrequently.

Marco and Fernando unloaded the luggage from the side baskets on the donkeys. Marco left to return to the barrio. It was some twenty minutes later before the old battered blue, green, red, and yellow bus crawled its way up the small incline. Clouds of black diesel fumes and smoke followed behind it and were sucked inside as there were no windows.

On the bus were simple peasants from other barrios. They carried live chickens on their laps and one enterprising young man had two chattering monkeys beside him in the aisle of the bus. An old woman chewed a cigar made of local tobacco that hung from her mouth. She sat on the back seat of the bus with her collection of noisy parrots. Such was life in the poor interior of South America.

The bus ground its way along the flat road, surrounded on each side by fields in which farmers could be seen plowing behind huge oxen. They soon came to the mountains. With much grinding of gears, the driver coached the ancient bus up into the mountains. Toward the top of the steep hill, steam erupted from the front of the bus and the driver pulled it to the side of the narrow winding road.

The driver stood and made an announcement. He asked all the men to help and to go and pee in the radiator of the bus as the water had boiled off climbing the hill. One by one the men obliged.

With both the bus and the men relieved, they continued their trip on into the city. A guitar had been found and for the rest of the trip, local songs were sung. For those unable to sing or with bad voices there was much laughter.

Throughout the trip, Jorge remained quiet wondering what Father Lopez was doing at that mine. He had preached to the villagers to stay away from it.

It was early afternoon when the old bus arrived at the bus depot on the outskirts of the city. Martinez's relatives were there to meet them. Rosita's eyes were wide. The city was bigger and busier than she had imagined.

While she had seen cars and farm trucks in the barrio, she had never ridden in a car. Now she would ride in a car for the first time on her way to stay at Martinez's relatives. She looked at her father. Jorge was in deep thought and did not seem to be present. She had seen this before when he was deeply troubled. She wondered what could be ahead.

Chapter 6

That evening, Rosita was in total amazement. The family sat for dinner. She had never expected or seen such opulence. Glistening silver cutlery was laid out on the white linen tablecloth and shone with the light reflected from the small overhead chandelier.

Food was brought to the table in brightly colored bowls and trays. She did not know the foods. They were completely different from those she was used to in the barrio.

Plates were handed around and the soup was served. Rosita watched as Martinez's relatives took a strangely shaped spoon and took some soup from their bowls to their mouths. In the barrio, they just lifted their bowls and drank from the bowl.

She was scared to eat with the cutlery provided. Rosita thought the meal had finished when a large white oval platter was brought to the table. A large roast of beef was centered on the platter, surrounded by roasted vegetables.

Slices were carved and served to each person's plate. Small dishes were then passed around that contained paste-like contents. Rosita spooned out some of the whitish creams onto her plate.

Not knowing what it was and trying to be polite, she put a spoonful in her mouth. The strong horseradish burned. Rosita's eyes watered and she coughed the contents in her mouth onto her plate. Jorge, Martinez and his relatives laughed.

She was embarrassed and immediately felt the strange demon inside her awake. She did not like being made a fool of.

Martinez's cousin, Jesus started the conversation.

"It is always good to see you Martinez, but what is so important to bring you here to the city with your friend and his daughter?"

Rosita's curiosity was aroused. Quietly she kept her head partially bowed and listened intently. Like a sponge, she soaked up every word.

"Jesus, we have a problem in the barrio. For over two hundred years we never had sickness or problems with the crops and livestock dying. Now it is happening all the time. Even young men who are otherwise healthy and strong are affected. There is something wrong. This only started in the last year. We have tried old cures but nothing works. We have come here to look for help. We need a doctor to come and find out what the problem is. We do not have very much money, only what we make by selling our extra crops. Since the birth of Rosita, there have not been any new babies born. There have been weddings of young people and they should have babies, but there is nothing."

Jesus sat and thought before speaking.

"What has changed in the last year? Are you using any different chemicals to spray or fertilize?"

"No. Nothing has changed. We have kept the old way of doing things."

"Have there been any new people who have moved into the barrio from other areas?"

"Sometimes we get a visit from one of the men at the mine. He comes to buy our corn liquor. He never stays and leaves "

"Have the young men who left the barrio also been affected?"

"No. I have never heard of any being sick or dying."

"Tell me more. What happens to the people? Does each become sick the same way?"

"Yes. They lose their weight and shrink until they are too weak to eat or drink. They are so weak some cannot walk."

"If I go to the authorities to report this and ask for help, they will close off the barrio. No one will be allowed to leave and visits will be restricted. I need to speak to an associate. I am sure he will have some ideas. Now, let us finish this splendid meal that my wife, Angelina, prepared."

"We cannot stay away for too long. There are many tasks to complete and we need to help the others in our little community with the animals and crops."

"Martinez, your friend Jorge has very little to say."

"I am sorry. I have been thinking and trying to understand why our priest was at the mine near our village. We saw him as we passed by it. He has always preached for us to stay away from it as he suspects there are evil happenings there."

Rosita blushed and fidgeted at the mention of the mine and Father Lopez. Jorge watched her and instinctively knew she had been going there.

"Rosita, I know that you and your friends have gone there against our instructions. What have you seen? Have you or any of the others taken anything from the mine back to our village?"

All eyes at the table bored into Rosita.

"No Papi. We just watched to see what they do there. They push these carts with dirt from inside the mountain to the river and empty the carts into the water."

"What is it they put in the water?"

"It is like a grey wet mud."

"You must never go there again. I will speak to your friends' parents. You have all disobeyed. It is forbidden to dishonor us like this."

Rosita's internal temper was rising. She didn't understand what was happening to her.

"Papi, I am not feeling well. I think I need to lie down."

Jesus's wife, Angelina stood and took Rosita's hand and led her to the bedroom. It was on the second floor of the large house. Windows overlooked the street below.

"Here Rosita. I have a nightgown for you. I guessed your size and bought it for you as a gift."

"Thank you, Senorita. I will treasure it."

"Now, please go and wash and clean your teeth for bed."

She led Rosita into a small bathroom off the bedroom. Rosita was impressed. It had a toilet with water. There was hot water. She was overwhelmed. Never before had she been in a bathroom of such luxury. In the barrio, the toilet was moved when the hole in the ground was full. Normally, the toilet would be buzzing with flies and beetles crawling on the wooden seat.

It was then that Rosita decided she would have all of this and better. Life in the barrio was no longer for her.

Chapter 7

Over the next five years, frequent visits were made to the barrio by doctors from the city. The problem continued to remain a mystery. No one could explain the sickness nor the cause of it.

Some of the residents left to go to other barrios. The population shrunk. What had been a happy community became a worried and desolate place. Rosita yearned to leave and establish a life in the city.

She was about to ask her parents to allow her to go and live with Martinez's relatives and attend school in the city when fate dealt its hand.

The family had sat and eaten their meager dinner when Rosa announced she was not feeling well. Jorge arose and assisted her from the table to an old couch at the front of the adobe. She sat quietly for almost thirty minutes before Jorge noticed a dribble of blood from the corner of her lips. Rosa had also been infected with the mystery illness. He tried to be strong but knew that there was no recovery once a person was infected.

Rosita looked on with a coolness. She loved both her parents but did not share or agree with their decision to live in almost poverty in the barrio.

She too realized her mother would probably be dead in weeks. The illness took people to the grave quickly.

Her plan to ask to leave the barrio was thwarted. She would need to stay and look after Jorge. He was tired and worried.

Rosa's condition quickly worsened. Father Lopez was making frequent visits to their adobe. He would sit and pray with Rosa but what Jorge did not see was his constant staring at Rosita's budding breasts. She was becoming a natural beauty and most of the men could not avoid admiring her. Even at her young age of fourteen, she looked much older.

It was on one of Father Lopez visits that he mentioned that soon she would be a Quinceañera. The Hispanic Quinca Años tradition of celebrating a girl maturing at age fifteen was nearing. Rosita would transition from childhood to maturity and become a woman.

Rosita resisted his request for her attendance.

"Father, we do not have the money for me to have a pretty pastel dress like the other girls will wear. I would like this very much, but it is not possible for me. My father works long hours helping others for us to survive. Besides, my mother is dying. It would be selfish of me to insist."

The priest continued to stare at her. He liked the defiance he sensed, but still wondered about the evil he believed she possessed.

"My child, there are many here whom you have helped. I will get the money for the finest dress for you. At the church service and the party afterward, you will be envied."

The strange sensation started in her again. Silently she thought how she would enjoy being better than all the other young girls. She decided she would be the princess amongst them.

When she glanced across at Rosa she noticed the weak smile on her face and Jorge holding her hand. It was obvious that death was not far away.

"Father, I would accept your kind gift."

"We will talk later. Now, I must pray alongside your parents. I will arrange to visit again tomorrow."

They prayed for a while and the priest stood and straightened his black cassock before walking to the front entrance. He left.

The next morning, Rosita awoke to the sound of deep sobs coming from her parent's room. Rosa had died a peaceful death during the night.

Rosita went to Jorge and pulled his arms from hugging the deceased Rosa.

"Rosita, you must now go to the church and tell Father Lopez. It is our custom we must bury our loved ones within a day."

Rosita sprinted to the church and found Father Lopez standing and talking to several of the village women. Upon seeing her running towards him, he instinctively knew that Rosa had passed. He held out his arms to embrace her.

"There is no need for you to explain. I will make all the arrangements. Now return to your grieving father."

The small group of women had overheard and immediately each began making the sign of the cross. It would only be minutes before the passing of Rosa Valquez was known through the barrio.

One of the women who Rosita recognized had been a good friend of Rosa crossed to her.

"Rosa was my special friend. It is our custom that someone must sit with the body. I will do that until she is taken to the church. I will help to arrange the celebration of her life after the funeral.

Please go to Jorge and comfort him. I will first pray then come to your home."

The woman shuffled away and into the church. Rosita marveled at their stoic approach to hardships and death.

She started her walk back to their adobe. Her mind was full of thoughts about the dress and the event. She surprised herself that she did not feel sorrow for her departed mother.

It was to be a long day.

Already visitors were arriving at the home. Jorge had not moved. He sat firmly attached to his beloved Rosa. The women moved around inside the little home with peculiar grace. It was almost as if they didn't want to disturb Rosa from her eternal sleep.

Rosita went to Jorge.

"Papi, you must let the ladies do what needs to be done. Come with me. We will go out to the church and you can pray. Others will help to prepare her for the service."

Jorge looked up into her eyes and for the first time, she realized how old he had become over the past year.

"Yes. I would like that. She was a good wife and mother. We must have the best funeral and wake. She had many friends. I want them all to come to the wake. We will celebrate her life and all the good things she did."

Clutching a large black leather-covered prayerbook, Father Lopez arrived.

"Jorge, do not be upset. She was a good woman and will now be with the saints. I am preparing for the funeral service. Do you wish to speak to the congregation or just take a quiet role?"

Jorge thought for a while.

"No. I do not need to stand in front of our people and say how good she was. They all know it."

"Tomorrow morning at ten I have arranged for her service."

Jorge nodded and stood to leave the room. He walked outside and down to the cantina. Upon his arrival, the conversation fell off. Men came to him to express sorrow. Several brought him bottles of the corn liquor.

He sat alone, speaking to no one. The men were unsure of how to react to him. He had been a mentor to many and highly respected. They did not know how to deal with Jorge in his grief.

Suddenly, Jorge stood and walked quickly from the bar. He headed in the direction of the church and turned to the villa where Father Lopez lived. He knocked loudly.

A disheveled and partially drunk priest answered the door.

"Jorge, come in. What can I do for you? Is it something for Rosa's funeral service?"

Jorge looked at him coldly.

"No. I think you need to answer some questions. Why were you at that mine with those men?"

Father Lopez raised his hands.

"Jorge, that is the business of the church. It is not for you to know."

"Why have you insisted the people stay away from the mine, yet you go there? I want to know. What is happening there?"

"Jorge, you must relax. After the service for Rosa, I will explain. There are also men there who need the services of a priest. I am the only priest in a hundred miles of here."

"I have lost some trust in you. I am not sure I believe you."

The priest stared at Jorge. He could not believe the insolence. No one spoke to a man of God that way.

"Jorge, you are distressed. Go home. Be with your friends and sit with Rosa. Later tonight, we will move her to the church and start the preparations for her mass and funeral service."

Jorge realized he had been dismissed. He no longer trusted Father Lopez.

Chapter 8

Weeks passed by after the funeral services of Rosa Valquez. Loneliness took its toll on Jorge. Rosita tried to substitute for her deceased mother but could not. Jorge was failing fast.

It was almost time for the Quinca Años. Several girls were coming of age and would be participating in the event. Rosita was worried. She had not heard from Father Lopez and his offer to provide her the best dress of all. She wondered whether she should be bold and ask him and then decided she would go to the church in the afternoon. There was only one week left before the ceremony. She worried about the dress.
What if it didn't fit? What if it was a horrible color?
Questions flowed through her mind.

Rosita prepared a lunch of chicken tacos, rice, and beans for herself and Jorge. Jorge picked at the food and ate little. He excused himself and went for a siesta. His health was failing fast.

Rosita tidied up and cleaned the plates and put away the food. It was time to visit Father Lopez and ask about the special dress.

Another heatwave was baking the barrio. As she walked from the front entrance of their adobe, a large brown dog ran to their door and lifted its leg to urinate on the steps she had cleaned that morning. She went to chase the dog, but it turned and snarled at her. For a moment she considered hurting it, but her love of nature calmed those thoughts.

As she walked towards the church the dog sidled along beside her. It had become her friend. She went to pat the dog but pulled her hand back when she observed the infestation of ticks in its head and along the back. She felt sad. It was like so many of the dogs in the barrio. No one looked after them and they continued to breed and walk the streets in search of any food they could find.

There was a narrow path leading to the imposing front door of the priest's residence. She rang the bell suspended on a bracket beside the door and waited. She heard shuffling inside and finally, Father Lopez opened the door.

"Father, I am sorry to disturb you. I was wondering if you had received the dress you promised me for the Quinca Años. It is next weekend. I want to make sure it is proper for me."

"Yes, I am sorry. I forgot. I have had many things to deal with. Come in. I will go and take it from the library where I set the box down."

A huge wave of relief passed over Rosita. She accepted the priest's explanation.

Moments later the priest returned carrying a large narrow box. He handed it to her.

"Go ahead. Open it. See if it is what you had hoped for."

Rosita lay the box on the large wooden table under the window. She opened the box. Wrapped in layers of tissue paper was a pale pastel pink dress adorned with lace and embroidery. It was everything that Rosita could have hoped for.

"Father it is so beautiful. I hope it fits me well."

Father Lopez cast his eyes at the young girl's full figure. He had allowed for such a figure when he had ordered the dress from a boutique in the city of La Iluminada. He knew the woman who owned the store. They had once been lovers until her jealous lover had discovered them. Father Antonio Lopez had stabbed him to death in a brutal manner. The police counted fifty stab wounds to the body. Antonio Lopez had fled and taken sanctuary in a monastery before taking the vows of priesthood.

"My dear, go to the room at the end of the corridor and try it on. Come and show me. I am excited to see how that beautiful dress will enhance you. That room is where the altar boys change. You will find everything you need there."

Rosita was not shy. She hurried to the room and stripped before sliding the dress over her head and flattening it out against her body. In the lopsided mirror, she looked at herself. The dress was beautiful but her hair was a mess. She spent ten minutes smoothing her hair before exiting the room to present herself to Father Lopez.

His jaw dropped as the transformed little girl walked in with the appearance of a twenty-year-old model. He rose and walked around her admiring the dress and in particular, the young lady in it.

"Father, thank you. This has made me so happy after all the bad things we have had to deal with. How can I say thank you?"

The priest walked to her side and kissed her cheek.

"You are a special girl. For you, I would do anything."

Rosita blushed and turned to him. Her feelings and emotions were boiling. The evil spirit was back.

The priest wrapped his arms around her and drew her into him. She felt his stiffened penis pushing against her leg. He slid his hand up to the top of the dress and released several buttons. The dress dropped to the floor. Rosita stood completely naked in front of him. He visually soaked in the beauty of her body before reaching and caressing her breasts.

Within minutes, he removed his cassock, laid her down on the tabletop, and commenced intercourse. This was not her first encounter. She had been curious about the white-skinned blonde Marco and what he looked like naked. They had found an area far from the farms and enjoyed each other and the total intimacy.

The priest plunged and groaned. Beads of sweat lined his brow. He was a fierce lover.

Rosita knew it was wrong, but her evil spirit egged her on. She felt exhilarated. She realized that she had the figure and looks to attract and control men. She intended to use her attributes.

A loud howl pierced the afternoon air as the priest exploded in her. In return, she felt nothing but contempt.

At fifteen she had learned a lot.

They lay there in silence. A loud knocking at the door occurred. He jumped from the table and rushed to a room to find a robe. He called the person at the door to wait while he dressed. Rosita ran to the room at the end of the corridor and dressed in her old clothes.

Father Lopez opened the door. There were two men from the mine standing there.

"Father, please come. A part of the tunnel has collapsed. We have pulled out the men who were inside. They are in poor shape. One wants you to bless him and give him last rites. Will you please come back with us?"

The priest turned away from them to fetch his bag containing holy water, prayer book, and other items. It was then he remembered it was in the room in which Rosita was hiding.

He returned to the men.

"Yes, I will return with you. Go and wait for me at your truck. I need to gather some items first."

The men left and Father Lopez hurried to the room.
"Rosita. I need to come in. I must take my bag from in there."

She opened the door and stood naked. "When you return, you

will do what I want."

Father Lopez looked at her in amazement. How could this young
innocent girl know of these carnal pleasures? He thanked God
right then for allowing him to be a man of the cloth in this
particular barrio.

He smiled and nodded before leaving to go to the mine with the
men.

He now had another secret to conceal.

Chapter 9

The collapse at the mine was far more serious than originally thought. Three of the men were critically injured.

After a long and private consultation with the priest, two of the men, obviously managers, reluctantly agreed to call for medical assistance.

Thirty minutes later, two military helicopters from the airbase at La Iluminada arrived and medical personnel ran from them to examine the men.

Rosita had returned home and had assisted Jorge to walk to the scene. He was exhausted from the long walk but watched the proceedings with the eye of an eagle. Not one little thing escaped his observation. He was particularly interested to see the interaction between the men and Father Lopez.

He turned to Rosita.

"That man is keeping something secret. I detect that he has a greater involvement at this mine and the reason he lectures us to stay away from it is to hide whatever he is involved with. I do not trust him any longer."

Rosita thought to herself that if he knew of the sexual antics of earlier that afternoon, he would take matters into his own hands. She knew that Jorge looked at her as his princess.

A decision was made to transport the men to the hospital at La Iluminada. Jorge and Rosita watched as there was an urgent exchange between the priest and the commander of the military medics.

After five minutes, the commander nodded and they watched as the men were loaded into the helicopter and Father Lopez climbed aboard.

Clouds of dirt swirled into the air and leaves and grass flew as the helicopters revved their engines and slowly climbed into the sky. The sound was deafening.

Rosita and Jorge watched as the helicopters became specks in the sky as they flew toward the city.

On the walk back to the barrio, Rosita did not feel guilty or ashamed. She was pleased that she had the power to manipulate others. She intended to use this power to get the things she now wanted in life.

Back at their adobe, Rosita prepared a goat stew with boiled potatoes and corn. She had received some loaves of bread from the neighbor. As she cooked, Jorge sat at the table in the center of the old kitchen and watched. With the heat outside, the kitchen was swelteringly hot. His clothing was damp with perspiration. He looked over at Rosita who appeared cool and calm. There was no perspiration on her to be seen. He thought it strange. He had worked in the fields and performed heavy work in temperatures that were hotter than this. He had never perspired, yet every part of his clothing was damp. Also, he felt tired again. He was not enjoying the process of aging."

"Papi, when the men go into the city next, can they buy us a radio?"

"Why do you want a radio? You can hear the music in the cantina and they speak the news of our country on that radio. I don't think we need one. It would be a waste of what little money we have."

Rosita was disappointed but was already scheming how she would convince another to get one for her as a gift.

She did not argue with him. There was no point. His mind was made up. Besides he did not look well. She was worried about him and did not want to burden him with other things. Since the death of Rosa, he was not the same man. In some ways, she felt sorry for him, but in other ways, she mentally criticized him for not taking them from the rural barrio into the city where they could have had both a better life and money.

"On Monday I am going to go to the government and speak with the officials there about the mine. It is not correct for us to not know what they are doing there."

She was worried. The officials were a corrupt and dangerous group. Without money or a bribe of something they wanted, a person could easily create a problem for themselves. There had already been incidents where some farmers had gone to dispute the price the government had paid for some of their crops. The farmers were never seen again. The rumor amongst the villagers was that the officials had bought the crops at a low price then resold them to the military at a much higher price. The officials had wanted no evidence.

"Papi, do not do that. Let me ask questions. I think that Father Lopez likes me. I will see if I can make him talk about the mine."

Jorge rested his elbows on the table and cradled his slim recently bearded jaw in his hands.

"If you can do that, it will be safer and easier for me. Do you think he will tell the truth?"

"Oh yes. I will be charming to him. I have seen the way he looks at me. Don't worry, Papi. I am not stupid in those matters, Mother taught me well on the ways of men and their desires."

Jorge looked adoringly at his daughter. She was everything his beloved Rosa had been but possessed a drive and quality he had never seen before in a woman. He hoped that she would achieve happiness in her life. He wished that Rosa could be with them to see what a fine person she had become.

Rosita had developed a skill for hiding the demons that lived within her. She had promised herself that no one would know the real Rosita.

Chapter 10

The priest returned two days later. He arrived in a military jeep driven by a young Colonel. He immediately went to the church to attend to any matters that may have arisen in his absence.

There were a few minor issues. A complaint from one of the eighty-year-old women who had missed making her pointless confession. A request for a new goat to be blessed to ensure it produced more milk. There was an envelope with a government seal on it. He ripped it open. There was to be an inspection of the mine and barrio to investigate the high number of deaths and illnesses. Father Lopez cursed words that would have blistered the ears of any criminal. He had a problem.

He returned to the jeep and suggested they go to the cantina for a beer and food. It was there that destiny was sealed.

The young Colonel walked in and encountered Rosita leaving. He stood in awe. He had known many women but never one so strikingly beautiful.

Rosita greeted the priest on his return and then summarily dismissed him as if he was a little boy. She had experienced a leap in her heart and a glowing feeling in meeting the Colonel.

He stepped forward and made a slight bow.

"Senora. You are a magnificent sight for my tired eyes. We have driven from La Iluminada. I do not believe there was a single thing we passed on the way here that could compare to your beauty."

Father Lopez was seething. How dare this junior officer move in on his recent prize.

"Colonel, I suggest we leave now and go to the mine."
"No. I wish to drink and eat. I anticipate a long session at the
mine and I am hungry….both for food and love."

Rosita gave a small enticing laugh. She looked at the handsome
Colonel. He had medals pinned to his uniform and possessed an
air of confidence she had never seen before.

"Senora, what is your name. Will you sit with the Father and I as
we eat and drink. Maybe I can tempt you to join in a drink."

"My name is Rosita and of course I will join you. Will you be
staying here in the barrio? Where will you sleep? We have no
places for visitors."

The Father thundered at that question.

"He will stay at the church. He will be a guest of God. No one
from the barrio is to interfere with him or the work he is to do.
That includes you, Rosita. You are a sinner. A whore. Now leave
us."

She stood and slowly moved to the corner of the table. She
reached down and removed a jug of water. She raised it and
slammed it over the priest's head. Blood spurted from the huge
gash and he fell heavily to the floor.

"You are a pig. Burn in the fires of hell, you hypocrite."

The young Colonel stared. He did not know what to make of the
scene that had just played out in front of him.

"Rosita! Was that a wise thing to do? "

"Yes. He is no good. He raped me. I was too ashamed to tell
anyone. My father is very old and ill. It would probably kill him
if this became known here in the barrio."

"I must get someone from our medical team to check him. He is unconscious and bleeding. I don't think I will stay at the church tonight. I will stay at the mining camp."

"You will not. I insist you stay in our humble home. I will make a meal and my father and I will enjoy the company. I want you to tell me about life in the city. My father, Jorge, will be happy to have company. Let us leave the good father here to look after himself. He has been nasty to many here. Let me take you to my home."

The young Colonel was unsure.

"We don't even know our names. I am Felix de Santos. I live in La Iluminada and serve in the investigative division of the Army."

"And I am Rosita Valquez. I live here in the barrio and help others when not looking after my aging father."

Felix bent forward and took her hand. In an exaggerated bow, he kissed her hand. They both laughed.

"Yes, I would love to come to your home. Are you sure your father will approve? What about Father Lopez?"

"I told you he can't do anything. I will tell all that he raped me. Don't worry. He is finished here."

She looked down at the sprawled heap lying on the floor. With blood flowing from his head and his cassock lifted to his thighs, he was a pitiful sight. He was not the domineering self-confident preacher anymore.

Felix escorted Rosita to the jeep. They drove the short distance to their home. Jorge was delighted to have a guest. Especially a military officer. He welcomed Felix into his house and then went to fetch a bottle of old expensive brandy that he had reserved for a special occasion.

Rosita accompanied Felix to a room and showed him a bed where he could sleep. He thanked her and they returned to join Jorge. It seemed he had become ten years younger with the arrival of the guest and distraction.

Rosita was happy. She hummed a folkloric tune as she prepared the evening meal. She had decided it would be a meal that was only made at special times of the year. Felix had captured her heart and she was determined he would not leave her now, or in the future. He had no idea.

Felix sat with Jorge and told him of his missions in the military. He described the action in foreign countries and espoused the political belief of the country's desire to be an international leader and not succumb to any other foreign power. Jorge was impressed with the young man.

As time passed, Felix spoke of his family and their respective lives. Jorge was further impressed. Felix was an educated and wealthy man. He silently hoped that Felix would fall madly in love with his daughter and then he could depart this life knowing she would be cared for.

Rosita observed them talking. She was pleased to see that Felix had adapted to Jorge's simple ways and conversation. Even though he was educated, Felix did not overwhelm Jorge with big ambiguous words or conversation so complex that it could not be followed.

The aroma of the spicy foods and the roasting pork seeped through the villa. Felix was hungry but suppressed his desire to eat. He had manners and did not want to offend Jorge, but in particular, he did not wish to appear rude in any way in front of Rosita.

When the meal was ready, Rosita set it at the table. Jorge and Felix were impressed. Jorge smiled. To him, it was obvious that

Rosita had made this a special meal to impress the young man.

They talked about life in the barrio. Jorge described a past life in which the people were happy and where poor health and death was uncommon. He spoke of the changes and how he had become unhappy with his life. He saddened as he thought of the close friends who had left or died from the mystery illness.

"Jorge, I have a suggestion I would like to make. Please do not be offended. I will need to return to my post at La Iluminada soon. I would like to invite you and Rosita to be my guests. You will be welcome to stay at my home. It is large and my family has servants who will attend to your needs. I will take you and Rosita to many of our country's famous statues and museums. You will see our culture and experience life in our beautiful city."

Rosita dropped a plate at hearing this. The plate shattered into many pieces and scattered across the floor. Felix sprung to his feet and kneeled to pick up the shards of sharp ceramic. As he slid a piece from under the table, it slipped in his hand and cut into him deeply. His blood immediately ran down his wrist and stained the cuff of his military shirt.

"I am sorry. I am so stupid and clumsy. I will bandage your cut and rinse the blood from your shirt. Come with me. We have a small bathroom and I will attend to you there."

Felix followed her down a narrow corridor into the bathroom. He tried to unbutton his shirt, but the cut in his hand made it difficult.

"Felix, let me do that for you."

Rosita unbuttoned his shirt and stripped it from his body. She felt a strange sensation as she looked at his muscular rock hard chest and firm stomach. In his uniform, it had not been visible that his arms had large strong muscles. There was a small tattoo of a cross on his shoulder. Rosita was curious.

"Why do you have that tattoo?

"It reminds me of the burdens in life that my family endured. I will say no more please."

Rosita stood immediately in front of him. He was the vision of a man she had dreamed of. She was not going to lose him.

She looked into his eyes and orchestrated a soft ambient look. She observed him twitch and then knew she had him. She thought how easy it had become since she had changed from the body of a little girl to a young attractive woman. It was like fishing, and the fish were hungry.

He held his cut hand over a basin and she moved around his side to rinse away the blood and then dried the area with a white cloth. As she did, she let her eyes fall below the line of his stomach. She could see that he had become aroused and turned to him with a devious smile.

The shirt was placed in a bucket with water and soap.

"Stay here and I will get you one of Papi's shirts while this soaks."

Minutes later she returned with a cream shirt that he pulled on. It was a little tight but he accepted it. In the cream shirt, his dark brown eyes and jet black hair framed his almost perfect face.

Rosita decided she would have trouble sleeping that night.

Chapter 11

Roosters crowed the morning awake. It was early. Rosita quietly arose and went to the kitchen to make some of the country's famous coffee. She took some eggs from a basket and laid them on the counter. Next, she chopped fresh tomatoes and onion. She had decided to make the scrambled eggs that had been the special breakfast her mother made the few guests who had visited and stayed overnight.

She reflected upon the discussion of last evening. Jorge had resisted the idea of leaving the barrio with so many sick and suffering. It did not feel right to him to leave at such a time. Rosita was angry at him but had disguised this anger. Now it was time to convince him.

There was a shuffling behind her and she turned to see a sleepy Felix stumbling into the kitchen. She laughed at him. He was wearing an old nightshirt her mother had wanted to throw out. It was bright yellow and green and far too short for him. The hem barely covered his crotch.

"Good morning, Felix. Did you sleep well? I heard you snoring."

"Yes. I slept very well. I think that delicious dinner made me sleepy after the day I had. Thank you. I loved that meal. I will be sure that you will enjoy a fine meal at my favorite restaurant in La Iluminada."

Rosita did a silent panic. She had never eaten at a restaurant before. Only the cantina and that was not class, but a place for everyone to meet and sometimes eat.

"Felix, that is a nice offer but I cannot go with you and leave Jorge here alone. I hope you understand."

"I do. I will speak with him further. Today I must contact my base. I am sure the situation with Father Lopez has been reported by now. He influences the Generals there. It may not be safe for you or Jorge to remain here. Do you understand what I mean? Do you remember those farmers who went missing after they complained about the prices they were paid? I don't want to see you or Jorge in danger. I need you to tell me when and how you were raped by Father Lopez. I may be able to create a situation where you will be safer."

"I will not. Either you accept my word or disbelieve me. It seems all men choose to think that women make up these stories. I can assure you that I did not make up this story. I will describe some strange things about his body that only a person who was in my situation would know."

Felix was surprised at her articulation for a girl just fifteen years of age.

"Then I will not ask again or pursue the matter."

Jorge arrived in the kitchen. Rosita went to give him a morning kiss. As she approached him, she was surprised to see that his expression seemed younger.

"Papi, I have made you a coffee and am preparing your favorite scrambled eggs."

Jorge looked across at Felix and winked.

"Why all this motherly attention?"

"Papi, you have not been so well recently. You must eat and build more energy in your body. I am the one to help you with that."

"Felix and Rosita. I lay awake for a long time last night. Felix you have made me think. I am becoming an old man. I do want to see the city before I die. I have decided to accept your invitation and visit La Iluminada with you. Now, I cannot speak for my young Rosita. Maybe she will want to stay here."

He chuckled knowing that Rosita would leave the barrio for the city on a moment's notice.

He looked across the kitchen at Rosita. She was glaring at him.

"Rosita. If you are to succeed in life, you must understand when a joke is a joke."

Felix looked at his watch. I must go to the government office and report back to my base. I will return in a couple of hours. But first, I must taste those eggs."

He left them and returned dressed smartly in his uniform. The shirt with the blood had come clean and dried overnight. In his uniform, he cut a dashing figure.

Jorge looked across at him.

"Felix, how long will you stay here in the barrio?"

"I will know after I visit the government offices. It will probably be a day or two. I am required to attend some functions at the home base. I will need to return for those."

Rosita laid two plates of the eggs down. One in front of Jorge and the other in front of Felix.

"This looks good. I am so hungry this morning. I think all the action yesterday made me tired and hungry."

He forked a huge amount of the scrambled but runny eggs to his mouth. As he did so, he could not suppress a huge sneeze. The hot sauce had tingled his sinuses. Scrambled eggs flew over the table and sprayed Jorge. The balance fell from his fork down the front of his uniform. The hot red chili sauce made a long stripe down the chest of his green military shirt. His tunic was covered in small pieces of chopped red peppers and onion intermingled with the bright yellow flecks of the egg.

Rosita laughed hard until tears rolled down her cheeks. Felix saw the humor and also laughed.

"What will I tell them at the offices?"

"Go and take your clothes off. I will fix it and no one will notice. You will need to have your jacket buttoned. That chili sauce will not be easy to remove."

She walked away and returned with an old robe for Felix to wear.

"I am going to prepare another meal. This time I ask you both to get it in your mouths. Honestly, you are both like little bambinos."

The men laughed. Jorge had not felt this way since before Rosa had passed.

"Are you sure that you want us to come and stay with you in the city?"

"Yes. I think you will enjoy it. My family will welcome you."

They ate their breakfast of eggs in silence.

"I enjoyed that. Now, I must dress and leave. I need to contact my superior officer and cannot be late."

Rosita went with him to his room and helped him clean off the food and to dress. When he was done, she reached her hand behind his neck and pulled him to her and kissed him passionately.

Felix was bewildered. He liked Rosita but had not expected that.

"I think I have fallen in love with you Felix. Please return soon. We will plan our trip to La Iluminada when you come back. I would like to leave soon. I am excited by all this."

Chapter 12

Early in the afternoon, Felix returned to the little adobe. He parked the military jeep and walked up to the entrance very slowly. Rosita watched him. It was obvious something was wrong.

Felix, you look worried. Is something wrong? Are you in trouble?"

"No, it is not me. It is you. Father Lopez has made a complaint and is requesting the Federal Police to arrest you. He has told them he caught you stealing in his house and when he tried to stop you, that you attacked him and tried to kill him. Because he is a priest they believe him. You are in a serious situation. They are planning on arresting you and taking you to a terrible jail near the city. I suggest we leave soon or it will be too late for me to help you.

This morning a new priest is coming to replace Father Lopez. His name is Father Dominic. I know him. He is a chaplain to the military. He is a good man and not stupid. I am not sure why he was chosen to replace Father Lopez but it is curious. The barrio is insignificant to the upper echelon of the church. He would be better suited to one of the larger and more wealthy areas. It is very strange."

While they had been talking Jorge had entered the room and overheard the conversation.

"Felix, I wonder whether Father Lopez asked to be relieved, or is he being recalled?"

"I heard at the offices he asked to leave here."

"What can we do? They will believe the priest. Rosita will not have any chance."

"Don't worry. I know the District Commandant for this area. He is a bit dimwitted. It is nothing that a thousand or so pesos will nor resolve."

"Felix we do not have that big amount of money. We will be in trouble."

"No don't worry. I can easily pay that for you. Now, I suggest you start preparing for the trip to the city. I am required to stay here and meet Father Dominic. He will need to take over the church's house. It is another strange matter that Father Lopez has already left the barrio. He was taken away by one of the men from the mine in a truck. It is all very strange,"

Rosita frowned and decided to ask the question that had been bothering her all morning.

"I don't know what to take. I do not have many nice clothes. We dress simply here, like peasants. I will be embarrassed in La Iluminada to wear those clothes."

"Rosita, you have been kind. I will make sure my mother takes you to get nice clothes. It will be my gift to you."

Jorge wondered at the source of wealth. He thought back to anything he may have heard about Felix's name. The de Santos family was known for owning businesses, but Jorge could not remember what they were. There were days when he could not remember the simplest things or names of old friends. He hated aging.

"Jorge, Rosita, I am required to be at the church before the new priest arrives. I have been given orders to take certain items back with me. I will need to leave now."

After Felix left, Jorge asked Rosita to make some coffee using the special beans from their region. She obliged and when the coffee was made they both sat outside on the open front porch.

"Rosita, I have been watching you. I think you are in love with this man. Be careful. You are young and he is an officer and has experience in life. You can get hurt. There are probably many women in the city who wish to have him. He is from a family with wealth and power. Those other girls will not give up easily. You will be ridiculed and fought with. It will not be physical fighting but nasty tricks and games played on you. They will try to manipulate you. Beware, this may not be the right thing for you."

"I am old enough to know what I want. Do not worry about me. If other girls wish to play those games, they have decided to play with the wrong person. I intend to marry this man Papi."

Without showing any emotion, Jorge was thrilled. A life away from the poverty-stricken barrio and in the city with wealth. He could not have hoped for more.

"Let us go in and pack what few things we wish to take with us."

Jorge walked through the house. There was very little he wished to take. He selected some of his best clothes and took them to Rosita who was laying her dresses on the bed. She took a sheet from the bed and started wrapping the clothing in a neat bundle in the sheet as they did not own a suitcase.

When she was done, she took any perishable food to her neighbor and explained they were going to visit friends. The neighbor asked questions but Rosita was scarce with answers. She was unable to tell the neighbor how long they would be gone.

Jorge was in his room looking through a pile of old books. He was looking for one he had read that featured La Iluminada. He was excited to be making the trip.

The day dragged on. Felix returned mid-afternoon. He seemed preoccupied.

"We must change our plans and leave in the morning. I have been asked to drive back to the city and it is too late today, plus I am tired. The military officer who accompanied Father Dominic briefed me. It contained some disturbing news. I cannot discuss it with you as I am in the investigative unit. It is a confidential military matter. I promise to tell you when it can be discussed, I will share all the details with you. Please understand."

Jorge nodded. He knew better than to probe into the business of government. No good came to those who asked the wrong questions.

"Felix, tonight I will take you to the cantina. It is owned by friends. I will have them make some delicious foods that are unique to our little village. You will relax and enjoy."

"I look forward to that. We will need to leave early in the morning. Our drive will be between six and seven hours."

He walked through the adobe and headed to the kitchen where Rosita was working. As he approached she observed something very different had been added to the uniform in which he had left dressed that morning. A large pistol in a black leather holster was strapped to his side.

Felix saw her looking at it.

"Why?"

"I told you that I am part of the investigations unit. When we are working we are required to wear a sidearm for our protection. Sometimes we have to deal with unpleasant people and situations."

"Since you are wearing it here does that mean you have started working on something in the barrio?"

"You know I cannot answer that."

His response was enough for Rosita with all her cunning to understand he was.

"Don't go bringing trouble to Jorge and I. We want no trouble."

Felix started to raise his hands to object.

"Felix, be quiet. Say no more. Let us enjoy the evening here."

"I will change my clothes. I don't wish to wear this uniform tonight. I want to be entertained."

The type of entertainment that ran through Rosita's mind would have shocked many a priest in a confessional. She smiled to herself and thought, "If he only knew."

The sun was setting as they strolled into the center of the barrio, and headed to the cantina. They were greeted by the owner who immediately hugged Jorge and Rosita before standing back and eyeing Felix.

"It is alright. He is a friend of ours and he came to our little village for government business. We have brought him here tonight for your special foods and music. His name is Felix de Santos."

The owner bent forward with an extended hand. He shook Felix's hand and then hugged him before leading them to a hand-carved wooden table near the rear of the restaurant.

After they were seated, a sultry young woman in a low cut turquoise dress came with a carafe of red wine. She bent excessively low as she placed the wine on the table in front of Felix. He could not help but view the vista in front of him, and it was plentiful. The waitress slowly and seductively straightened herself and smiled a disarming smile at Felix. Rosita felt the fury rip through her. Her hands were shaking. She was trying to control both her temper and the force of the evil inside her.

Felix was loving the attention. He had no idea that Rosita was in a murderous mood.

Chapter 13

The owner returned and recommended the churrasco steak with chimichurri sauce and lime butter. While they waited, a lone guitarist softly played some old Spanish guitar tunes.

Their steaks arrived. They were cut thin with the spicy sauce poured over them. Knobs of serrano butter decorated the top. The customary fried egg sat at the edge of the plate. The aroma of the fresh parsley, oregano, and onions wafted up from the plates.

While they were eating, several men filled up the cantina. Most stood drinking at the long dark wooden bar.

They had finished the meal when the guitarist was joined by two other men and flamenco music erupted. At that moment, the waitress in the turquoise dress spun from the kitchen, and with her hand extended pulled Felix up to dance. Rosita almost flew over the table. Jorge sensing the impending crisis restrained her.

"Rosita, please do not give her the satisfaction of a bar fight. Only the men will enjoy watching the two of you. You are young and pretty. She is older and will soon turn to seed like the plants. Men will be bored with her sooner than she would care to know."

He held Rosta's wrist firmly. He was surprised at her strength. He relaxed his grip as she started to sit back down.

The flamenco dancing waitress looked seductively at Felix as she twirled and clicked her castanets. Jorge again moved quickly when from the corner of his eye he saw Rosita slide a knife from the table.

He vowed that the night was over and when the spectacular

performance ended, he would take Felix and Rosita away from the cantina and back to the adobe.

They were about to leave as the music stopped but halted when two men walked in. One was dressed in military dress and the other wore a priest's garments. The military man recognized Felix and headed toward him after pointing him out to the priest.

"Felix, this is Father Dominic whom I brought here to the barrio earlier today."

 Felix introduced Jorge and Rosita.

The priest shook hands and spoke very softly. He was unlike Father Lopez. His demeanor was that of creating trust in him with those to whom he spoke.

"Come and sit with us for a while if you can. I am interested to speak with someone who has lived here in this barrio for so long."

They were reseated at the table and again the owner arrived to introduce himself. Much to Jorge's surprise the priest ordered a bottle of the local corn liquor and offered to buy them all drinks. Jorge was impressed.

The turquoise robed waitress looked markedly at the table and scowled at Rosita, who gently smiled back at her. She had won this round.

After much small talk, the priest became serious.

"Jorge, you have been here so long. Have you ever seen the people getting so sick before? Did any die from sicknesses like this?"

"No, Father. The men worked hard on our farms and we were very healthy. Children got the type of sickness associated with their age. Things like mumps, measles, and chickenpox but never was there any strange illness. The women would wash in the river and a little further up from where they wash their clothing is a pool from where we take our drinking water. Some of the farms have dug wells where possible, but in some areas, there is too much rock to dig through."

There was a pause in the conversation before Father Dominic spoke again.

"I was sent here to replace Father Lopez. It is too soon to tell you why, but he was involved in things that the church claims to know nothing about. Tomorrow, some scientists and doctors are coming here. I am asking if you can assist them?"

"We are leaving for the city in the early morning. Surely there will be others to help."

"I suggest you delay making that trip if you can. Father Lopez has made some astounding claims about the things your daughter, Rosita has done. He has threatened to have her arrested by the Federal Police. I think you should stay for a while. It will only be for a few days. I am unable to tell you more until we have certain evidence. It will be best for you to stay."

Felix placed his hand on Rosita's arm.

"I can request to stay and assist my fellow officer. I too know of the issues he speaks of and his advice is excellent. Please stay. I will also be here. There are going to be several difficult days ahead. Don't run from them. It will make it harder for you."

"But I have not done anything. I went to see him as he had my new dress for the ceremony of Quinca Años. I was trying it on when he stripped me and raped me. He is a monster."

"Rosita, my child. Please be calm. You will be able to tell the church and police authorities what happened. That is another reason for you to stay. Quinca Años is always fun and I will ensure it will be special for you."

"I will not wear that dress. I have nothing to wear. I am not going."

Jorge watched the interchange without speaking. He was amazed at Rosita. A few minutes ago she was acting like a vixen protecting her prey, and now she was again a teenager worried about a dress and how she would look to others.

Jorge decided it was time to speak.

"Father, I think there is a solution to the problem of the dress. There is an older woman here in the barrio. She used to make clothing for many of us when she was younger. I know her well. Let me go and visit her. It is still early and she lives close by. I will return. Come with me, Rosita."

Felix arose.

"Should I accompany you? Will you be safe?"

Jorge roared laughing.

"Felix after sixty years here in the barrio I don't think there is much for me to be scared of. I've seen it all. But I thank you for your kind gesture. Wait here for us."

Ten minutes later they were at a darkened little mud-brick house. It had bright yellow window frames and on the front porch, there were old wooden boxes with flowering plants of all size and color.

Rosita calmed. It felt like home.

Jorge knocked on the thick wooden door. He heard shuffling inside and the door creaked open on its rusty hinges. An old lady stood in the doorway and upon recognizing Jorge moved forward to embrace him. She stood back and admired Rosita.

"Jorge, is this the little girl I would look after when you and Rosa needed to be away from your home?"

"Yes, Senora de Silva. This is my sweet Rosita. We have come here to ask for your help."

"Come into my simple home. Wait while I make us a coffee. Come Rosita and help me. My you are a handsome one little Rosita."

They sat and drank their coffee and spoke about friends and some who had passed away with the strange illness. Finally, it was time.

"Senora, my little girl has Quinca Años this weekend at the church. There has been a problem and the dress she was to wear is no longer available for this event. We have come to offer you money to make her a dress if you can make one."

"I still make some clothes and since she is so pretty I think it will be easy to make a fine dress. My problem is I do not have a lot of different materials to make such a dress. Does the church want it to be white?"

"No. It is a joyous celebration. We are allowed colors."

The old lady sat for a while speechless, then stood and turned up the brightness of her oil lamps and left the room. There were some banging and thumping. Rosita looked to Jorge in panic. He held up his partially raised hand in a gesture to remain quiet.

Senora de Silva returned with a bulk roll of material that was almost the same size as she was. She may have been old, but she was tough and strong.

"Will this do, my dear?"

She unfurled a satin-like bright peacock blue material. Rosita was immediately in love with it. It was so far from the pink dress the priest had bought and the material had an expensive-looking shine.

"It is better than anything else I have ever seen. Yes, I love it."

"Tomorrow morning you come here early. Please do wear some underclothes. I am going to make exact measurements. You will be the best dressed and best looking young lady at the ceremony."

"Senora, how much will this cost. We do not have lots of money."

"Jorge, your dear wife Rosa was a special friend. She helped me with many things and I am sure you were never told of those things. I owe Rosa now as she rests with God. It is my turn to help you. There will be no cost to you. I will do this in the name of Rosa."

Rosita looked at Jorge in the soft yellow light of the lamps and saw the huge tears flowing down his cheeks. He stood and walked to the old lady and bent and hugged her for the longest time.

"My Rosa was a special woman. I think she will be a saint one day. It is only now since she passed that I am finding out about the many things she did for people."

"Jorge, go now. You are making my chair wet with those tears." She stood and started toward the door before stopping and turning to Rosita.

"I have a favor to ask you, Rosita. Promise me that you will live and be kind like your mother was. That is all I ask of you. Remember this as you grow and experience life."

The words struck Rosita hard. She would never forget them.

They returned to the cantina to find the others involved in heavy conversation. The atmosphere was filled with noise from the men at the bar. The flamenco dancing turquoise belle was sprawled across one of the men's laps in a drunken state. She attempted to call to Rosita in a slurred voice but was unable to get her words out.

Rosita smiled. Now she knew she had won.

Chapter 14

Felix rose to hug her and take her to a seat next to him when they returned from arranging for the dress. She felt supreme and in control. She looked across at the turquoise flamenco dancer with disgust and an air of superiority.

"My dear Felix. I saw how that bitch danced with you. It was not about dancing. She wanted you. It would have been your mistake to make. Now, look at her. A drunken whore. Is that what you would have liked tonight?"

Jorge was astounded at Rosita's outburst.

"Rosita, we have only known Felix for a short time. It is wrong for you to speak to him like this. You do not know him. I was hoping you would act like a young lady. You are disappointing me."

"I intend to look after you and me. We will go to the city and we will never return to this barrio. You will have a better life my Papi. You will see."

"I love you, Rosita. I cannot think of my life without you. You are from Rosa and me. We had only wanted good things in your life, but here in this country, it has been too hard. We are only small people. The Generals and those in power take all the money and riches of our country for themselves. We are left with nothing. I have known men and ladies who could be the best doctors, yet they have been robbed of the opportunity to receive an education because the privileged want those schools and university opportunities for their children. They pay for them from the money that we, the poor, pay in taxes and bribes to be allowed to live on our farms. Our life has been hard. Now you have an opportunity with Felix. I ask you to think carefully. An opportunity like this will never come to you again. I believe that your dear mother, Rosa, has intervened and blessed you as her child with this chance to escape the poverty that is growing here in our community. Be wise. Take the rose that is offered to you. Be careful and ask the right questions. You are my daughter. I love you and want you to have a life beyond here."

It was then that Felix returned, after having excused himself minutes earlier.

"I have spoken to my superiors. My continued stay here is approved. I will be required to assist Father Dominic and the church with an investigation."

It was then that Felix looked at Rosita. As he looked at her, it seemed the image of her beauty changed from a young girl to a beautiful woman in front of his eyes. He was bewildered as the image moved back and forth in his mind.

He asked Rosita to dance with him and threw some large peso notes to the guitar and violin player.

Moments later harmonious music filled the cantina. Felix held Rosita tight as they danced close together. She was enraptured by the music, the heat, and the scent of his body, and the heady atmosphere of the cantina with the smoke that filled the air and the loud laughs of the men at the bar.

They slowly danced as a couple tied together in an embrace. The turquoise decorated waitress decided to make a last attempt at seducing Felix. She pried herself off the lap of the drunken friend at the bar and attempted to interfere with their romantic dance. Before she reached the small area in which they were dancing, she fell face down. Vomit spewed from her mouth. The evening's margaritas were being recycled.

Felix decided it was time to leave. He bid farewell to Dominic and his military companion and with Rosita and Jorge they left to return to the little adobe.

Felix escorted Rosita out of the cantina. Jorge walked a slight distance behind them. Slowly they wound their way back to Jorge's simple house. Inside, Felix spoke to them.

"Don't worry. This investigation will end tomorrow and we will leave for La Iluminada the next day."

"I am worried about Rosita. Will she be arrested? She has done nothing wrong. She is young."

"Jorge, I am aware of how they wish to proceed. Rosita will be protected. Many serious matters will be exposed. I will make sure she is protected. I must ask Rosita to stay away from others and remain here. It will be best. Father Lopez had a huge following and many will be upset when he is exposed.
Rosita will probably be attacked by other women. It is for her safety I ask that she hide until we leave for La Iluminada. It will only be for a day or two. For me to keep you safe you must promise me this."

"Felix, she cannot do this. She is to attend the Quinca Años. We can leave to drive to the city after the ceremony. Why are you concerned that other women may try to attack her?"

"It seems that Father Lopez had a very active life with many women here."

"Tomorrow Rosita must go to Senora de Silva as they will be starting to make her dress for the special ceremony this weekend. She cannot miss that. The Senora is expecting her."

"I will escort her there. I will make sure she arrives safely and then when she is ready to return I will bring her back. Jorge, I cannot say too much, but what is about to be revealed in this barrio is going to cause big problems. It is best we are leaving for the city."

"We must stay for the ceremony. Rosita will be a rose amongst the thorns. I ask you to delay the trip."

"Tomorrow, I will contact my superiors and request we stay until the end of the weekend. Then we must leave. I have urgent matters to attend to in La Iluminada."

"I will pack our few belongings for the trip. We will be ready to leave on Sunday night."

"It will be a long day for Rosita. The trip will be tiring."

"I am sure that her excitement in visiting the city will overcome any tiredness she may have. She has wanted to go and stay in the city for many years now. It is her dream coming true."

Felix laughed as he made his way to the door.

"I must visit the other officer now. I will return later."

Rosita's eyes lit up. Felix would be there for the night.

"I will make a delicious dinner. We will wait for you to return."

Rosita stared at him and smiled a provocative smile while thinking of the task she was about to perform.

"My plans will happen. I need to attend to an important matter before we leave. I will go for an hour Papi, then I will return and make us that dinner."

Rosita excused herself and outside started her determined walk back to the cantina.

She arrived back at the cantina and found the man she was looking for. He was drunk and stared at Rosita's firm body. She allowed him to undress her with his eyes. She knew his reputation and in her mind, he was a human-pig.

"Senor Pepe, you like what you see? It can be yours if you help me take the flamenco dancer home. She is too drunk to walk alone."

Pepe continued to stare at Rosita's firm body and in a crazed voice responded with enthusiasm that he would assist with anything that would result in an hour's pleasure in bed with Rosita.

Rosita knew she had him hooked.

"I have some things I will need to carry with me. Go and bring her out. We will take her for a walk to sober her up. We will walk her up the river to the start of the jungle and then take her home. If she stays so drunk, then maybe you and I can enjoy our encounter in the growth of the jungle, far away from the prying eyes of others."

Pepe could barely control his excitement and left to get the flamenco dancer for what would be her last walk.

Chapter 15

Days passed slowly until the Sunday ceremony. Rosita made frequent trips to the home of Senora de Silva. Felix spent more time at the Villa talking with Jorge.

Rosita's obsession with Felix grew. Her early teenage crush developed into lustful thoughts and desires. At times she found herself blushing at the images she conjured up in her mind.

"I am determined to have him as mine."

Felix seemed oblivious to her infatuation and assumed she was just being polite and friendly.

On Sunday morning, Rosita arose early and slipped away to her room to dress and prepare for the Quinca Años. She was determined to look, be the best dressed, and the most charming. She did not think this would be hard, as she considered the other girls to be ugly and somewhat stupid.

Felix and Jorge were sitting in the shabby little kitchen drinking coffee and smoking cigarettes made from strong-smelling local tobacco when Rosita emerged.

Rosita watched their eyes absorb her.

"It is a quite acceptable dress." She twirled in front of them.

Her shiny jet black hair was pulled back tightly. She had copied a picture she had seen in one of the magazines their friends had brought from the city.

The bright peacock blue dress accentuated every curve of her young body. A pale pink sash hung loosely around her waist.

She presented the picture of mature and wise beauty, not the image of a young girl.

"I believe I have your attention, Felix. Will you dance with me at the ceremony?"

"How could I refuse such beauty."

Jorge sat and watched his daughter's overt flirtation.

"Felix, please escort me to the church. Here take my arm."

The three walked from the little adobe. The heat had remained, and even at that hour of the morning heatwaves shimmered off the surface of the mud packed path that led to the church.

Outside the church, families stood talking while the young Quinceañeras ran between families giggling and chattering like monkeys.

Rosita watched the gathering and thought.

"Those girls are not like me at all. I am better, more clever, and beautiful than any of them. They are just stupid little girls."

A silence fell as Jorge, Felix, and Rosita approached. The locals looked in astonishment at Rosita who had her arm draped through Felix's. The envy of the other girls soon became obvious. Rosita heard the comments.

"Nobody wears blue to a Quinca Años."

"Look at her hair. It is filled with chicken fat to shine like that."

"She has sinned with that man. She shouldn't be allowed here today."

The comments went on, but silently and secretly, all the girls yearned for a Felix.

Jorge observed a group of men standing together away from the others. There was a look of hostility on their faces. He was about to cross over to them when Felix spoke.

"Jorge, I told you that there was going to be trouble. Rumors have started already. We should leave immediately after the service. The reasons for the presence of the other military have become known. If I stay with you tonight, I fear I will be placing both you and Rosita in danger. We leave tonight."

"I am ready. I packed some clothing for Rosita and me, and food to eat during the trip."

The priest stood on the small step at the front door of the church.

"It is time for the Quinceañeras to make their procession down the aisle to the special chairs that await them at the altar. We will then have the mass, after which I will do the traditional presentation of a young 'woman' and each family to God. Today we will need to share the tiara, as there is only one crown for these princesses to share. After the crowning, these young ladies will be the princesses of God. We will celebrate that with a reading from the bible and a rosary. The young ladies can then place flowers at the feet of the Virgin Mary after which each will be given a ring by me to symbolize the love of God. Now let us commence."

The girls walked the narrow aisle as proud parents watched. Some mothers dabbed away tears from their eyes. The Quinca Años (Fifteen Years of age) proceeded and hours slipped by. The ceremony concluded and the celebration moved to the village cantina.

All of the girls sat and performed the customary changing of shoes ahead of the traditional Quinceanera waltz.

An old battered accordion squeaked out the notes to the waltz. The girls danced with their fathers, with one exception. Dressed in her bright peacock blue dress, Rosita held Felix close and tight. The priest frowned. This was not the behavior he expected from a fifteen-year-old. Especially at a Quinca Años.

He arose and went to Jorge.
"She needs to be controlled and learn virtues."
"Father, she is a good girl. I think she is confused. She has no mother and no one to speak with. She means no harm to anyone."

"I will speak to her after the final custom is performed."

The Father then left to announce the ceremony of the dolls. Each girl was given a doll that was to be passed to a younger girl. This symbolized the end of childhood for the older girl. She was now a woman.

Rosita refused the custom. The other girls had been watching her with envy. In her peacock blue dress, she was the most obvious and beautifully groomed Quinceanera, and she had a handsome and debonair partner.

Rosita was enjoying every moment of mentally torturing them. She had no love for any of them.

Jorge was embarrassed. He had never witnessed her behaving like this

There was a moment when the festivities quietened as the families and the girls talked together. Jorge took this pause to summon Felix.

"I think we should leave. Rosita is causing discomfort amongst the others and especially with Father Dominic."

"I will tell Rosita it is time for us to quietly leave and start our night drive to La Iluminada."

Rosita stood displaying her dress to a group of older women and complimenting the work of Senora de Silva. Seeing Felix approaching, and the determined look on his face, she excused herself and brushed by some of the other girls on her way to him.

"Rosita, the time has come for us to slip away from the barrio and take our trip to the city. I have asked my fellow officer to travel with us. He will take his jeep and follow behind us. He needs to return to the military base and bring some others here. The coming week here will not be safe. There are some here who are secretly contributing to the problems of the barrio. The government and the military will be involved in a raid to stop these criminals next week. You and Jorge must be safe. You will be at my home. Please don't ask any questions. At your villa, be quick and take only those items you need. We can retrieve your other effects at another time."

Rosita turned to him and looked directly into his eyes with a piercing intensity.

"Felix, I will agree this time, but you must never keep any secrets from me."

Part 2

Ascending in a New Life

Chapter 16

The sun was still setting and the sky reflected the orange and pink of the dwindling rays on the scattered clouds.
The country's proximity to the equator meant that sunset was late and the twilight time was short until darkness enveloped the land.

Felix wanted to leave before darkness descended.

As they packed their basic belongings and some light food to eat during the trip, another jeep silently rolled to a halt behind Felix. A tall dark man unwound from his position behind the driver's wheel and stretched his lanky legs out of the open door.

Felix beamed as he introduced the man.

"Jorge, Rosita this is Major Sergio Alvares. He will drive with us to La Iluminada. Jorge, why don't you ride with him for a while. We can change during the trip and you can join me."

"Yes, I would like that. Is the Major from La Iluminada? I have many questions. Hopefully, he can answer them. I feel like a little boy about to embark on a new adventure. I am excited for Rosita and myself."

Rosita was watching the exchange. She had a blank expression on her face. Her mind was assessing what lay ahead and questions formed.

"Will I be free, or will Jorge be in my way?" She wondered and frowned. This was not the way she had planned to leave for a life away from the barrio.

Jorge had been a good father and provided for her. She didn't understand the emotions she was experiencing and felt some shame at wanting him away from her life. He had done nothing wrong, nor did he deserve any scorn from her. She dismissed the thoughts and went to help finish packing their belongings into the jeep.

She entered the Villa, in which the hot dusty air hung. There had been no breeze that day and the sweltering heat had baked the interior. Smells of stale clothing and recently cooked meals had been released by the intense heat.

"I won't be sad to leave this place."

She was walking out with clothes in her arms when a stray dog sidled up to her and lifted its leg to urinate on her shoe. Her fury erupted. The dog yelped in pain as she kicked it hard in its genitals. A huge feeling of relief swept over her. No one had witnessed her humility at being used as a latrine.

She looked back at the Villa to see Jorge standing alone and staring at the little home.

"What are you doing?"

"My life with Rosa was here, and then you were born to bring so much happiness into our lives. While I wish to live in the city, I will miss our humble little home here. We had many friends here, but many have died from the mystery illness and others have left. The barrio is not the same. There are people here now that I do not know. At the church, there was a group of men who stood and stared at me. I did not know any of them. They did not look friendly. I believe they must be from another barrio in the country. Their dress was simple and of the type that the peasants wear. I did not trust the way they looked at everyone. Who are those men? I do not feel like it is my home here any longer."

Felix arrived and interrupted them.

"All your possessions are packed in the jeep. It is time for us to leave."

Jorge turned and held Rosita. She hugged him tightly.
"Don't worry Papi. We will make a new and interesting life in the city. I have many ideas. You will be fine and happy."

He looked at her. She was dressed in black shorts and wore a white blouse. The peacock blue dress had been packed for the trip. Rosita had transformed from a scraggly child in front of his eyes.

Major Alvares called Jorge to join him in his jeep. The jeeps were open with no windows. In the heat, there was no need for the rooftop covers.

"It is going to be a long drive tonight. I hope you like bad jokes. I have many. By the time we reach La Iluminada, you will probably have heard all of them."

The Major roared laughter at the prospect of entertaining Jorge for hours with his repertoire of jokes. The sunlight was starting to fade as Felix and Major Alvares fired up the jeeps and crawled slowly away from the barrio.

Once out of sight of the other adobes of the village, Felix removed his tie and rolled up the sleeves of his military tunic. He looked over at Rosita, who had curled herself into a comfortable yet somewhat seductive position on the passenger seat and door. She was examing his physique and allowing her imagination to run wild. She dreamed of situations where they stopped and he took her into the heavily overgrown grasses beside the road. She imagined him naked in a giant bed with her in a luxurious hotel. She had seen pictures of movie stars in such rooms in the magazines she had been lent.

Rosita was determined that the trip would not be boring…either for her or Felix. She wondered how they could elude Major Alvares and her father for them to enjoy such an encounter.

Felix drove ahead of Major Sergio Alvares, occasionally glancing in his mirror to ensure they were still close.

Felix felt a cool sensation on his arm and looked to see that Rosita had slid her hand up to his rolled-up sleeve. He smiled. She was such a child.

They continued the drive south. Other than several beat-up old farm trucks, there was no traffic in this poor part of the country.

Nightfall was closing in fast. The sky was darkening.

Behind Felix and Rosita, Jorge was enjoying his conversation with Major Sergio Alvares, who seemed so natural.

Jorge looked over at the man. He was all muscle and sat rigid in his seat. An unlit cigar dangled from his lips. He chewed at it and had remarked to Jorge that his wife demanded he stop smoking and this was his silent escape from her. They had laughed at this.

They were fast approaching the mine operations. Jorge was surprised. The compound was lit with bright Klieg security lights. This was new. He had been in the area before with other men when they hunted wild boar at night. The mine had never been lit.

Ahead of them, Felix slowed to take in the view of the mine compound. He sensed that someone had leaked the information about the planned raid.

As Major Sergio Alvares slowed to a crawl to observe the situation, Jorge let out a gasp. He saw the two heavily armed men at the front gate near the barbed wire enclosed fence. They were the same men he had seen earlier at the church. They were not local men. They appeared to be either Mexican or Colombian. In the light, Jorge could not tell.

Hurriedly he ducked down out of sight, but it was too late. The men had seen him.

He rose after a minute and looked back. The men had left their posts and were running back toward a Ford F-150 truck equipped with a row of extra lights attached to a bar running across the truck's roof and there were bars welded across the grill. The truck had been ruggedized. As he watched, the men jumped into the truck. The wheels spun throwing up clouds of the reddish dust.

It was soon apparent to Jorge and Major Sergio Alvares that they were being pursued by the men. The distance between the jeep and the truck was diminishing by the minute.

The Major sounded the horn of his jeep continually to attract the attention of Felix and then grabbed the microphone for the military radio. He tried to radio Felix. There was no response. He next dialed up a number to attempt to contact the base in La Iluminada. A weak voice responded through the static. They were too far away from the base for the radio reception to be clear.

Within minutes, the truck sped by and slewed to a halt in front of them, blocking the narrow road. The armed men jumped from the truck and roughly grabbed Jorge and Major Sergio Alvares, pulling them from the jeep.

Jorge was thrown to the ground. The butt of a rifle was smashed into his forehead. Blackness ensued as he lost all consciousness and spasms of pain wracked through his twisted body.

On the other side of the jeep, there was a ferocious confrontation as Major Sergio Alvares fought back his attackers. He used every ounce of strength and trick he could remember from his territorial training. He had no intention of surrendering to these men.

Minutes passed until another truck from the mining camp screeched to a halt behind the jeep. More men jumped from the back and ran to assist in subduing Major Sergio Alvares.

It was pointless to resist.

Ahead, the jeep with Rosita and Felix had sped on, unaware of the drama unfolding behind them.

The sun was sinking below the hills and cactus-strewn landscape when Felix decided to stop and wait for Major Sergio Alvares. Within minutes he became alarmed and realized something was wrong. He checked the jeep's radio transmitter and found it had been accidentally turned off. He switched it on and tried to call the Major. Static crackled. He dialed the frequency for the base and broadcast a message for help. It was soon answered by a broken and somewhat garbled response.

Felix sat worried and thought about the situation. He had been briefed on the possibility of an interception. Both he and Major Sergio Alvares had been provided intelligence regarding the arrival of a large shipment of equipment and suspicious men at the mining camp.

For the first time since he had visited Nos Grande, Felix sensed great danger.

He looked over at Rosita who was softly humming a local folk tune. She was unaware of the danger in which they were in.

Felix attempted to radio the base again. With the sun setting and nightfall descending it seemed the reception was improving.

He considered the situation. He was with a sophisticated teenage girl, and except for the uniform dress pistol he was unarmed. Between the two of them, there was little they could do.

Felix made his decision. He would drive at high speed to the base and brief the others before mounting a mission to return and rescue Jorge and Major Sergio Alvares.

He reached across the seats of the jeep and squeezed Rosita's cool wrist. It gave him a feeling of exhilaration and hope. He slid the jeep into gear and quickly drove through the dirt roads and tracks to the main highway.

Major Sergio Alvares had been correct. When the information of the mine was known, there would be major trouble within Nos Grande and the military.

Felix despised that he had been recruited into the investigations unit within the forces. It had cost him friends and the other men were always guarded and suspicious of him.

Finally, the day had arrived when the corruption and treachery would be revealed. Felix hoped that this would assist in his regaining friendships and the trust of his peers.

He wondered how Rosita would react to the information. He considered her strong but had concerns that what was about to be revealed would push her to the point of hostility and hatred.

Suddenly he realized that he had fallen far more into his friendship with Rosita that just that of a friend. He had fallen in love with the young woman.

Chapter 17

They sped down the highway toward La Iluminada. Rosita started to sing an old Spanish love song. She was carefree and happy to be away from the barrio and on her way to a new adventure.

During the trip, Rosita asked Felix to stop at various times to visit the dirty bathrooms of the country's run-down gas stations. Each time he stopped, concern for their safety increased. He trusted no one at this point. He was uncertain whether they were being followed. He could not tell Rosita of his fear.

The highway was poorly lit. Heavy jungle vegetation had crept down and bordered on the road. There were very few cars traveling at that time of evening and since turning onto the highway they had only passed half a dozen old farm pickups on their way to La Iluminada where the farmers sold their produce. There were wire cages stuffed with chickens piled high on the rear trays of some trucks. Others were laden with fruits and vegetables. Felix wondered how the farmers survived.

They had traveled thirty minutes since the last gas station. As Felix turned the steering wheel of the jeep to start the climb up a mountain pass, they encountered a military roadblock.

"Rosita, stay calm, and say nothing. I will talk. This is a military vehicle and I am in uniform. I'm sure we will not be detained or experience any difficulties."

"Felix, there is no war or unrest in the country. Why are there these roadblocks and checks?"

"They are just routine. The government is concerned about the possible infiltration of militia from our hostile neighbor. That country is rife with corruption, drugs, and political assassinations. We patrol to prevent their influence from entering our country. Now be quiet while I go and speak to the commander of this unit."

As Felix swung open the door and kicked his legs out of the jeep, two very young soldiers approached. They did not seem impressed with the rank of the uniform that Felix wore. They jeered at him and cracked crude jokes before one reached into the jeep to touch Rosita.

She had seen the attempted move before the soldier could reach her. With a mighty force, she lunged at him with her fingers extended. The fingers sunk into the soldier's eye sockets blinding him.

The second soldier witnessed this and immediately swung his Uzi sub-machine gun at Felix.

"Don't give me any reason to kill you. I will. You are nothing but one of those bourgeois privileged officers. You take bribes and make the rest of us suffer. It would give me pleasure for you to do something stupid so I can pull this trigger."

On the ground beside the jeep, the incapacitated soldier moaned and lifted his head. Rosita's strike had been effective and damaging. The whole eyeball of his right eye dangled from the socket. A mucous ran down his cheek. He alternately whimpered or cried in pain.

Felix looked to his partner.

"I think you should now concentrate on your friend here. Before you leave I want your ID and papers. Where are you stationed? Which base? Who is the base commander?"

The young soldier looked unsure.

"I have enough information on you and this event to commence a nasty proceeding against you. The military, even the corrupt ones, don't like the men raping young girls. I will be reporting that the two of you attempted to rape my passenger and she attacked your accomplice."

There was no bravado left in the soldier's demeanor.

"He meant no harm. Just fun. It has been boring here. Nothing but chicken farmers and the odd pig being taken to market. Please don't report this. I will get my friend looked after. I plead you do not make a report. We are poor people. This job as a soldier means we can eat and have a little money."

Rosita felt the strange cold sensation arise in her chest and around her heart. A feeling of anger was developing.

"Felix, these men meant to hurt us. They would have robbed us and done other terrible things. Give me your pistol, they do not deserve to live."

She reached forward to his waistband in an attempt to snatch his pistol.

"No Rosita. That will not help. We are going to need the assistance of soldiers like this in the days ahead. I am sure I can convince them to support the efforts that will start in the next days. You must trust me."

Rosita scowled at him before her face softened into a radiant glow. She smiled.

"Of course, Felix. You are wise and have experience. I am just someone young and silly. I am not thinking."

The soldier stood confused. He looked at his partner still writhing on the ground.

In the jeep, Felix picked up the microphone and attempted to call the base. A reply came back that was clear and without the static.

"Base, this is Felix de Santos. I am returning from my mission in Nos Grande. There have been incidents. Major Alvares has been taken captive by men I do not know. We are at a checkpoint at Kilo 92. The soldiers manning this post have been attacked. One is serious and needs help immediately. The other has been shot."

The soldier had listened to the transmission and his eyes widened as Felix aimed his service pistol at him and shot him in the leg.

"Now you will be with us and take our orders. Do you understand? I needed to shoot you to convince the officers at your base. It is only a small wound. You will be fine."

The radio crackled back to life and an excited voice exclaimed that additional men had been dispatched to Kilo 92 checkpoint. The voice also commanded them to take cover until the other soldiers arrived.

Felix turned to the soldier.

"I think it is time I knew your names. I am Colonel Felix de Santos, Lead Investigator for the Supreme Command."

The soldier looked at Felix in awe, considering and wondering how such a young man could hold the rank of Colonel in that role.

"I am Pedro Juarez and my wounded friend is Ricardo Cassillio. We are both from the same little village about 5 kilometers from here."

"Then Pedro, help me move him to the cover of the jungle growth. Your leg wound is minor. I am an excellent marksman and could have done major damage. I chose to give you a slight injury to make your story seem true. I will drive the jeep into the jungle. If any banditos come by they will not detect us."

The four of them cloistered themselves in the thick growth of the jungle vines. After thirty minutes Rosita tapped Felix on the shoulder when she heard the sound of the approaching helicopters. She and Felix pushed their way through the growth and stood in the center of the highway. They could see the flashing of the strobe lights on the choppers as they came closer and dropped in altitude. The noise from the blade slap and the whine of the jet engines was almost unbearable. As the lead chopper dropped toward them, the high-intensity searchlight was illuminated. The chopper landed on the road. The two remaining helicopters hovered overhead with their spotlights scanning the dense jungle growth on either side of the highway.

The chopper remained on the road while the accompanying units flew off.

Felix ran to the open door of the cockpit and introduced himself. The pilot was a Captain. He extended his hand to Felix.

"The others have flown on to the Nos Grande area in search of the Major and his jeep. I am to take you and the injured soldiers to the base in La Iluminada. They will receive treatment at the hospital there. Let's get them aboard."

Felix turned and called into the jungle. Minutes later the scraggly group stumbled out of the growth. Pedro had his arm draped around Riccardo and was limping noticeably. Rosita held his other side. The helicopter Captain stared at them as they moved toward the chopper.

"Colonel Felix. Who is she? I cannot take civilians on this craft. It is strictly forbidden. I will not allow her on board."

"Captain, I am a Colonel and order you to allow her to accompany us. She is critical to the mission that is planned at Nos Grande. She has lived there all her life and knows the situation. She has been cooperating with me and the Intelligence group. I do not wish to exert rank over you, but you will fly her to La Iluminada. That is an order.”

“With all respect, Colonel, will you place that order in writing here in the flight logbook?”

Chapter 18

In the chopper, the sound of the engines and rotors made conversation impossible. Rosita sat in awe and was entranced as they flew southward toward La Iluminada. As they slowly approached the city more lights of houses shone up into the sky like little jewels on a black velvet sheet. The closer to the city they flew, the lights of office buildings illuminated the sky. Brightly lit colored neon signs flashed below them.

The chopper banked and quickly dropped altitude. Ahead of them, a rotating searchlight marked the landing area at the military airport. Runway lights brightly defined the edges of the tarmac.

Rosita strained to see the area. Off in the distance, she could make out the shapes of huge military planes. Parked beside them were trucks and some tanks. Felix had been watching her.

"Rosita, those planes and that equipment are being prepared for the action that is planned at Nos Grande. Soon you will understand."

"Felix, I am not a child. I demand you tell me what is going to happen to my barrio. I do not expect you to keep any secrets from me."

"Rosita, I cannot. I am sworn to secrecy. I can tell you that what will happen will only improve life at the barrio and remove some dangerous and destructive forces. You must just accept that for now. Tomorrow I will be able to fully explain the situation. Please, I ask you to understand."

Again she sensed that cold sensation in her chest, but as she admired his handsome and rugged face, the feeling subsided. She intended to fully seduce him that night.

As the engines were cut, a dark green ambulance with a red cross painted against a large white circle raced to the helicopter. After screeching to a halt, attendants in white coats rushed to the rear door of the chopper's fuselage. They helped Pedro and Riccardo to the ambulance and sped off with the siren blaring. Felix and Rosita stood in silence waiting for the special jeep for senior officers to arrive.

Rosita looked around, soaking in all the sights and sounds at the base. Beyond the high barbed wire lined walls, she could see the high buildings of the city and the glow of lights. She was eager to make her presence in the city known.

As she stood absorbing the surroundings, she began to wonder whether Felix would remain part of her life or had she used him just enough to get out of the barrio. She decided the next days at his family home would help to determine that. Again she felt the odd coldness grow in her chest. The frequency of the occurrences was increasing and the intensity of her emotions was growing.

A white jeep sped across the tarmac to meet them. Two flags attached to stanchions mounted on the jeep's front fenders flapped in the wind. It was then that Rosita realized Felix was a man of importance and stature. The cold feeling in her chest dissipated immediately.

A junior officer in a dress uniform and wearing a peaked hat marched to Felix and gave a crisp salute. This made Rosita happier. This was the life she had hoped would exist for her in the city.

The junior officer moved quickly to the door and assisted Rosita to the rear seat before helping Felix into the vehicle.

Before driving away from the helicopter, the pilot crossed to the jeep and handed Felix the logbook.

"I need you to sign and authorize the transportation of a civilian." Felix grabbed the logbook and pen and hurriedly scribbled his signature and rank on the form.

They stopped at a building set far back from the runways and operations buildings of the airport. Two armed sentries stood either side of the front entrance. Rosita glanced at them. It was obvious from the weapons they held that they were not there for ceremonial purposes. Each one possessed the look of hardened, mean, and determined men who had seen plenty during their lives.
They scared her and she tugged harder on Felix's arm. She had known men like these to visit the barrio. The men of the barrio soon encouraged them to leave.

Again, the junior officer sprang from the jeep and opened the door. Upon entering the building the two sentries snapped to attention and delivered formal salutes. Felix responded. One of the sentries turned and walked to open the entrance door for them.

Inside, the interior belied the look of the exterior. The floor was lined with ornate marble tile and polished to a radiant shine. Artwork and portraits of officers and leaders hung from the walls in huge gold-gilded frames.

While Rosita was admiring the portraits an adjutant walked quickly toward them.

"Colonel de Santos it is good to see you back here. May I have the pleasure of an introduction to this young lady."

"Yes. Thank you. This is Rosita Valquez. Rosita is from the barrio of Nos Grande."

At the mention of the name Nos Grande, a noticeable look of concern quickly passed on the adjutant's face.

"Welcome. Will you stay long in La Iluminada. Is it for a quick visit with relatives?'

"No, Rosita will be a house guest with my family. Besides, she has important information that will help us with our mission."

"We must hurry. The Generals are assembled and awaiting your arrival. They are impatient."

"Rosita, please wait in the area the gentleman escorts you to. I will return momentarily."

Felix opened the door and walked into the large smoke-filled room. Five Generals sat around a large mahogany table in luxurious chairs smoking cigars. Felix saluted them upon his entry. In return, he received several nods. There were no returned salutes.

"Good evening gentlemen. As you may be aware, we were ambushed on our trip here. I ask your indulgence to provide me an hour to prepare. I have a guest to take to my home. I will change and return within the hour."

A large obese man with short blonde cropped hair and acne-pocked face looked to the others.

"Why not allow this? I have more of that fine bourbon I brought with me from Tennessee."

Felix observed him. He had heard of this military advisor from the United States who was advising the army. He took an instant dislike to him.

"Boy, I'm Brigadier General Cutz, CIA liaison officer for the United States Army. Scoot along now son. Just be sure to have your arse back here in an hour. These good ole boys will do as I tell them. They know what side their bread is buttered on."

Felix again saluted and excused himself. The smell of cigar smoke and alcohol fumes filled the room. He was relieved to be leaving and dreading his return. He wondered what condition they would all be in. He was worried. His confidence in these men to lead an attack on that mining camp was low. They were not true military officers, but hacks who had been promoted to high salary positions by the crooked politicians they now served. Felix had no idea of how they could effectively rid Nos Grande and the camp of the criminal influences that had infiltrated the lives of the residents. Then it dawned on him. They were all involved. His job had just become more complex.

He met Rosita in an anteroom and walked with her to the entrance. The adjutant telephoned and a driver and jeep arrived to take them to the home of Felix de Santos.

They drove through the heavy double-armed gates on the compound out onto the street. The route to the home wound through several business districts before they encountered houses in a leafy section with large flowering gardens. Rosita looked on with silent approval.

It was so unlike the adobes of the barrio. There were no cantinas or food stalls on the sidewalks selling produce and shabby clothing. Expensive cars were parked in driveways.

With a sudden turn, the jeep started to climb a small hill. The trees and decorative vegetation were prolific. Felix was watching her surreptitiously as they turned into a winding driveway where a castlelike house stood in magnificence. The front façade was lit by spotlights mounted in the garden.

Felix turned to Rosita.

"Welcome to Villa Magnifico."

Chapter 19

Her face beamed as she examined the beauty of the architecture. Villa Magnifico was far beyond anything she had imagined.

The driver opened the door for them. Rosita left the jeep but Felix seemed to have gone into a trance, unaware that he was to leave the jeep. Suddenly he snapped back into reality. The task he faced with the Generals was consuming all of his attention. He needed to devise a plan within the hour and at the same time have Rosita welcomed and settled in the Villa.

Before they made it to the top of the stairs a gracious woman dressed casually in what Rosita knew were expensive clothes, rushed to meet them.

"Felix, are you alright? We heard from one of your friends at the base you had been attacked. Who is the young lady with you?"

"Mother, please meet Rosita Valquez. She will be staying with us for a while. She is from Nos Grande and assisted me while I was there. Her father will be joining her soon. They are moving to La Iluminada for Rosita to start a new life and career. Rosita, this is my mother, Carmine de Santos."

"I am pleased to meet you, Senora Carmine."

"I will have her bags taken to a guest room."

Rosita blushed and placed a hand over her mouth. She froze on the spot.

Carmine looked at her in bewilderment.

"What is wrong?"

"My bag is with my father. I have no belongings with me."

Felix looked to his mother and signaled her to drop the conversation.

"I am sure we can offer you some things until your father arrives with your bags. Did Felix mention he has a younger sister who is around your age. I am sure there will be clothing and items you two can share."

Felix was not sure the bags would ever arrive, nor did he think his less than kind sister would share anything with Rosita. The visit was not off to a good start.

"Mother, it was a difficult trip. I am required to return to the base to brief the command. I am sure that Rosita is both tired and hungry. I am going to change into a fresh uniform and return. Will you please look after Rosita in my absence? It is going to be a long night and possibly tomorrow I will be required to return to Nos Grande and the mission. Tonight I will sleep at the barracks."

"I will look after Rosita as if she were my own. She seems a charming girl."

Felix left them in the beautifully decorated foyer and proceeded to his room to shower and dress in a new uniform. He was disturbed thinking about what lay ahead. He was about to leave when an idea struck him. He raced back to his room and snatched up the phone and urgently punched in numbers. Impatiently he waited until a groggy voice answered at the other end.

"It's me. Felix. I cannot explain now. Be ready in full uniform. I will pick you up in ten minutes."

He rushed downstairs and called farewell to Rosita and his mother before jumping into the jeep.

"Driver, we are going to make a stop on the way back. Another officer will be joining us. Are you clear?"

"Yes, sir."

Felix gave the man driving directions. The driver's expression conveyed the fear he had. The district into which Felix had directed him was one of the most violent in La Iluminada.

The driver drove cautiously through the narrow cobblestone streets and finally stopped in front of a dilapidated two-story home. It had not been painted in years and the weeds in the garden could feed a herd of the local wandering goats for months. On the street outside the broken front gate, a gang of youths dressed in baggy jeans and smoking marijuana taunted the military men.

Felix jumped from the jeep and ran up the cracked concrete path to the front door. Before he could knock, his friend Caesar Kuhn embraced him in a bear hug. Caesar was a giant of a man. He stood close to seven feet and was all muscle and brawn. His head was shaved of every hair. To those who did not know him, he was a terrifying sight. To those who knew him, he had the heart of a kitten. In his full uniform, he represented the fearful figure that most army recruiters looked for on posters.

His father had fled the Kriegsmarine of Nazi Germany during the war and lived with a local barmaid. Caesar was the product of their union.

Together they walked to the jeep. The gang of youths sprinted away at the sight of Caesar. He chuckled.

"They are so full of bullshit."

"Caesar, we will sit in the rear together. I need to explain the dilemma I find myself in."

Caesar had an uncanny ability to consider the logistics of situations and digest them before offering several alternatives. He listened carefully to Felix's description of the events at Nos Grande and the ambush on the way back to La Iluminada.

For most of the trip, Caesar was silent. As they pulled back into the base, he leaned forward. "Driver, take us over to the mess. I need to get a coffee and a snack. I did not eat tonight and this is going to be a long evening."

At the mess, Caesar and Felix sat for a few minutes before Caesar delivered the solution.

"Felix, you are in great danger. There are Generals in there who know of the goings-on in Nos Grande. If you disclose what you have found, I fear it will be the end of your life. Here is my idea for you." He sat and for five minutes delivered a precise plan, which when he had finished had Felix smiling.

"That is brilliant. I have a favor to ask. If I implement a force to resolve all this will you be part of it with me?"

"That is a question you should not need to ask."

Felix left Caesar at the mess and with newfound confidence walked to meet the Generals.

Chapter 20

Felix entered the conference room. He could barely see through the haze of cigar smoke. At the head of the table, Brigadier General Cutz slouched. His tie was ripped open and his giant bulbous-belly seeped through his tunic shirt where the buttons had parted. He was drunk and slurred a welcome to Felix who looked around the table and tried to assess the condition of the other officers. Two had fallen asleep.

Felix moved to the wall and turned the air conditioning system to full and opened the exhaust to the outside. He hoped that within minutes this would clear the room of the stench of the cigars.

He walked to a table at the front of the room and poured a tumbler of water. Upon seeing this, the Brigadier attempted to stand and move to Felix with an extended arm while grasping a bottle of Bourbon. There was a resounding crash as the Brigadier fell onto one of the two sleeping Generals.

Curses in Spanish were shouted. The Brigadier hit the floor with a squelch and grunt. He knocked the sleeping General off his chair and had landed on top of him. The General was unable to move under the weight of the Brigadier General. The weight on his stomach resulted in the General vomiting violently. The sickly smelling vomit flew over the Brigadier General's shoulder and coated one of the chairs.

Felix strode to the head of the table.

"Generals, there is no one here this evening who is sober enough to act rationally and hear my report. I am using my rank to suspend this meeting under these conditions."

He furiously strode from the room, carrying the portfolio of papers beneath his arm. It was then he decided that it was in the interest of his country to find a way to replace those Generals and their old-style thinking and ways. He had met many aspiring young men at the academy who were well educated and had the drive and desire to improve the life and country's international stature which had suffered greatly during periods of civil war and unrest. Felix was annoyed as he thought about the state of the country and the inaction of those corrupt politicians and Generals. "One day," he thought," I will change it all."

He crossed to the quartermaster's stores and demanded the use of a jeep. He then drove to the mess and found Caesar embroiled in an arm-wrestling match with several of the young privates. Although gambling was prohibited on base, Felix noticed the pile of bills at one end of the table. A young private quickly placed his hand over the bills, but not before Felix looked into his eyes, smiled, and gave him a nod. Amongst the men, Felix was close to admired.

Staff Sargeant Caesar Kuhn looked at Felix quizzically.

"I thought you were to brief the Generals. I was expecting to be here for hours."

"Caesar, it would be inappropriate for me to discuss the situation here in front of these men. There is a private office here where we can go. I may wish to call others later, but first, let us discuss the situation."

Before leaving the mess, Felix ordered an urn of coffee and trays of sandwiches to be delivered to the office. The private who took the order grumbled until Caesar stood and walked very close to the open area of the counter where the private was exposed and not protected by the shelves containing food platters of hot dogs, pies, and general slop consumed by the hungry troops.

"It will be at the office in ten or fifteen minutes, Sir. I will prepare and deliver myself.”

Caesar beamed at the boy who could not have been many days over eighteen.

“That’s what I like to hear. With such a good attitude, you will be out of the mess soon and working on the latrine detail.”

Felix could barely suppress his laugh. The private was too dumb and accepted Caesar’s proclamation as a compliment.

“Come Caesar. What we need to discuss is no laughing matter. We have serious problems confronting us.”

In the private office, Felix went to the wall and disconnected the phone. He then went to the lectern at the front of the room beside a large blackboard. He unplugged the microphone and removed the power from the projection system and other equipment.

“I want to remove the possibility of any listening devices picking up on the conversation. I know this room was scanned for bugs less than a week ago. None were found. It is not a popular place for meetings.”

Caesar was by now confused and getting worried.

“Felix, what the hell are you up to. You are making me scared and I don’t scare easily.”

“Over the past week, I have learned a lot of things. The trip to Nos Grande has opened my eyes to things that are happening here with the blessing of the Generals, politicians, and senior members of the church. It is time.”

Before he could continue, Caesar held up his hand and exclaimed,

"If you are talking or planning a coup, you can count me out, There is no way to reverse the depth of deception and corruption in this sick country of ours."

"I do not propose a coup. We have many bright and educated young men and women in our communities. None are really happy. We can harness that force of minds and the will to democratically bring about change to our land and future generations. I saw the desperation in that barrio. Too many are living badly in this wealthy country while that wealth is stolen by the greedy few. I believe we can show a nonviolent way of change, and the masses will gravitate toward us.

Tonight I saw the worst of our ruling 'elite.' They were drunk and incoherent. I was shocked and still do not understand why an American United States Army Brigadier who is a CIA liaison officer was present to hear a briefing on what is an internal matter. We do not need foreign military here to solve a domestic problem unless there is a lot more we do not know.

Any change we plan or try to implement will not happen quickly. There are only five Generals. They are getting old and some are frail. We need to populate the replacements with good men we know, and not necessarily military men. Slowly we will manipulate these criminals out of power."

Caesar sat quietly and considered everything Felix had said. He did not speak for ten minutes. As he went to speak the young private arrived with the coffee and an assistant carrying trays of fresh sandwiches. His assistant left the room but the young private remained and went to Caesar.

"Sir, I hate working in the mess. The men are mean. Can you get me promoted to the latrine squad?"

Caesar nodded seriously. After the young private left, they rolled in their chairs and roared with laughter.

For hours, Felix and Caesar sat and talked of the risk and possibilities of forcing a change in the direction and leadership of the country,

Felix named several other officers he trusted, along with a banker and an avocat.

It was shortly before midnight when Felix called them and summoned to meet him at his home.

Chapter 21

On the drive to his home, Felix explained to Caesar that there was a mission planned for the next day at Nos Grande and he suspected criminal involvement of some of the Generals in the targeted actions. Felix worried that if it was to proceed it would be a bloodbath and many good troops and citizens would be unwittingly trapped and killed.

He needed to get orders issued to abort the operation.

He drove quickly in the jeep he had commandeered from the Quartermaster. He swung into the driveway of his home and accelerated to the front entrance. He slammed on the brakes and the jeep screeched as it skidded to a halt on the asphalt drive.

Lights flicked on in the upper part of the house. Felix jumped out of the jeep and sprinted up the stairs. He waited until Caesar lumbered up behind him and then threw open the door. They had barely entered when Carmine came down the ornate stairway.

"Have you boys been out drinking. Look at the time. Felix, you told me you had a meeting at the base and would not be back tonight and now here you are with Caesar. What is going on?"

"I will explain it all to you very soon. Where is Rosita? I have called some others here to the house for an emergency meeting. Please do not ask any questions. I can assure you that you will be proud and pleased with what we are doing tonight. Please just accept that explanation for a little while."

Carmine reflected on his words.

"You have never been dishonest or done anything to bring shame or disrespect to this family. I hope that what you are doing will not change that. Rosita is sleeping like a baby. She is a most charming young woman. Maybe one day a young one like that will fall for the old ugly grump you are."

Carmine laughed and started to walk away, but stopped.

"Can I have one of the servants prepare sandwiches for your meeting?"

Caesar and Felix roared laughing again.

"No thank you. We have trays of sandwiches in the jeep that the aspiring latrine squad leader has provided."

Carmine turned and looked at them with the most confused look on her face. She considered them both mad. This had the effect of causing more mirth and merriment.

Carmine shook her head and climbed the stairs while muttering, "Men, I will never understand them."

Over the next hour, different men and women arrived at the Villa. Felix had arranged for the main salon to be set up as a conference area. The atmosphere was almost like that of a social function until Felix called the group to order.

" You are all probably wondering why I have called you here this evening at such a late hour. Please trust me when I tell you this is one of the most difficult and important things I have had to do. Many of you know I have a position of rank and privilege in the military and within society here. Tonight I wish to share with you my deepest concerns and thoughts for our country. I can almost hear the sighs of 'Why couldn't this wait until the morning?' When you hear what I have to say those thoughts will soon evaporate. I have called my attorney here to assist me, as the subjects I wish to speak about could lead to charges of treason. I feel that would be a travesty and abuse of our system of justice."

Felix was about to continue when he looked out to the stairs and saw Rosita standing there dressed in a stunning long dress. She had heard the arrival of people and had decided to join the party.

Felix was at a loss for words. This was no sixteen-year-old standing on the stairway but a transformed and beautiful young woman of an age that could not be guessed.

"My guests, I would like to introduce our house guest, Rosita. She has traveled here from Nos Grande and has been assisting with our understanding of life and recent incidents there. Rosita and her father were outstanding hosts to Major Alvares and me during our recent assignment there."

The guests continued to stare at the beauty and gave her a short round of applause. She smiled and gave a natural bow toward them. Felix was shocked at her grasp of the situation. He needed to find a way to exclude her from the meeting.

"Rosita, come and let me introduce you to the guests, and then we will need to meet. It will be a boring meeting and I suggest you sleep to retain your radiance for the morning. I am sure Carmine will have a busy day planned for you."

Rosita sensed her gentlemanly dismissal.

"No Felix. I will stay. I am most interested in your work and now your friends."

Felix pondered the situation. In time she would learn. Was she too young to understand the gravity of the events he would speak of later that night?

Rosita descended the stairs and joined Felix. He extended his arm for her and slowly he introduced her to the group of friends, officers, and associates. Outwardly, she was at her most charming best, but inwardly she was making an inventory of each person and decided who was trusted, false, or dangerous.

Fortunately, she found the majority to be honest and trustworthy. She had reservations about two of the women, but then that could just be her jealous nature clouding her judgment. Overall she was satisfied.

Rosita drew Felix aside.

"Felix, they don't know my background or my age do they? Have you deliberately hidden that?"

"No. Until this evening I have not spoken about you to any of them. This meeting was convened on an emergency basis. Please leave us now and let me conduct some most important business."

Rosita turned and smiled at him and gave him a seductive look.

"No Felix. I will stay and listen. If you are to be my lover and possible future husband I want to know everything there is to know about you. In our time together I have realized and found you to be an honest and caring man. I like that. Please don't force me away from something I think is very important to you. If it wasn't, then why have you brought these people here so late at night? Be honest with me."

Felix was shocked at her outward expression of affection and interest in him.

"You may stay and listen. Do not speak or in any way interrupt the meeting."

"You will be happy I stayed. I think I know what your plans are. Maybe I wish to be part of them."

For all his military training and education, Felix felt flustered by the young woman. He wondered what power she possessed.

As Rosita moved through the room to find a seat, she felt the cold feeling rise in her chest and heart. She would protect Felix at all costs from any of these people should they try to hurt him.

Chapter 22

The assembled group pulled their chairs into a crescent-shaped formation so each could see and hear Felix. Rosita sat at the outer wing so she could watch each person. Nothing would escape her attention.

Felix walked to the center of the front row of chairs. He hesitated before starting.

"I have asked you all to come this evening as we are experiencing what could develop into a national crisis. I am not exaggerating this matter in any way. As you all know, I am an officer with the Investigative Division of the army. As such I am privy to certain information. Most of it is classified and deals with foreign and national issues that could affect the security of our country. Recently, I was on assignment with another officer from the division. What we uncovered has the massive potential to throw us into a civil war. I have asked you here tonight, as I cannot report my findings to the Generals or other politicians. Tonight I was to debrief and disclose what we had found and to expose the names of people and the roles they played. What we found out is shocking. At the debriefing tonight I could not understand the presence of a United States Army Brigadier General. Normally an officer of this rank is greeted and hosted by representatives of our government. This was not the case. He was drunk and wielded some sort of power over our Generals as they were content to tolerate him. At the debriefing, all of our Generals were drunk and incoherent. This, my friends, was on the eve of ordering a major assault on a clandestine operation located at Nos Grande.

In fear of being charged with treason for disclosing secrets, I will explain. Our investigations were done over a long period. We planted an operative in the barrio. He is well disguised and to the best of our knowledge, he has not been compromised. He has been able to verify information that we managed to extract from an unwilling participant in our questioning.

Our investigations have led to identifying the Generals who rule our country as responsible for serious criminal acts including major drug trafficking, money laundering, murder, and coercion of other officials here and in other countries.

It is time to orchestrate their removal. I am proposing the formation of a political party to force them from power and that they are held accountable for their crimes. They have raped millions of dollars from our economy. It is hidden in private accounts in unfriendly Mid-East countries.

Tonight I am ordering all my fellow officers to abandon any action that is planned for Nos Grande or the nearby regions. I ask you all to witness this command I give. Are there any officers present who do not wish to obey this command?"

Nervous looks were exchanged amongst the attendees. Finally one of the older men spoke.

"Felix, this is interesting but why all the urgency to meet tonight?"

"Almost everyone here tonight has dealings with the government. What they have planned is so horrendous that there will be civil unrest and you will all suffer. I must be specific now."

Felix moved to the blackboard and wrote a list of the names of each General. He then wrote the areas of criminal activity. When he reached the last name he added another. The name of the priest who had raped Rosita. Father Lopez. Besides his name, he wrote several crimes and the name of the church. Next, he listed names of well known Mexican and Colombian drug lords and criminals. He then continued and listed names until there was no room left on the board. He turned to his fascinated audience.

"Now it is time for me to explain how this all works. But before I continue are there any questions?"

One of the women stood. It was a question from Julia.

 "Felix as you know, I am the senior lawyer charged with overseeing that crimes such as the ones you mentioned are brought before the courts. How do you explain that this has gone on and been unaccounted for?"

"Julia, it is unfortunate that some of your peers and many senior lawyers and officers in the police are on the payroll of these Generals. Let me explain more of how this has been working and you will understand the complications."

The woman sat down but seemed unconvinced. Rosita watched her and made a mental note to consider her for retribution.

"This is how the operation has been working for years. Outside of Nos Grande is a mine. To the locals, it is a small mine and the miners there have essentially kept to themselves except for wanting supplies on occasion. The mine is supposedly owned by a Canadian mining firm. Our detailed investigation with the Security Services of the Royal Canadian Mounted Police and their subsequent visit here to Nos Grande identified some of the individuals involved. They are powerful figures in the Montreal and Woodbridge, Ontario, Mafia. These are ruthless gangs and also use the Hells Angels, The Banditos, and others to perform executions and other nasty business for them. These gangs are well organized and have huge distribution networks in the US, Canada, and The Netherlands where the Hells Angels motorbike gang run the operations.

I digress. The mine is rich in gold. This fact was known to all of the Generals who then conspired to cover this information up.

The gold is contained in seams and embedded with the ore. To separate the gold, the ore is sluiced with arsenic. The gold extract is removed and the oxide and arsenic trailings are dumped into the river. This is the river in which the village women of Nos Grande wash their clothes and draw the water for cooking and other domestic purposes. That has resulted in many deaths, deformities, and is the reason the women of Nos Grande cannot bear children."

Felix was unable to continue.

Rosita screamed in fury and swore an act of revenge like one that had never been heard of before. Several of the officers rushed to restrain her. She sobbed until the sobs represented more of a snarl. The cold sensation was back. It was not a minor discomfort, but rather like a solid spike of ice piercing her chest.

In the audience was a doctor and he withdrew a syringe from the little case he carried and ran to her.. Rosita was injected with a powerful sedative and slumped forward in a deep sleep. Felix called his friend Caesar to take her to an upstairs bedroom.

Burly Caesar pushed through the others and with a single lift he draped the inert Rosita over his shoulder.

When he and Caesar returned, Felix suggested a break for coffee before continuing. The assembled group wanted to continue without a break.

Felix continued.

"The gold is then exported using government aircraft. It is sent to friendly states and deposited into hidden accounts before it is converted into currency, then the money is split. Some funds are directed to the accounts of the Generals, but the main part is sent to accounts and holdings of the powerful Colombian drug cartels. Each of our Generals has been blackmailed and threatened by these criminals.

Upon receipt of the monies, cocaine, heroin, and marijuana is loaded onto small planes in Colombia. These planes are originally from the United States and are flown through friendly farming airfields in Venezuela to Honduras. Many planes are abandoned there after the drugs dumped in the sea not far from the coast, or rivers. The drug cartels pay the local peasant farmers well to retrieve and collect the cargoes. Any that try to cross the cartel is executed in front of the others in gruesome ways. They have a very loyal workforce to gather the drugs and help track them northward then through Mexico before they are sent onto the United States, Canada, or the Netherlands.

Our politicians, police, and military are complicit in this trafficking. It is dragging our country to its knees. The United States has placed us on a blacklist of countries involved in International crime and money laundering. They have established links between certain individuals here and terrorist organizations.

My investigation has unearthed other serious matters. The drug cartels have established caches of weapons that are hidden at the mine in Nos Grande and other locations. The Generals intended to seize these weapons. It seems they were to be sold to those Mid East countries they have conspired with.

I am not attempting to start a military coup nor am I suggesting violence. Everyone in this room is a prominent member of our society and yields significant influence.

Tonight I am announcing that I will voluntarily run for election to the governing council. If I am successful, I will expose the deals and weaknesses of those Generals. I will push for the election of civilian citizens to make the laws and govern the country.

It will not be easy. I expect I will be confronted with hostilities from those loyal to the Generals. I do believe they will attempt to have me arrested and my family harmed….both physically and financially.

I know the risk I am taking. I do not need the power for financial gain. Our family grew its fortunes over the last two hundred years through cattle farms, fruit, produce, and land development. All of this family's fortunes were made honestly and are open to scrutiny.

Tonight I am asking for your support."

The assembled friends and associates sat in silence.

It was John J. Carter, the leading lawyer in the country who spoke.

"Felix, this is an ambitious plan you have. The ruling party is tightly controlled by those Generals. I do not think you have any chance of succeeding or replacing any of them. They have friends buried deep in the system. You will be challenged for every move you make. I admire your drive and principle. You will have my full support. I suggest that those who wish to support Felix indicate this. We will need to plan and prepare strategies and the roles others will need to do in assisting him in fulfilling this goal. When I leave here I will contact my legal counterparts in New York, London, Sydney, and Hong Kong. My office will prepare and send out a press release that will emphasize the change that is planned and in progress for the country. We will fire the first salvo and catch the Generals off guard.

I will wait outside the room and take the information of anyone who wishes to join this historic challenge."

John J. Carter walked from the room with a small group following him.

Felix returned to the front of the room and in a loud voice summoned the military officers present to come forward.

The cluster of officers stood tightly together.

"Gentlemen, I understand it is going to be difficult to delay, and in some cases, ignore or challenge orders. I am issuing an order now that I expect all to obey. The attack on Nos Grande and the mine is canceled until we have more information. I fear we may lose incriminating evidence if we move too quickly. I will convene a meeting with the Generals and explain that the conditions for an assault were wrong. They will not argue with me. They have no idea of military tactics. Does anyone wish to differ or have any questions?"

A young red-haired officer introduced himself before asking the question.

"Do you know when the attack will likely take place?"

"I suspect it will happen within the month."

Chapter 23

Sunlight peeped through the windows of the second-floor bedroom. Felix arose and walked down the corridor to the room he had recommended his friend Caesar sleep in, as the meeting had finished late. He heard the shower running and cracked open the door to hear the tortured sounds of Ave Maria being sung loudly and off-key in the bathroom.

He pulled the door closed and proceeded to the room next to his mothers. He went to knock but hesitated. He put his ear to the door. It was quiet. He moved to his mother's room and knocked. There was no answer. Confused, he returned to his room and dressed in casual civilian clothes. He had decided to relax at home for the morning and face the Generals that afternoon. He doubted many would have shaken off their hangovers and would be pleased the meeting was delayed until noon.

He heard the deep baritone voice of Cesar attempting a Luciano Pavarotti tune as he headed toward him.

"Please. It is far too early to listen to you killing the great songs of the masters."

Caesar laughed and in a fake girlish voice started to sing 'My Favorite Things' made famous by Julie Andrews in 'The Sound of Music'. Felix groaned. It was going to be one of those days with Caesar.

As they arrived at the bottom of the stairs the aroma of freshly brewed coffee, toast and bacon hit them. After yesterday and the events of last evening, they were starving.

Felix walked into the kitchen to find Rosita smartly dressed and eating a huge breakfast. Carmine sat across from her with a copy of The International Herald held open. She popped her head from behind the pages. Her reading glasses sat on the tip of her nose.

"Mr. Politician, I suggest you serve your guest and yourself breakfast. I'm too busy reading of the planned political upheaval that is happening here in our country spearheaded by a certain Colonel Felix de Santos, who the papers are calling the Spoilt Rebel with a Cause."

Felix sensed the iciness in the air.

"When the hell did you decide on this stupidity. When were you going to tell me? Now you have dragged our friends into this. We will all suffer at the hands of those fools, the Generals. Look at this. Mr. John J. Carter the leading legal expert in the country predicts that the change will happen sooner than later and the people will be shocked and horrified by the revelations of crime and corruption. He is suggesting that the assistance of foreign governments, including the United States of America, will be needed to stop any interference. He continues that all steps will be taken by the new political party to prevent any massacres.

Felix, are you crazy? You are wrecking a perfect career and possibly the fortunes of our family."

Rosita sat and watched. She had a slight smile on her lips and was enjoying the sight of Felix being admonished like a schoolboy. It made him all that more appealing to her. She was determined that when the chance arose she would have him. As she continued to eat, her mind slipped to lustful scenes. She envisaged him naked in a giant bed and then a scene stripping him in a horse barn after they had been riding and he was all sweaty. She squirmed as her thoughts deepened in both detail and heat.

"Mother, I had full intention of telling you of the plans. You have known since I attended at the university that I was intrigued by politics and intended to pursue a career in politics one day.

Yesterday all hell broke loose. For the first time, I saw with my own eyes the situation as it sat right in front of me. I was disgusted. What the Generals had planned was the sacking of Nos Grande to expand and promote their filthy operations. I needed to act and stop them."

Carmine put down the paper and looked softly at her son.

"Felix, I know you are a good person and only want what is right for our people. I worry about whether you will succeed. I will be unable to continue living if anything happens to you. It was hard enough when they killed your father."

Rosita dropped her cup and spilled coffee over the crisp white blouse she was wearing.

"They killed your father? That is horrible. They must be punished. I will help you."

Carmine smiled at Rosita. "You are little more than a child. How can you help?"

"Oh Mrs. de Santos, I will. On that, you can trust me. I have my ways and thoughts."

Carmine wondered, "Just what is Rosita's Way?"

Felix went and hugged his mother.

"Rosita go and ask the maid to assist you with a clean blouse. When you return I will tell all that has happened and give you details of last evening's meeting."
Rosita sprang from the table and ran to the stairs, eager to change into a new shirt and the return to hear the story.

Carmine assumed a motherly face and posture.

"Felix, before she returns I have a direct question for you. What are your intentions with that young lady? I see a spark in her eyes every time you speak or are near her. She is extremely bright and likable. I hope you are not playing some foolish game with her. I feel you will both live to regret it."

Caesar had been staying out of sight and in the background of the kitchen. Hearing Felix getting the motherly lecture was too much for him. A whooping laugh exploded from the shadows. Soon they were all laughing when the humor of Carmine's lecture to her thirty-year-old son was realized.

Rosita came bounding back into the room and sat back down waiting to hear the story.

Felix went to refill his coffee before launching into the details of the previous day and the events of the meeting at the house. When he finished there was total silence. Carmine stood and went to him. She hugged him and kissed his cheek.

"Now I understand, Felix. You have done the correct thing. Those monsters must be stopped. When I return I will be contacting others. We must leave now. Rosita and I have some very important business in downtown La Iluminada There is shopping to do for a wardrobe for the young lady and we will lunch at La Fenice. Rosita tells me she has never experience fine French foods before. It will be an adventure for her. I have asked Enzo to be our chauffeur for the day. I hope that fits with your plans."

As they were walking to the front door, Rosita turned and smiled the most impish smile Felix had ever seen. Caesar was watching.

"Felix my friend, I think you are a done man. Now let's get to work. It will be noon before too long and you will require a very strong story to present to those skeptical Generals. They may be corrupt and monsters, but they are not stupid."

"Come, we will work in my basement bunker."

The name 'basement bunker' described the office exactly. Due to Felix's rank and importance a complete radio and data communications center had been installed in his home. The systems were secured with a high-security military-grade system. Only Felix and a few fellow officers were cleared for entry into the bunker. Banks of rack-mounted equipment lined one wall. Blue network cabling snaked overhead from one rack to another. There was a long and wide console that ran the length of the opposite wall. Three flat-screen displays flickered with the Army logo displayed on them. One was a huge display and was mounted to the wall. Rows of backup batteries populated the last rack in the room. It was a fully operational control room and in the event of an emergency could take over the command of the country's forces.

Caesar looked at the impressive setup.

"I wonder whether you will be allowed to keep this now you are publicly challenging them?"

"I will not mention it to them. I am sure that they are unaware of a lot that goes on within the forces."

The telephone that was an extension of his base phone shrilled and startled both of them. Felix snatched up the receiver and frowned as he listened to the woman's voice on the other end. He slowly lowered the phone back into its cradle and picked up the remote control which he pointed at one of the screens. He pressed buttons until it flipped to regular television. A local news show was in progress.

He sunk into the chair at his desk and motioned to Caesar to do the same. He adjusted the volume. On the screen, a female reporter whom he despised was giving a dramatic account of Felix's defection from the Military and inciting unrest in the forces and within the population by claiming he would offer improvements in the suffering economy and an improvement in the quality of each citizen's life. The reporter droned on, and at one point took out a clipboard and started to recite a long list of de Santos owned businesses. She continued and called the de Santos family hypocrites, as they owned factories, farms, and apartment buildings. She exclaimed that the de Santos family was in large part responsible for the suffering of the people. When she finished she turned to passersby and stopped them for quick on the street interviews. In each case, she posed a loaded question regarding the de Santos family and how the individual benefitted from them. In all cases, the interviewee was unable to list one thing. After she had stopped around eight people and received the same reaction, she smugly summarized the situation, branding Felix a fraud and his family as criminals.

She continued and gave a detailed account of the situation and the plans Felix had discussed the previous evening.

"How did she get that information on the meeting and the businesses. The companies are private. Outside the family and the professional firms who manage the financial and legal affairs, no one has that level of information."

"Felix, I hate to say this but there was a rat in the meeting last night. We need to review each person who attended. She had details that were only discussed last night. Your opposition has started. I think you have already gotten too close to something big."

Felix heard the upstairs phone ring. It was answered by one of the maids. She called down the Felix. He instructed her to take a message. The phone then started ring consistently. The maid was taking messages down, but the phone was ringing faster than she could write them down. Then Felix heard her shriek."

He called up the stairs from the basement.

"What is it?"

"Mr. Felix, must I write down the rude ones and the threats?"

"No. Unplug the phone. If I need to contact anyone I will call them. Are there any important messages?"

"Some are containing the rudest possible words."

Felix returned to the room and resumed watching the reporter. She was standing in front of the building which housed the senior management for all the armed forces. It was where the civilian support staff worked and some of the officers. As he was watching her, she spun to the right and started to run to the building. The camera jerked up and down as the cameraman ran behind her. Felix chuckled and pointed at her backside. Running in her tight coral colored skirt with high heels greatly exaggerated the rise and fall of her buttocks.

"Reminds me of those pink bobbleheads on sticks we had as kids."

Caesar chuckled.

"Felix., even in these dark moments you see the humor. That in part is one of the reasons I like you."

As they continued to watch, the reporter caught up to her prey. Felix gasped as he turned. It was the General responsible for Justice. He stopped and turned to face the camera.

She led in with a controversial question. The General thought for a minute before he moved closer to the camera and looked directly into the lens.

"You have asked for our official position regarding the recent announcement made by Colonel Felix de Santos. I can tell you that we will be examining his comments carefully before taking steps. I can tell you from personal experience with him, including early yesterday evening that the man is a dishonest fraud of questionable character."

The reporter was lapping up his words.

"How is that, General? Can you elaborate? Can you share some details?

"Certainly. It is only fair and correct that the people know what sort of man the Colonel truly is. Late yesterday, the Colonel was to brief the joint members of the ruling military party with details of a raid that had been planned for today. The Colonel showed up to the meeting slovenly dressed and reeking of alcohol. He was so drunk we had to postpone the briefing and arrange for the Colonel to be driven to his home. It was a major embarrassment as we had a special guest at the briefing. That guest was the Brigadier General from the United States who is responsible for cooperation between our countries. The Brigadier was so offended he has departed this morning. His report to the officials in the US and Europe will reflect poorly on us. In addition to this incident, we now have a major matter of insubordination. There was to be an operation carried out on the edge of the jungle near Nos Grande. The barrio there has been harboring suspected terrorists. Men from Cuba, Mexico, and Colombia have been reported as creating problems in the barrio and there have been gang killings in the area. The mission was to capture these men and destroy any cache of arms and equipment they had. We have reports that detailed their planned attacks on our country. The Colonel canceled this operation. We have been informed that he and Major Alvares were operating with these criminals and providing classified information to them.

That is the sort of man who is attempting to create problems amongst the people. I say that everyone needs to stick by us. We have delivered stability and wealth to the community. Now I must leave. Thank you."

"General Cruz, thank you for your time."

"My pleasure."

The camera followed him a short way before it turned back to the reporter.

"Now viewers I must ask you. Is Colonel Felix de Santos a true reformer or a traitor. This is Carmilla Vesco, VTV News Live signing off. Now back to the studio."

Before Felix could switch off the TV a commercial for laundry detergent featuring men filling machines with obviously fake stained laundry blared from the set. Felix grasped the control and powered the TV off.

"Now what do we do? It seems the battle lines have been drawn."

Chapter 24

Enzo drove Carmine and Rosita into downtown La Iluminada at a quick but safe speed. Other cars raced by them. He did not care. There was no need to rush. He had taken Mrs. de Santos on many shopping trips. He knew the routine. Before turning onto the stretch of highway that led to the financial district, he turned off and drove down the Avenue of Golden Doves. This was the home to most of the Parisian and French fashion houses.

Rosita's face was glued to the window of the car as they passed stores and restaurants. Along the way, Carmine had pointed out places of interest and explained their history. Rosita was thrilled and forgot the earlier turmoil of the morning.

Enzo slowed and pulled to the slower curb lane as he approached the stores he knew she would want to stop at and visit.

As he had anticipated, she asked him to stop outside El Balaciano, one of the finest women's apparel stores, to select clothing for day outings and casual club nights. Inside the store, Carmine was greeted by a well-groomed sales clerk. She introduced Rosita and explained they were looking to purchase a new summer wardrobe of casual clothing. The clerk listened attentively, but the usual charm and politeness were gone. The clerk was professional but lacked the warmth that Carmine normally received at that store. They selected a range of casual clothing. It was early summer, and already the temperatures were soaring.

Rosita was lost in the racks of colorful garments on display. She had never seen such a selection. The sales attendant took her measurements before directing her to the area that contained clothing of the size.

"I do not wish to be in any way insulting, but I would suggest you select underwear from our collection. I am afraid that what you have on will not make our designs look at all flattering."

Rosita felt the now familiar icy feeling creep into her chest.

They selected the Balaciano selection, a very cool range of cotton dresses and accessories. Carmine selected some scarves and a lightweight fashionable coat for the days when there were winds and light rains.

When they had finished their shopping, the clerks carefully wrapped the purchases in fine tissue and placed them in the store's designer bags, and a bill was handed to Carmine.

"Please put these purchases on the de Santos account."

The salesgirl became flustered.

"I am afraid these cannot be charged to your account."

"Why? We have shopped here for years. Is there a problem?"

The salesgirl blushed.

"I will go and bring the manager. He can explain".

Minutes later, she returned with a petite man dressed in a three-piece pearl-grey suit, with a pale cream vest and a blue and white striped high neck shirt. He was wringing his hands nervously as he approached them.

"Welcome, Senora. Who is the lovely young lady with you?"

Carmine introduced Rosita.

The store manager made a fuss over Rosita. He took her hand and kissed it before making a slight curtsy.

"How can I assist you ladies today?"

"I wish to charge these purchases. There seems to be some problem. The girl tells me they cannot be charged."

The manager took the bill and looked at it.

"Senora, I think it would be more discreet for you alone to join me back in my office."

Rosita stayed to look at other garments. Together, Carmine and the manager walked behind the counters down a corridor lined with original Spanish oil paintings. Carmine recognized some of the artists.

The manager opened the door to his plush office and ushered Carmine in.

"It is early but would you like to join me in an Apéritif. I have some of the finest Italian Campari. Let me fetch us a glass each."

He stood and went into the small enclosed room off his main office. He returned with the drinks in crystal glasses.

"Carmine, if I may address you that way, I am under instructions not to extend any credit to your family, whether you purchase directly or through your staff. These instructions were phoned to me this morning by the son of the owners. It is not my decision."

He paused and sipped at the Campari. Minutes passed in silence. Finally, he spoke.

"If it was my decision alone I would not hesitate. I have known you, your former husband, and children for years. You have all been good and kind. I am embarrassed and upset by this. It seems that your son Felix, whom I admire, has upset the owners. They have other businesses that supply uniforms and other items to the forces. It is not personal. They do like the de Santos family, but they, like many others with whom you deal, received the notice this morning that should they continue to help your family or any of your businesses, they will be permanently prohibited from dealing with the government or the forces. This was broadcast on the news and in special bulletins by radio this morning.

I am sorry to tell you this. If I, as a friend had not told you, then others would have and the circumstances may have been worse.

Please understand I am trying to inform you of today's reality.

I listened to the news and I think that Felix is brave and morally right to fight those corrupt Generals. On a personal level, please tell him he has my support. Be careful. Those men are powerful as well as corrupt. Unfortunately, their money buys loyalty from other crooks."

Carmine nodded. She neither smiled nor flinched as he delivered the news. Instead, she opened her purse and removed a black American Express card, and handed it to him. His eyes widened. He had heard of these valued cards but never seen one. He took it from her and was surprised at its thickness and weight.

"I will process your purchase. Here let me get you another Campari."

He returned with a fresh glass of the nectar for her and left to complete the purchase. When he returned he helped her and Rosita to the car and assisted with the bags. As she was about to enter the car, he reached out and gently took her wrist.

"Senora, please relay a message from me to Felix. I am sure he and his friends will need money for the venture. I wish for you to tell him I will contribute."

She smiled and thanked him.

When they were done, Carmine looked to the front of the car and was shocked to see a sloppily dressed cop standing with his foot raised and resting on the front bumper. He had a book in his hand

and was writing a ticket. An exasperated Enzo looked at Carmine and shrugged. The de Santos cars were well known and displayed custom license plates. In all the years of shopping at this store and Enzo waiting for her, they had never received a ticket. She attempted to speak to the cop. He ignored her and ripped out the ticket from the book and stuffed it through the window before mounting his motorbike and roaring out into the traffic.

So far the day was not going well. Rosita had not noticed. She was thrilled to be in the city.

Their next stop was at Palermo Galleria. The eclectic store brimmed with both designer and handmade handbags, totes, and purses. Rosita was again overwhelmed. The smell of freshly tanned leather perfumed the cool air in the store. Rosita selected a Fuschia colored handbag that seemed to blend with any color. She was thrilled.

They left and were driving deeper into the center of the city when Carmine suggested they take an early lunch. She directed Enzo to take them to the artisans' open-air market area. She invited Enzo to join them for lunch. Carmine treated all her staff as extended family and was rewarded in many ways for doing so.

Enzo took them to the entrance of the French bistro Les Jardine and drove off a short distance to park the car.

Rosita was at a loss for words as they entered Les Jardine. Inside was a large wine bar and at the rear of the bistro, high leaded glass windows opened onto a cobblestone patio with small iron chairs and tables. Each table was painted in a tasteful yet subdued color. Planters dotted the courtyard and the borders were planted with low brightly colored flowers. To Rosita, it was a paradise.

Within seconds of them entering a man in his late thirties walked briskly to them. He stretched out his arms and hugged Carmine.

"Regardless as to what is being said, I know the truth about the de Santos family. You are always our friends here and welcome at any time."

"Thank you, Marcel. Have you been back to your home in Paris recently?"

"No, I am hoping to make a special trip next month with Pierre to celebrate our anniversary."

He had no sooner spoken when a tall thin man with thinning black hair and eyes so dark they matched coal, joined them.

"Pierre, It is nice to see you again."

Pierre made a huge fuss over Carmine and Rosita and almost danced them to a shaded table on the patio. He looked the part of a typical restauranter. He was dressed in a starched crisp white shirt and tight black trousers. He wore expensive black sneakers on his feet A long white and navy striped apron was tied at his waist and dropped almost to floor level. He was the true image of a French waiter.

"Pierre is working with Gaston in the kitchen today. We are celebrating the arrival of summer with a special menu featuring fresh local produce. We have salads that are so delicious at this time of year.

I recommend Les Jardine delight. It is a light salad and is made from tender greens, including lamb's lettuce, fresh spears of asparagus, grated carrot, arugula, two cold filets of poached salmon flavored with a hint of fresh lemon and surrounded with diced slivers of red onion picked this morning. We drizzle our specialty mayonnaise dressing over the greens. There is a small wait for this exquisite salad as the salmon is freshly poached and chilled and the mayonnaise dressing is freshly made for each order."

Carmine licked her lips.

"I will take that. What would you like Rosita?"

"I am not sure yet. The events of the last few days have made me very hungry."

"In which case, I recommend our delightful rack of fresh lamb. It is seasoned with our special rosemary and thyme seasoning, served with seasonal Parisian potatoes, fresh beans, and served in a red wine reduction. One of our most requested specialties."

Rosita looked up at him and smiled her disarming smile.

"Yes, that sounds like something I would enjoy."

They were completing their order when Enzo arrived. Pierre and Marcel hugged him before he could sit.

Marcel looked at Enzo.

"Let me see. I think I know what you will order. The New York Luncheon strip steak grilled medium and served with a knob of melting garlic butter and a baked potato, steamed asparagus, and baby carrots."

"Marcel, you know me too well."

They all laughed. Pierre arrived back at the table with an ice bucket containing a large bottle of chilled white wine.

"We did not order any wine," Carmine said looking at him and frowning."

"No you didn't, but this is a gift from Marcel and me to celebrate the news that Felix is standing up to those evil bullies that bring disrepute and sadness to the country and especially our little community."

Carmine smiled and thanked him. She knew how hard it had been for those in same-sex partnerships. The Generals had instituted discriminatory policies against them.

"Thank you, Pierre, but we can only accept this kind gift if you and Marcel join us in a toast to my lovely but foolish son."

"We will do that. Let me get him."

After they toasted, Marcel and Pierre left them to attend to their order and greet others arriving for the lunch hour. Marcel paused several steps away from their table and turned. He addressed Enzo,

"Enzo, I know you do not drink heavy wines or spirits. Is there something I can bring you?"

"Yes please, Marcel. I would love one of those ice-cold Saint Omers French beers."

"Excellent. Refreshing and not too heavy."

Over lunch, the conversation was light and political issues never surfaced. It was almost two hours later when they left the bistro to continue shopping.

Both Carmine and Rosita were happy and a little carefree after the wine. They drove onto the next store Carmine had selected.

"Rosita, you are going to need some fashionable dresses if you are planning to accompany Felix to any events. You are also going to need some formal dresses as I am planning events at the Villa that will require you to dress appropriately. Now let us go and have some fun."

Enzo pulled to a stop in front of Papillion with its imposing front façade. It was the fashion house for the wealthy.

Carmine was received as though she was an old family friend. She and Rosita had barely entered before they were seated in the reception area and an attendant arrived with flutes of champagne on a silver tray.

Carmine was then escorted into a private room. Rosita's measurements were taken and questions were asked regarding the events to which the dresses would be worn. The sales clerk dutifully wrote notes in a small leatherbound book. When they had completed detailing their needs, the clerk left to select some items. Another attendant arrived with more champagne for them.

Ten minutes passed by before the clerk returned. She was accompanied by a young man pushing a wheeled rack from which a large selection of dresses, blouses, pants, and shorts hung.

For the next hour, Carmine and Rosita chose the garments that appealed to them.

Rosita was very much enjoying the day. The barrio seemed a long time ago and a long way away.

Chapter 25

Feeling a slight buzz from the glasses of wine as they left, Rosita laughed and was giddy with the prospect of visiting one of the leading fashion designers to select shoes for different occasions. Carmine had described the store and the vast selection of footwear available. It has always been a secret desire of Rosita to have a large and fancy collection of fashionable clothes and shoes. Living in the barrio though, she could only dream of such a thing.

Enzo opened the car door and they stumbled in, the effects of the wine now evident.

With Carmine and Rosita laughing and giggling like little girls, Enzo drove to Avenida des Torres and drifted to a halt outside the elaborate frontage of the French fashion store, Pied Elegance.

Rosita's eyes were saucerlike when she looked at the massive glass window display. There were shoes of all colors and styles on display. With her enthusiasm bursting, Rosita pushed open the door before Enzo could reach it. She ran across the sidewalk and into the store. Carmine took great delight at watching Rosita's impetuous behavior. She was liking Rosita more, but still had reservations about her.

The next two hours were spent with both Rosita and Carmine trying on different footwear. They regaled themselves trying on outlandish and weird shoes that were meant to be fashion statements. The wine was having some effect and they laughed until tears streamed down their cheeks. The store attendants were not amused.

Enzo had waited outside and was leaning against the side of the car smoking a pungent-smelling cigarette. He dropped the

cigarette and rapidly walked to the store entrance to assist
Carmine and Rosita with the many boxes containing their
purchases.

"Enzo, please drive us out to the coast. I want to stop at La Vista
for cocktails before we return to Villa Magnifico and all that
awaits us there."

Enzo nodded and turned the car across several lanes of traffic to
get to the road to the coast. He loved the coast and often took his
son fishing off the rocks below La Vista. He wished his son was
with him and decided that he would take him fishing the
upcoming weekend.

They arrived at the restaurant thirty minutes later. It was a
magnificent structure. The restaurant was modern and
suspended from the cliff and over the ocean below by huge
cantilevered beams buried into the cliff face. Inside, the
windows ran from the floor to ceiling and provided a view out
to the ocean. Below the restaurant, large waves crashed in on
the black volcanic rocks that lined the shore.

As they entered, Carmine was immediately recognized and they
were taken to a private seating area with an unobstructed view of
the coastline and the ocean.

Carmine looked out of the window. The sun was just starting to
set and was slipping down toward the horizon. At this time of
day, the sun's rays glowed orange in the sky and created a
greenish hue on the ocean. It was Carmine's favorite place and
time of day.

Rosita was speechless. She had never seen such opulence.

"Enzo, please come and sit with us. I am sure you would like a
drink after all the driving today."

"That is kind of you, Madam."

The trio sat and admired the view. Carmine ordered a bottle of fine Chablis and Enzo ordered a Campari and soda. As they sat chatting, a waiter arrived with a large complimentary tray of sushi.

Rosita was confused.

"Carmine, the fish is not cooked. It is raw. Do not eat it. You will be ill. Send it back to be cooked."

Carmine and Enzo laughed.

"No, Rosita. It is called sushi. It originated in Japan. If you look at it you will see some are rolled around special fillings. There are delicious sauces and other accompaniments in those little dishes. It is a delicacy."

Rosita did not seem so sure. She placed a seaweed roll on her plate and heaped the pink ginger and pale green wasabi on top of it. She did not wish to appear ungrateful or naïve and pushed the roll and wasabi into her mouth. The heat hit her at once. Tears streamed down her face and she immediately gagged. Rice and salmon sprayed across the table. The pink pieces of ginger fell from her mouth into her lap.

"It is an acquired taste, my dear. We will need to get you educated on the art of fine dining. You will need to learn these things for the occasions when you will attend functions with Felix or our family."

Rosita swore to herself that no fish was going in her mouth again, but smiled politely at Carmine.

Wait staff with large yellow cloths arrived to remove the exploded sushi mess from the table and floor.

Carmine felt sorry for Rosita.

"Is there something you would like? The sushi is not your favorite."

Rosita looked up at the waiter who was standing ready to take an order.

"Can you get me some donkey meat sausages?"
Carmine was shocked. Her late afternoon cocktail gathering was spiraling into a disaster.

"I am sorry but we do not have that specialty here. May I suggest the fine skewers of spicy beef. They are excellent and very popular with our esteemed customers."

This calmed Carmine and restored her composure. To be recognized as esteemed boosted her ego.

"Yes, please bring enough for all of us, and please bring another Campari and soda for Enzo and another bottle of that fine Chablis."

For the next hour, they ate and drank. Carmine asked Enzo about his family before steering the conversation to explore Rosita's life in the barrio. What she heard shocked her.

Chapter 26

Upon their return to Villa Magnifico, they found several cars parked in the driveway. The lights were on in the living room and shone brightly through the tall windows out onto the lush garden.

Enzo stopped the car at the front stairway entrance and opened the door to assist a slightly tipsy Carmine and Rosita up the stairs. He then returned and made an additional three trips to carry in their purchases of the day.

Felix had watched the action through one of the front windows. He excused himself and advised his 'guests' he would return in minutes.

He walked out into the long hallway, where Rosita and Carmine were laughing and giggling like little children.

"Mother, I am holding a serious meeting. Please do not join. It seems that you have had a nice afternoon. I suggest you relax a little until my meeting is finished and then we can all sit and talk. I will be finished very soon."

Carmine wagged a finger at Felix.

"See, Rosita, this is my son telling his old mother off because I had fun today. He is a sour man."

"Mother, it is important I return to the meeting. Please take Rosita and change. I will take us all out for a light dinner and dance a little later. Now, please go."

In Felix's mind, he was happy to see the bond between Rosita and Carmine developing. He watched as they walked away. Rosita no longer seemed to be the young girl he had met at the barrio.

Felix opened the door to the living room and as he entered saw all his ' Guests' were standing around the television set. Other than the loud commentary shouted by a reporter in Spanish, the room was quiet. No one spoke. They all stared at the television. Felix craned to look over them and understand the situation.

Caesar pulled him by the arm and took him aside.

"They have just announced that General Cruz has been assassinated and you are believed to be the killer."

"But I have been here with you all. When did this happen? Where? How was he killed?"

"He was found dead in his car. It was after that interview he gave to that reporter, Carmilla Vesco. His head had been cut from his body."

"I did not like the man, but my God, that is horrible."

"Felix, you are now in real danger. We must find a way to get you to a safe location."

"No. I will stay. I have no reason to run away. I am not guilty of any offense. Arrange for me to be interviewed. Get that Camilla Vesco and have her come here to the Villa."

"The other Generals are calling for your blood. Are you sure this is a safe thing to do? They may come here."

"I have nothing to hide. These Generals have raped our land of its nature, customs, and money. It is time to correct the situation. Many will agree."

Suddenly there were excited whispers from those gathered around the television. Felix pushed his way to the front. The screen showed the Generals sitting at the table to conduct what was a hastily convened press conference.

They looked a particularly dour group. The camera turned and focussed on General Perez. He leaned forward and pulled several microphones toward him that had been placed on the table by various reporters.

General Perez was a heavyset man with huge black eyebrows, black wavy hair that was slicked back, and a face scarred with the remnants of acne he suffered as a youth. In his dark uniform festooned with medals and braids, he looked a foreboding character. He held up his finger and silence descended.

"Tonight is a sad night for our country. My fellow officer and good friend General Cruz has been found brutally murdered. I will spare you, good citizens, the horrible details of his death but know they leave us in no doubt that this was a political assassination. Before the announcements and threats made by our insubordinate officer, Colonel Felix de Santos, we had already suspected he had dangerous motives and had investigated him. We now have evidence that Colonel de Santos was responsible for this murder and treasonous act. Tonight we will find him and bring him to justice."

He no sooner stopped speaking when the reporters bombarded him with questions. He listened for a few minutes before again raising his hand.

"We have information that will prove that Colonel de Santos is guilty of this murder and other crimes against our country. Recently, the Colonel was on assignment to the barrio of Nos Grande. There has been trouble at the barrio and we have confessions already from the peasant men he hired to kill General Cruz. We cannot let this man corrupt our country or political system any further."

Felix stood in disbelief. His 'guests' were looking at him.

"There is nothing further from the truth. I uncovered corruption and activities that are directly tied to those crooked Generals.

They are looking for ways to silence me. You all must leave here immediately. Caesar, you will stay with me.

Please believe me and accept that I am not guilty of the claims General Perez has made. I need the assistance of you all. We must have reform in our country."

Most of them nodded their heads. As they moved to leave every person, except one, came forward to shake Felix's hand and offer support.

Felix watched as the female lawyer, Julia, picked up her coat and folder and left. He sensed a problem with her.

"Caesar, were you able to contact that reporter? We must move quickly. I need to tell my story to the people. All they know are the lies of General Perez."

"Yes. There is a crew on the way here now."

"I need you to help me during and after the interview. I want you to go down to my command center. The communications equipment works on all military frequencies. The Generals will dispatch others who are complicit with them to arrest me. I want you to go and broadcast conflicting directions and instructions. While you confuse them, I will escape the broadcast."

Caesar was grinning. The idea of issuing false and conflicting directions to the Generals' goons appealed to his sense of humor.

"I will need Enzo and the gardener to assist us with my plan. Please find Enzo. I am going to find Rosita and Mother and explain the latest development."

He was about to leave when the phone rang. He snatched it up.

"Felix, good evening. It's J.J. Carter here. I have some startling information. I saw Perez's performance in that press conference. I have information that will completely contradict his claim. We need to meet. I am worried for your safety. Their corruption is a lot deeper than I think you realize."

"I am at the Villa and awaiting the arrival of Camilla Vesco and a TV crew. I intend to dispute the claims that Perez has made and disclose some of the information regarding the barrio at Nos Grande."

"Please do not speak to them until I arrive. Will you retain me as your lawyer immediately?"

"Yes, of course. When can you be here? I will find a way to delay them."

"It will take me at least twenty minutes. There are heavy rainstorms and traffic will be slow. Let's hope it is slowing the TV crew as well. It is imperative you and I speak before that interview."

Felix looked out of the larger front window. He had not noticed the change in weather. The night was dark and strong wind lashed at the trees and bushes. Torrential rain was falling. The weather matched his mood.

"Drive safely. I will see you soon."

Felix hung up and left to find Rosita and Carmine.

Chapter 27

Carmine sobered quickly when Felix finished telling them of the situation. Rosita sat puzzled. She thought about the barrio and wondered if there were men there who could have killed the General. She was unable to identify any who would do such a thing. The barrio was not large and she knew almost everyone. Even with the recent troubles, no one was so desperate to kill for money.

The front doorbell chimed. They heard voices and Felix left to find J.J. Carter in the foyer with another short wiry man. He appeared to be Hispanic. He had the strong facial features of men from rural areas of other countries in South America. Felix was curious.

"Good evening J.J. Thank you for coming. It seems I have some rather serious problems to solve. I believe my fight will be long and hard."

"I am here to help with that. First I must warn you that there are some friends you trust who are not your true friends. I have found some communication from Julia to certain judges that have influenced trials. It seems that certain acquaintances of the Generals have been able to prove their 'innocence' under some very strange circumstances. I have brought this man, Jose Martinez, with me tonight to share some important information. He is from Mexico. Be warned that what he will tell you will not be nice."

Felix was curious. He excused himself to find Caesar and Enzo before he would sit with J.J. and Jose Martinez. He found Caesar in his communications room twirling knobs and listening in on were privileged military communications.

Caesar turned to Felix.

"They have just left the base. Four men are coming for you. Enzo is in the little office area in the back. What do you want him to do?"

"Let us meet him and I will explain."

They walked back and entered the smoke-filled room. Enzo sat dressed in casual clothing. He was with a tall man who worked as a gardener at the Villa. There was a striking resemblance between Felix and the man.

"Enzo, I need your help tonight. I want to create confusion. Caesar is going to issue false information to those who have been sent for me. You will drive our fastest car through the city to some of the poorer locations. Our friend here will double as me. They will think you are driving me to a safe shelter to evade them. I will provide you with a two-way radio on the military frequency. You will be able to hear the directions Caesar gives them. After a long chase, you must allow them to stop you. My double will have been dropped off in an area that I hope they will be unfamiliar with. When questioned you will tell them you drove a friend home. He had been with you to play cards. You must act surprised when they finally stop you. They will ask you where he went. I suggest you tell them that he was going to a lady friend and you do not have the address. He just wanted to be dropped near her house."

From the grins on their faces, it was obvious that Caesar and Enzo were looking forward to the task ahead.

"I want you to be ready and drive away from the Villa just as they are arriving. I expect it will be a high-speed pursuit. I will leave you now to plan this with Caesar. I have people here to see me."

As he ascended the stairs from the basement, he encountered Rosita standing at the head of the stairs. She was dressed beautifully in casual clothing. Felix looked into her face and was surprised to see her eyes were almost black like coal.

"Rosita, are you alright. Maybe the day with Carmine was too much for you."

"No, Felix. I am not stupid. I know what these men are trying to do. It is right that we stop them. I am going to be with you during that television interview. This is my country too. Those men must pay for what they have done to the innocent people in the barrio and elsewhere. I have ideas and you will include me. I will not agree to be removed from this fight. I am determined that we will win."

"Rosita, I must go and speak with my lawyer before the TV people arrive. It seems he has some important information to discuss."

"Then I am coming with you. We are in this fight together. I will not have it any other way."

Felix was surprised at her determination. He decided that it was not worth fighting about it with her.

J.J. Carter was sitting in the living room talking to Jose Martinez, who seemed nervous. As Felix and Rosita entered he attempted to stand but his knees buckled and he fell back. Flustered he raised himself and stood firmly in front of Felix. His little dark eyes flickered between Felix and Rosita. It was clear he was not comfortable.

J.J.Carter placed his hand on Jose's shoulder and guided him back into a sitting position.

"He is very nervous. The information he has could result in both his death and that of many others."

"I hope whatever information he has is accurate and worth our while. The Generals have sent men to arrest me. We are going to try and distract them, but ultimately they will find me. I don't have time to waste. The TV crew will be here very soon."

J.J. Carter nodded and then asked Jose to tell his story.

It was a long story told by an illiterate man. Felix needed to stop him often to clarify matters.

When he had completed his story, J.J. Carter spoke.

"Felix, let me summarize the situation. Jose was in the employ of a Mexican drug cartel. He was involved in getting drugs sent through the country to the United States. By mistake, he stumbled into a trap laid by the US Drug Enforcement Agency. After months of interrogation and negotiation, the DEA contacted me, as Jose had identified some powerful people here in our society as being involved and I agreed to cooperate. We are talking to the top people. The DEA is not prepared to go to trial yet but is prepared to assist you with your goal of removing the Generals. It has been proven that they are all involved with the cartels in Mexico and Colombia. There are more than just drugs involved. Huge amounts of money are being laundered through our legitimate government institutions. There are large exports of gold and other precious metals. Disgustingly there is also sex trafficking. The country is being drained of valuable assets that could overhaul the way of life for all citizens. I have been retained to assist in devising a plan to bring about this change.

Jose knows who killed General Cruz. It was not men from Nos Grande. They are gangsters from Mexico who are working and stationed at the mine. We believe that the attack on you when driving here from Nos Grande was staged by them.

I am authorized by the United States to arrange for you to seek shelter and asylum for yourself and your family until the murder

of General Cruz is exposed. The strategy is one of deception.
The Generals are not to know that their underground businesses
have been penetrated. The CIA has infiltrated the mine and other
areas with men who are undercover CIA operatives. We must
not do anything to jeopardize this operation. In the TV
interview, Jose will admit to knowing the men and claim that
General Cruz was heavily involved in the drug trade and had not
paid some huge debts. These men had threatened him and been
sent to execute him as an example to others. General Perez sees
it as opportune to frame you. After tonight, Jose will disappear."

Rosita sat with her mouth hanging open. Felix had a deep frown
burrowed into his forehead.

"Is all this true?"

"Yes. I am to arrange meetings with you and others to help
replace each of the remaining Generals. You have some
powerful support. You must be very careful. As I have told you
others are posing as your friends. You cannot discuss this with
anyone, especially Julia. She is involved in a major way. She
has caused the failure of cases from proceeding. There has been
lost evidence, witnesses disappearing, and the manipulation of
officials."

Rosita snarled. "I knew it. I could see she was a bitch. Let me at
her."

"No, Rosita. The best way to win this war will be through charm
and politics. The Generals must not suspect anything."

Before she could answer there was a heavy knocking at the front
door. Felix left to open the door. Standing on the doorstep were
two US officers in full uniform.

"Good evening, sir. We are here to be present alongside Jose
Martinez when he speaks in the TV interview and to escort him

to safety afterward. There will be other armed US Marines arriving shortly to escort you and your family to the Embassy."

Felix was confused. "How did you know of the interview?"

He turned.

J.J. Carter was standing smiling.

"I figured we needed a strong plan and support. Please advise your mother to pack for a few days away. Again, I request you do not say too much. Tell her you are to be special guests at the US Embassy until the allegation of your involvement in General Cruz's murder is resolved.

Chapter 28

Inside Villa Magnifico, activity reached a fever pitch level. Rosita and Carmine consulted and chose dresses and shoes. Carmine anticipated there would be formal functions in her honor and therefore commanded Rosita to include formal wear.

They were busy packing when Camilla Vesco and the TV crew arrived. The weather was foul. Rains drummed against the huge glass windows. In the distance, thunder rolled. Wind and leaves swept into the foyer of the Villa when the door was opened. Camilla Vesco stood soaked. She was not happy.

"I am going to need our makeup people immediately. Where is the bathroom? I need to prepare. I cannot go on the broadcast like this."

Felix was shocked at her brusqueness and lack of manners. He was apprehensive and developed a feeling of immediate distrust toward her.

He called a maid to assist Camilla with her preparations. The crew was dragging wet and dirty equipment up the front stairs and into the foyer.

Felix walked to them and held up his hand.

"This is my home. I request you treat it with respect. Those cases are not to be taken into the living room where the interview will occur. You will unpack and carefully carry in the equipment you need. I want nothing damaged or soiled by you all."

Several of the crew mumbled a response and opened the heavy cases. They lifted in a special chair for Camilla Vesco and a table on which they arranged fake flowers. Cables were run across the floor and plugged into outlets. Three cameras were set up at different angels and focussed on the chairs that Camilla Vesco and Felix would use. J.J. Carter called for two other chairs. The senior crew member queried him why they were needed. J.J. Carter explained there would be a surprise participant and he would need to be sitting beside him to advise him if needed.

This information caused great consternation. The live news producer marched up to J.J. Carter and demanded to know the details. J.J. smiled sweetly and told her the minimal. The producer stormed off to find Camilla.

Camilla appeared wearing a makeup robe. Her hair was wet and hung like strands of black spaghetti. Her overdone makeup had run in the rain. In the flesh, she did not possess any of the beauty or grace she cleverly displayed on the TV. She was ideally made up for a role in a horror film.

Felix found the whole circuslike atmosphere amusing. He was watching from a corner of the room when suddenly Caesar ran into the room. He was laughing.

"Felix, I am having so much fun. I directed them into a major construction zone. Their vehicle is stuck. They have called for assistance. I told them it is on its way. Of course, it isn't, but they won't know until its too late. I have bought you some time. Perez is on the air. He is swearing at them and madder than hell."

Felix thanked him and returned to the TV crew.

"Let's get this over with. I have things to attend to."

The producer objected. "Camilla is not ready."

"She has less than five minutes and then there will be no interview. I will be leaving."

The producer threw down her clipboard and stomped away to get Camilla.

Soon the reporter arrived. The transformation was remarkable.

Felix thought to himself. "Pity the poor guy who falls for her all made up and wakes up in the morning to reality with her on the pillow beside him."

She fronted up to Felix. He sensed what was coming.

"I will be asking you some direct questions and I hope you will answer straightforward and not be difficult. It seems to me you have a lot riding on this interview and need to convince many of your innocence if that's possible. I understand there is another here who will be participating. Please explain."

"I am accompanied by J.J. Carter my lawyer and he has evidence in the way of a witness who will shatter any illusions others may have about my guilt."

This perked up Camilla who was now seeing headlines and her news report running on networks around the world. Her manner to Felix softened.

One of the crew member's two-way radios crackled. The studio was calling to check progress to feature the interview on that evening's late news.

Camilla motioned Felix to sit across from her for one camera to remain on her, yet the other camera to switch back and forth between Felix and her. The third camera was focussed on J.J. Carter and Jose Martinez.

The producer looked through the cameras and called for an adjustment to the lights. When she was satisfied she called the cameramen to start. Camilla led in.

"Good evening viewers. It has been a wild day of accusations and allegations regarding the murder of General Cruz and the involvement of Colonel Felix de Santos. We understand that Colonel de Santos is about to be arrested by the military police, so we will start this interview with him without delay.

Colonel, did you murder General Cruz?"

Before Felix could answer, J.J. Carter intervened.

"Miss Vesco, I believe that it is unnecessary to continue with that line of questioning. Tonight I have with me Jose Martinez, who has full knowledge of the murder. He is prepared to make a confession and provide the details of this grisly matter."

"Please, ask him to proceed."

Jose was sweating profusely. Beads of sweat ran down his forehead and dripped from his nose. He wrung his hands together and then looked directly at the camera and told the whole story of the drug cartels, his involvement, the corruption of General Cruz, the names of the men from Mexico who killed him, and where they were.

Jose spoke for ten minutes without any interruptions. When he was finished, Camilla sat and looked at him uncertain how to proceed.

"There you have the confession of a drug dealer and criminal. Ladies and gentlemen, I don't think this person is credible nor does it exonerate Felix de Santos...."

Before she could continue, J.J. Carter stood and commanded Felix and Jose to leave. As Jose walked from the interview couch, the two US officers walked forward and placed their hands beneath his arms to take him away from the scene and the Villa.

"Felix de Santos has no more to say on this matter. Thank you. This interview is concluded."

Camilla stood dumbfounded. Members of the crew who had little respect for her snickered.

She glared at J.J. Carter and Felix. She addressed J.J.

"One day I will get something on you. What a smarmy bastard you are."

Chapter 29

The interview played on all stations. At the military base, the Generals were huddled in front of a large screen television. The mood was dark. By the time the military police arrived at Villa Magnifico, Felix was long gone. They had observed Enzo speeding out the gate with a passenger in the rear. Believing it was Felix making an escape they chased the car for miles until it turned into one of the poorest and roughest areas of the city. As Enzo stopped to let out his passenger. The military police rushed them. Shouts and anger followed when they realized they had been fooled.

Carmine and Rosita were taken to the US Embassy for their safety. J.J. Carter left with Felix. Instead of going to the US Embassy, they headed for Carter's office.

"Felix, we are going to need the help of some very important people to achieve our goal of replacing those corrupt Generals. Tonight, I am taking you to my office to contact some of those friends. My office is probably the last place they will come and look for you."

"J.J. I don't understand. You are a high ranked member of the legal profession here. Why are you so involved in the politics of this country?"

"I thought you would ask that question. I had expected it a long time ago. I am head of the CIA Field Operations office here. I have access to our highest ranked officials. The CIA has been building a dossier on each of the Generals over the past few years. Starting tonight, certain information will be leaked. Events that may have seemed strange and unexplainable will be revealed. That interview will have been watched by our intel people in Washington and Virginia. It is going to be a full night for many. We have a private plane that is kept fuelled and ready for immediate departure at the La Iluminada airport. It is disguised as a medivac plane. In an hour, you will be on it and heading out of the country to a safe destination. It will not be the United States of America. We cannot be implicated in any plot to overthrow the Generals."

"I am not prepared for this."

"I don't believe you are prepared for the certain death that awaits you if you stay here and are captured."

"I will not leave Rosita behind. You must arrange for her to leave with me."

"Felix, what is so important about her? Why are you so enraptured with her? She is young. You are an old grizzled specimen. Leave her to find her way and meet others of her age and social stature."

"J.J. you are a friend who I trust and respect. Stay out of intruding into my private life. I intend that one day, Rosita will be my wife. Now, I have said it. That will end this discussion. Either she goes with me, or I will go nowhere."

"I am not sure I can arrange for her to travel with you."

"In that case, please take me to the US Embassy. I will take my chances there."

"Felix, this is not like you to be so irrational. Let us go to the office. I will see what can be done. We have secure communication facilities set up there. I cannot promise but I will try. I will contact the Secretary of State and make a case for you. It will take a few hours as authorities in another country will need to be briefed and approve. Please, just be patient. I promise you that if we cannot get her out tonight, then we will within a few days."

They pulled into the opening to the underground garage at J.J's office building. Torrential rain was still falling and visibility was poor. J.J muttered a few curses. He had stopped too far from the security key reader and was unable to back up over the spikes embedded in the cement to stop traffic from exiting. He opened the door and as he exited the car, was soaked by the rain and buffeted by the howling wind.

The security gate slid open and J.J drove down two levels and stopped at yet another security gate. This one was heavily reinforced with steel panels and blocked the casual observer from seeing what was behind it.

J.J stopped beside a console and removed the ruggedized telephone handset attached to the side of the unit's cradle. He held it to his ear waiting for someone to answer. Barely thirty seconds passed before J.J was reciting a series of numbers and letters. The gate flipped open. As they drove into the private garage area, Felix was amazed at the number of high- end security cameras monitoring the area.

"Felix, welcome to our little command center. It is here that we coordinate our South American covert operations. The existence of this place is only known to a few, including the President of the United States. Unknown to you, all your vital information has been gathered as we drove through that last security barrier. You now have a high profile file on the servers in Langley, Virginia. Your height, weight, blood type, and X-rays along with countless other facts will have been gathered from banks, courts, travel

records, and filed. You will now be in the databanks of world
leaders on who we have a special interest."

Felix was shocked.

"I wish you had told me all of this. Maybe I would have refused."

"The reason for establishing your file is simple. We maintain
files on those leaders or possible leaders with whom we have
friendly relations. You have been observed for some time now
and after you stated your desire to see a change in this
country, our Administration decided to support you."

They left the car and entered the inside of the building through
dual security locked doors. The interior was sterile. A long
narrow corridor snaked straight ahead. Overhead bluish-white
fluorescent lights lit the passageway with their harsh light. The
floor was tiled with linoleum of a nondescript light grey color.
The light reflected up from the highly polished surface. Felix
felt claustrophobic in the space.

At the end of the corridor, there was an elevator. The doors were
polished stainless steel. J.J moved to the side and put his head
into an enclosure for a retinal scan.

The doors silently opened and Felix and J.J were whisked up
several floors before exiting into what seemed the offices of a
regular law firm. There was nothing to denote the true operations
that it fronted.

Several men sat at computer terminals and ignored J.J's arrival.
He continued to a plushly furnished office. Inside he lowered the
blinds to cover the glass panels on either side of the door. When
he was sure they were secure he took a key from his pocket and
opened a lock beside the tall bookshelf. He then slid up the

shelving containing various legal books. A terminal and phone automatically rose from below the surface of the shelving.

"Felix, I am now going to make the calls to arrange for your departure. I am sure they may wish to speak with you. Are you ready? Would you care for a Scotch? I have a fine one here."

"No. Can we just get this done? I am anxious."

J.J lifted the phone. As he did so an emblem of the United States CIA lit up on the screen of the computer. After a few lines of snow flickered on the screen a figure appeared. It was the Secretary of State.

"Good evening, gentlemen. It is good to see you are both safe and right on schedule. We have a lot to get done tonight. First, though, I think I should update you with the latest news. I am sure you have not heard it yet.

Two of the ruling Generals have been found dead. It seems they committed suicide, though that is speculation on our part at present. General Perez is howling mad. We were able to kidnap those two Mexican murderers. They have been fully "cooperative" in return for something most precious to them….their lives. They have given us far more information than we had hoped for. In return, they are going to be surgically altered and given new identities in another friendly South American country. That is all I have to say about that matter. Now, the information they gave us allows us to confront the Generals and their associates. Their impenetrable wall is crumbling. We must get Colonel de Santos out of the country now."

"Sir, we have a problem. He is refusing to leave unless his partner accompanies him."

Felix watched the screen as the Secretary frowned and looked at his fingernails.

"What sort of foolishness is that?"

J.J indicated to Felix to stand and move in front of the camera to address the Secretary.

"Sir, with all due respect, the young lady has been and will be key to our discoveries in the barrio of Nos Grande. I am also affectionately involved with her. I insist she accompanies me."

The Secretary sat back and stared off into the distance. He was considering options.

"J.J please contact our ops man and arrange it. Make sure suspicions are not aroused. We must not be visible in this whole affair."

"Yes, Sir, and thank you."

Chapter 30

At the Embassy, Carmine surveyed her accommodations. She had expected a more opulent room. The room was clean and basic. A double bed was placed against the wall across from the doorway. The bed was made with military issue linens and blankets. The ensuite bathroom was equipped with a shower, toilet, and vanity. It was not how she had envisaged the interior living quarters of the Embassy.

She left her room and crossed the hallway and knocked on the door to Rosita's room. Her room was smaller than Carmines and was equipped with a single bed. The bathroom was basic with a shower and a bath. A small circular mirror was mounted on the wall. The room was tiled in pale cream. It was depressing.

A sudden loud knocking distracted her from completing the examination. Rosita went to the door. A young Marine addressed her.

"Good evening, Madam. I am requested to ask you to come with me. You are to be taken to meet with Colonel Felix de Santos. He is waiting."

Rosita cheered up at this news.

"Carmine, I will go now, and when I return we can chat."

Rosita grabbed her coat off the bed and joined the Marine. They took an elevator from the third floor to the lobby. He marched her through the lobby and past some guards and out the front door to a black car that was waiting and moved forward when she exited the doorway. The young Marine opened the rear door for her. Once inside he slammed it closed.

Rosita attempted to speak to the driver. Her attempts failed. She looked around the interiors of the car. There were no door handles or window switches. She was a prisoner in the car. She screamed at the driver. He activated a glass shield and isolated himself from her.

She sulked and sank back into the seat. Unable to understand what was happening or if indeed she was going to see Felix, she felt the anger in her grow at the hopelessness of the situation.

The driver drove quickly but safely through the center of the city. He was careful to obey all traffic signals as he did not wish to attract any undue attention.

Almost thirty minutes passed before he pulled into the entranceway to the parking area that Felix had been driven to an hour earlier. The same security processes were repeated.

The car was met at the entrance door by two men. One opened the door and greeted Rosita.

"Please do not ask me or my partner any questions. We know nothing and cannot answer you. It will soon be explained."

Five minutes later she was taken into the room where J.J and Felix were sitting. Papers were scattered on a desk in front of them.

Felix stood and went to Rosita. He hugged her. She was shivering.

"I am sorry they had to bring you here like that. It seems that I am in extreme danger. The Generals have dispatched military and criminal teams to kill me. I am being taken somewhere safe until the situation calms. I insisted I would not leave without you. In some ways, it is my fault you have been made to worry."

"I am not that scared. I am angry. Why is this happening? The people in my country are nice. In the barrio, we did not have problems until those workers came for the mine. Why did the country decide to replace the King and his family with the ruling Generals? I don't understand."

He hugged her tightly and he felt her taught body relax.

"Rosita, many of our people are asking that same question. Nobody understands how we have arrived in this bad situation. I remain determined to see those Generals gone. If we are to succeed in our goal, we will need the help of these men here. Are you happy to come with me?"

Before answering, she raised herself on her toes and kissed him with passion.

"You are my love. Of course, I will go with you."

J.J. Carter was embarrassed and tried to look away but the show was too much for him to miss.

"Young love," he thought.

"I hate to break this up, but there is a lot to be done. You both must come with me now."

The trio left the office and walked back to the area where the men were working on the computers.

"The first thing we will need to arrange is American Passports. I need to have your appearance changed, Felix. We have trained theatrical makeup artists here. They will make enough changes to change your appearance for the passport photo. You will stay in makeup until you are on the plane. Rosita will be made up differently. To get you safely on the plane and through security at the airport, we have a subterfuge planned. The plane operates under the cover of a medivac service. You will be given identification as a worker at the Embassy and Rosita is your

assistant. You were both in a car accident. You will both be made
up to look injured. You will be taken to the plane in our
ambulance and loaded onto the plane on stretchers. Do you have
any questions?"

Felix smiled at the simplicity of the plan. He knew the Generals
would be actively watching the airports, seaports, and borders.

Rosita was frowning and looking back and forth between Felix
and J.J. Carter.

"What plane? Where are we going?"

"That we will not know until you are on board and the plane
has taken off. The pilots have sealed instructions."

Two young women arrived and asked Felix and Rosita to go with
them to an area where the makeup would be applied.

They seemed to be in the makeup area for hours, either sitting in
barber style chairs or laying on narrow beds.

Eventually, the process was complete. Felix gasped when he saw
himself. His natural wavy hair was now blonde, and they had
aged him. He looked at Rosita and could not contain his laughter.
She now appeared as a redheaded stern-looking woman. The type
Felix associated with government clerks at typewriters in days
long past.

The two of them enjoyed the brief interlude in the otherwise
serious proceedings.

With pictures taken, passports were manufactured. Felix was
impressed with the operation. He wondered at the legality of it all
on the soil of his country.

When they left the area to return to J.J's office, they found he
was gone. The two men in dark suits who had taken Rosita from

the car upon her arrival reappeared.

"The ambulance is waiting."

In the basement, the fake ambulance was idling. It was painted precisely as the local hospital's ambulances. It was fitted with lights and siren and even government-issued ambulance license plates.

The two stone-faced men removed gurneys from inside the ambulance and went about positioning Felix and Rosita on them in such a way to show their 'injuries' to anyone who looked closely.

Again, Rosita started giggling. The seriousness seemed lost on her. She was in convulsions when the two men removed their suits and dressed in white hospital gear. It was perfect, with one exception. The machine pistols each wore on their backs.

Chapter 31

With siren wailing, the ambulance sped through traffic to the airport where it turned off at a sign that read **'Private Aircraft'** and continued down a narrow poorly lit road to a fence and security gate. A small group of soldiers was standing guard at the gate. The ambulance slowed and stopped. One of the soldiers challenged the driver and then demanded the rear doors to be opened.

Several soldiers looked in with horror on their faces. One young soldier turned back as he was leaving. He put his face down close to Felix's. He stayed looking at Felix for a couple of minutes and then smiled. He tapped Felix on the shoulder. Felix squinted an eye open. He knew the young soldier. He was no longer on latrine patrol.

The ambulance drove into a cavernous hangar and over to the side of a white Gulfstream jet. The two men jumped from the ambulance and removed the gurneys. Some soldiers walked around at the sides of the hangar, bored with their duty.

The two men climbed the ramp with Rosita first. As he lay waiting to be loaded onto the plane, Felix opened his eye slightly to observe the situation. He looked at the lettering on the side of the jet's engines. He did not recognize the country of registration. It started VH- He could not remember which country used that registration prefix.

He was bumped and almost dropped as he was carried into the plane. Once aboard, the two stone-faced men wished them a good trip and left. The cabin door was closed from the outside and the sound of the jet turbines spinning and starting filed the plane. It shuddered a little as the force from the jets grew. Before they started to taxi from the hangar, the cockpit door opened and J.J. Carter emerged followed by one of the pilots who completed locking the cabin door from the interior.

"J.J what the hell are you doing here?"

"You didn't honestly think I was going to let you take this holiday alone did you?"

"Do you know where we are going?"

"I have just been informed by the Captain that we are headed to Australia."

J.J had barely finished speaking when a muscular tall man in a short-sleeved white pilot shirt came to speak to them.

"Well gidday, mates. Welcome aboard as guest of the Royal Australian Air Force. My name is Bob Thorne and assisting me is Cam Cross. And we're gonna have to watch him on this flight with a pretty sheila like you aboard. He's a bit of a Casanova with the pretties. It's going to be a long night. We are shooting over to the west coast and then south over the Pacific and expect to touch down in Sydney in about 16 hours. The other traffic over the Pacific has reported strong tailwinds that will work in our favor. Now, unlike real tourist planes, the RAAF hasn't installed videos or TVs in the planes. If you want entertainment just tell me and I'll sing Waltzing Matilda for you. Now I better get back to the controls before the fun starts. We filed a flight plan to Miami, but soon that will attract attention as we turn west. We have been issued a special military id for the overflight of the countries we need to cross. So folks, sit back and enjoy."

Felix was in shock. Rosita had no idea where or what Australia was and wondered what the strange language was that she had just heard.

J.J turned to Felix and spoke.

"We had considered either Canada or Mexico but the concern arose that the drug cartels and the Generals have many contacts in those countries. We cooperate with Australia a lot. I hope you get to see a bit of the country. It's a great place, but I fear you are going to be very busy. I suggest we try and sleep. When we arrive there will be things you will need to attend to."

They collapsed the seats back into a sleeping position. J.J was in front of Felix. Across the narrow aisle, Rosita settled in. She lay on her side. Her eyes were focussed on Felix with the look of wonderment. What life had she gotten herself into?

Chapter 32

Sleep on the plane had been difficult. Twice the pilots called J.J to the cockpit for secure communication back to Langley.

The plane started its descent into Sydney's Kingsford Smith airport. As their altitude dropped and they flew over the famous Sydney Heads entrance to the harbor on approach, strong thermals threw the plane around like a toy. The turbulence was fierce. Rosita was terrified. Felix reached across and took her hand to pacify her. She looked at him. He was so calm and just smiled back at her.

The pilots rapidly dropped height. The smoothness of the Gulfstream's flight returned. Felix looked from the left side of the window at the sparkling waters below. In the distance, he saw the Sydney Opera House with its distinctive sails. As the plane turned, he saw the Sydney Harbor bridge. From the air, it looked to be a beautiful city.

At eight-thirty, the pilots taxied the plane to an apron away from the main terminal. Felix looked out and noted several airforce helicopters and large planes parked. The pilots cut the engines and the whine of the turbines spinning to a halt filled the cabin.

Captain Bob Thorne opened the cockpit door and attempted to stretch his tall body in the narrow confines of the plane.

"That is one long trip to make. Going to get some sleep then call some mates to go fishing."

He had just finished speaking when the cabin door opened. An officer in a lightweight khaki uniform boarded the plane.

"Gidday mates. I hope you got some rest on your flight. Got a couple of formalities to complete, and then we will take you to your home for the next few days."

Another man in a white uniform crawled up the little ladder and into the plane.

"Welcome to Australia. I am Jeffry Strong with the Australian Department of Home Affairs. I will handle the Customs and Immigration procedure for your entry into Australia. I have been briefed on the background. The paperwork is a mere formality. I am aware of the circumstances why you are here and wish you a safe and enjoyable time in Australia."

J.J had been quiet for a long while. He called the government official and handed him a large manila envelope. The official opened and removed the passports and some paperwork. Felix was not sure what the papers were but noticed a US State Department insignia on them. The official scanned them, and without any further delay, handed the passports back to J.J. They were now in Australia.

They gathered up the few items that they had brought with them and climbed down the stairs to the tarmac. The heat was already high in the early morning. Captain Bob Thorne and Captain Cam Cross stood at the base of the stairs. They wished Felix and Rosita well. Cam moved forward and gave Rosita the biggest hug she had ever experienced before slapping a kiss on her forehead. Captain Bob laughed and exclaimed.

"That's Cam."

J.J was talking with the men dressed in suits. A GM Holden SUV stood at idle. J.J and the other men laughed at something and Felix and Rosita found themselves guided to the car.

Inside the SUV the air-conditioned cold air blasted out the hot humid Sydney air. J.J climbed in and the driver headed for the exit from the airport. He wheeled out of the airport and onto General Holmes Drive, a wide busy highway. The early morning traffic was snarled and crawling. Felix could hear the curses and unique Australian swearing coming from the driver. Although dead tired he smiled and was enjoying the experience. He was eager to get somewhere and remove the residual makeup that had been applied to disguise their escape.

An hour later, they drove into a residential area of old Victorian houses in the city. The roads were narrow and it seemed that small Greek and Italian cafes and stores dotted every corner. The houses were all two and three-story-high and narrow. The sidewalks were lined with small blue gum trees planted at the edge of the sidewalk. Felix found it different from what he was used to. He found it pleasant.

The driver slowed and stopped in front of an elegant red brick-faced house. He climbed from the driver's seat and opened the rear door to assist Felix, Rosita, and J.J. Carter out and into the house. J.J was curious.

"Where are we in Sydney?"

"You are in Surry Hills. This building houses the honorary consul for your country. It is not marked as such and has very little consular traffic. The consul has severed ties with your country's rulers. It has been on the news here the last day."

Felix was excited. "Please tell me more. Has there been more news?"

"Yes, but it is best you go inside and I am sure the consul, Hector Moreno will provide you with a full update. I am not authorized to discuss matters of this nature."

The red wooden door swung open and a portly olive-skinned man bounced down the stairs holding onto the black ornamental wrought iron railing.

In rapidly spoken Spanish he welcomed Felix and Rosita. He hugged Felix and then made a major production of kissing Rosita's hands and giving her his arm to help her up the stairs and into the house.

Rosita was exhausted. The last day's events had caught up with her. The consul's wife, Emeralda, greeted them. She immediately saw the fatigue on Rosita's face.

"Rosita, my dear, come and we will get you a warm shower and then send you off for a comfortable sleep. These men! They never think about us. They only care about their games. Come! I will take you to your room and make sure you have everything you need."

Rosita was taken up a set of narrow stairs to the second floor and taken down a hallway until they reached an ornately carved wooden door with a crystal handle and imposing locks.

As they entered the room, Rosita gasped. It was decorated in Victorian style. The enormous bed was covered with a floral duvet. Paintings depicting pastoral scenes adorned the walls. The floor was polished wood with a huge area-carpet. Rosita loved it. She smiled and thanked Emeralda, who gestured to another door which led into a very feminine bathroom.

"I will leave you now. There are some new nightgowns in that chest. Please find one that you like. Now, you shower and sleep. I will be here when you wake up. I am going to go and control those men."

Rosita stripped and stood under the warm running water for ages. She felt herself drifting off into a sleep and hurriedly left the shower and after drying off, rolled naked into the cool sheets of the bed. Within minutes she was in a deep sleep.

Chapter 33

J.J. Carter requested an update on the recent events that had occurred since their departure. Hector Moreno invited them into the official consular office. On his desk were printouts of newspaper articles that had been sent to him over the Internet.

The articles were in Spanish so Felix scanned them and pointed out the major parts of the story. It seemed that the confessions of the Mexicans had caused significant damage. There had been a rash of murders and gang hits that were suspected to be related to tensions amongst the different drug trafficking gangs. General Perez was pleading ignorance of the actions of the generals who had committed suicide. He announced a judicial inquiry into the claims of drug and money laundering, while also professing his innocence. The other Generals had not been seen since the crisis broke.

There were reports of the search to bring Colonel Felix de Santos to justice for his involvement in the attempt to destabilize the country. The reporter Camilla Vesco had interviewed those loyal to the Generals who were calling for the death penalty by firing squad for both Felix and J.J. Carter. She had included her vitriolic editorial denouncing all that Felix had exposed. Claims of treason, betrayal, and deep criminal activities were made. Her article was endorsed by Julia, the senior lawyer for the government. The article carried an interview with a businessman who was suspected of operating one of the largest drug gangs. Felix knew of him, but had never met him or had any dealings. The businessman was offering a reward of $500,000US for the capture of Felix.

It was now clear to Felix why the US government had arranged to hide him.

He turned to the consul.

"There are others who share the same concerns and aspirations as I. We were starting to develop a plan to replace the corrupt and evil with a true democracy. I will need to contact a number of these people. Will it be possible from here. Will my location be exposed?"

At this point, J.J. Carter jumped into the conversation.

"We will be providing the technology to allow that. Do not use any of the phones or other equipment here. They are not secure."

Hearing this, Felix thought of a scheme. He leaned toward J.J.

"Why don't we use it to have a little fun?"

"What are you thinking?"

"Have your people in Washington send messages to this and other consulates without secure facilities. Initially, indicate the US is interested in finding me. Then later send messages that I am in Spain. Throw Perez and his gang off the trail."

J.J. Carter grinned ear to ear. He loved the idea.

By now, it was mid-morning and Felix was starting to feel tired.

"Hector, I am wondering if I can go shower and take a rest. After the trip, I feel I need to freshen up."

J.J concurred and Hector led them up the stairs to their rooms and then left them to attend to other businesses. Felix could hear the sound of soft music playing. He went to the window which looked out onto the street. Sitting across the street and in the shade of an old gum tree, there was a young man playing guitar. Felix listened for a moment before turning away and preparing for his shower.

After the shower, he lay on the bed and dropped into a light sleep. Many things were running through his mind. He was woken by the presence of a soft sweet smelling weight on his chest. He sat up startled only to see a naked Rosita stretched on the bed beside him. His arousal came quickly.

Rosita was gentle and seemed to float with him in rhythm.

Finally, she looked directly into his eyes and whispered, "We will get our way. We will rule our country. We will win the people Rosita's way. I know my countrymen. I will win their support."

She slid from the bed and wrapped herself in a gown before returning to her room.

Felix felt no guilt, instead, a deep passion for Rosita was developing. He dressed and went to join Hector and J.J in an early lunch.

Emeralda joined them.

"Where is your friend, Rosita?"

"She is in her room. She is waiting for me to take her to the stores for clothes. We left in a hurry and she did not have the opportunity to pack anything."

Emeralda threw back her head and laughed.

"Felix, here in Australia it would be a very rare and unusual sight to see a man buying clothes with a woman. You stay with Hector and I will take her."

Felix was relieved. The thought of going around looking for women's stores in a strange country and with all that was happening did not appeal to him at all.

"I will need to provide you with money. I will need to go to a bank and make arrangements."

The words had no sooner left Felix's lips when J.J. Carter boomed in.

"You will do no such thing. Are you stupid? You will blow the cover we set up. We made you leave in a hurry so Rosita's new wardrobe will be courtesy of Uncle Sam."

Felix could not believe how stupid he had been to think such a thing.

Emeralda left to go to Rosita and plan their shopping trip. The men were huddled in a conference discussing strategies when Rosita and Emeralda appeared.

"Hector, I am going to need to take our chauffeur for the afternoon. I imagine it will be late in the afternoon when we return. We will take our guests out for an Australian dinner tonight."

Hector nodded his agreement.

J.J left Hector and Felix and went out to the street to hail a taxi. He did not want to use the phones at the consulate.

An overly chatty cab driver swooped in and picked up J.J

"Gidday. Where you going, mate?"

"Please take me to the US Embassy on Martin Place."

"Oh, so you're a Yank. Whatcha doing here then? Taking a holiday with the missus or did you come alone to see all our beautiful sheilas?"

"Just a quick business trip."

"How do make your bread, mate?"

"I'm in logistics. Arrange for the handling of special cargo."

"That sounds bloody boring. You ever think about suicide having to sit around and do that?"

"No, I can't say its ever been that boring."

They were in the middle of downtown Sydney when a bicycle courier cut them off. The driver wound down his window and let fly with obscenities and words that left J.J in total awe and astonishment.

"If nothing more, these Aussies certainly know how to swear," he thought.

The taxi pulled over at the Embassy. Marines stood on duty outside. The security at the entrance was heavy. J.J walked up to one of the Marines.

"I am here on official business. Here are my ID card and rank."

He flashed his wallet in front of the young Marine, who was impressed to be talking with such a high ranking official.

"Yes, sir. I will report that you are here. Please accompany me."

J.J followed the Marine past a queue of people waiting to conduct other business. There were visa applications, lost passport reporting, US government business issues that US citizens needed help with, and other issues. J.J was surprised at the size of the queue.

At the main entrance, his credentials were taken and he was asked to wait in a barren reception area with a giant grinning portrait of the President looking down at him.

The wait was not long. In minutes the senior CIA agent arrived.

"Welcome. We have had no warning that you would be visiting. Has someone forgotten the protocol? I'm sorry but we weren't prepared for your arrival."

J.J raised his hand and calmed the man down.

"I am here on active duty. It is a top-secret mission. It was assembled quickly by the Secretary of State with the endorsement of the President. I will not need much support from you but do require some items. We immediately need an encrypted communications system. Can you arrange that? We need it immediately."

"Follow me. I will take you to the group who will assist with that."

J.J was escorted from the room to a bank of elevators. A sentry guarded access and checked J.J's credentials before inserting a card and pressing a button that opened the doors.

The interior of the elevator was large. J.J surmised that it was used to move equipment.

The doors closed and the elevator glided smoothly downward for some time. It came to a smooth stop and the doors opened to an immense area that was contained behind bulletproof glass. Inside men were hunched at desks or working at benches strewn with electronic equipment.

The CIA man observed the look of curiosity on J.J's face.

"This is the HQ for the South Pacific region. We have excellent relations with both Australia and New Zealand, who are active participants in activities directed from here."

J.J had heard rumors of this operation, but it had never been confirmed.

The CIA man beckoned a tall skinny man to the doorway. He was in his early forties, skinny with pale skin and a huge crop of wild black hair that flopped as he walked. In J.J's mind, he epitomized the mad professor look.

"No names are used here. I will explain your needs to him."

The sliding glass door hissed open and the man joined them.

"This man is here on a top-level assignment. He requires a secure system to communicate. Can you please assist him and fulfill that requirement?"

"I believe we can. Please hand me his security pass. We will need to scan it to ascertain the system his security level is authorized for."

He took J.J's white plastic card with the embedded microchip and returned to the area and vanished behind a cubicle.

Minutes later the man hurriedly left the cubicle and walked quickly to the door. His face was flushed and he was eager to accommodate J.J and the request.

"Come with me. I will take you to the communications lab. When your security ID was scanned we received a notification from Langley advising us of the features and type of system you will need. It is one of our best, so please look after it and under no circumstance lose it or leave it anywhere it could be stolen."

They reached a nondescript wooden door that opened into a room lined with metal shelving containing an array of phones, laptops, and some ordinary-looking suitcases.

The man reached high on the shelves and removed one of the suitcases. It was a reddish-brown leather-clad case. He lowered it onto a table in the middle of the room and bent over it. He fiddled with the combination lock until there was an audible click and the case sprung open.

J.J peered inside the case. There was a flat-screen display, a keyboard, and on the right side, a strange headset with a microphone attached.

"This is Apollo. It is our most advanced mobile unit. It contains a complete broadcast, messaging, video calling, and encryption computer. It accesses the global network of military satellites by pressing this switch."

The man continued to explain the functions of the device. When he was finished, he turned to J.J.

"Even though all communication sent from Apollo is encrypted, it can be used to call civilian numbers. The outgoing calls are scrambled and get directed through our servers. The calls are all monitored so don't call your favorite dating service or any of those girlie numbers."

This was the man's attempt at humor. J.J gave an obliging smile.

The CIA man requested the paperwork to allow J.J to take the case and leave.

Chapter 34

Rosita had enjoyed her time with Emeralda. The day had worn on it was late afternoon before J.J returned with his case. Felix and Hector had finished whatever business needed to be handled and had just sat down for a glass of one of Australia's finest Chardonnays. Always eager to try a new wine, J.J joined them on the garden patio.

The conversation veered away from the troubles Felix was hiding from and turned to stories of life in Australia. Hector and Emeralda regaled J.J, Felix, and Rosita with humorous stories of their arrival in Australia and adapting to life there.

They sat drinking and talking until dusk. J.J looked at his watch.

"I think we need to consider dinner and stop eating all these grapes. I will treat everyone to dinner at my favorite Aussie restaurant "The Sheep and Shearer". It is in the downtown area near the docks in a place with a weird name. Wooloomooloo. The food is beyond description. I suggest that you all try the Balmain Bugs."

Looks of apprehension appeared on the faces of all. J.J laughed.

"No, it's not what you think. Not those types of bugs. It's seafood, like a mix of a lobster and a crab. Australians love to grill them. They are only found in the shallow waters around Australia."

There were looks of relief on the faces of the others, followed by more laughter.

Hector spoke. "This is what I was explaining. The Australians have strange names and sayings."

Before leaving for dinner, Felix asked J.J to assist him in placing a call to Carmine who was still sheltered at the US Embassy in La Iluminada.

Felix dialed the coded number for a secure link to the Embassy. The call was answered by a member of the staff and switched through to Carmine.

"Felix, where are you?"

"I am in Australia and under protection. The consul here has limited the exchange of communication. What is happening there?"

"There have been changes and the people are questioning and protesting against the ruling Generals. It seems that by exposing corruption and treasonous activities, their rule is weakening. Strikes have been threatened and the Generals have ordered brutal actions against those who gathered to protest. There have been demands to hear from you. The people are worried that you have been captured and taken to prison.

When will you return? I miss you. How is sweet Rosita? I miss her like a daughter."

" I do not know when I will be able to return. I am safe here and Rosita is loving the time here. At present we are safe. I cannot speak for long. I have an idea I need to discuss with J.J and the consul. I will call again tomorrow."

Felix closed the secure link and glanced at his watch. They had ordered a taxi for seven-thirty to take them to the restaurant. He wanted to discuss his idea with J.J. He went to the living room area and found him casually dressed and waiting for the others.

"J.J I have something to discuss with you. I have spoken to my mother who has told me of recent developments. It seems that the population has accepted the news and disclosures I made. The absolute control of the Generals has been weakened. I wish to record an announcement and rally cry to the people. Will your government assist me?"

"You will never be able to get any radio or TV station to broadcast any message from you. They are censored and controlled. I will speak to others in Washinton and present your wish. It may be possible. I cannot guarantee it, however."

"It will be a simple message. I will explain I needed to flee for my safety and that it is not my desire to create political upheaval, but rather to introduce positive change and make those in control accountable for the actions they take. I will publicly ask the Generals to agree to reform and allow me and my family and political associates the freedom to bring about that change. I will ask for them to agree to allow for my return and a position that will allow me to work to bring about the change that the people are requesting."

"That will be a difficult thing to arrange. I will attempt to get you as much support from the US as is possible before we are condemned for interfering in the internal affairs of another country."

Felix sat outlining his desired address but was interrupted by Hector announcing the arrival of their taxi.

Rosita and Emeralda joined them. As they walked down the front stairs to the curb, Felix was surprised to see another young man playing guitar beneath the tree across the street. It was a different person. He wondered about it for a moment and then climbed into the taxi for the quick trip.

Early evening traffic slowed their progress. The driver suggested another route and swung his taxi on a course that took them down to the edge of the harbor and past the famous Sydney Opera House. The sails were illuminated with soft colored lights.

They arrived at the entrance to the restaurant and walked down a pier to the doorway into the establishment. It was busy and the lighting set at a level to enhance the ambiance.

Felix then realized how hungry he was when the rich aromas of steaks, Italian pasta dishes, and seafood intermingled in a heady mix. His stomach emitted a huge gurgling rumble. Rosita was holding his arm and felt the vibration. She could not contain her laughter. The others had not heard the rumble.

"It's better you get that out here and not during the passion I have planned for you later."

He looked at her and saw the look of devilment in her eyes.

"If you keep that up, I will be a worn-out old man before my time."

"Don't be silly. I will keep you young in mind and the body. You will see."

They were waiting to be shown to their table when the proprietor arrived. He immediately recognized Hector.

"Good evening, Hector. It is always a pleasure to see you and the adorable Mrs. Moreno and I see you have brought friends. I will see if one of the private dining areas is available. Please wait in our lounge. I will arrange for complimentary drinks."

The group followed him to the small lounge off the main restaurant. It too, like the décor of the restaurant was rustic. The walls were bare ancient wooden boards interspersed at intervals with exposed brick. Real gaslights burned and flickered overhead. The flooring was dark hardwood. Plush chairs were arranged around low slung tables. Newspapers and magazines were arranged at the end of the tables. Felix felt a sense of relaxation envelope him.

He was liking Australia, and especially the company of Rosita. A bottle of Chardonnay and a bottle of famous Australian Shiraz arrived shortly after they were seated. Felix thought back to his time with Rosita earlier and immediately felt his arousal start. If it hadn't been polite to stay at the restaurant, he would have taken her to a discreet location and made love to her with a wild and uncontrolled passion.

Rosita sensed his thoughts and reached across for his hand. He felt a tingle like electricity rush from her touch. She smiled a sly grin at him, knowing full well his thoughts.

In their cocoon of private enrapture, they had drifted away from the conversation. Felix looked across at the others who were all looking at him. It was obvious that something had been addressed to him but he had not heard. He simply smiled and shrugged. J.J looked at him as if he was mad.

"Felix, Hector was asking about your plans when you return. You just shrugged to indicate that you don't know. That is crazy."

"I am sorry. For a moment there, I was deep in thought."

Emeralda knew exactly what the thought was. She had noticed the increased bulge in Felix's lightweight trousers. She smiled and thought to herself, "Lucky girl."

They had just finished their drinks when a waiter wearing a white shirt, tight red pants, and a long apron arrived to escort them to their table.

After they were settled and another drink order was taken, the waiter launched into his glowing description of the specials for that evening.

Emeralda and Rosita ordered the endive salad and the men selected escargot in garlic butter.

The waiter continued until Hector interrupted him.

"Can you recommend an Australian dish for my overseas visitors?"

"Yes, of course, there are several. Tonight we have grilled emu, Scallops, and Broccoli in Abalone sauce, but the best is the Surf and Turf Australian style. It is Balmain Bugs drizzled with a champagne sauce and served with an eight-ounce rare pan-fried Kangaroo steak and fresh asparagus and Petites Pommes de Terre. For dessert, I would highly recommend the Cherries Jubilee. We use only the freshest cherries from our private orchards in Tasmania. We receive them daily."

After the meals arrived conversation floated around the table. They all agreed on the excellence of the meals. Hours passed and Hector summoned the waiter to request a taxi be ordered for them.

As they stood to leave, the proprietor rushed to them.

"I hope all was fine with your dinner and evening. I look forward to seeing you here again."

"We will George. Thank you for a wonderful evening."

They walked the short distance along the dock and found their taxi waiting. Thirty minutes later they were home and preparing for bed.

Chapter 35

Rosita spent considerable time in the bathroom. She emerged in a revealing negligee and looking beautiful. Felix admired her and wondered how he had gotten so lucky.

Felix decided to shower before retiring for the night. Feeling relaxed, he joined Rosita in his bed. She smiled and put her arms around his neck while drawing him to her. Their embrace tightened and long passionate kisses followed.

Rosita giggled as he lay on his back and she crawled on top of him. Her intent was obvious. As she reached down for him, he froze. He reached and pushed her gently to the side of the bed and sprinted across the room for the bathroom. He had barely sat on the toilet when voluminous diarrhea started. He was shocked at the foul odor that filled the small bathroom air. He sat for the longest time. It seemed that the flow would never stop. His anus stung from the acidic fluids that had streamed from him. He felt dirty and desired to take another shower. He attempted to rise from the toilet but dizziness prevented his attempt. He slunk back onto the toilet for a repeat performance.

Rosita was calling to him from outside the door.

"Felix, are you alright?"

He was too weak to respond. She forced open the door to find her lover on the toilet and in total disarray. Ignoring the situation, she helped him to his feet.

"I want to shower. I cannot be dirty like this."

Rosita helped him into the shower. Given his weak state, she stripped and decided to shower with him for his safety. When he was satisfied, she helped him out of the shower and dried him down before guiding him to the bed, where he fell heavily onto the sheets.

For the next five minutes, she watched him as he drifted off into sleep. When he was deeply asleep, she decided to visit the kitchen to find a juice he could drink to prevent dehydration.

She quietly crept from the room and proceeded along the corridor to the stairs leading down to the lower level where the kitchen was located. She was no more than six stairs down when Hector rushed up the stairs with his hand over his mouth. He threw open the door to the shared toilet off the corridor. She heard the roar and bellow as he projectile vomited.

Rosita was worried. She decided to go to the private quarters and find Emeralda. On her way to her room, Rosita heard more toilet flushing through the pipes as she passed J.J's room.

At Emerald's room, she rapped loudly on the door. Emeralda opened the door, surprised to see Rosita standing there. She was wearing a sequined night mask.

"What is it? Is something wrong?"

"It seems all the men are sick. I need your help."

Emeralda visited each of the men and then called the Consulate doctor, who took close to an hour to arrive.

The doctor examined them before declaring they each had a bad case of food poisoning. He asked about the foods they had eaten. Emeralda described the dinner. It was then she realized that the men had eaten the escargot and she and Rosita had the endive salad.

The doctor seemed worried. He checked their temperature and blood pressure.

"I am worried about them. I want to ensure we get them treated to prevent botulism. It can be fatal. I suspect the garlic oil with those escargot was the culprit. I will need to inject each with an antitoxin. It will stop the toxins in their bloodstream, but they will suffer for a few days. I will need to report the restaurant to the authorities. Their cases happened quickly meaning that the food is heavily contaminated.

I will stay here the balance of the evening to be sure their situation does not worsen. Is there somewhere I can rest between checking on them?"

Emeralda showed him into the library on the ground floor.

"I will be upstairs if you need me. We have some staff who sleep here. I will alert them to check on you and if you need food or coffee, just ask them."

The balance of the night was without further disturbances.

The doctor left early when he was satisfied that none of the men had worsened during the night.

Chapter 36

A weak and pale Felix arose and attempted to dress. Rosita
watched his feeble effort before rising and fetching a robe from
the room closet.

"I have never felt so sick. My stomach is on fire. I am too ashamed
to leave our room. I must stay near the bathroom."

"Felix, don't feel bad. The others are suffering the same way. I will
speak to Emeralda and ask her to call the doctor. I am sure we can
manage to make you feel better. In the barrio, we had some cures
for this. You must drink a lot."

Rosita left to speak to Emeralda. She found her in the kitchen
preparing a large pot of a cream-colored mixture.

"Good morning. What are you making?"

"It is oatmeal. It should help settle their stomachs. I spoke with the
doctor's office this morning. They assure me that this will help."

One by one the men arrived in the kitchen and took seats at the
large table. Each looked haggard and grey. Emeralda placed bowls
of the steaming oatmeal in front of each of them. Felix looked at it
and experienced a rumbling in his stomach and felt an immediate
pressure build in his bowels. He pushed back from the table and
sprinted to the closest bathroom. The others sat in silence as a roar
similar to that of an exploding volcano echoed through the ground
floor. Rosita was worried and wanted to rush to him, but
instinctively knew his pride would cause him to shun any

assistance.

A long time passed before Felix returned to the table. He was embarrassed. No one commented other that Emeralda who advised him to try and eat the oatmeal.

The silence was broken by the shrill ringing of the secure consular phone. It stopped and a female voice could be heard answering it. Minutes later, one of the secretaries to the Consul knocked at the kitchen doorways.

"Consul Hector, there is an urgent call for you. The person asked to speak directly to you. He claimed he has been requested to call you by General Perez."

Anxious looks were exchanged around the table. Had Felix's shelter been discovered? Rosita scowled.

"I must go and take this call. I have no idea why they are calling here. Maybe someone has leaked the information that you are taking refuge here. I will assure them I do not know where you are hiding. I will suggest you went to Spain."

Hector hobbled away from the table at a slow pace toward the office area in the old home.

It seemed that Hector was gone for hours. Felix had consumed the oatmeal and already felt his stomach settling. Emeralda had served J.J and Felix a weak coffee without cream or milk. As they sipped the coffee, Rosita went to Felix. She was dressed for the heat of the summer day that lay ahead. She looked at Felix and bent to kiss his forehead.

"You are a strong man, Felix. This will pass quickly I am sure. You must drink lots of fluids today. I am going out with Emeralda today. Will you be alright here with J.J and Hector?"

Before Felix could answer her, Hector returned. Even though he was suffering the effects of food poisoning, there was a look of satisfaction on his face.

"Felix, there is news from home. With the loss of the other Generals, Perez has made some sweeping changes to the governing party. He has forced the retirement of several of the politicians and promoted two officers to the status of Generals. He has addressed the nation and shifted the blame and responsibility for the country's problems to the politicians and Generals who are no longer in the ruling elite. He is covering things up. Things are getting worse with the masses. There have been huge rallies calling for reform. Perez's family has left the country for an undisclosed location. Several business owners have also departed. It seems you have exposed the situation in a way that the people can understand and relate to. Perez has broadcast an appeal for you to return and help in restructuring the control of the country and assist in bringing in the reforms. The person I spoke with told me he is contacting our embassies and consular offices in his search for you. It will only be a matter of time before we are contacted."

Felix sat in silence, digesting the news that Hector had delivered.

"Did you get the names of the Generals he has promoted?"

"Yes. One is Ricardo Sousa and the other Xavier Ruiz. I was unable to find out anything about them or the names of the new politicians he has appointed."

"I know both Sousa and Ruiz. They would kill their mothers for a penny. This is not good news. We must find out who the new politicians are and their roles in the governing body. I am suspicious of them."

J.J had been listening to the conversation and spoke.

"If Perez has started a hunt for you, then we must look at moving you and Rosita from this location. I will contact the US Embassy and my contacts there. We must move quickly."

The shrill ring of the consular phone pierced the air again. They were silent, fearing that the hunt for Felix had arrived. Instead, it was the same spokesman who had phoned minutes earlier. Hector was summoned to the phone and listened in silence. When the person speaking was finished, Hector thanked him and returned to the kitchen.

With all the activity and the evolving situation, the men's food poisoning issues were diminishing.

"I was informed on that call that Perez and the new governing party have issued a Proclamation of change and announced that the formation of political parties will be allowed, and these parties will be allowed to participate in open elections. It seems that these new parties will need to meet certain criteria which will be decided by members of the ruling party. General Perez has issued a direct invitation to you, Felix to try and beat them. You have been publicly challenged."

"It is a trap. He has no intention of allowing me to participate in any election. I know too much. I am sure his position is simply that if he cannot convince me to join with them, he will find a way to assassinate me. I do not exaggerate."
J.J considered this.

"But, Felix. What if his offer is real? I think we should explore it further. Some ways come to mind. I suggest you make an international and public appeal to the United States to protect and assist you. As you are aware there are many US interests in your country. I am sure we can make a strong argument for them to protect you. We will present an argument whereby Perez will not be able to interfere or reject their assistance. If you agree, I will go to the Embassy here and arrange another place for us to stay and start the discussion for their help in having you safely returned and protected during the formation of a party and the election. All you have to do is say, Yes."

Felix nodded. He looked at Rosita who was beaming at the idea of the prospect of being associated with one of the leaders of the country.

"Please Felix. Consider this. You have a lot to offer our nation."

"I will take some time. I need to speak and confer with others before I decide. J.J please go to the Embassy. I agree that we must move from here if Perez has set a search for me in motion."

J.J stood and excused himself. He fetched an umbrella from a stand in the hallway as heavy thunderstorms were predicted for late morning and early in the afternoon. J.J anticipated his business at the Embassy would take long. Some powerful people needed to be contacted and in agreement. He suspected that the US would want its allies to support any move to assist and support Felix.

Chapter 37

It was dusk when J.J returned. He looked tired and upon entering the home told everyone he wished to rest for a while as the food poisoning had caused him fatigue, as that afternoon as he negotiated with the Secretary of State and awaited the reply of the President. As he had suspected, the President reached out to certain allies to brief them and obtain their support. It had been a difficult process. As a courtesy, the President had insisted some other countries be involved. Russia and China had been less than accommodating but finally relented when other inducements were offered. It had taken the White House administration hours to determine the benefits of supporting Felix, and then to convince the opposition of this. He was exhausted.

While J.J slept, the others talked. Emeralda and her assistants prepared a meal that was recommended for people recovering from food poisoning. She had advised her staff to prepare a clear broth and a dinner of baked chicken and boiled new potatoes.

Felix and Hector sat for hours discussing the situation with General Perez and his proclamation. At around eight J.J reemerged from his room and joined them for the dinner.

"I am starting to feel much better. This afternoon at the Embassy I engaged in detailed talks with the Secretary of State and others. Your country has many resources that are important to the United States and therefore there was great interest in reversing the direction it has been taking. I received the full backing to proceed. We must still be cautious and on our guard to protect you, Felix. I am expecting to hear of the plan to move you to another safe location in the morning. I suggest you and Rosita pack what possessions you have so we can leave with little delay in the morning. The relocation was approved, but with the condition that the move is performed by the Marines from the Embassy. They will be dressed in civilian clothing not to arouse suspicions."

"Where will they be taking me?"

"That was not revealed to me. I suspect we will be taken somewhere outside of Sydney."

"I will want to contact friends who will want to be involved if there are elections."

"That is premature. I suggest we wait a few days and see what Perez and his gang are up to. During that time we can strategize how to proceed."

Felix began to wonder whether he was to be relocated somewhere other than Australia and questioned J.J.

"No, I don't believe they will move you from Australia. Your presence here has gone undetected. To fly you to another location would involve the risk of exposing you. Please have Rosita ready to leave early tomorrow morning."

"J.J, I have a question. Have you seen those men who sit beneath that tree across from the house for hours playing guitar and collecting money from passersby? It seems strange. They are there for almost the whole day and night."

J.J looked at Hector and Felix and after some minutes spoke.

"Yes. Those men are highly trained special forces. Their job is to keep the consulate under surveillance in case of any unwelcome visitors. They are not alone. There are others with them. They are heavily armed and would not hesitate to spring into action if required."

Emeralda entered and advised them that the dinner was ready. The men arose and shuffled to the dining area. The meal was served and the conversation drifted to the situation that the Generals had created. Ideas to restore civility and wealth in the country were expressed. Throughout most of the meal, Rosita had been silent. There was a lull in the conversation and finally, Rosita spoke. The group concentrated and listened to her with great interest. Felix was surprised at the eloquence and intensity of her speech. Even with the minimal education Rosita had received in the barrio, her natural drive and intelligence were evident. He glanced around the table and observed the others were in deep thought, listening to her opinions.

J.J was the first to speak when Rosita finished.

"I had no idea you were so patriotic. I am very impressed. I hope that you can convince Felix with some of your ideas. We need new fresh concepts and young people to help rebuild our country."

"If I am given the opportunity, I will help. I am not pleased to see so many suffering when their lives and living conditions could be easily improved."

Felix had remained quiet. He was deep in thought and trying to understand the rapid pace of events that had unfolded.

As they sat finishing a dessert, there was a loud knocking at the front door. Hector arose to accompany an assistant to the door. It was unusual for anyone to visit the consulate at such a late hour.

Upon opening the door, two men presented their plastic-clad credentials identifying them as members of the Marines. Hector ushered them in.

"We are sorry to arrive unannounced. For security reasons, we were directed not to call but to come here directly. We are to escort the following people to a new location. Felix de Santos, Rosita Valquez, and J.J. Carter. We will wait inside here while they pack their personal effects."

Hector showed the Marines into the living room area and left to fetch J.J.

The Marines stood and saluted J.J as he entered.

"Good evening. I am surprised that you have arrived here at this time. We had expected an escort in the morning. Of course, we will come with you but need an hour to pack our belongings. Can you tell us where we are being taken?"

"It has been determined that it is no longer safe in Sydney for your friends. We are to take you to a safe house in Surfers Paradise, just south from Brisbane by about one hour's drive. You will be met there and given further instructions. We are on increased alert as it seems someone unfriendly has discovered the presence of Felix de Santos. We are eager to leave here as soon as possible."

J.J was angry. With all the security how could their whereabouts have been found? He surmised that there was a traitor in the service and had probably sold out for money or some other gain.

“We will be ready soon. How are we to travel?”

“It is not ideal, but you will fly on a private plane that is waiting now. You must hurry.”

Chapter 38

At the airport, a Cessna Citation had been prepared and was waiting on the tarmac. The Marines stopped the car at the foot of the narrow stairs leading up to the door into the aircraft. The pilot stood beside the plane and greeted them. Introductions were made. He was young and a little too eager to help Rosita up the stairway and escort her to her seat. Felix watched with mild amusement. It was obvious the pilot was taken with Rosita, but he knew that her aspirations far exceeded those of a pilot.

When they were all on board and seated, the young pilot addressed them.

"My name is Larry and please let me know if you need anything. We will be taking off in about ten minutes. I am just waiting for the approval of the flight plan. Maybe the young lady would like to join me in the cockpit for takeoff."

Rosita was thrilled. It was evident that the young pilot was more than just slightly attracted to her.

She went forward into the open cockpit and was told to sit in the seat to the pilot's right. He spoke quickly into the microphone of the headset. Technical jargon bounced back and forth between air traffic control and Larry. He reached behind Rosita and pulled out another headset which he passed to her. She pulled it on with great enthusiasm. Larry proceeded to explain some of the instruments.

She jumped slightly as the loud voice of the air traffic controller announced the flight was cleared to make the trip north to Surfers

Paradise. Rosita watched in amazement as Larry turned knobs and pressed buttons at a rapid pace. There was a whine that grew in intensity as he fired up the plane's jet engines. Minutes passed and the jet jerked forward in a slow roll toward the runway he had been allocated.

Rosita could barely contain herself. She looked out of the cockpit window at the flashing lights of other aircraft and the brightly lit terminal. The pitch of the jet engines rose as Larry accelerated. In seconds the small jet started to lift from the runway and Larry applied more thrust and they rapidly climbed. He leveled off and made a sweeping turn. Below the lights of Sydney glistened. They cruised without any changes for a few minutes and then, responding to the instructions from air traffic control, Larry accelerated and climbed to a higher altitude.

"OK Rosita, the exciting part is over. Now we will just glide along up the coast for the next hour and a bit. Did you enjoy that takeoff?"

In the passenger cabin, Felix was watching as Larry and Rosita chatted. He was pointing to various instruments and occasionally out of the cockpit window at something unseen by Felix. Rosita was chattering constantly. Felix could not remember her being so excited.

J.J had fallen into sleep and Felix was starting to feel tired. His eyes were heavy and involuntarily falling shut. His rest was interrupted when he looked forward into the cockpit and saw Larry's hand resting on Rosita's upper leg. He had had enough. In a loud voice, which woke up J.J he called to Rosita.

"Rosita, please come back here. I have some important things to discuss."

In the cockpit, she hesitated and then gently removed Larry's hand before standing and crouching to return to sit with Felix.

"Felix, I believe you might be a little jealous," she teased and burst into laughter.

"Be quiet. I have very serious matters in my mind. I cannot spend time on silly frivolous behavior."

Rosita sulked and Felix drifted back into a deep sleep. His snoring was loud enough that Larry heard it. He turned the Rosita and blew her a kiss. She was flattered.

For the next hour, they flew on smoothly. Larry's headset erupted into life with instructions to change to a different frequency for approach. There were constant communications on the new frequency from inbound planes from over the Pacific heading into Brisbane and Sydney. The traffic this evening was heavier than normal. Larry needed to pay careful attention to other aircraft in his vicinity. Again instructions were radioed to him and he turned to a new heading and reduced both speed and altitude. In ten minutes they would be on the ground at Gold Coast airport. More instructions directed Larry to commence descent into the airport. His mind wasn't full on the task. He was wondering how he could get a message to Rosita and convince her to meet him while in Surfers. He glanced back at Felix who had awakened and fixed his eyes on Larry. Resigned to defeat, Larry abandoned any further ideas.

The landing was heavy, and the little jet bounced and rocked to side a little. Felix was not impressed with the rough landing. He was tired of Larry.

Upon leaving the plane, they were met by a group of casually dressed men, one of whom seemed to be a friend of J.J.

"Felix come and meet an old friend. This is Ben Giles. Ben and I were in training together for our respective roles. Ben will be looking after our stay here in Surfers Paradise."

Felix shook hands and engaged in some small talk. He turned back to the plane and saw Larry gesticulating wildly. Rosita stood in front of him in a firm stance. Whatever Larry was suggesting was wasted on her. She looked over at Felix and waved. Larry turned and stormed back up the stairs into the plane.

Rosita ambled across to the group who were gathered around the two large black vans that were waiting to take them to their accommodation.

After twenty minutes they pulled into the entrance of "The Board and Sand" hotel. It was a smaller hotel on the beach and with magnificent gardens surrounding it. A fountain lit in soft white lights played in the garden at the front of the hotel entrance. Tall palm trees were also lit and the light reflected over the gardens filled with hibiscus and bougainvillea.

Attendants dressed in colorful shirts, tropical shorts, and sneakers moved quickly to open their doors and assist with luggage. They were surprised at the small amount of luggage these three guests were bringing but greeted the group with great friendliness. Rosita was enjoying the attention and the appearance of the hotel.

The staff recognized Ben Giles and welcomed him back. Felix was confused and turned to J.J.

"Those young men certainly seem to be familiar with Ben. Does he come here often? Maybe he stays here on vacations?"

"No, it's not like that at all, years ago when NASA was working on the Apollo program and when the Vietnam war was raging, the CIA purchased this land and had this hotel built. There are floors of the hotel that are secure and off bounds to guests and staff. We will be staying on one of the secure floors."

Felix digested this information. He was surprised at the level of involvement of the United States in Australia. He intended to discuss this with J.J. in private.

Ben Giles directed Felix to the entrance. There were no check-in formalities and once inside, the marines who had been accompanying them left. Ben led them down a long corridor to an elevator that required a special security pass for the doors to open. They rode up to the top floor of the hotel. The décor was different from that of the ground floor. It had an office like appearance. Ben laughed when he noticed Felix and Rosita looking around.

"Uncle Sam didn't want his servants living in luxury here. You get to stay in standard-issue furnishings but with a great view."

Felix liked Ben. He found him to be an affable character who seemed to be permanently optimistic. His humor was at its peak when he showed Rosita and Felix their room. It was decorated in the style of an army barracks. Ben couldn't resist commenting Felix about the military maneuvers he could practice with Rosita.

"OK, I will leave you to settle in while I discuss some business with J.J. Good night."

Rosita walked across the room and slid open the tall glass door that opened onto a wide concrete balcony. Standing on the balcony in the pale moonlight she could easily make out the long curving white sand beach below and hear the crashing of the surf. She gazed out to sea and watched the white caps of the waves as they rolled into the shore with lazy ease.

Felix joined her on the balcony and slid his arm around her waist. She rested her head on his shoulder. A feeling of contentment enveloped her.

"Rosita, I watched the overtures that Larry the pilot made toward you. As you are aware, I have many important decisions to make and actions to take. If you are planning something I suggest you leave me now. I have no time or desire for any foolish behavior."

She spun toward him. The streak of evil in her arose, but then subsided when he looked deeply into her eyes.

"Felix why do you say things like that. I have no intention of leaving you now or in the future."

She reached up on her toes and while embracing him, kissed him fiercely. Within minutes they were entwined together making passionate love on the creaking metal-framed bed. Rosita laughed as the sounds from the bed reminded her of an old tractor one of the farmers in the barrio had owned.

Chapter 39

The morning sun streamed through the sliding glass door into the living area. Rosita awoke refreshed and happy. She looked at Felix beside her. He was in a deep sleep. Deciding not to wake him, she gently left the bed and went to the small kitchen area where she found some cups, a pack of coffee and milk. After making a coffee she went out onto the balcony and sat looking out at the rising sun glistening over the waters of the ocean below. The air tasted of salt from the spray rising off the surf breaking at the shoreline. Rosita considered it to be a paradise and understood why the area was called Surfers Paradise.

She sat with her eyes closed soaking up the sun's early rays. Except for the occasional cry from a passing seagull, there was total silence.

Her tranquility was interrupted when Felix reached over her shoulder and hugged her from behind.

"This is beautiful, Felix. I wonder if I can buy something to go and swim in that ocean?"

"I will speak to Ben. Today I will need to attend some meetings with J.J and others. I will be busy all afternoon. This morning we will go and explore and enjoy our first freedom."

Felix had no sooner finished speaking when the phone inside rang. He turned and muttered as he answered the intruding interruption. The call was from Ben.

"Felix. Are you up? I would like to join you for a little while."

"Yes, we are having coffee on the balcony. Come and join us."

"I'll be there in five minutes."

Ben arrived precisely on time carrying a bag of fresh pastries. Together, they all sat on the balcony enjoying the early morning and chatting.

"Ben, I would like to go and swim but I need a bathing suit. Is there somewhere close by to purchase one?"

"Yes, but you will need an escort. I will arrange for one of the members of the security team to follow you. I assume Felix will go with you? I intended to advise you to get some surfing clothing and look like tourists. We do not want to draw attention to you. I suggest Felix goes tropical in a bright tacky shirt and shorts with sandals, and you get some beachwear. Tell me when you want to leave and I will arrange for the security man."

"Rosita and I were about to leave and find somewhere on the beach to have breakfast and then go to the stores."

"If it's alright, I will join you. There is a great place not far from here. Wait while I advise the security men of our plan. Even though they will be watching and guarding you, their presence will not be obvious."

While Ben made his phone call, Rosita and Felix dressed. Ben was in high spirits when they left the hotel. They walked along the beach for almost a quarter of a mile until they reached the restaurant. There was a patio that extended down onto the beach. Although it was early, there was a crowd waiting to be seated. The host noticed Ben and waved him forward. Several people complained as Ben, Rosita and Felix moved ahead of the queue. The host raised his voice and announced that they had reservations. While walking across the patio, Ben thanked the host. A table at the front of the patio with a view of the beach and ocean was offered. Rosita was thrilled. She was enjoying every moment of her unplanned stay in Australia.

The service was impeccable. Rosita ordered a fresh fruit plate, tea, and a Danish. Before Felix could order, Ben decided he would order for him and chose "The Australian" for them both.

"What is "The Australian"?"

Ben chuckled.

"It's an old Australian favorite of their traditional steak and egg breakfast you won't forget."

After a leisurely breakfast, Ben excused himself and signaled the waiter to charge the breakfast to him at the hotel. He threw some money on the table as a tip and bent to kiss Rosita on the cheek before departing. As he was walking away he turned to Felix,

"Please be available at one this afternoon. We have a lot to cover and there will be several meetings. I suspect we will work until the early evening. Rosita, you will be alone for a while. I can arrange for a companion you if you wish."

"No thank you. I will be happy walking and resting on the beach."

Ben removed a roll of banknotes and handed them to Felix with the instruction to use them for any purchases.

With breakfast completed, Felix and Rosita wandered back to the coastal road and walked to a group of stores that were focused on catering to tourists.

The first retailer they encountered was a sportswear store. A salesclerk descended on them the minute they entered. Felix explained they were on holiday and looking for some casual clothing.

"We have a new line of shirts that I believe you will like. Let me choose some for you."

Shirts were laid out on the counter, along with some surfer and dress shorts. Rosita selected three shirts and four pairs of shorts for Felix.

Sensing an opportunity, the clerk suggested they look at the selection of sandals and sneakers.

Fifteen minutes later they left the store. Felix felt stupid. He was now wearing the new clothing as Rosita had insisted, dressed in a pale cream linen shirt with embroidered pineapples and beach umbrellas on it, a pair of bright orange shorts and open-toed roman sandals. He was uncomfortable until several passing ladies complimented him on his unique appearance.

Rosita gasped in glee as they encountered a ladies' swimwear store. In the windows, mannequins were dressed to display a range of different styles.

"Felix, I have seen the one I want. Let's go inside."

She half dragged Felix through the door and into the store. They were no sooner inside when Rosita pointed to a pink and white polka dot bikini. The salesclerk nodded and left to take one from a shelf behind the counter. Felix removed some bills from the roll of money Ben had provided. Rosita was eager to return to the hotel and change to visit the beach. She tugged impatiently at Felix's arm.

Back at the hotel, they changed into swimwear and were about to leave for the beach when there was a loud knock at the door. Felix went to the door.

J.J asked to enter their room.

"Felix, go and enjoy a few hours at the beach, but you must be ready to attend some meetings here at one this afternoon. There have been some major developments and I am advised you are to receive a full briefing. I do not have much information, but they must be very important to replace the original meetings that had been scheduled."

Felix frowned. He wondered why there had not been a secure call on the communications system J.J had obtained. This sudden development worried him.

"J.J do you have any idea what the briefing is about?"

"No. I do know that it has been scheduled by the most senior people in the White House. I asked several people I know there and none were prepared to speak. It seems that whatever the topic is, that it is extremely sensitive."

"I will be ready. Now I am going to take the impatient and demanding Rosita to the beach. It will be interesting to see if she can swim."

They left the room with J.J and proceeded to the private elevator. A man dressed in casual clothing followed them onto the elevator. He smiled and nodded to Felix.

"I will be overseeing your safety at the beach. Don't be concerned I will not interfere or be visible. Enjoy your morning there."

Chapter 40

Their time at the beach passed quickly. Rosita proved to be an excellent swimmer which surprised Felix. He swam with her and later dozed beneath the rented umbrella. The travel and stress had made him tired and now the relaxation intensified this.

While Felix was in a deep sleep Rosita bathed in the sun watching others on the beach. Her peace was broken by their security escort signaling and pointing to his watch. Rosita shook Felix awake and advised him that it was time to leave. Reluctantly they left the beach to return to the hotel.

Back in their room at the hotel, Felix found a message waiting for him. It advised him of the room number for the meeting. He showered and dressed.

"Felix, I will be on the beach. I will have a light lunch before going."

"I wonder why this meeting and all the sensitivity around it?"

Felix left the room and was escorted to the meeting room. It was a converted suite and housed a conference table. There was an enclosed office area containing various communications equipment. A large screen television hung on the wall at the head of the table.

J.J was already seated and was involved in an intense conversaison with Ben Giles and another man who Felix had not met.

"Felix, welcome. Please meet Charles Clark. Charles is the liaison between the White House and the operations here. He has been provided with information regarding your situation and the next steps that have been planned for your return.

Charles Clark nodded to Felix. He struck Felix as a dry personality, lacking any sense of humor.

"Good afternoon. Last night and early this morning, The Secretary of State and the President received assurances from General Perez and others in command, that they guarantee your safe return to participate in the elections. The United States has sought and received certain collateral in support of their claim. There is substantial doubt their offer is the truth. The President has authorized the mobilization of troops and naval assets. In seeking to guarantee their sincerity and to protect you, a demand was made by the US to have you escorted back to the country by US Marines along with a commitment to allow troops to be stationed in the country until after the elections and any transfer of power. General Perez agreed to this but with a lot of reluctance. Our belief in his guarantees is slim.

We are not announcing this publicly. In the event of any betrayal by Perez, we are establishing legal methods to seize all assets that any members of the governing party have either in the country or invested abroad. Furthermore, we have enlisted the support of Britain. Members of their Special Forces will be sent with others to monitor the election process.

Felix, we want you to hold a press conference tomorrow night and announce your intention to return voluntarily to the country. We are not announcing the role the United States is playing as it could impact the world's financial markets. As you are aware, South America is a politically volatile region and in the event we have to take action, it is anticipated that other countries will get involved in an armed conflict. Our sources in certain countries have established without any uncertainty the loyalty many have to General Perez and his cronies. Please be prepared to leave to return tomorrow evening. It should be obvious to you that major steps are being taken behind the scenes. It is not necessary to brief you on these."

Charles Clark sat back in his chair. He neither invited and accepted questions from J.J or Felix. The meeting was over. Charles Clark stood, handed Ben an envelope, and then briskly left the room.

Ben Giles, J.J, and Felix were silent, thinking of the situation. It was J.J who spoke.

"I suspect there is a lot more going on behind the scenes that we are not being told. For the US to be involved to this extent means that someone very high up wants it kept quiet. I will attempt to find out from my contacts what is happening. I am concerned that Felix is being used as a pawn in a powerful game."

Ben Giles opened the envelope that he had been handed.

"I have instructions here regarding the balance of your stay and the plans for tomorrow. You are to be flown by military plane to Hawaii tomorrow morning. There you will hold your press conference. It is being arranged as we speak. After the conference, you will be flown back to your country. It is a clever move to stop in Hawaii. Your presence in Australia will not be disclosed. You must never reveal your time here."

Felix pondered the situation. As he sat there, Ben Giles handed him a folder in which was the press release and the points he was asked to make during the press conference.

"This is going to be our last night here together. I suggest we go for a nice dinner this evening and spend some social time. Tomorrow morning you will need to be updated on any recent happenings and then taken for your flight to Hawaii. Let us go and freshen up. It's getting late. We will all meet in the downstairs lobby in one hour. I have been told of a club in Brisbane that is a fun dinner theater. I will arrange for reservations."

An hour passed and Felix and Rosita found J.J and Ben waiting in the lobby. They were casually dressed and in high spirits.

"I have arranged a company car to drive us to Brisbane. It is a bit too far for a taxi and I wasn't sure we would be able to get one later this evening to bring us back here. The driver will wait until we are finished."

The trip from Surfers Paradise was uneventful. Ben asked Felix many questions about living in the country. He was intrigued when Rosita revealed the life she had in the barrio.

It was just over an hour when they arrived in Brisbane. The driver had consulted an intelligence map and found the location of the club. Fifteen minutes later they stopped outside a huge complex. A sign garishly lit up the night sky declaring the club's name to be *'Life's Pleasure'.* Under bright pink flashing and strobing light the group left the car and entered into the cavernous interior. The club's interior was softly lit with a deep maroon carpet, mirrored walls, and five doorways leading off to other bars and lounge areas.

They were greeted by a short man dressed in a pink three-piece tuxedo. His shaved and polished head glistened as he passed under the beams from the little halogen lights mounted in the ceiling.

"I see your group is booked for dinner and the show in the Cave Room. It will be an exciting show tonight. We have one of our best groups entertaining this evening. I'm sure you will enjoy."

As they walked past other tables on the way to the Cave Room, Rosita found the women who were seated at them to be extensively made up. The women seemed to be artificial and wore too much lipstick and makeup. The hairstyles were like those of stage performers or movie stars. She found the men to be dressed oddly as well. Many had open vests exposing naked skin. Others wore sailor hats and tight black leather pants. She wondered if this was the style of clothing that was considered appropriate for a night out in Australia.

The Cave Room was reminiscent of an older style movie theater. At the front was a stage that ran from side to side. An old curtain hung from the ceiling to the floor of the stage. On each side of the stage, there were banks of spotlights pointed at different areas of the stage. Throughout the room, elaborate tables were set with silverware and expensive-looking glasses. Small flags on silver shafts displayed the table number for the reserved guests.

After being seated at a table directly in front of the stage, a waiter dressed in an apricot suit arrived to take an order for their drinks. After he left, Rosita looked around at the other tables. Waiters dressed in a variety of different colored suits buzzed around them. Some were dressed in coral, others in primrose yellow, and some in powder blue. While it was colorful, she found the club, its staff, and its patrons to be strange.

After the food poisoning incident, the men decided to order foods they considered safe. The men ordered cuts from a roasted hip of beef and Rosita opted for the fish dish of Barramundi. While waiting for their meals they sipped on some superb wines. Rosita's curiosity finally needed to be satisfied.

"Ben, is this a normal club? Do people in Australia always dress like this?"

"No, Rosita. It is a special theater club. We are lucky to be here. I was able to get a member to arrange for us to dine here tonight. Normally you must be a member. It seems they like to dress up a little, and some of it strangely. I am told the food is excellent and the acts very worthwhile."

They had finished their meals, and the dinner service concluded at nine-thirty. The brightly dressed waiters hurried around the tables that seated the approximate two hundred diners, clearing off plates, glasses and then returned to take drink orders before the show commenced. At ten, the lights dimmed and two of the small spotlights lit up an area at the center of the stage. The curtains parted and the emcee for the night's entertainment walked out and into the lit area. There was a round of applause from the seated diners. The overhead lights went dark.

"Good evening friends. Tonight we have some very patriotic acts to present. The theme of the show is that of highlighting Australia's contribution to music and the arts. Please take the time now before we begin to go for a tinkle or refresh your drinks. The show will start in fifteen minutes."

Quiet well known Australian music softly started to play, led in by a short instrumental version of 'Waltzing Matilda'.

At ten-fifteen, the curtains rolled back to reveal a live band seated and ready to accompany the performers. The emcee stepped back into the center spot.

"Ladies and gentlemen. Tonight the performance will be kicked off with our favorite group, *"The Estro Ginettes."* In keeping with the theme of tonight, their opening number is the song made famous around the world by our own Aussie singer, Helen Reddy.

The drums rolled and the cymbals crashed as *"The Estro Ginettes"* rushed onto the stage. Rosita gasped and J.J and Ben burst into laughter. The group was composed of four big muscled and burly men in drag as blondes. All were dressed in tight bright red dresses. Below the dresses, their hairy thick legs protruded. One of the group approached the front of the stage and shouted into the microphone.

"We start tonight with a tribute by presenting the song *'I am woman'*.

The group burst forth in a disjointed but harmonious version.

The irony was not lost on either J.J or Ben. Rosita and Felix were not sure what it meant. Rosita turned and spoke to Ben.

"Ben, what is happening, and what is this place?

"Rosita, my dear it is a drag club. Those are men and a lot of the woman you see here are guys made up in drag to look like women."

"But they look like women. Do they still have their bits?"

It was too much for J.J or Ben. Tears of laughter streamed down their faces.

The group continued to play other well known Australian artists, including '*I've got to get a message to you*', after which the audience clapped loudly. Suddenly the group stood and rushed to the front of the stage. As they ran forward they stripped off their dress and blonde wigs, Revealing them wearing short shorts. They threw Australian digger hats on their heads and broke into a raucous version of Rolf Haris' *'Tie me Kangaroo down sport'*. The audience loved it and joined in. It was quite the show.

The next act was an elaborate cabaret show with performers in white satin gowns, dressed as flappers from the 1920s and featuring Australian adaptations of the Charleston and other popular tunes of that period.

By the time the show was over it was midnight. They slowly walked to the exit of the club. At the front door, J.J stopped and turned to them.

"It was a great night. I will not see you tomorrow as I am required to attend to some business in Sydney. I will see you back in our home country. I must leave now for Sydney. Take care and safe travels."

Rosita and Felix were sad to see their traveling partner leave. The trip back to their Surfers Paradise hotel was quiet. Other than discussing some of the show, it seemed there was nothing to discuss.

Upon reaching the hotel, Ben opened the door for Rosita and Felix.

"I too must say goodbye. You will be escorted tomorrow by some other agents. Please stay in contact with me. I wish you the best of luck and hope you succeed."

They returned to the room to sleep for a long day ahead.

Chapter 41

The morning arrived too quickly. Felix arose remarkably refreshed.
The previous evening's entertainment had drawn his mind away
from the problems and tasks that lay ahead. He was about to shower
and dress when Rosita called him back into bed. She lay with her
head propped up on her arm and pillows surrounding her. Felix
gently sat on the bed beside her. She threw her arms around him
and passionately kissed him. He turned to embrace her and as he
did, she slipped her hand lower on his chest. She felt his arousal and
smiled sensually at him, pleased that she had such power over him.

Felix rose to the occasion. Passionate lovemaking ensued. Rosita
sensed the strength and control of their relationship. It amazed her
that she had such power and influence. As they lay spent, Rosita
started thinking of ways she could use that power, as well as the
inner streak of evil she knew she could now control.

"Felix, we should go and eat a large breakfast. The day ahead of us
will be long and tiring. You will need to be relaxed and alert when
you meet the press in Hawaii. I am sure that Perez will have one of
his informers there. Be careful with what you say and don't trust
anyone."

"Rosita, you need not worry about me. I should be worried about
you. It seems that the role of being my partner suits you too well.
Now, come on. Let's dress and go for breakfast."

Felix found it lonely at breakfast. He was missing the presence of
J.J and Ben. He barely listened as Rosita chatted on about things.
His mind was focused on the return trip and what lay ahead.

They had finished eating and were sipping on coffee when a tall man with a blonde crewcut approached. He was American and military.

"Good morning. I am Lieutenant Charles Horn. If you are ready, I am to drive you to your plane at the Amberley Airforce base. The drive will take us over an hour and a half. Please take a few minutes to gather your possessions together. I will help you take them to the car."

Felix and Rosita returned to their room and gathered the few items they had accumulated over the short stay. They returned to the lobby area. The lieutenant took the small bag from Rosita and the case that Felix carried. Outside there was a dark blue van waiting. Lieutenant Horn opened the rear doors and carefully place the luggage on the floor.

Rosita and Felix climbed into the row of passenger seats. Felix looked at the interior of the van. It was not an ordinary van. Adjacent to the driver was a bank of electronics including a computer screen and a console festooned with switches and LED lights. The interior had been equipped with a fridge and a bar. The seats were soft and upholstered in plush reddish-brown material. The windows were tinted and at the seat armrests were telephones.

Lieutenant Horn jumped up into the driver seat. He started the van and immediately Felix realized that the engine had also been enhanced. There was a deep throbbing roar as they accelerated away from the resort.

The Lieutenant turned back to them.

"You will find some water and soft drinks in the fridge. There are other snacks and sandwiches if you get hungry."

As they drove inland and away from the coast, Rosita was surprised as the trees and other vegetation thinned and it reminded her of the lands around the barrio. She suddenly felt pangs of homesickness. She thought of the families and friends she had at the barrio. She wondered about her father. Had he been caught by those men? Was he dead? Rosita's spirits sank.

"Felix, I'm feeling sad. I want to go home. I miss too many things and my friends."

"Rosita, we will be back in the country within a day."

"No, that's not what I mean. I want to return to the barrio. Those are my people. This has been nice, but it is not my life."

"But Rosita, you wanted to leave the barrio and see the city and life beyond. You have now seen other countries. You have met powerful people. This is what you told me you wanted."

"There are things that I miss. Felix. Things that make it my home. I miss the smell of the foods cooking over wood fires. I miss the sounds and music. I miss the simple laughter and friends. These are our people. These are the people who need a true leader. Felix, if what you say and believe is true, then you must find a way to help those who have worked so hard to build our little country. It is not there for a few rich Generals and their political friends to rape."

Felix sat quietly thinking of the words that Rosita had spoken. He reached across to smooth her hair as her head had fallen and rested on his shoulder. He stroked her cheek and his hands immediately were wet as he felt the tears that rolled down her cheek.

"Rosita, I promise you that I will dispose of those who have created so much hardship and evil in our country. I need you to be strong and stand with me. It is not going to be an easy fight, but I need you to be with me. I have fallen in love with you. We are both young and can change the future for the people. We have many friends who are waiting for me to declare that I will stand up against those Generals. We have the opportunity to bring change to our country. I desire to bring back our royal King and Queen and give them the ability to restore a peace that we have not enjoyed for many years. Will you help me? It is not going to be easy."

Felix looked down at the young woman resting her head on him. He wondered how one so young could have such compassionate feelings. A surge of soft emotion ran through him. He was amazed at the deep and profound feelings for this young girl from the poverty of the barrio.

Lieutenant Horn turned to speak with Felix.

"Sir, in a few minutes we will drive out from these hills and be at the Amberley base. My instructions are to travel to the main gate and present you for secure access. The base is also an aviation heritage center, so the public does visit on open days and at other times. We will need to get a clearance for me to drive you to the party who will be transporting you."

At the gate, armed sentries approached their vehicle. The Lieutenant handed them an envelope. They were ordered to park in a small fenced area while the contents of the envelope were read.

Minutes passed and a uniformed sergeant walked to the car. He smartly saluted Felix, then sat in the front passenger seat.

"Welcome to Amberley. We have been expecting you. I will accompany you to your plane and ensure everything is in order."

They drove away from the entrance and Felix was amazed at the huge shelters under which fighter jets sat in shade. There were no walls, and the shelters and looked like long open-air hangars. Felix was surprised at the number of fighter jets and the large transport planes parked at the base.

They continued past several hangars with closed doors and security outside of them. Felix wanted to ask the reason for the guards, but before he could speak, the sergeant spoke.

"We are at your departure location."

The Lieutenant pulled to a halt. The sergeant jumped down from the van and walked briskly to the guarded door. The guards saluted and opened the door for him.

After a brief wait, the main hangar door arose to reveal a Gulfstream jet waiting. Unlike other private jets, this one did not have any decorative painting or decals. It was painted a drab olive. The Lieutenant opened the door and helped them out of the van. He retrieved their sparse luggage, before climbing back into the van.

"I will be leaving you now. The sergeant will handle things from here. I wish you the best of luck, and personally, hope you succeed in your plans."

Chapter 42

Aboard the aircraft, Felix and Rosita settled into the plush seats for the nine-hour flight to Honolulu. They had been in the air for approximately two hours when the pilot invited Felix to join him in the cockpit. The copilot vacated his seat and sat with Rosita to chat with her. Felix was fascinated and the pilot described the various roles of the instrumentation. Felix asked meaningful questions and displayed keen interest and understanding.

The pilot was impressed by Felix. He made a decision.

"Sir, I was formerly a flight instructor with the airforce. Would you like to take the controls for a bit? I will disengage the autopilot but will have my hands on the controls at all times. There will be no risk."

Felix beamed a huge smile. This had always been a dream of his. He put on the headset and microphone the pilot handed him, and gingerly took the controls. The pilot advised him on adjusting the altitude and making small turns. Felix was enjoying the little maneuvers when the headset crackled. The air traffic controllers were calling in instructions to change altitude and course bearing. The pilot acknowledged and nudged Felix to increase the altitude. The pilot then changed the coordinates and they continued toward Hawaii.

Felix returned to his seat and was surprised to find he had spent over an hour in the cockpit. He decided to learn to fly and become a pilot after the business he had started was complete.

Rosita had watched Felix closely. She was concerned that Felix was becoming distracted and worried that her plans were in jeopardy. "Felix, you must stay focused. We have major obstacles to overcome. I will not allow other interruptions that may cause you to change our goal. I intend to work with you to win and remove those Generals."

Felix looked at her and wondered about the intensity with which she spoke.

"Rosita, you have become very dedicated to the plan. I am surprised. You are young. It is still my intention to proceed and win over our people and defeat the ruling party. Why are you so intent on making this happen?"

"While I miss my life in the barrio, I am convinced that I can achieve a better life. I do not intend to be stopped. You will continue to force a change. I will be beside you the whole time. I will speak to the people. You are from a rich and privileged family. I grew up poor and understand the people, their needs, and my affection for the country. I will not be dismissed by either you or the others who say they will support you."

Felix was shocked. The young girl he had known from the barrio was disappearing and a fierce spirited young woman was evolving in front of his eyes.

"Rosita, There are many other strong people who wish to see the change happen. I need them to help. I studied politics and can work to organize these people to assist. I fear that you have no political experience or understand the processes. I love you, but you must not interfere."

The inner demon in Rosita flared. She raised her hand and slashed it toward Felix's face. He was faster and grabbed her wrist. Rosita arose from her seat with a surprisingly strong force and twisted her wrist from his grip. She clenched her fist and delivered a blow to his cheek. There was immediate swelling.

"Stop, Rosita. Have you gone crazy? What is wrong with you?"

Rosita continued beating at Felix, finally collapsing back in her seat.

"Felix, don't you ever speak to me in that way again. I intend to be a part of the plan and I will make it happen. Never try to push me away again. I will make us win. The people will want us and no one else. We will prevail and have power."

Felix stood beside her in shock. He had never experienced such an outburst.

"You have a lot to learn. I will express how I feel and what I believe in. I am not going to be dissuaded from my objectives. You are entitled to have your opinion, but never behave like that again."

Rosita looked up into Felix's face. A nasty blue bruise was rapidly forming where she had hit him. She immediately felt sad and guilty. Her inability to control that inner urge worried her.

"I am sorry to have hit you. I don't know why I did that. I just want us to win. I don't want to see you distracted. I feel strongly for the people of our country. We must go ahead and win."

Felix nodded and bent forward to kiss her forehead.

"I forgive you. You have such passion."

Rosita stood and went to the rear of the aircraft cabin and removed a tray of ice. She returned to her seat and held a piece of ice over the bruised area on his cheek.

For the rest of the flight neither spoke. The pilot turned and called to them.

"We are starting our descent into Honolulu. We will be touching down shortly after midnight. I have been informed there is a group of reporters waiting at the arrivals area to meet you. We will be met by Customs and Immigration officers on the plane. I understand that your arrival here on this aircraft is to be kept a secret and special preclearance been arranged. After you leave the plane, you will be met by US Military personnel who will be assisting you and flying you to Panama. I hope everything works out well for you."

The small jet commenced a series of turns and the engines revved and slowed as they maneuvered on approach. Felix glance through the cockpit windshield to see the bright lights illuminating the edge of the runway. He felt a surge of excitement.

The jet had barely glided to a halt when the cabin door cracked open and two men in uniform crawled in.

"Welcome to the United States. My partner and I are here to assist you with this part of your journey home. Please gather your possessions and follow us."

Felix and Rosita followed the officers down the stairway from the plane and across the dark tarmac to a dimly lit building. Inside, they were greeted by men who displayed their CIA identification cards to them.

"It is late now, but a small contingent of reporters is waiting in the main terminal area to interview you, Felix. The group has been carefully selected by us. They will not be allowed to question where you took refuge and we request you do not provide that information. If you are asked, you appealed to the United States after General Perez declared you would be welcome back. As far as the press needs to know, we are just providing secure transport for you and Rosita back to South America. Do you wish to take a few minutes to freshen up and enjoy some light food?"

Rosita again sensed her anger arising. She resented the fact that others were controlling their lives.

"We will use this opportunity to tell the world of our intention to restore our country to its former glory. Felix has ideas and a plan that will help all the people."

"Rosita is optimistic. I wish to have the reporters to include in their articles the guarantee that General Perez issued, stating that Rosita and I will be safe upon our return. For us to succeed in bringing about any reform we will need the assistance of other countries by keeping our struggle visible. I understand you have a briefing to give me regarding what I am to say at the press conference. I wish to read it and take time before meeting with them. I am asking to delay any conference until I have read the brief and we have slept. It has been a long and exhausting day."

The CIA men huddled and spoke in low voices.

"We agree and will announce the new time for the press to meet with you."

Chapter 43

After a few hours of sleep, Rosita and Felix were taken the short distance to the main terminal. It was early morning, and already the Honolulu airport was busy with flights arriving from Asia and departing for mainland USA.

At the main terminal, they were taken in a side entrance and up on an elevator to a room with a plaque announcing it to be a VIP room. The room was filled with approximately twenty reporters and photographers. The group surrounded Felix and Rosita. Cameras whirred and flashed as the reporters swarmed them. Their arrival was recorded on video for television and still photos for the newspapers.

The questions came fast, with the reporters shouting over each other. Felix looked around the group confused and unsure how to address the never-ending barrage of questions.

A man in a dark blue suit, who Felix had not noticed stepped forward to address the press.

" Good morning ladies and gentlemen. I am James Ruby, the Press Liasion officer for the US Airforce, Sacramento base. I am afraid we have limited time here with you this morning. I suggest you calm down and ask your questions in an orderly manner."

"Why is the US Airforce, Sacramento base involved with the return of Felix de Santos to his country, and where was he in exile?"

"The US Airforce has agreed to provide a safe passage for the return of Colonel de Santos to his home country. We will not answer any questions relating to where he sought safety, nor those who were with him. I will, however, stress that it was not any part of the United States. Now I will ask Colonel de Santos to answer questions. Please state your name and the news organization with whom you are affiliated. Keep the questions short, and they will be limited to one question and a followup if required."

Felix hesitantly started to walk to the microphone. Rosita joined him and linked her arm around his. He increased the pace to a steady and confident walk.

"Good morning. Thank you for your interest in the politics of my country and our desire to implement reforms that will be for the betterment of everyone's life there."

"Good morning, Colonel de Santos, I am Chuck Salter, Foreign correspondent for the New York Lives. Can you explain why you feel you are qualified to form an opposition to the existing regime, and how you will achieve success?"

"I think my academic background and the disciplined military training and experience I have will assist me in forming a credible political party to challenge the current regime and to expose and correct the corruption and abuse of power they have created since the people voted to replace our then Royal family. The regime has caused our people great suffering with the implementation of socialist values and rules by fear and torture. I am disappointed that other countries and the U.N. have not assisted in preventing this situation. I have gathered together some of the strongest business leaders, lawyers, and academics to help in building a political party capable of defeating the regime. It is not, and I repeat, not my goal to ferment the public or the military to bring about a coup. I envisage a process where we will democratically deal with the issues."

"Good morning. Robert Jackson, Latin American analyst, ANT Television Network. What steps have been taken to create this party?"
"There have been preliminary meetings at which key figures have been selected. Besides, financial resources have been committed."

"A second question. You are accused of murder. Are you not afraid that you will be arrested upon your arrival?"

"General Perez has declared to the world and assured them of my safety and he welcomes a challenge to the ruling leaders in an election. I must rely on this and if he takes actions otherwise, I hope the other countries who have been involved in negotiating the terms of my return get involved."

Before the next question could be asked, Rosita pulled Felix's arm. He leaned forward and lowered his head. She whispered in his ear. He then continued.

"I should continue and advise you, that my partner, Rosita Valquez was born and grew up in a rural area of my country. She and her family and friends have experienced living in poverty, fear and suffered tragically as a result of the corruption. The village has almost been destroyed by the actions of General Perez and his other Generals who allowed the establishment of a mine nearby that poisoned the waters and killed many of the residents. We have evidence of the financial involvement of the Generals in this mine."

"Good morning, Colonel de Santos. Tony Chestnut from The Enquiring Voice. Please explain the relationship you have with Rosita Valquez. Is she your lover? What more can you tell us? Is she part of the group you have assembled to try and overthrow the government? Please tell us more. Who is she and why is she so important? Why was she in hiding with you? What power does she have over you? Seems she is very young. In the United States, I don't believe she would be of legal age. Please tell us all why you have her there by your side."

Felix stayed silent while wondering how to respond. Before he could speak, Rosita reached up and pulled the microphone toward her. Felix placed his hand over her arm in an attempt to stop her from speaking. She wrenched her hand out of his grip. The inner demons had been awakened.

"I am Rosita Valquez. My age is not important. I have seen and lived the situation created by the existing rulers. I have lived amongst the peasants. I have personally experienced the crime that their corruption has allowed. I know Felix and I will stand by him and support his efforts. I warn you all not to underestimate me nor the powers I possess to help him. I desire to see the change. I love the poor people in our homeland. I am there to represent them. I will be active and visiting and helping them. No university can teach the kindness and emotion needed to help them. I have that spirit and fire within me. Instead of asking all these questions of Felix, I suggest you investigate and tell the real story of what the Generals have done and created."

The reporters went quiet as they absorbed Rosita's outburst. Various reporters continued to pepper Felix with questions until James Ruby walked to the microphone.

"Thank you all for coming. This press conference is now closed. The transportation aircraft is scheduled to leave shortly and we need our guests aboard. Thank you all."

Felix and Rosita were led back out the side door to a waiting car on the tarmac. After a short drive, they arrived at a dark military grey Boeing jet. The door was opened for them and Rosita and Felix were taken to the mobile stairs that led up to the entrance door

Chapter 44

Felix was surprised as he entered the cabin of the aircraft to find J.J seated and smiling at him.

"J.J, I never expected to see you here. I thought you would either stay in Australia or be taken back to the US."

"Relax Felix. Nice to see you too. The powers in Washington decided that since we are flying into Panama, and then on to your country, which we consider hostile at the moment, that I am to travel with you as the diplomatic representative. The fact of my presence is going to be sent in advance. The State Department is making it known that the US, while not directly involved or participating in your plan, is actively supporting you. We are creating a mild threat so they do not attempt to change the agreement they made for your safe return. If they do, then they will face some nasty consequences."

Rosita was not happy to see J.J. She had a plan and it did not involve him. His very presence would detract from her scheme. She feigned feeling fatigued and slightly ill and requested to be taken to a row of seats where she could lie down. She did not want to engage in any discussions with J.J. She needed time to think and strategize, now that her original idea had been wrecked by his presence.

The attendant lowered the customized luxury seats the plane had been fitted with, into a reclined position. Rosita lay down and continued to act ill. The attendant and Felix offered her help.

"No, I just wish to sleep and have some time alone. I will be fine. I am very tired."

The attendant provided her with a blanket before he and Felix returned to the front of the cabin. Rosita closed her eyes and pretended to drift into sleep. In reality, she was fuming but found control over her inner demon. Her carefully devised plan was coming apart. She was convinced Felix had believed her earlier act of homesickness. She was especially proud of the fake tears and knew she had him believing she needed to return to the barrio. The presence of J.J. would likely interfere with that. She needed to get a message to certain 'friends' that their original plans were now jeopardized.

Rosita lay quietly and pondered other alternatives. Her quest and pursuit of the life she envisaged were now delayed. She smiled to herself at the thought of it only being a delay and not an action that would kill her goal. Rosita's way would prevail.

She was drifting asleep when Felix joined her.

"This is going to be a long flight. The pilot estimates a thirteen-hour flight. We are not stopping but flying direct. She is asking if you are feeling better. If your condition worsens they have a contingency plan to land in Los Angeles to get you help."

"That won't be necessary. I am already feeling much better. I think I was overtired. I need to eat and have a long sleep. I will be fine."

Felix sensed her attitude was different from the girl he had known at his home and in Australia. He considered this but dismissed it as a reaction to the amount of traveling and the situations she had endured in the past few weeks. He returned to his seat and ordered a scotch with J.J. Together they sat huddled discussing politics and a strategy to remove General Perez and his cronies. Little did they know of the plans that were festering in the evil mind of Rosita.

239

Part 3

The Unforeseen

Chapter 45

City of La Luminada

Their night arrival back in La Luminada after an uneventful and boring flight was discreet and went unnoticed by many. At the airport, Rosita was thrilled when Enzo arrived to drive her and Felix to Villa Magnifico. She recalled the fun day she had with Enzo when he had chauffered Felix's mother, Carmine, and Rosita on their first shopping extravaganza in La Luminada.

"Rosita, Felix, welcome back. I am pleased to see you are both safe and looking well. I was very worried when General Perez was making those claims. I knew you were not guilty. I prayed so hard for your safety.'

Enzo retrieved the small amount of luggage they had and started to walk out of the airport to the waiting car.

Felix turned and scanned the crowd. He spotted J.J. deep in conversation with a military officer in full uniform. He was concerned.

"Enzo. Wait. I need to speak with my friend before we leave."

Felix strode across the shiny tiled floor of the terminal toward J.J.

"J.J. Is everything all right? What does this man want with you?"

J.J. laughed. "Don't worry, Felix. This man is a relative of mine. He is updating me on the mood of the country, especially in the army. It seems you have created a lot of discontent by exposing Perez and his gang. You have supporters already. I think we should move quickly to hold a rally while these events are still fresh in people's minds. Tomorrow I will contact our friends who volunteered at the night meeting you held at Villa Magnifico. Now is the time to organize."

Rosita listened. She stayed quiet. She was determined to be a major part of the effort. Before she would take any actions, there was the business to look after at the barrio in Nos Grande. She wondered if the man who knew her secret was still living in Nos Grande. She remembered the threat that he had once made to her. He needed to be silenced before Felix started the campaign. As she thought back to those days and her misery, the demons started to scream in her head and she felt dizziness. Enzo was watching and quickly moved forward to steady her as she started to stumble.

"Thank you, Enzo. I am afraid I seem to be a lot more tired from the trip than I realized."

"My pleasure to assist. Let me help you to the car."

While Felix continued to talk to J.J., she was escorted to the car. In the car, Rosita watched Felix and J.J. Standing a short distance behind them were two men who would occasionally lower their newspapers and watch Felix and J.J. with a certain intensity. Rosita realized that they were under observation.

"Enzo, please go to Felix and tell him to hurry. Those two men are watching him. I fear that General Perez has arranged a few nasty surprises for us."

Enzo left the car and approached Felix and J.J. He made a show of pointing to his watch and then the car indicating there was some urgency to leave.

Slowly, they made their way across to the car. Enzo jumped into the driver's seat and as soon as Felix and J.J. were in the rear seat he gunned the car away from the airport. Enzo constantly looked into the mirrors, concerned they were being tailed.

As they sped toward Villa Magnifico, the traffic thinned. Enzo slowed to a more leisurely pace and relaxed. He continued to navigate through the back streets to avoid any possible confrontation.

Felix and J.J sat without speaking. Rosita rested her head against Felix's shoulder, pretending to be asleep, but in reality thinking and watching everyone's movement. She wasn't sure of J.J. There was something that bothered her. She thought back to the night they had held the meeting at the Villa and those women who had spoken with him. She had decided they were not to be trusted and had already devised a plan to eradicate them from her and Felix's life. There was nothing that was going to stop her.

They were all thrown forward in the car as Enzo braked sharply. There in the entrance to Villa Magnifico were two white cars with the word POLICIA emblazoned on the doors. Enzo brought the car to a stop only a few feet from the cars.

"This is what I expected. They are going to harass me and my family. Perez and his henchmen aren't going to make it easy for us."

The doors of the police cars opened and two burly cops exited and walked toward their car. Enzo lowered the driver window.

"Good evening. What seems to be the problem? I need to pass as this is where we live."

Felix looked out at the officer. He was large with a sloppy appearance. His long greasy hair oozed out from the edges of his peaked police hat. His shirt was stained and around the area of his beer bloated belly, the buttons fought to keep his blubber contained. His uniform trousers were creased and over time had aged and developed a shine around the crotch. On his feet were military-style boots.

Felix decided he was not one of the law-abiding officers, but one who was crooked and for a few extra pesos would willingly use his position to threaten or extort. Felix wondered who this goon was working for.

"I need to see all your IDs. Now. Don't keep me waiting. I have a busy night ahead."

"Why are you stopping us? This is where I live. We have never been stopped nor have we ever had any issues here that required intervention by the law."

"I have my orders. Now just shut up and give me the papers."

Rosita studied his face and committed every detail to memory. She would ensure his fate would not be pleasant.

"Officer, I urgently need to use the washroom. I cannot wait."

"Well, senorita you have two options. Either you piss yourself where you sit, or my partner will take you and wait while you pee in the bushes."

Felix bristled with anger. He decided it was time to challenge the bully.

"You have no right to speak to us in that manner. Give me your name, ID number, and the area commander's name as well. Which station are you from? I will have you disciplined for this. You are disrespectful. You epitomize the corruption and fear that our so-called leaders are accused of."

" You can ask but you're not getting any information from me. If you don't like it, then I suggest you write a complaint. Don't expect it to do any good. You are not liked by the other officers."

Felix started to open the door to confront the cop and take details of his badge and the license plate and patrol car number. The cop showed surprising speed and grabbed Felix as he left the car. He twisted Felix's arm and forced him onto the ground. His partner joined in the scuffle and dropped to the ground firmly pushing his knee into Felix's back and pinning him to the ground.

J.J. attempted to leave the car, but the burly cop kicked the door shut on J.J.'s leg. J.J. let out a cry of pain. The cop laughed and menacingly turned his attention to a terrified Enzo.

"Now give me the papers before I deal with you too. Your treatment won't be so gentle as I will be taking you to a special cell where we get information from unwilling participants."

Rosita sat frozen with fear, yet still felt the anger rising and her demons awakening. Her ploy to leave the car had been thwarted.

Chapter 46

The altercation ended abruptly with the arrival of Felix's military friend, Caesar Kuhn.

The lights of the military jeep Caesar was driving lit up the scene. Felix was pinned to the ground and J.J. was struggling with the other officer as he struggled to get out of the car.

Caesar jumped from the jeep and rushed forward to separate Felix and the officer. As he did so, the officer spun toward him and lashed out at him. The sound of a gunshot and a scream emanated from the car. Caesar grasped the officer's arm and twisted him to the ground before delivering a powerful karate chop to the rear of the man's head. The officer immediately folded into a limp state.

Caesar ran back to their car. Rosita was in the corner of the back seat staring at the slumped over J.J. who was motionless. His head was twisted in Rosita's direction and the lifeless eyes stared at her.

Caesar heard the sounds of the other officer running back to the police car to attempt an escape. He sprinted after him and tackled the officer as he tried to open the door. Caesar drove his fist into the officer's face with all his might. The officer crumpled to the ground in a state of unconsciousness. Blood streamed from his nose and the split skin beneath his eye.

Felix unsteadily rose to his feet and stumbled to find Rosita. He pulled open the rear door of the car and pulled Rosita out and held her tightly.

"Are you all right? I heard that shot. Are you injured?"

Felix looked into her face. What he saw shocked him. There was a look of hardened defiance.

"I was not injured. These men must suffer. Do not allow them to return. Imprison them in your Villa. It will help us in our quest to overthrow those corrupt leaders. We will call the press and put them on display. J.J. is dead. Leave him there. Let the photographers come and take their pictures. Call that Carmilla Vesco, the reporter with VTV television. These stupid cops have helped us to start our campaign. The public will see the assurances of General Perez were worthless."

"Rosita, we cannot do that. We must show dignity to J.J. It would be wrong to use this for our purposes. I am angry and upset, but we must act correctly."

Caesar had dragged the cops to his jeep. He bent and picked them up from the ground and threw them into the jeep.

"Felix, what Rosita said is correct. We cannot pretend this did not happen. We must take them and detain them. I will ask Enzo to take you and Rosita to the house, then Enzo and I will take these cops there and secure them so they cannot escape. Enzo will take you in the jeep and then return to help me. We will leave the car with the body of J.J. in it to show the press, then take them to view those two cops. Do not come out of the Villa until I arrive there. I am going to handle this with the press. Now please go."

Felix looked at his dead friend J.J. He wondered what the result of his death would create with the Americans. They had not discussed or planned for a situation such as this.

This was not the start of the campaign Felix had hoped for. Doubt started to creep into his mind.

Enzo drove them to the Villa. He had no sooner stopped when Carmine appeared in the entranceway.

"What is going on? I heard a gunshot. Why is our car in the driveway entrance? Why are you here in a jeep? Is there trouble?

"Mother I will tell you all in a minute. We must get inside quickly. Bad things are happening."

"Is my dear Rosita fine? Has she been hurt? I missed her during my horrible stay at the US Embassy."

"Mother, please go inside. Rosita is fine. We are both fine. Enzo needs to go and assist my friend Caesar. He must hurry."

Carmine looked confused but obeyed and followed Rosita and Felix into the Villa.

"Felix, I fear that no good will come of this venture of yours to reform the leadership. I did not enjoy having to leave my home and friends and hide in the Embassy. This is not the way I wish to live. Please stop this nonsense now."

Before Felix could respond, Rosita went to Carmine and hugged her.

"Carmine, please do not panic. Felix is a good man and has strong supporters who also wish to see the ruling party changed. I intend to see that it happens. I will win over the public to support us and those corrupt Generals will not harm me, or any of us, for fear of alienating them. I do not intend to be silent or allow any harm to come to you. There are things I can and will do. I ask you not to ask."

Both Felix and Carmine sensed a strange power in her words and actions.

Felix heard the sounds of shouting and the scuffle at the front door area. He excused himself and left to investigate. Caesar and Enzo had bound the officers' feet and dragged them into the foyer. Enzo had found handcuffs in the police car and both men had their hands cuffed tightly behind their backs.

"I want to know who sent you to my home. I will not be very patient. My friend and colleague have been killed. I intend to see you both punished and those with whom you are working. Answer me now."

The greasy-haired cop spat blood and saliva at Felix's feet.

"Go to hell. I'll tell you nothing. You are stupid if you think we will be punished. Many hate you and what your wealthy friends stand for."

There was a rush from behind Felix as Rosita ran to the officer. She raised an ornamental vase from the wall side credenza and crashed it down on the officer's head. Blood gushed from his head as he rolled unconscious to his side.

"Rosita, you should not have done that. I'm sure he would speak when we turn him over to the Americans. They are going to be seeking revenge. J.J. was an important figure in their secretive operations.

"Felix, I don't care about the Americans. I care that we win and assume the leadership of our country. Besides, look at his partner. He is terrified. I should give him some special treatment as well."

"No. I am sure he will talk. We will find out who was behind this. Caesar has contacted the press and they will descend on this like vultures."

Felix had barely spoken when there was a pounding on the door. He went to the door and opened it. Miss Carmilla Vesco, the reporter for VTV stood there with a cameraman and two other assistants. Behind her on the driveway, cameras flashed, recording the gruesome death of J.J. Carter. The TV camera was already recording. Carmilla Vesco as she launched into an aggressive questioning of Felix.

"Who is dead in the car? What is his relationship with you? Did you arrange this incident for publicity? Is this how you want to get people feeling sorry for you? Did you do this to try and place blame on our good General Perez?"

Felix stared at her before turning away and ignoring her questions. Carmilla pushed past him with the cameraman and immediately ordered him to record the images of the handcuffed officers, especially the one lying in the now large pool of blood. She positioned herself in front of the camera.

"People, witness what is going on here. Felix de Santos refuses to deny he staged this attack. Take a close look at how he and his gang have brutally attacked these law-abiding officers. Don't you find it strange that Felix de Santos disappeared for days in hiding and this is how he repays the generosity of General Perez and his colleagues? They pledged and guaranteed that Felix de Santos could return to his home safely and without fear. Look how he is repaying our kind leaders. Felix de Santos is not to be trusted. He has fooled us into believing he is an innocent man. He is not. He has the blood of many on his hands. I will now take you outside to the car where an unknown man has been assassinated."

Before she could leave the Villa, Rosita pushed in front of the camera and spoke loudly.

"I am Rosita Valquez. Do not believe any of this. I am the partner of Felix de Santos. What this reporter is saying are lies. She is working with Perez and his gang. Do not trust her. I am one of you. I am not privileged. I was born in a poor barrio. I know how hard life is for many of you. This reporter has not suffered the indignities we have all suffered while the ruling class has benefitted from our hard work and sacrifices. I beg you to support Felix de Santos...."

Before Rosita could finish, Carmilla Vesco pushed her into the arms of the two men who had accompanied her. She underestimated Rosita's strength. Rosita wrenched free and tackled Carmilla Vesco to the floor. Her inner demons erupted in full fury. Blow after blow landed on Carmila's face, chest, and head. Her attempts to ward off the blows were futile.

"Rosita, stop. This will gain us nothing. She is in my house without permission. Let Caesar deal with this."

Caesar stepped forward and grabbed Carmilla. Her two henchmen attempted to intervene but had sadly misjudged the strength of Caesar. He threw them back against the wall and proceeded to pick Carmilla up. He exited and with a single stroke threw her headfirst into the rhododendron bushes that flanked the stairs.

Chapter 47

Sirens wailed in the distance as police cars sped to the Villa. Caesar ran from the Villa back to the car containing J.J.'s body. Photographers swarmed the car. Some shouted questions to Caesar as he approached. He was in no mood to answer them. He considered driving the car up to the Villa but quickly decided against that when police cars screeched to a halt. Heavily armed police ran from the cars toward the Villa while others surrounded the car.

The cop in control looked at Caesar, who was dressed in his military uniform.

" I am Commander Santiago. What is going on here? Who is the man in the car? Where is Felix de Santos and Rosita Valquez? How did this happen?"

Caesar told the cop of the ambush on Felix and his party. He pointed to the now empty police cars that the assailants had arrived in. Commander Santiago was puzzled. He crossed over to the cars and opened the driver's door of the car closest to the Villa. Inside were some weapons. Confused, Santiago walked around the car surveying it. He stopped and looked at the identification numbers, before walking back to his patrol car. In his car, he radioed headquarters and requested details on the two cars. There was a long pause before the radio crackled with a response. Santiago listened in surprise as he was informed that the identification numbers he had provided were false. The cars were not real police cars. The paint, decals, interior containment cage, radio, and windshield decals were all forged.

"I will have my men call an ambulance and remove the body. First, they will need to record the details. I will have them cover the body and prevent those photographers and news reporters from any further access. Take me up to the Villa. I am curious who those two 'officers' are."

Caesar commenced the walk up to the Villa accompanied by Commander Santiago.

"How did you know about this? I had just called the incident into the station and yet I heard the sirens while I was reporting the assault."

"The report that Carmilla Vesco was making was broadcast live. We saw things were out of control. That Rosita Valquez certainly removed any uncertainty we had. She is very assertive. I liked her little speech. Is she still in the Villa?"

"Yes, she, Enzo the driver, and Felix are in the Villa and guarding those two cops."

"This will be interesting. No officers under my command were dispatched to the Villa this evening. Something is wrong. Those cars they have are extremely well disguised to look like real police cars, and I did not send any officers here."

Upon entering the Villa, Santiago examined the men. He asked for their details, but neither would speak. Frustrated, he called for other officers to assist him and take the false cops to the cells at the police station for questioning. As they were being dragged from the Villa, a distraught Carmine confronted Santiago.

"How do we know you are telling the truth? How can we be sure you are not involved with those who oppose the plans Felix has to replace the corrupt leaders? I have lost trust. It seems that almost everyone has some link to General Perez and his crooked gang. Can you prove to us that you are not under their control?"

"I could have made things very difficult for Felix, instead, we shadowed Felix and Rosita to ensure that no harm came to them. Had I made it difficult, they would not have been able to leave the country and seek asylum. We watched him and were aware of every action he was taking. It would have been easy for us to apprehend him and Rosita. We could have locked them away for months pending a trial."

Carmine considered the response from Santiago.

"I will accept what you say, but I am not convinced. It seems that Perez can buy almost anybody."

"As Felix takes action to challenge Perez, he is going to be exposed to other attempts to silence him. I will be assembling some of my elite officers to accompany him. We will also guard you and Rosita against any attempt to endanger your lives. If I was not in support of Felix, I would not be doing this."

Rosita had been listening to the exchange between Santiago and Carmine and then spoke.

" I share Carmine's concerns. If you truly support Felix, then use your powers to arrange an interview for him with the TV and newspapers. I will accompany Felix and I will speak and appeal to the ordinary working people who are not amongst the rich and privileged. They are the real people who make this country work. I come from a background that they will relate too. They will listen and believe me. We need to move quickly. We cannot wait and allow Perez and his gang to create more problems for us."

Santiago had listened and after a few minutes, spoke.

"As Commander of Police here, I do have the authority to schedule a press conference. I will have the newspapers and media contacted tonight and arrange for it to be held at the police headquarters tomorrow morning. It will give me and my men time to question the two thugs who have caused this mess. We will find out who is responsible."

As Santiago finished speaking and commenced walking back to the car containing J.J's body, a shiny black government car slid to a stop at the entranceway to the Villa. The rear door opened and a military officer in the uniform of a General stepped from the car. He walked briskly toward Santiago and gave a salute which was acknowledged by Santiago.

The General and Santiago remained engaged in conversation. After a few minutes, Santiago pointed up to the stairs of the Villa, where Felix was standing watching with curiosity.

Santiago and the General strode toward Felix.

"Felix, this is General Jiminez. He is on the political committee of General Perez. He has been dispatched to speak with you. If you wish, I can leave the two of you to speak."

"No, I would like you to remain and hear what General Jiminez has to say. These are proving to be dangerous times here and I do not trust anything that Perez is involved with."

General Jiminez shrugged and smiled.

"There is nothing confidential. Can we go inside and sit. I have a letter from General Perez and I will explain the details."

Inside the Villa, Felix, Rosita, and Santiago sat in the immense living room. Felix dismissed a servant who entered with an offer of refreshments. He was all business and felt no goodwill toward one of Perez's cronies.

General Jiminez removed an envelope from the inside pocket of his uniform. He handed it to Felix, who carefully opened it and sat back to read the many pages of the letter. The room was silent as Felix took his time reading it. He flipped back and forth clarifying certain points. When he was finished he placed the letter on the table in front of their chairs and cradled his chin in his hand. Rosita reached forward to pick up the letter but Felix grabbed her wrist and restrained her.

"No, Rosita. I need time to think about what I have just read. There will be time for you and the others to read the letter."

Carmine arrived and sensed the atmosphere was not one of a social get together. She quietly took a seat next to Rosita. Felix continued to sit without speaking. He occasionally picked up the letter and flipped to different sections to reread them. Finally, he spoke.

"This letter I have here is from General Perez and the ruling politicians. In the letter, general Perez encourages the formation of a political group to join in a public vote. In the letter, there are excerpts from our constitution outlining the legality and processes that must be followed. I need time to study this further."

General Jiminez shifted uncomfortably in his chair.

"General Perez has requested your response this evening. I am to report back to him. If you need some time I can wait."

"There is no point in your waiting. Tomorrow morning we will be holding a press conference to discuss the attack here this evening. At the press conference, I will distribute copies of this letter and provide my answer publicly. If this letter reflects the truth then neither General Perez nor the politicians should have any concern. Any steps I take to establish our party will be open and communicated to the population. There will be no secret arrangements. That is my answer for you to take to General Perez."

General Jiminez unhappily rose to leave.

"Felix de Santos, if what you claim is indeed how you wish to proceed, and there are no secret motives, then I am sure General Perez will wish to be in attendance at the press conference to respond and state his position. Please be aware that we will be in attendance. I will have an adjutant obtain details of the time and location. Now, good evening."

General Jiminez stood and was escorted to the front door of the Villa.

Chapter 48

The next morning at the police station, reporters and TV crews crowded the conference room. At the front of the room, a large oak desk had been set up. Microphones jutted up from the desk like irreverent bunches of flowers. A pile of printed papers was positioned at the end of the desk. A water jug and glasses were set in front of the various speaker's chairs.

At nine in the morning, a press officer for the police entered the room and addressed the assembled reporters.

"The conference will start in fifteen minutes. I am going to hand out some materials for you all to read ahead of the conference. I am sure you will all have questions after you have read them."

There was a rush forward of reporters, eager to get the documents. As the reporters read, the room fell silent. A few whistles and sworn exclamations could be heard.

At the back of the room, cameras flashed and reporters rushed to the aisle as General Perez and several other men entered. A staccato of questions was hurled at General Perez. His bodyguards pushed the reporters back and guided him to the front row of seats.

It was the first time that Rosita had seen him, other than in photos. Strangely she felt an attraction to him. He was tall with dark wavy hair and a brilliant white smile he flashed often. Underneath his uniform, Rosita imagined a muscular body. He looked directly at Rosita and smiled one of his most charming smiles as he proceeded to cross over to where she stood. He extended his hand but quickly withdrew it and kissed her on her cheeks. The perfunctory kisses went on longer than she expected. Rosita blushed and a redness colored her cheeks.

"I saw your little speech on the news, Senora. You are a dedicated and lively young woman. I think I will need to keep a close watch on you."

Felix had watched the exchange and was not pleased, yet decided against giving Perez the satisfaction of intervening. Rosita looked across the room at him and gave a slight smile and shrugged her narrow shoulders.

At precisely nine-fifteen, Felix walked to the desk and seated himself at the center behind the microphones. He waited for the others to sit and the general noise of the reporters to stop before he spoke.

"Good morning. I welcome you all this morning. As many of you are aware, I have been accused of insubordination, illegal activities, and murder. All the accusations have been proven false.
Last night while returning to my home with my partner, Rosita, and a guest were ambushed in my driveway. There was a scuffle and my guest was fatally shot. The criminals who did this were dressed as police officers from this area and drove police cars. Upon checking it was found these were not real police cars but cleverly disguised cars to fool us.
The police are investigating this matter, and I will ask Commander Santiago to speak and answer your questions next.
It is this state of lawlessness, corruption, and terror in our country that has prompted me to embark on a mission to bring about major reforms. There are those amongst us this morning whose fingerprints are all over the problems we live with daily. I say that it is enough. It is time for reform. It is time that General Perez and

certain politicians relinquish their positions and face the people of our country in democratic elections. I intend to establish a political group to win these elections and restore our great country to wealth and happiness. I have studied our constitution and hold the firm belief that our former Royal Family was deposed using an illegal process. It is my intention, if elected, to restore our Monarchy.
I already have committed members of our society who have contacted me and pledged support and resources.
I ask the press to be fair and cover our election in a professional manner and in a way that all our people can understand the issues.
The attack on me last night was politically motivated. As we progress with our campaign, I'm sure there will be more threats. I will not back away from them.
I now ask Commander Santiago to tell you all of what the investigation into last night's attack has uncovered."

The room erupted as questions were shouted. Felix held up his hand and returned to the microphone.

"I will speak again after the Commander. I will be discussing the letter from General Perez and some other matters. Now please hear Commander Santiago."

The Commander walked very slowly to the center of the stage. He studied the line of seats at the front before speaking.

"Last night, Colonel Felix de Santos, his partner Rosita Valquez and one of our prominent lawyers, J.J. Carter were ambushed as they turned into the driveway to their Villa. I'm sure many of you saw the video that Carmilla Vesco of VTV broadcast shortly after the event. Naturally, many thought this to be a continuation of recent hostility between de Santos and General Perez and certain ruling politicians. We have investigated and questioned the two men we took into custody at the de Santos Villa. Our inquiries continue, but we have established these men are from outside the country and are associated with certain businesses supported and financed by some of the very people that Felix de Santos wishes to expose and eventually have held criminally responsible for the hurt both to our country and its citizens.

We are still questioning these men and already have the names of individuals who wish to harm Felix de Santos, his family, and friends.

At this time, I have no more to say as this investigation is new and is proceeding. There will be updates at a later date when we have accurate information."

Commander Santiago stared at the seated General Perez and his colleagues as he walked from the room.

Felix leaned forward and spoke into the microphones.

"If you have read the documents that were available to the press, you will see that one is a copy of a letter delivered to me last night after the attack. It is from General Perez and some ruling committee members. On the surface, it offers safety and claims that anyone working to establish the new political party or help in the elections will be protected from any form of violence. I wish I could believe that. There are significant amounts of dirty money involved that the present regime supports. Those involved have interests that extend to businesses and individuals far beyond our shores. I am aware that certain members of the press are in the employ of General Perez and his gang. I warn you that we will expose you and the public will not be fooled."

Felix was about to continue when General Perez stood and approached the desk. He turned to face the assembled reporters.

"My good character and intentions are being impugned here this morning. I deny the allegations that have been made here. I have taken many actions to protect Felix de Santos since he announced his intention to challenge me and the ruling political party. There was no need for him to run from the country and hide like a scared rabbit. We welcome his participation in an election. He will soon learn that the people of our beloved country are happy and will vote to maintain the existing rulers. I can assure you all that since Felix de Santos was declared innocent of the horrible murders of my associates, we have done everything to respect him and ensure his safety.

The General then motioned to an aide to join him. He took an envelope from the aide and made a scene of opening a single sheet letter.

"I have here a petition that has been signed by my fellow Generals and all of the ruling politicians. The petition, which you may view and photograph, requests and recommends the promotion of Felix de Santos from the rank of Colonel to that of a serving General in our army."

The room erupted with shouted questions and several reporters running from the room to announce the news. At the desk, Rosita stared at Felix in disbelief. The police press officer stood and announced the conference was over.

General Perez turned and walked to Felix with an extended hand. Felix attempted to ignore the attempt at hospitality. Perez moved along to where Rosita sat.

"My dear, we will be meeting again and very soon."

Chapter 49

The next few weeks were hectic. Meetings were held to select candidates, financing, and plans for rallies to address the public. Since the press conference, Felix arose in prominence. The people were fascinated with his bold approach to reach the position of leadership and even more curious about his relationship with Rosita. She was with him at every function and was soon seen by many as almost a movie star. Invitations to social events arrived at the Villa daily, requesting both her presence and comments on the elections. Rosita graced these events with style and a dominant presence. As time passed she became a significant influence. In public, she was graceful and easy to relate to. She never tried to hide her past and life in the barrio. She spoke of improved life for the poor and especially the need for medicines and help for the women in the poorer rural areas of the country.

Privately, she seethed at the stupidity of the people but played to them to reach her goal of power and money. She saw less of Felix as he traveled the country and undertook his military responsibilities. It was during a period of Felix's absence that Rosita planned her return to the barrio of Nos Grande. There was a matter to be dealt with there and Felix was not to know. She needed to devise a plan that would allow her to make the trip, yet keep it a secret. As she pondered this, Carmine arrived in her room.

"Rosita, I am going into the city today. Since you are alone, I thought you may wish to join me."

"I thank you for the offer, but the relatives of Fernando, my neighbor from the barrio, have invited me to stay with them for a few days. Fernando is going to be there. I thought I would stay with them while Felix is away on army business. Sometimes I miss my friends from Nos Grande. It will be good to see Fernando and hear what has been happening in the barrio."

"How long will you be staying with them?"

"I suspect for three days. Is it possible for Enzo to drive me to their home?"

"I will arrange that for you. When do you wish to leave?"

"This afternoon. I promised to be there for the dinner they arranged to welcome Fernando."

"Enzo is driving me into the city. I have a luncheon with friends. I will have him return for you. My lunch is going to be long and quite liquid."

After Carmine left the room, Rosita packed he casual clothing and the items she would need at Nos Grande. She would require protective clothing in the jungle-like area where the task needed to be performed. She only intended spending one night with Fernando's relatives and return with him to the barrio the next morning.

Rosita wondered how she could explain to Enzo the tools that were bundled together for the trip. An explanation came quickly. She would tell Enzo that Fernando had asked her to purchase them as he was unable to do so in Nos Grande.

Doubt crept into her mind. It had been many years since the incident happened and she wondered whether the item she hid would still be there.

Rosita left her room and waited for Carmine in the salon. She wanted to be sure that Carmine was gone from the house before she retrieved the tools from the garden shed where she had hidden them.

"I will see you in a day I hope. It will be lonely here with both you and Felix away from the house. I have become so used to you being here. I will miss you."

"You can enjoy some quiet time without us bothering you and having constant visitors and phone calls. It will be busy when I return, as Felix plans to address the public at many rallies. I imagine we will have many helpers who will be coming to the house."

"I wish Felix would abandon this silly scheme of his. No good will come of it. The men he is challenging are devious and have access to a lot of money and powerful friends both in the country and abroad. Furthermore, there are some I know who claim they are working to help Felix, but are keeping themselves aligned with General Perez and his gang."

"I am aware of a couple. There is a certain woman I observed and I believe she is spying on every plan we make and reporting back to Perez. She is playing a very dangerous game. I intend to see it ends when I return."

Rosita felt the internal frothing of the cold demons as she recalled the night of the first meeting when she had observed the actions of the woman.

"Rosita, who is it that you believe is working against Felix?"

Rosita hesitated, unsure whether to tell the truth or mislead

Carmine. The answer was simple.

"The night Felix called his friends together to announce his plans, I carefully watched the reactions of people. There was one in particular that I did not trust. It was that lawyer, Julia. She is trouble."

"I share your concern. There is something about Julia and Felix you do not know. Several years ago she attempted to seduce Felix and tried to manipulate him. She claimed privately that he had made her pregnant and demanded that he marry her. She created a huge problem and threatened Felix and our family with public shame. Of course, she wasn't pregnant and the matter died. Felix has always watched her closely since that incident."

Rosita could barely control the rage that was consuming every inch of her. Visions of death and inflicted injuries flashed through her mind. The thought of her Felix in a sexual relationship with Julia was too much. Rosita let out a blood-curdling scream. Carmine retreated toward the door. The outburst from Rosita scared her.

"Rosita, please be calm. There is nothing between them. Felix has assured me that she means nothing to him."

"I will deal with her. I need to discuss this with Felix. She will regret those actions. I intend to see to that."

"Please Rosita. That was years ago. Leave the matter alone. It is still possible for her to do a lot of damage, especially now that Felix is so prominent. She could wreck his chance of success."

"She will pay dearly."

Chapter 50

Rosita enjoyed the evening with Fernando's relatives as there was laughter, traditional food that she missed, and singing accompanied by Fernando playing guitar and a nephew on his harmonica.

As she dressed the next morning for the trip back to the barrio of Nos Grande, Rosita thought how different the evening was, compared to the nights with Carmine and Felix at the Villa Magnifico. She enjoyed being amongst her people. They were hard workers and did not expect much from life, only happiness and health. Rosita thought about the contrast between that life and life with the de Santos family. She realized that eventually, she would have to choose and choose carefully.
She finished dressing and joined the family for breakfast. There was laughter and loud conversation as the family ate and prepared for their day. Rosita was quiet as she considered the day and night ahead. The need for secrecy and deception was great.

Fernando was eager to leave for the long and difficult trip back to the barrio. He did not understand Rosita's desire to return.

"Rosita. Why are you returning? It wasn't long ago when you wanted to leave for the city. What can be so important there to make you want to return?"

"Fernando, I wish to speak to some old friends before Felix starts to make his speeches. I hope to convince people to support him."

"Why are you taking tools? We have tools there. I don't understand."

"I was asked to take these to a farmer who cannot afford them.

They are not expensive in La Iluminada. They are my gift to the old man."

Fernando was not convinced but chose not to say anything

The family gathered to wish Rosita and Fernando a safe return trip to the barrio. Fernando hoisted the bundle of tools over his back and picked up his small battered suitcase. Rosita carried a small bag, and together they departed for the bus terminal for the long trip to Nos Grande. At that early hour, the city of La Iluminada was bustling with workers setting out for offices and factories.

At the bus terminal, Rosita looked at the waiting passengers. The women were dressed in their brightly colored ponchos and colorful dresses. The men wore straw hats and white shirts with well-worn trousers of varying colors. Some were holding treasured purchases of items only available in the city. One man held a large shiny black china bull with a ferocious face in a snorting posture. Many of the women stood with handwoven flax baskets stuffed with cans and items of clothing. Rosita reflected on how different these treasured items were to the simple peasants when compared to the fashionable clothing she had purchased with Carmine. It was at that moment that Rosita realized she was no longer part of the life lived in the barrio. She wanted more and intended to demand it. She reflected on the length of time she had been living away from the barrio. It seemed to her she had only been gone a few weeks, but then thought of all that had happened. The trips, the time in Australia, the visits she had made to other locations in the country with Felix or Carmine. It was only then she realized she had been gone from the barrio for over a year.

Her thoughts were shattered as the old bus ground its way to a halt in front of the assembled group. There was a rush by the women to be the first on the bus and commandeer the best seats. The driver left his seat and assisted men at the rear of the bus to tie items onto the rusted racks that had been installed to carry large pieces of luggage. Rosita watched as her bundle of tools was firmly attached and Fernando joined her. He waited behind Rosita until she was on the bus. They found a seat across and behind from the driver. The seats were torn and dirty. The feces of some animal was streaked over the cheap covering. Fernando found some crumpled newspaper on the floor and covered the seat.

Rosita was not happy to be returning to Nos Grande. If it wasn't for the important task to be done, she would have probably never returned. As the bus lurched away from the terminal with black diesel exhaust fumes belching from behind, Rosita turned to look at the activity of the city. Her vision was obscured by the smoky exhaust. She was already regretting her decision to leave La Iluminada.

The traffic thinned on reaching the outskirts of the city. The bus lurched and swayed as they drove onto the dusty country road. Rosita looked from the window opening and watched the men and women who walked at the edge of the road, leading their donkeys or carrying wrapped goods on their backs. In the fields, she saw farmers working in the fields. Occasionally bluish smoke drifted skyward into the perfectly blue sky, as the brush from cleared land was burned. Rosita thought of the speeches Felix had made in which he claimed the people would have a better life without the corruption and loss of money because of it. She recalled these promises as she watched the workers labor in the oppressive heat performing back-breaking work.

Rosita was determined to help Felix in his campaign, but first, she needed to deal with a matter that could stand in their way.

For hours the bus labored on through the flat farmland and into the mountains. The driver finally pulled the bus into a dusty clearing. He had no sooner shut the engine off when the passengers climbed down and headed to the two weathered wooden huts that served as toilets.

As Rosita approached the hut, flies buzzed and swarmed around her head. She swatted at them, and thankful to be at the door, she pulled it open. The stench of urine and feces assaulted her nostrils. On the bare mud floor, giant beetles crawled around the wooden supports holding a plank that acted as a seat over the open mud trench below. It reminded Rosita of her childhood days and the primitive baños in the barrio.

The relentless sun beat down and the passengers took shelter in the shade of giant trees at the edge of the jungle's growth. Rosia joined the group but stayed far away from the edge of the clearing. Chattering monkeys and brightly colored parrots in the trees squawked at the assembled passengers.

Fernando joined her and held out a ceramic jug to her.

"Rosita, have some freshwater. I brought this with us as the water at these stops is dirty and often has a disease. I have some food with me. There are cheeses and some fruit. You must drink and eat. We still have hours of travel ahead."

"Thank you. I will drink some and eat the fruit."

"That is good. This sun and heat can make you sick. I do not ever remember heat like this. It is strange. I also noticed that some of the jungle was on fire. That is unusual as the soil is often damp and nothing burns. There is something wrong in our world."

Chapter 51

After thirty minutes, the driver called the passengers to board the bus for the rest of the trip. The bus lurched and bounced along the dirt road that traversed the top of the mountains. Every so often the bus would swerve to avoid the large rocks and boulders that slipped down from the cliffs that bordered the road.

Rosita settled back and watched the people. On occasion, the bus would grind to a halt to pick up the odd person standing at the roadside. Large clouds of sandy dirt arose from the rear of the bus and blew into the windowless bus. Rosita wondered who these peasants who got onto the bus were. She tried to understand whether they lived in these barren mountains or had walked from some other location. She was tempted to ask them, except one of them withdrew a small pan flute and started playing. All the passengers either hummed or sang along with the ancient country tune he played. A serenity developed on the bus.

The afternoon was dwindling as the bus descended from the heights of the mountains and started across gently rolling land. Rosita looked out at the plantations in disgust. These were lands that belonged to the people, but General Perez and his men had devised a clever land use scheme and encouraged large international corporations to farm and develop the lands. Any profit made went to the corporations and the ruling party. The hard-working laborers on the farms received little compensation.

Rosita noticed heavy black smoke and flames leaping into the air as the workers burned off more shrub and forest to clear land for more crops. As she watched, she recalled Felix discussing the control these international corporations had over the government and the certain members. They were too powerful to control. She remembered him wanting to review the agreements and modify them to share the profits with the local workers and develop medical facilities and schools. She wondered if it would ever be possible. It seemed to be a task too large for the government of their small country. General Perez had agreed to terms with both the Russians and Chinese who operated the plantations in return for loans to finance the new Buena Viva airport and the trains for the capital. The country was at the mercy of the Russians and the Chinese. They controlled the terms of the finances. General Perez and the ruling party had sold out the country in return for the lucrative bribes and lavish luxuries they had been afforded.

Rosita dozed off into sleep as she thought of Felix and the plans he had. The rocking motion of the bus and the drone of the engine lulled her into sleep.

Fernando shook her awake.

"Rosita. We are almost home to Nos Grande. We will be passing the mine in minutes. It is time to get ready to leave the bus."

She looked out into the dusk. Minutes later they were passing the mine. Rosita felt the fury rise within her. She recalled her father, Jorge, and how the thugs hired by the mine had beaten him. The mine had increased in size. There were more buildings near the river and a huge fleet of trucks. She promised herself that she would take her revenge on these people. Once she and Felix were in power she would have access to information that would reveal who was responsible and the names of others involved in the illegal activities of the mine.

There was a renewed level of activity on the bus as they lurched the short distance to Nos Grande. Rosita was more curious than excited. She wished to see the change that had occurred since she left. The bus slowed and turned onto the narrow road that led into the town.

Rosita observer small groups of men standing and talking. She found it unusual that there were no women to be seen. She studied the men and did not recognize many. There were many new faces in the barrio. Rosita suspected they were men who had arrived to work at the mine or manage the large plantations.

The bus slowed and as the brakes were applied they emitted a shrill squeal caused by the build-up of dust and the overheating. An acrid smell filled the bus.

"Rosita, we will take our luggage and your equipment and walk to my adobe. It is not far. I want to walk after having sat for so long on this bus. You will enjoy a nice dinner with us and then tomorrow you can look after your business."

"No Fernando. I will be pleased to dine with you and your family, but afterward, I will need to find the man who will need to assist me. I suspect I know where I will find him."

Fernando was curious but stayed silent. He had a bad feeling about the reason Rosita had returned. She had evaded all of his questions and been vague when pressed. He also considered the timing of her trip. It seemed strange she was traveling while Felix was away on military business. It made little sense to him.

Fernando removed his luggage from the rickety overhead rack. Rosita walked in front of him and went to the rear of the bus to retrieve her bundle of tools. She heaved them over her shoulder and walked with Fernando. They turned off the main road onto the cobblestone lane that led to Fernando's home. Next to it was the adobe in which Rosita had grown up with Rosa, her mother, and Jorge, her father. She felt a twinge of sadness as she thought about them and the carefree life she had enjoyed in the barrio. Those days were gone. If her parents knew of the wicked act she had committed they would have left the barrio. In some ways, Rosita felt ashamed, but in another way, she was glad she had taken control. Now it was necessary to remove any evidence that could impact her and Felix's pursuit of power and leadership.

Fernando opened the front door to the adobe and was greeted by both his cheerful wife and the overwhelming aromas of the stews and baking. The inside of the adobe was warm and welcoming. The light from oil lamps flickered on the walls casting a dance of yellow designs.

"Rosita, I am so happy you have come home. Fernando had told us you might return with him. How long will you stay? What do you need to do here? Can we help? Will you stay with us tonight?"

"Yes, I would love to stay with you tonight. I will take my equipment and store it in our old home next door. I will be leaving early in the morning and will not want to wake you. Thank you for the offer to help, but this is a personal matter. I will return in the afternoon tomorrow."

Rosita swung the bundle of tools back over her shoulder and left to store them in her old home. As she entered the door, she was pleased to find the house was empty and not feeling abandoned or looted. The house was dark and dusty and lacked the atmosphere of the home she had known. Rosita was feeling confused.

Chapter 52

After depositing the tools in a safe location in the house, Rosita returned to Fernando's adobe.

"I am so hungry after that trip. It will be nice when there are new modern buses. It is such a hard trip, especially for the elderly. Is there any help I can offer in preparing our meal?"

"No. Please come and sit with us. We want to hear about your adventures in La Iluminada. Tell us about your man, Felix. We have heard the reports on the radio. He is going to be a good leader. Those men there now have not helped people like us or in other barrios. They only care to help the cities and the big corporations. They ignore us and our needs and troubles. Will your Felix be able to change that?"

"I will be with him when he wins and I will work with him. We will change things together."

Fernando quietly watched. There was something that was not right.

"Rosita, what is this business you have here?"

She thought for a moment before replying with the lie she had just formed.

"Before my father was killed, he had made a business arrangement with a man here. There is money that is owed. I intend to collect that money. The man contacted me and I need to sign papers. It is all very simple."

"I am confused. Your Papi, Jorge was not a rich man. He did not do business. He was a poor worker like all of us. This does not make sense."

Rosita sensed the doubts that Fernando was having. She needed to convince him that there was nothing to be suspicious about.

"Fernando, I will answer you, but Jorge wanted all this kept secret. You must promise me this."

"Rosita, I was a friend of Rosa and Jorge for many years. We were not just neighbors but very close friends. He would not have kept any secrets from me. I find all this strange. I will agree to keep anything you say a secret. Please tell us."

"Before my father was killed, he had planned to move with Rosa and me to a new villa. He had found the land and wanted to build. The only problem he had was money. He found a man who wanted to buy our home. The deal was agreed upon. It is the man I must meet. It is the reason that the house has been empty since I have been gone."

Fernando sank his head into his hands.

"I had no idea. Why did he want it a secret?"

"Papi did not want to upset you or others in the barrio."

Again, Fernando was doubting her story.

"Tonight I need to go and speak with the man. Tomorrow his wife will be arriving here in Nos Grande and they will sign all the legal papers. I have arranged a meeting tonight beforehand."

"Rosita, you must be careful. Do not go to the cantina alone. Since that flamenco dancing waitress disappeared there have been other attacks on women who go there alone. Would you like me to accompany you?"

Rosita became angry with Fernando and her demons started to wake. She fought to control them.

"No Fernando. I will be fine. I know most of the men there. If there is a problem I am sure they will protect me."

The conversation drifted to other topics and waned as dinner was served. Rosita helped to clear the table and wash dishes when the meal was finished. She then groomed and prepared for her meeting.

Rosita was wary of Fernando when she left the house, so along the way she stopped to talk with people she recognized, all the time watching to see if Fernando had followed her. When she was convinced she had not been followed, she proceeded to make her way to the cantina.

The cantina was already full. A few drunken patrons lingered on the street outside, shouting obscenities as she passed them. Inside the cantina was filled with cigarette smoke and noise. She studied the tables until she found what she was looking for. There at the far end of the bar, sitting with some other rough-looking men was Pepe. He still had the look of a pig about him. Nothing had changed. She pushed her way through the men until she reached his stool.

"Pepe, I need to speak with you. It is important. Come with me outside. It will be easier to speak."

The other men jeered and made lewd suggestions regarding the purpose of meeting outside. Rosita ignored them. Pepe had not been expecting Rosita and immediately slid off his stool and followed her.

"What do you want? Why are you here? What is so important you are here and want to talk to me about? Our business is long finished."

"No Pepe it isn't finished. In the city of Il Luminata, the police have been looking at the disappearance of people, That slut is one of them. I heard a rumor they have discovered the body where we buried her. Very early tomorrow morning you and I will go to the area in the jungle where she is buried. We need to be sure she cannot be found. If you do not come with me, I will speak to authorities I now know in La Iluminada and tell them it was you and that you have committed other crimes here."

 "I don't think you would dare do that. I can have witnesses who will support me."

"Pepe don't be a fool. Since I left Nos Grande I have changed. I am now in contact with many powerful people. Felix de Santos is my lover and partner. He has a strong position in the military. You are in no position to bargain with me. You will meet me at five tomorrow morning on the track past the church. I have brought tools. We must find out if she is there and maybe move her."

Pepe's face became contorted at the thought of moving a decaying corpse.

"Rosita, we hid her well. She will not be found."

"I cannot take that risk. I will make sure you are well rewarded after Felix wins this election. You will never need to work for money again."

Pepe's concerns quickly disappeared.

"And, Pepe remember that I paid you to dispose of the body. You will have to explain a lot. I will see you at five in the morning."

Rosita gave him her best smile and turned away from the confused and worried Pepe.

Chapter 53

It was still dark when Rosita left Fernando's home. She pushed open the door to her former home and entered. She walked back to the kitchen and reached beneath the old stove to retrieve the set of tools she had brought for the gruesome task that lay ahead. With the tools secured and strung over her back, Rosita started the walk to the church and along the dirt track that ran beside it. If Pepe was on time, they would be at the location before sunrise. Rosita was happy to see very few people out in the barrio at the early hour.

A voice called a greeting to her as she entered the center of the barrio, but it was just an early worker leaving for the fields. She had been startled but settled down when she realized she was alone.

The dirt track was baked hard and well worn. A few pebbles dotted the surface. She slowed and scanned ahead. In the distance, she saw the form of Pepe huddled against a tree smoking a cigarette. She was angry. The smell of smoke and the glow could easily expose him and draw unwanted attention.

Rosita continued toward him. She snatched the cigarette out from his lips and threw it to the ground.

"Are you stupid? Do you want others to see us leaving here at this hour? Take these tools and we leave immediately. I just hope no one saw you."

Pepe went to resist her verbal attack but decided it would only worsen the day that lay ahead. He had plans for Rosita once they got into the jungle. Pepe was still fuming from the previous night. He intended to punish Rosita for her comments and treatment.

Pepe took the sack containing the tools that she thrust at him. He studied her for a moment. She was dressed in military-like fatigues which she intended to abandon in the river after the task was completed and change into the casual clothing she had brought. She did not worry about Pepe's clothing as she planned for him not to return.

"Pepe, you lead the way. I will be right behind you. We should reach the location in about thirty minutes and hopefully, we can check the situation and return by noon. I will come back first and alone… You will wait a while and then return. If you are asked, you were looking at the area before going hunting."

Pepe gave a sullen nod and commenced the trek along the track. The further they moved away from the church, the denser the vegetation became. Unknown animals scurried out of their path. Pepe was terrified he would step on a snake in the dim light. If it wasn't for the money she had offered and the need to know the body had not been found, he would have refused to go with her.

"Pepe, do you remember the exact location? There is more growth here than I remembered."

"It is where the river bends to the right. There are some large rocks on the riverbank. We are almost there."

As they continued, there was a rush of sound and fluttering and cries as the disturbed a flock of nesting birds flew into the sky. Pepe was hating the walk.

Soon the path became obliterated. Vines hung from the branches of tall trees. Thick jungle grass tangled with spiky shrubs. The path was at an end.

"We will need to push our way through this growth. We are very close now."

"I am going down to the riverbank. It will be easier to travel along the edge of the river."

Rosita thought of this and agreed.

"Yes, it will be easier and quicker. We just need to be careful. There are alligators and at this time of the day it will be hard to see them."

Slowly they pushed ahead until Pepe pointed to some large rocks where the river abruptly turned.

"Rosita, we are there. I will climb up and locate where she is buried. Follow me. I will start to dig. It seems unlikely that there has been anyone here. There are no signs the vegetation has been disturbed. Are you sure the information you heard is correct?"

Pepe stopped and stared at her. She did not answer him but started to pull herself up the incline from the river.

"Don't worry Pepe. I am sure the information was correct. Now let's finish this. We will be back in Nos Grande before siesta time and you will be able to relax with a cold Cerveza."

Pepe grinned at the thought of the money she would pay him, and of sitting on the outside verandah of the cantina drinking beer and watching the women walk by. His life was getting better. He considered how he could help Rosita and Felix with the election in return for the large payment she had mentioned. He could not believe his luck had changed from that of a poor laborer to someone about to benefit through helping Rosita with these grim tasks.

"Pepe, I am feeling a little weak. Please go ahead and start digging where you think we buried her. I will rest for a minute."

After climbing up the incline, she fell back against the trunk of one of the huge trees that populated the jungle. The sun was rising and the jungle was awakening. Birds called, monkeys screeched and every so often she heard the growls of the large wild cats that roamed nearby. She was eager to get finished and get out of the hell hole.

She stood as Pepe excitedly called to her.

"I have found the location. It is exactly as we left it. I think we should just leave it and return. No one has been here. The grave is untouched."

"No, Pepe. I want to be sure she is still in that grave. It would be easy for the police to cover up the surface. Please start digging. I will assist in a minute."

Pepe shoveled with force. The soft alluvial soil was easy to penetrate. He dug down exposing layer after layer until the shovel hit an object. He stopped and called to Rosita for the broom she had brought, to brush away the last layers of soil.

Rosita walked to the edge of the grave and handed Pepe the broom. She watched as the remains of the flamenco dancer were unearthed. She looked down as the bright blue dress was exposed. She felt nothing. The flamenco dancer's remains were in a state of decay. The flesh from her face was gone and a skeletal skull lay twisted to one side. Beetles and worms crawled through the crevices where her ears had been. Her arms were splayed in front of her as if trying to break her fall. Large holes exposed white bone where some creature had eaten through her flesh. What flesh remained resembled a milky scum, dissolving and saturating the soil.

"Pepe, dig more. I want to be sure that nothing is missing."

"Rosita, there is no point. She has decayed. If someone had moved anything, she would be in pieces."

"Pepe, do as I say. I agreed with you."

Pepe thought of the money again, and the riches that possibly lay ahead. He turned and started shoveling furiously. He did not hear Rosita approaching from behind. She raised the ax above her head and crashed it down on Pepe's head. His skull burst open and pink matter sprayed out. Rosita thought of an exploding watermelon. She kicked her leg forward and into his back. Pepe fell face down on the decaying flamenco dancer with a sickening squish.

Rosita leaned back, satisfied that now no one would be able to jeopardize the chances of Felix or her rise to power. The last evidence was gone. Now she needed to complete the job and return to Nos Grande.

With strength she didn't realize she had, Rosita filled the grave with soil and pulled vines and branches across the completed grave. She was pleased with the result she achieved.

She took her small bag, along with the little sack of tools down to the river bank. She stripped naked and threw the clothes into the swiftly flowing river. They would be carried away from Nos Grande deeper into the jungle. With all her might she threw each tool out into the river. Rosita dressed in the light clothing but kept on her boots for the return trek to the village. The day had started well.

Chapter 54

It was late morning when Rosita walked past the church and down into the open farmers market. She stopped and spoke to the farmers she had known while living in the barrio.

The farmers told her of the conflicts, violence, and attacks that were occurring since the expansion of the mine and the development of the plantations. The foreign men who worked in them visited the barrio and created many problems. They told her the barrio she knew no longer existed and asked for help.

Many asked her about life in La Iluminada, and in particular her life with Felix and his desire to lead the country. She promised them to hold a rally in Nos Grande during the campaign and asked for their support. The farmers who had suffered over the years were only too eager to commit their support.

After a few hours, Rosita decided it was time to return to Fernando's home. As she walked past the cantina, she observed Pepe's empty chair on the outdoor verandah where he normally sat each afternoon with his friends. "That seat will be empty for a long time now, " she thought.

Rosita encountered friends she had known at school and some others she had met while living in the barrio. She was courteous and took time with each. It reminded many of the delightful young girl they had known growing up. No one knew of the festering demons that resided within her.

Finally, Rosita reached the adobe of Fernando. She pushed open the front door and was surprised to find him at home sitting with his wife.

"Fernando, why aren't you at work? Are you not well?"

"No, I am tired from the trip and I wanted time at home. I just returned from the village market. I have told my wife about your plans to sell the house. How was the meeting? Have you now sold the house?"

"I could not. I met the man last evening. He explained to me his wife and her family would decide today. I went to meet them this morning. The family does not have the money. The house has not sold. There is no need for me to stay here any longer so I will take the bus back to La Iluminada tomorrow. I am disappointed."

Fernando listened but stayed quiet. He said nothing. Unbeknownst to Rosita, he had watched her leave his home that morning and retrieve the sack from her adobe next door. He had watched as she walked off with the sack over her shoulder, dressed in military fatigues, and yet here she was now dressed in casual summer clothes. He did not trust her nor the lies he knew she was telling.

That morning he had been tempted to follow her but decided there was no point in searching for trouble. In the barrio, it was too easy for trouble to find you.

"Yes, I agree with you. If there is no business here for you you should return to Felix. I am sure he needs your help and support at this time."

Rosita was surprised. She had expected more questions. After a few more minutes of conversation, she excused herself and left to pack her few belongings for the long trip back to La Iluminada.

While packing, Rosita froze when she heard the wail of a police siren pass by the home. She needed to get away from the barrio forever. There was nothing left that held her interest or emotion. She knew she would never return. It had become a sad and depressing village.

She turned away from the case on the bed and found Fernando standing in the doorway watching her.

"Rosita, I don't know what secret you are keeping or what trouble you are in, but I suggest you leave tonight. Take the night bus. Some do not want you here. I heard things in the village. It is no longer safe for you. Felix has enemies here. There are men at the mine who want him dead. You must leave. I will arrange to have you taken from the village to a safe location where you will be able to board the bus. Do you understand?"

Rosita instinctively knew he was in part lying to her, yet she was pleased to run from the barrio sooner than she had planned.

"Yes, I understand. Thank you."

"I will have food prepared for you to take on the trip."

An hour later, Fernando arrived in an old farm truck driven by a friend of his.

"My friend and I will take you to the shelter on the main road where the bus from the next barrio will pick you up. We will wait with you until you are on the bus."

Chapter 55

Villa Magnifico, La Iluminada

Felix paced the floor of the salon.

"Mother, have you any idea where she went? You say the relatives of a neighbor from Nos Grande, who live here. I asked Enzo to take me to the address she went to. He took me there. It is in an unsafe poor class neighborhood where there is lots of crime. I went into the house. No one would speak to me. I am worried. Did she say why she was going there?"

Carmine watched. Felix continued to pace. She remembered him as a young boy when he would pace if he had been caught in trouble.

"Not exactly. She said there was some business in Nos Grande but did not elaborate. She may have gone there with her former neighbor, but surely she would have told us. It is unlike here. She is a strong woman, Felix. I am sure there is an explanation and she will be safe."

"I don't like it. Why would she leave like this with no explanation? I am concerned. I will call Caesar and ask him to make inquiries. He knows people who live and work in that district. Maybe he can find out something."

There was the sound of someone arriving at the front door. Felix heard the voices in the foyer and the door opened. Rosita walked in.

"Where have you been? We were worried. You should have told us what was happening."

Rosita thought of a plausible excuse. The lie she had concocted for Fernando had worked. She decided to lie again, as much as she hated to lie to Felix and Carmine.

"Relax, Felix. I was invited to spend time visiting with my former neighbor who was visiting La Ilumunada. He had an envelope with a letter for me. Our former home in the barrio is empty and this man was interested in buying it. He wanted to meet. Fernando agreed that I should accompany him on his return to Nos Grande and stay at his home while I met the man. We met but while he wanted the house, he did not have an amount of money to purchase it. I left immediately to return and be with you. It all happened very quickly."

"Rosita, you took a huge risk. We are now well known. For you to travel alone was stupid. You should have told me. I would have arranged a proper escort for you. Never do something like that again."

She felt the demons stirring inside her. She wanted to rebel against Felix and his lecture. He did not own her and had no right to speak to her in that manner. Rosita was tired from the travel and chose not to fight with him. It was best that the affairs in Nos Grande quietly fade away.

"Tell me about Nos Grande. Has it changed since you left?"

"I did not like it. The village is not the same. There are workers from different countries who work at the mine or the plantations. They are not like the local people. There have been arguments, fights, and killings. Nos Grande has changed. It is no longer a sleepy and peaceful little barrio. I do not wish to return there."

Carmine watched Rosita's performance. She detected that Rosita was misleading Felix. She wondered what was so important in Nos Grande that Rosita would lie to her son. She waited until Felix left the room and fixed an icy stare on Rosita.

"You may fool my son, and think you are fooling me, but you are not. I believe you are involved in something terrible or you would not be telling such lies to cover up the truth. For your sake, whatever you are involved in had better not impact the de Santos family. As much as I like you, Rosita, I will put my family before you. I will see you destroyed before you hurt Felix or negatively impact de Santos' name or businesses. Do you wish to tell me the truth now?"

Carmine had trapped her. Rosita bit her lip and looked at Carmine.

"Before I met Felix, I was involved in a bad situation in Nos Grande. Felix is aware of some of the events that occurred. I needed to finish the business. It is now done. Please do not ask any more questions. That part of my past still haunts me."

Carmine continued to interrogate Rosita.

"Is this about that business with the priest who raped you or other matters?"

"It was related. That is all I am going to say. I am tired and am going to rest for a while. Please relax Carmine. No harm will come to Felix."

Carmine watched as Rosita turned and left the room. She wondered whether Rosita's behavior was insolence, defiance, or aggression. She decided to keep a close watch on her.

Chapter 56

The next three months passed and Felix was busy holding meetings with candidates who wished to represent different areas of the country. No one spoke of Rosita's solo trip to Nos Grande. It simply faded into the background.

A date was established for the day the election would be held. The advisers to Felix prepared a schedule of appearances for him at political rallies throughout the country. Strategy meetings were held and controversial speeches prepared. The press continually sought interviews with Felix, who was happy to oblige. He attacked General Perez and his men, pointing to corrupt contracts, questionable transfers of money, and suspicious dealings with foreign governments. General Perez fought back with attacks on Felix and the family's businesses. The campaign became heated and nasty. The worse it became, the more interested the public became. Arguments and debates occurred between friends and strangers in bars and at sporting events. There was a high level of interest in the election as it would be the first true attempt at establishing a democratic government. To counter the attacks, Rosita took a role, appearing with Felix at his side. She did not dress in the latest fashions. She wished to appear as an ordinary person and in interviews, she played up her background and life in a poor barrio. The women loved it and easily related to her. The only liberty she took was to wear a bright yellow rose to each rally. The press has asked her what the significance was. Her response to them was that the yellow rose represented spring and fresh new beginnings. The public loved it.

Attendance at the first rallies was not at the size Felix had hoped for. It seemed that the interest amongst the public was high, but most were resigned to the belief that Felix stood no real chance of defeating General Perez.

At the rallies, the crowds were loud and on occasion, some would rush toward the stage. Felix worried for his and Rosia's safety. He decided to establish better security for Rosita and himself.

Back at Villa Magnifico in the afternoon, Felix met with his party members to review the rallies and plan for the future ones. He steered the discussion to how security would be handled at the events.

"Gentlemen, I am concerned. At the last rally, we had several men run toward our stage and some were able to reach the podium. I believe these men were just enthusiastic, but if one of them intended to harm me or Rosita, it would be very easy for them. I intend to hire a full-time security detail to protect us. Remember who we are challenging. I do not trust that they will not resort to such things."

The assembled men concurred. It was late when their meeting finished. Felix was exhausted. He noticed Caesar at the side of the room speaking to a couple of the candidates. He signaled to Caesar to join him.

Caesar showed the other men out of the room before returning to sit with Felix.

"Caesar there is something I want to speak with you about. I am increasingly concerned about the safety of Rosita and me. As you heard me tell others, I am going to hire a security detail. I want you to run it. Please resign from the army and head it up. I have known you for years and believe you will be loyal and execute the role with dedication and determination. Will you accept my request?"

Caesar was shocked. He looked at Felix and waited a couple of minutes before responding.

"It would be an honor to serve you in that capacity. But what about my military career?"

"Caesar, I intend to win this election. You will have a future with me. I will personally compensate you with benefits from our family's private business. You will be hired by the company. Not only will you handle security for Rosita, Carmine, and me, but you will also manage all security for our companies. You will need to hire staff. I am sure there are some good military men you know. Do I have your answer?"

"Yes, I will accept this position with pride."

"I would like you to review the schedule for the upcoming rallies. We will be traveling into country areas and speaking at a venue in our largest city, Santa Flores. I am concerned about that particular location. It is where General Perez is from and he looks after his friends there very well. I suspect we will not have a friendly reception there."

"I suggest we send men the day before and check the venue. I see on the schedule it is two weeks away and the last speech before the election. You are right. For this rally, we need to be extra careful."

Caesar sat and looked at the calendar to the upcoming rallies.

"I see that the next rally is in the industrial city of Mendoza. That should be interesting. Most of the factories there are owned by Perez supporters. It could be a noisy rally."
"Yes, but many of those workers are unhappy with their lives. The

factories do not pay them well and the conditions are bad. Every year lives are lost due to the accidents that occur. It is somewhere where we can establish support."

"Felix, I will leave now. I am going to the military base. There are some men there I wish to speak with. If I can convince them, you will have an excellent security force."

Caesar left. Felix sat thinking of the challenge that lay ahead. There were only three more rallies before the day of the election. The more he thought of the reaction of the people at the past rallies and the obstacles ahead that he needed to overcome, his self-doubt grew.

As the hours wore on, the late afternoon sun-faded, and the room darkened. Felix sat alone thinking. Like the darkening of the day, Felix's mood sank. He reflected on the past year and questioned the decisions he had made.

"Felix, what are you doing sitting here alone in the dark? Is something wrong?"

Felix looked up at Rosita. In the dimly lit room, her appearance looked different. She seemed much older.

"No, Rosita. I am thinking of the past year. I am not convinced we will win this election. Perez has too many supporters embedded in almost every business and social group in the country. I do not. I had an ideal. I thought it was something worth striving for. I wanted to beat them at their games of corruption and worse. I now know I may have made a huge mistake. I am one person. I cannot defeat them alone."
"Felix, you must not speak like this. You are not defeated. You

have many supporters who want you to win and make the changes this country needs. I will not let you think this way. I am going to speak with Carmine. I have an idea."

"Please, Rosita. Accept that we have very little chance of winning. I am concerned about what will happen to us if we lose. Perez will exact revenge. We may need to flee the country."

Rosita stared coldly at Felix.

"Then we must not let him win."

Chapter 57

Caesar arranged to spend part of the night meeting with several officers at a bar located far from the barracks. It was a rough neighborhood in the dock area.

Two bare lightbulbs hung on long wires from the ceiling and flickered. Flies and other nocturnal bugs buzzed around the lights. The pungent smell of stale beer, rotting food, and human sweat filled the place. Sailors from the merchant ships drank heavily, played pool or darts, while some engaged in gambling or the arm-wrestling matches. It was an unfriendly place. Caesar had chosen it as he did not want the possibility of any other officer or soldier accidentally stumbling into the meeting he wished to hold. Dressed in civilian clothing, the officers easily passed as simple laborers. Upon entering the bar, the patrons had looked at them suspiciously but soon ignored them and returned to whatever game they were playing.

They sat at a dirty table. Caesar signaled the barmaid. She was a stocky woman in her early thirties. Caesar looked at her somewhat sad and hardened face. Her makeup reminded him of a skimmed coat of cement and her eyes were sunken in the abyss of the circles of black eyeliner. Artificially colored red hair rose in spikes from her scalp. She wore a bright and tight lemon-yellow t-shirt and jeans that were so tight, Caesar questioned how a human could even get them on. Caesar decided that he would avoid any possible actions on their part that may invoke this woman's wrath.

"Bring a pitcher of beer."

"Whad ya gonna drink from? No glasses here. You want pitchers then get one for each of ya. I'm not runnin around for youse guys all night."

Caesar decided to err on the side of caution.

"Yeah. Sounds good. Bring us a pitcher each."

"OK, pretty boy. Ya think I'm fuckin stupid. Seen guys like you before. Getcha money out first."

Caesar reached into his jacket and withdrew some bills. He laid them on the table and the barmaid snatched them within seconds.

"I'll getcha the beer now. No trouble from you guys or I'll crack ya fuckin heads open."

Caesar loved the hospitality of the place and started to laugh. It was the ideal setting to recruit his security team. The others joined in the laughter.

Caesar huddled with the others and discussed the need for Felix's security. Questions were asked. A couple of hours went by. Several more pitchers of beer were delivered to their table. Empty pitchers lined the table.

During a lull in the conversation, while his fellow officers considered the offer, three burly police entered the bar. They went to the tables of the sailors demanding identification. One of the cops looked at Caesar and his companions. He crossed over to them.

"Who are you guys? Looks to me like you don't belong here. Maybe you are the ones responsible for those murders up the street."

Caesar went to put his hand inside his jacket to pull out his military identification. The cop scared that a different scenario was about to unfold, grabbed Caesar's wrist, and twisted him to the floor. The others stood and the two other cops raced across the bar with their guns drawn.

"You idiots. I'm an officer. I was reaching for my ID. Let me go you baboon."

The cop twisted Caesar's arm further as he helped him to his feet. He wanted to inflict as much pain as was possible. No one was going to call him a baboon and get away with it. Slowly he released his grip on Caesar. The two other cops kept their guns trained on Caesar while he extracted his ID.

The cops asked for all of their IDs and examined them.

"I suggest you get out of here. There has been a gang fight and a number have been killed. Get out and leave now."

Caesar needed no further prompting. He gathered his papers, threw some additional money on the table, and with the others they quickly left the bar and headed to their cars.

It was late when Caesar pulled into the entrance of Villa Magnifico. The downstairs was fully lit. Caesar assumed that Felix would still be awake and working. He parked off to the side of the front stairs.

He found Felix sitting alone in the salon.

"Caesar. It is late. Is there something wrong?"

"No, in fact, it couldn't be better. All three of my officers are now your security team.”

“That is excellent. What will you need?”

“I wish to take the company’s private plane to Miami. I will need to purchase a few items there to equip the men. I would not trust anything purchased here. As you are aware, most communications are monitored by the government. I know the technology they use and will be able to procure devices that cannot be detected by their monitoring equipment.”

“When do you wish to leave?”

“If the plane can be readied, I will leave tomorrow.”

Felix thought for a while before responding.

“Caesar, I am tired. There has been a lot of pressure and travel since I announced my intent to create the demand for an election and then run as a candidate. I am concerned it has affected my relationship with Rosita. Please wait here as I will go and ask her if she would like to go to Miami with me for a short vacation. Tomorrow is Friday. I do not have any appointments. I would like to take Rosita and spend the weekend in Miami with her. We need time together away from here. Our next rally is in Mendoza and it appears there will be a large crowd. I need to rest a little and prepare.”

“Felix I think that is an excellent idea. I am sure Rosita will wish to go.”

Felix left the salon to find Rosita in her upstairs bedroom.

“Rosita, there is a need for Caesar to travel to Miami tomorrow. I would like you to come with me on a little weekend vacation. I promise that there will be no work. Just time for the two of us."

"I would like that. You must promise me you will take me shopping and to a famous restaurant."

Felix laughed.

"Rosita, you are making it so I cannot afford you."

Chapter 58

Felix and Rosita returned to La Iluminada refreshed after a leisurely weekend. That night, Felix retired to his office and prepared the speech he needed to make at Mendoza the next evening. All indications suggested it was going to be a larger gathering as that day was a national holiday and the rally was to be held in the huge sports stadium. Before the rally started, the crowds would have been watching an international football game. If the favorite team won, the mood would be festive.

While he and Rosita had been in Miami, several reporters had left messages for Felix. He scanned through the messages and was surprised to find some from reporters from the international press.

It was close to midnight when Felix joined Rosita in the salon.

"I feel like a drink. Will you join me?"

"Yes. I am not tired as the passions you unleashed in Miami are still arousing me."

Rosita stood and walked to Felix and embraced him tightly.

"I am going to Mendoza with you. I want to be there to support you. It is going to be one of the most important rallies. It is already in the news here with claims it will be the largest ever held in the country. You must win over the people. This rally will decide who wins this election."

"I think the people have seen enough of how Perez and his officials have hurt them and the country. My speech will discuss how life will be after we win."

Rosita felt a strong urge to have him at that moment.

"Felix, forget drinks. I have something more important in mind."
She wrapped her arm around Felix's waist and led hin up to their
shared bedroom. They were barely inside the room, when Rosita
aggressively kissed him, before pushing him back onto the bed. She
stood at the side of the bed with her arm stretched out and resting
on his chest.

"Wait for me. I will be back in a moment."

Felix smiled and relaxed on the bed. The door of the ensuite
bathroom opened. Rosita walked to the bed naked, except for the
diamond and ruby necklace around her neck. The rubies shone
against her tan colored skin and accentuated her red lips. A gift he
had bought her in Miami.

Rosita moved seductively toward him and fell onto the bed.

"Now I want you to show me how you intend to rule. A trial run
before the election."

They played out their passions for hours. Depleted and exhausted,
they succumbed into a deep sleep.

Felix awoke early and quietly crept from the room. He was excited.
He planned to spend the day preparing for the early evening rally.
The newspapers and news broadcasts covering his speeches were
favorable.

Before her return trip to Nos Grande, several magazines had

interviewed Rosita and published flattering articles, in which they dramatized her days in the barrio and her struggle to assist Felix with his goals. The public hung on every little reference to Rosita, whether it was a statement she made or events or places she attended. Rosita was becoming the idol of the masses.

In the kitchen, Felix was served coffee and pastry by a maid. He reached for the morning papers and left to read them in the salon and enjoy his breakfast. The newspapers were filled with articles speculating on the size of the crowds and interaction that may occur between Felix and Perez who planned to attend the rally. Mendoza was his home town, and Perez had looked after many friends there. The newspapers speculated that there would be friction.

Felix was engrossed in the papers and did not notice the arrival of Caesar.

"Good morning, Felix. This will be a big day. Today we will decide who will win this election. I hope you are relaxed and prepared for the rally tonight. Where is Rosita? There is a reporter outside who wishes to interview her."

"Rosita is still sleeping. Who is the reporter? Which newspaper does he represent? Is he friendly toward us?"

"I must correct you. It is not 'he', but a lady reporter. She writes one of those social columns in the paper. Her past articles have been favorable toward you and Rosita. I think it would be of value for Rosita to meet with her."

Felix considered this, before leaving to awaken Rosita.

"Tell her to come inside and wait. Have the staff serve her a coffee.

Fifteen minutes passed until Rosita joined them. She was dressed in a crisp white blouse and bright red capris, with a pair of ostentatious blue sandals that she had bought on the shopping trip with Carmine.

Felix watched as she graciously welcomed the woman to their home. He sat silently observing Rosita and listened as she spoke.

"Caesar, observe the way Rosita is speaking to the reporter. It is not the Rosita I know. There have been many times recently when I think I am watching and hearing a completely different person. The Rosita I know is young and gentle and does not seek power or prestige. I have mentioned this to her and she responds as the Rosita I know. I am confused by her actions."

"My friend, Felix. I did not want to say anything but I too have seen the changes of which you speak. I noticed that she was calm and happy with you during the weekend in Miami. It seems that when there are reporters or people who could hurt or damage her, she becomes a different personality. Is it possible she is not well? Last week I watched her berate one of your female staff. Her temper flared and the woman she was attacking was cowering in fear. You are right. Something has changed and she is presenting herself as a saint to the masses at the rallies. Since the last few rallies, Rosita is in demand to speak with different groups. Her popularity has grown tremendously. As a friend, I caution you to be careful. Something is not right."

Felix digested Caesar's words without comment. He had seen the changes and knew Caesar was correct and wondered what was causing Rosita to act so differently. The thought of drugs flashed through his mind, but he dismissed that idea. He decided it was time to consult privately with his trusted doctor before the situation worsened.

Chapter 59

Political Headquarters, La Iluminada.

In the drab grey monolithic building in the center of La Iluminada, General Perez sat at the head of the conference table. Around the table were his loyal staff. Generals and the politicians he had favored over the years. General Perez looked at the worried faces around the table before speaking.

"Gentlemen, we have a serious problem developing. I never believed that Felix de Santos would ever represent a risk to us. I was wrong. The public has become sympathetic toward him, but that is mainly because of the little speeches and articles that Rosita Valquez has given. She is the one who is putting us in danger of losing control. Our efforts to frustrate Felix de Santos have not worked, and in fact, may have created support for him. This evening, we have one last chance to stop him at the rally in Mendoza. I am asking any of you to present ideas that may disgrace him, but more importantly Rosita Valquez. I had asked some loyal friends to visit the mine and barrio of Nos Grande and look for anything damaging. They were able to produce some very damning information, and we even have a witness who was involved. I will ask my assistant to bring him in to address us."

There was a loud murmur as those around the table consulted and wondered what information had been found, and who the mystery person could be. The rear door of the conference room opened and assisted by a military guard a tall lanky man entered the room. No one recognized him. General Perez beamed and beckoned for the man to join him at the podium.

"My friends, let me present Father Lopez who was the parish priest of Nos Grande for many years. He intimately knew most of the villagers in the barrio, but none more so than Rosita Valquez. She prostituted herself to Father Lopez in return for a dress and special favors. To keep matters quiet, Father Loez was reassigned by the church and eventually quit the church. He has played an important role in helping us develop our mine at Nos Grande. It was his knowledge of the private matters for certain villagers that allowed us to expand the mine and keep the locals quiet. Father Lopez has damaging information on many. He threatened to use that information if any of them attempted to interfere with the mine.

Before the rally tonight at Mendoza, Father Lopez will be holding a press conference to dispel the beliefs many have about Rosita Valquez. He will discuss how he was raped, her continual lewd actions, and how she seduced other young boys in the barrio. We have one of those boys in our custody, but he is being a bit reluctant to speak. We are presently providing treatments that will make him speak soon.

Rumors are circulating in that barrio regarding a missing flamenco dancer and an older man Rosita Valquez was seen with. My men are investigating that situation.

By the time the rally starts tonight, we will have destroyed the aura that Rosita Valquez has created. We will damage her beyond redemption."

Around the table, the assembled men and single woman clapped and cheered. They knew General Perez would not let them down.

One of the older, distinguished politicians stood to ask General Perez a question.

"General, will you be in attendance at the Mendoza rally this evening?"

"Yes. Mendoza is my home town, and besides today is a national holiday which is being celebrated with the football matches at the stadium. I will attend and along with several of my officers and other friends here, we will be seated at the edge of the front row of the stands behind the podium. I will be there to present the cup to the winning football team. I suspect that Felix de Santos and Rosita Valquez will not wish to speak for too long after the news we will release after this meeting ends. I have retained a special reporter to help us. She is here now and it will be my pleasure to introduce Carmilla Vesco of VTV Live News. Carmilla has a personal interest and an old score to settle with Felix de Santos."

The door opened again and Carmilla entered. She was dressed to kill. All the heads at the table turned to take in her outer beauty.

"Good morning Gentlemen. It will be my pleasure to assist General Perez in telling the people about the corrupt and evil couple that Felix de Santos and Rosita Valquez are. Immediately following this meeting, my film crew will be recording my interview with Father Lopez. I am delighted that he has in his possession many photos as evidence. We will also be flying to Nos Grande to obtain interviews with villagers and some workers at the mine. You can be assured that this report will severely impact the plans of that couple."

"Miss Vasco, I will arrange for you and your crew to be flown by military helicopter to Nos Grande. The interviews and reporting you are about to undertake are of national importance. There must not be any delay. You must advise me of anything else you require."

There was polite applause for Carmilla as she finished and excused herself. As she was leaving the room she signaled Father Lopez to join her.

In the private room off the conference room, Carmilla threw her arms around Lopez's neck.

"It is up to you now. We have both Perez and Felix de Santos where we want them. Felix de Santos and Perez will no longer be a problem after tonight's rally. Our comrades and friends in the military and those hiding in the neighboring countries will soon be able to seize control of the country. It has taken us many years to infiltrate the military, the press, the government, and the banks. Our people have waited patiently. It is now their time."

"Carmilla, I have the photos of Rosita you had suggested. We found a woman who looks identical to her, but who in reality, is a porn star. For a few dollars and a large supply of drugs, she was only too willing to pose for us. The pictures are very revealing. You will see some in which I posed with her in my priest's cassock. Of course, I am exposed while she stages the acts on me. For reality, we armed her with a knife and a pistol. To those who see these, I am the 'victim'. Now let us return and show these to Perez. That ignorant pig won't know it isn't Rosita in the pictures."

Lopez chuckled to himself as they turned to leave the private room and rejoin the others. Both he and Carmilla were looking forward to the events of the evening ahead.

Carmila thrust the pile of photos into Perez's hand. He scanned them, nodded, and smiled. He had no idea what lay ahead.

Chapter 60

Velo Sports Stadium, Mendoza.

The stands of the stadium were packed. The crowd was boisterous and loud. They cheered and shouted as the commentators egged them on to cheer for their favorite team. The match between Chile and the Netherlands was fast and heated.

Children ran up and down the stairs of the aisles. Men drank beer and other beverages and waved flags of orange in support of the Netherland team. The roars erupted as the Netherlands scored time and again. The atmosphere within the stadium was carnival-like as they celebrated both the game and their national holiday.

It was late afternoon when the match ended with the Netherlands winning by a huge margin. The crowd went crazy. Instead of filing out of the stadium, more people were arriving to participate in the political rally and to hear Felix speak. The women hoped to see or hear Rosita speak.

While the crowd waited, stirring music was played through the sound system of the stadium. The locals shared tacos and arepas filled with seasoned meats and exotic spices. The men challenged each other with tales of bravado and the women compared babies and gossiped about other women.

The afternoon sky started to darken with the onset of the evening. The crowd was starting to become restless but was placated when a marching band filed onto the playing field playing arousing music. After the band finished, several of the country's famous singers performed.

There was a period of relative quietness while everyone awaited the arrival of the dignitaries.

Black sedans started to arrive at the stands that had been erected on the playing field. General Perez and his party took their positions in designated seats. More cars arrived and politicians and other prominent citizens soon filled the stands. The party of Felix de Santos and Rosita had not arrived. The crowd was impatient and started chanting for Felix and Rosita. Perez looked into the stands with contempt. He had no time for these low-class mortals. He decided he would deal with them when re-elected. They would soon come to respect him.

Excitement rippled through the crowd when Felix and Rosita walked out from the team entrances below the spectator stands and walked across to the playing field toward the podium and guest seating. As they walked, they waved to the crowd. Every so often, Rosita would stop and turn to face different parts of the stadium and blow air kisses. The crowd loved her theatrics.

A discreet distance behind them, Caesar and his new security team followed all the time scanning for any potential trouble. The couple was halfway across the playing field when Caesar observed a poorly dressed woman running at speed towards them.

Caesar shouted to Felix to run, while he sprinted to intercept the woman. Rosita observed the situation and held up her hand and called to Caesar to stop. The woman slowed, yet still proceeded toward Rosita.

"Madame, I need help. I have nothing. I have nowhere to go. My baby is starving. Please help me. You are a kind person."

Rosita studied the woman in front of her. Dirty black streaks marked her porcelain white face. Her clothing was worn and the grey dress had small tears. The front of her dress was open and she held a small baby to her breast. Rosita felt compassion build within her. She went to the woman and embraced her.

"Felix, can we help this woman? What should I do?"

Felix motioned to Caesar to send one of the other security guards to help.

"Please take this woman back into the office inside the stadium. We will return there after the speeches."

A silence had befallen the stands as the crowds watched on.

Caesar was not happy. He thought of the hostilities that Perez and his cronies had created. He did not believe that Felix or Rosita was safe.

The couple and their small security entourage continued toward the podium. Felix looked into the seated guests and saw Perez sitting at the end of the first row of seats. He gave a small wave of acknowledgment before walking up the stairs of the lectern to address the crowd.

The crowd roared its approval when Felix reached the top and waved to the masses. He launched into his speech, but lead into it in an unplanned way.

"Patriots of this country. My friends. I had a speech prepared to deliver and once again tell you how bad things are in our land for the good hardworking men and women. I don't need to tell you all that again. You all saw it tonight when that poor woman rushed out to us in distress. She is an example of the suffering that is happening to many. I don't need to explain hunger or the inability to live in a decent home. These past rulers have raped our land and the fruits of your labors are in the hands of a few wealthy and other foreign interests. I will change that.

I know that many of you would like to hear my dear Rosita speak."

Felix turned to Rosita and waved her to join him on the podium. Rosita slowly arose and started to walk to the stairs. Felix extended his arm and escorted her up the narrow wooden stairs.

The crowd went wild. For five minutes the sound of cheering and whistling continued.

Rosita moved to the microphone.

"Thank you all. As Felix has said, it is time to stop the injustice. I will personally help to arrange programs to help the unfortunate and those in need. There is no need for poverty. We live in a country that is blessed with resources. We have oil, gold, crops, and other wealth."

Rosita continued to extol the beauty and strength of the country and all she would do as Felix's partner should they be elected. She finished her speech to a roar of approval.

Rosita looked across to the spectator stands and observed a small girl walking to the podium with a large bouquet. She stepped down from the podium and started to walk toward the girl. Caesar shouted to her loudly.

"Who is she? Who are those flowers from? This was not discussed or in the program. I want….."

Caesar's sentence remained unfinished.

There was a bright flash and deafening explosion as the little girl lifted the flowers to present to Rosita and the radio-controlled bomb exploded. The complete stadium shook from the blast. Smoke and dust enveloped the guest's stand. The wooden seating, chairs, and lumber flew into the air. Rosita's mangled body was thrown into the air and landed at the stairs leading up to the guest seating. Felix was blown from the podium and lay twisted in a pool of blood. Perez was surrounded by his guards and dragged out from under the splintered timber from the stands. Body parts from the flower girl lay strewn around the field. Screams rose from the now panicked crowd. Dense grey smoke quickly filled the stadium.

 The national holiday was over.

Sirens wailed as soldiers and emergency personnel rushed across the playing field to the pile of debris that had been the guest seating area.

Sheltered in the tunnel that led from the playing field to the locker rooms, Lopez and Carmilla watched the pandemonium. They had never intended to make the trip to Nos Grande that Carmilla had promised Perez.

"Carmilla, now our revolution has started. The others will be performing other disruptions. Perez will fall. Felix and Rosita are finished. The country will belong to our comrades. We will win."

Chapter 61

In the emergency department of the hospital, the doctors slaved feverishly to save the badly injured Rosita and Felix.

Felix had been standing beside Rosita when the bomb exploded and had been partially shielded. His body was burned and laced with shrapnel, but the most serious injury was the loss of his right arm. It had been severed at his shoulder.

In the extensive care unit, doctors worked in an attempt to stabilize the critically injured Rosita. The blast had impacted her stomach and chest area. Her hair and face were burned, and shrapnel had penetrated her scalp. X-rays showed a piece of metal barely penetrating her brain. The prognosis for recovery was poor.

News of the bombing spread quickly throughout the country. Those loyal to Perez disavowed any involvement and threatened revenge on those responsible. Accusations were made by neighboring countries and the United States, claiming it was a plot by Perez to kill Felix and Rosita.

In the streets of the cities, a swell of anger developed. Rosita's admirers and supporters were angry. Protests were held and wide-ranging strikes crippled the country. Perez's ruling party attempted to quell the protests, which only led to violent riots. The country was in turmoil. Buildings, cars, trains, and shipping docks were set on fire. Anyone or anything associated with Perez was attacked. The country had descended into a civil war.

Lopez and Carmilla Vesco remained silent throughout the upheaval. The events were all they had hoped for. They met with other terrorists and plotted the next moves. It seemed that the task of seizing control would be easy. The masses were leaderless and refused to accept the authority of Perez.

The weeks turned into months and the civil unrest continued. Felix recovered and attempted to resume his life. Rosita remained in the hospital receiving treatments. Her progress was slow. The injuries to her face and body healed, but the brain injury had resulted in a loss of memory and affected her ability to function.

At Villa Magnifico, Felix continued to recuperate. The atmosphere at the villa was subdued. Carmine and the staff missed Rosita and their expressions displayed the sorrow and sadness. Caesar had moved into the Villa to assist Felix. He was a changed man after the attack.

Felix was reading an account of uprisings in the countryside when Caesar joined him.

"Felix, I have just received a call from the hospital. The doctors have decided that Rosita is well enough to return home. That is great news. I will prepare to drive you there."

"Caesar, I am worried. I do not know how she will react. I am not the same man. I am partly disabled and not the young healthy officer she fell in love with. I am concerned she will reject me."

'You are worrying too much. I must caution you. The doctors have indicated that Rosita may act differently than before. They have been unable to perform the surgery to completely remove the metal splinter from her brain. They have contacted some of the leading neurosurgeons in the world. The operation cannot be performed here, and she will likely need to travel to Colombia or Switzerland for the procedure to be performed. Before we can remove her from their care, the doctors wish to meet and discuss signs to look for and treatments that can be administered here at the villa. I think it would be a good idea to take Carmine with us to that meeting. You will need help in caring for Rosita and I may not always be here when she requires assistance."

"I agree with you. Carmine is strong, but this has disturbed her greatly. I think it will help her to be involved in looking after Rosita. Please find her and ask her to come back here with you. We need to plan this carefully as I am sure Rosita would resist efforts to care for her. I fear she will attempt to pretend all is fine and live the life we had before the explosion. She will be weak and with that brain injury, she will need to be kept calm. When she learns of the massacres and violence throughout the country, I suspect she will try to get involved. The masses are still shouting out her name at the riots. They want her. I am pleased that the full extent of her injuries has not been released."

Caesar excused himself and left on his mission to find Carmine in the sprawling villa. He found Carmine sitting alone on an antique bench in the garden. As he approached her, he realized that she was weeping. He placed his hand on her back and caressed her.

"Carmine, cheer up. We have some good news. Rosita is coming home today. Felix has asked me to escort you back inside the villa as we need to discuss how to look after her."

"Caesar, my life is a mess. It doesn't matter that our family is wealthy. I lost my husband and now Felix is hurt. The country has gone crazy and I blame Felix. If he hadn't started that effort to replace Perez, then none of this would be happening. There are riots between men who were formerly friends. Families are torn apart.

The cities are filled with crime. Things are worse now than they ever were under Perez. I don't think Felix and his friends will be able to fix it. I am not sure I wish to stay here any longer. I may move to Europe away from all of this."

"Carmine, don't give up. Felix is strong in his mind. He is watching events closely and I hear him speaking of plans with others. You must have faith. Now, come with me. I know that Felix is eager to bring Rosita home."

Caesar waited patiently while Carmine left to freshen up before the drive to the hospital. She returned to find Caesar standing with an impatient Felix.

"Let us go. I am anxious to bring her home. Caesar, are you taking one of the cars we bought for the security team? I would feel safer if we used one of those cars, as our private cars are well known and we may be stopped."

"Felix, I am way ahead of you. The car is prepared and waiting. As a precaution, I have had guns placed inside for our protection. I will drive to the hospital using a route that runs behind the city and should be quiet at this time."

The trio left the villa and drove through the outskirts of the city and then looped back into the city where the hospital was located. On the sidewalks, groups of people with hand-scrawled posters stood in protest. Felix attempted to read the posters as they sped by.

As they turned onto the road leading to the hospital entrance, Felix gasped as he read the messages. There were several different messages, but each called for revenge for the bombing and injury to Felix and Rosita. The posters blamed Perez and his ruling party for the crisis and demanded retribution. Others called for Rosita to lead the country.

"Caesar, we are at a point of civil war. The masses are angry. I fear that the rioting will lead to Perez taking actions to suppress the uprising. I need to convince him to step aside for the good of the country. I have given this situation a lot of thought. I have a proposal to make to him. He and his crooked friends have established relationships with dictators and other criminals in foreign countries. I will convince him that if he steps down from the leadership, we will grant him safe passage from the country and never pursue him or the others complicit with his regime. I will announce this to the people. I suspect that Perez will wish to leave as he has lost control of the country and the masses."

"Felix, that is a huge risk. If he refuses, civil war will certainly happen. I suggest you satisfy the people of your intention to lead and assure them that Rosita will assist. I hope she will be able to help and her injuries will not prevent that. She has won over their hearts and would be a strong influence."

Felix sat quietly in the back of the car and thought of a plan to convince Perez to yield power. He was still deep in thought when the car stopped at the entrance stairs to the hospital.

Chapter 62

The doctors greeted Felix and Caesar and ushered them into an office. The hospital was busy with staff running in the corridors to attend to casualties of people injured in the riots. Felix disliked the hospital and its septic atmosphere.

"Doctors, what is Rosita's situation. Will she recover? Are there any effects she will suffer from brain injury? Will she be able to function normally?"

"We cannot perform the surgery to completely remove all the shrapnel. She still has a minute shard embedded in her brain. It does not seem to be affecting her in any way. We are surprised by this. We have assessed her cognitive and functioning skills and the results indicate that except for slight delays in her motor skills, she is fine. Until some more time passes and she heals, you can expect some differences in how she handles situations. She is going to need a lot of rest in the next few weeks. I advise you to monitor her carefully. The operation that is needed to remove the fragment cannot be performed here. I have written to the specialists in neurosurgery in New York and Switzerland and provided a complete dossier of her injuries. Further surgery that can only be performed by them may it become necessary."

"Is there anything special I will need to do? Will she need any medications?"

"No. The wounds on her face and scalp will heal naturally. The area of the incision into her skull is bandaged and she will need the dressings changed every day. I will arrange for a nurse to assist. The nurse will also observe any indication of infection."

The doctors continued to discuss her situation with Felix, though he was feeling nauseous and wanted to leave the hospital without any delay.

"Is it possible for us to hire a nurse to attend to Rosita during this sensitive time. I fear that while we will try the best, our efforts may overlook some crucial aspects of the needed care".
The doctors considered Felix's request.

"Yes, I do believe there is a nurse who will help. She is older and retired from the hospital last week, but still wishes to work. I will call ner. Her name is Juliana Gomez. She is a true professional. In my opinion, she should have been a doctor. Many times she advised us."

Felix nodded appreciation and acceptance of the doctor's advice.

"I am still not well. I will wait in the lobby until Rosita is brought down from her ward to take the trip back to the Villa Magnifico."

Felix waited sometime before a stern-looking nurse. The nurse stopped and introduced herself.

"I am pleased to meet you, Felix de Santos. I have heard much regarding you. My name is Juliana Gomez. I understand you wish to employ my nursing services."

"It would be a great help. As you can see, I too suffered some injuries that are making it difficult for me."

"I have been told of your injuries. Rosita will not be returning with you. She needs special treatments that can only be administered here at the hospital. It will be several days, or maybe a week or more before she can return home.”

“Are you prepared to come and help her? We will pay you well. My Rosita must recover. To me, she is the very reason I live.”

“I am quite aware of the deep bond of affection between the two of you. I have watched the rallies on television. She is very popular. She is a very strong woman for such a young person. I admire her, so yes it will be my pleasure to nurse her and help her back to health.”

Caesar had been standing and observing the interaction. He was initially curious about Nurse Juliana Gomez, but after observing her he decided she was not a threat to Felix or the household.

“Colonel, there is no purpose for you to stay here at the hospital.”

“But, nurse, we were contacted to come and take her home.”

“Colonel Felix de Santos, if you wish to use my services, then you will adhere to the treatments and advice I give. She is to stay here, and when I feel she can be moved, we will contact you. Now, goodbye as I have other patients to attend to.”

Caesar smiled watching Felix receiving the lecture.

“Now, please leave. I need to spend time with my patient and not waste it on the frivolous conversation with you. I will arrange contact when the doctors and I agree it is an appropriate time for her to go home. Goodbye. I will keep in contact and you will be informed of her progress.”

Chapter 63

It was another 2 weeks before Rosita was able to return to Villa Magnifico. The staff were pleased to have her return but were greatly concerned for her well being.

Felix had often been away from the Villa at medical appointments as the doctors worked on fitting him with a prosthetic arm and assisting in training him on its use.

During the next four weeks, the atmosphere at the Villa became somber. Carmine seemed distant and no longer interested in the daily affairs of the staff and her social life. Visitors to the Villa had dwindled.

The presence of Nurse Juliana Gomez created nervousness amongst the maids, who were unaccustomed to being ordered about. The nurse had managed to alienate almost everyone in the short period she had been at the house. Enzo had observed the nurse's behavior and decided to discuss the problems she was creating with Carmine that evening. He was deciding how to present the issue when he heard the front door open and Felix and Caesar enter. They were loud and laughing. Enzo was pleased. It was the first joviality in the Villa in weeks. Enzo walked quickly to greet them.

"Felix, I am happy to see you in such fine spirits. May I ask why? It has been many weeks since we had laughter in this house and we need it."

Caesar and Felix howled with laughter and tears streamed down their faces. Felix pulled off his coat and good-naturedly lunged toward Enzo while brandishing his new arm. Enzo recoiled in shock but soon joined in as they joked about Felix's new superpowers. They did not notice Carmine descending the stairs as they joked.

"What is going on here? I heard you all from my room upstairs. It seems you are having fun. Why? We have had to deal with too many terrible things recently."

Felix pushed his arm out to Carmine with the pride of a young boy with a new toy train.

"Mother, please be calm. Look. I have my new arm now. I can do things with it that are amazing. I am happy that the procedures went well and with this result."

Carmine looked at the arm and gloved hand.

"It is not the same, Felix. I much preferred you before that bombing."

"Mother, how is Rosita?"

"She is becoming impossible. She will not rest. Today she watched the news and was angry with the demonstrations. Felix, please be careful. The mobs in the streets are violent. They want Perez gone. The farmers and rural villagers are demanding you and Rosita take control. This worries me. Perez will not give up power easily."

"There is no way for Rosita to appear with me in public. She needs to recover. I will speak to her about this."

The conversation fell awkwardly silent as each thought of the severe situation in the country. Enzo seized the opportunity.

"May I please speak candidly to you Carmine? I believe that Felix should also hear what I have to say. There is great discontent in the house amongst the staff. The nurse, Juliana Gomez is creating much unhappiness."

Felix listened intently as Enzo described the situation.

"Caesar, please summon the nurse and drive her away from our Villa. Her services are dismissed."

Neither Felix nor Caesar were aware that Nurse Juliana was spying for Perez and his gang.

Caesar left to climb the stairs to the nurses' private room. He stood in the hallway and knocked loudly on the door. There was a rustling inside the room and finally, Nurse Gomez called.

"Who is there. I will be a minute."

Caesar stood and listened. He heard objects being moved. He knocked again. Finally, Nurse Gomez answered.

"Good evening Caesar. How are you? Can I help with something?"

"Yes. I need to speak with you. May I enter?"

"Please, but I was about to prepare for bed. Is it that important? Maybe we can speak in the morning."

Caesar gently pushed his way into the room. He looks around and noticed maps and handwritten sheets of paper on the bed. Nurse Juliana's eyes followed Caesar's to the bed.

"That is nothing. I am planning a trip with my sister when I am finished here and hopefully, the demonstrations in the country have ended."

Caesar walked over to the bed and looked down. He was startled to see the maps were of the villages and stadiums that Felix and Rosita had planned to hold future rallies. He spun and looked at the nurse.

"What are these? Why do you have these maps? These are not places anyone goes to take a holiday. What are you up yo?"

"Rosita had told me of the plans for her and Felix to visit and speak at these locations. I would need to travel with Rosita to ensure her health remains stable after the terrible incident."

"Nurse Juliana, that won't be necessary. I have instructions from Felix de Santos to advise you that your services are no longer required and I am to drive you tonight to where you would like to be taken."

The nurse scowled at Caesar and moved back toward the bed. Caesar quickly scanned it for any weapon. He did not notice the sounds behind him until the door slammed and he turned to find Rosita standing there dressed in a long white nightdress.

Rosita spoke. She felt the cold fury building within her.

"Caesar, she is lying. I never told her of our plans. She has been creating many problems. I suspected her of attempting to disrupt our plans a while ago. She must leave here now. She is planning something bad."

The nurse ran toward Caesar and attempted to smash a glass pitcher in his face. Caesar was too fast and delivered a powerful karate chop to her neck. The nurse crumpled like a deflated balloon to the floor.

"Caesar, I am well enough to drive. Help me get her into a car. I will deal with this now."

Caesar was surprised. He had not anticipated Rosita's arrival, nor her strength. He went to object but Rosita quickly silenced him.

"Caesar, if you wish to be a part of our plan you will help me with this. Go now and bring a car to the entrance and then come back to help me carry her down to the car"

Realizing he was not in control, Caesar left to perform the task.

With Caesar gone from the room, Rosita examined the collection of drugs and syringes on the nurse's bedroom table. She took a small bottle and filled a large syringe with a steroid she had been prescribed at the hospital then stabbed it into the unconscious nurse's neck. The nurse's breathing became shallow. Minutes passed before Caesar rejoined her.

"Get this bitch to the car. I will personally deliver her back to the hospital. You will stay here and guard Felix."

Caesar bent and picked up the nurse. For her size, she was amazingly light. On his way down the stairs, with the nurse over his shoulder, he was stopped by Felix.

"Caesar, what has happened? Is she not well?"

"Felix, the news of her dismissal was too much. She attempted to attack me with an object. I needed to stop her. I am taking her to the car. We will be driving her back to the hospital and reporting this incident."

Caesar had no sooner finished speaking when Rosita joined them. She had changed from her nightdress into jeans and an old gardening jacket.

"Caesar and Felix I am going to drive her. Caesar, please wit with Felix until I return. The hospital can have this despicable woman back."

Felix was concerned. He did not want Rosita to drive.

"Rosita, you are still recovering. Please let Caesar drive her."

"No. Besides I am tired of being trapped inside the Villa every day. It will do me good."

Felix shrugged. He knew there was no [point in arguing with Rosita. He had experienced this stubbornness before.

Caesar continued out the front door and heaved the inert form of the nurse onto the rear seat of the car.

Rosita gently kissed Felix on the cheek and then quickly ran from the room to the car. Moments later the car sped away from the house.

Chapter 64

Rosita had learned a lot about La Luminada. She knew where the affluent areas were and also the run-down slums where the drug addicts and homeless lived on the streets.

She drove away from the direction of the hospital. Her mind had been made up for her by the internal fury that had been building. She had hated the nurse. It was time for sweet revenge.

She turned the car into a narrow street. Buildings either side were spray-painted with graffiti and crude messages. She laughed at one particular message directed at General Perez. What it suggested was humanly impossible.

After turning another corner Rosita drove slowly past the drug addicts and drunks lying on the ground or propped up against the grimy walls of the decrepit buildings. The area was hell on earth.

Rosita slowed as two men approached her begging for money. She stopped the car and examined their features. Both men may have been in their thirties but the faces were ravaged by drugs and the effects of living on the street. Both had long filthy beards. Food and dirt were caked in the beards. Their clothes were torn and their skin was grey with dirt.

She cracked open the driver's window and recoiled as one of the men spoke to her and his foul breath entered the car.

"If you help me, I will give you money. Lots of money."

This excited the men. They were eager to get money for their next hit of drugs.

"Help me take this woman in my car and make her disappear."

The men raced to the car's rear door and pulled it open. They then dragged the nurse's lifeless body out and back into a dark and dirty doorway.

One of the men returned to the car for the money. He snatched it from Rosita's hand, while the other drug-crazed man pulled his ragged trousers down and engaged in necrophilia with the nurse. Rosita watched but was appalled at their depravity. The man who had taken the money returned to his friend and started urinating on the dead nurse.

Rosita had seen enough. She revved the car and sped from the scene narrowly missing several of the derelicts.

After fleeing the area, Rosita smiled to herself. The authorities would never be able to trace the events back to Rosita. The injection in the neck, the fact that she had been sexually violated. The police would assume that the 'good nurse' had gone into the drug zone in an attempt to help the addicts and met her fate there.

Rosita was pleased and hummed a folksong she had learned in the barrio as a little girl. She surprised herself as she had never sung or hummed that song since she left the barrio but it was fresh and strong in her mind. She thought it strange but dismissed it, yet wondered about the recent memories that raced through her mind since the bombing. She wondered whether the injury to her brain was causing frequent flashbacks.

As she drove back to the Villa, Rosita read the many messages scrawled on the walls and sides of buildings. She passed the shells of burned-out cars that had been torched during the street demonstrations. The streets were littered with rocks and pieces of wood some of which still had protest messages on cardboard affixed to them.

She was close to the villa when she read a particular message that had been freshly painted across a billboard advertising underwear. The message was an appeal to Felix and her to try to end the unrest and take control of the country. Rosita stopped the car to read the long message beneath the large headline. As she read, she felt a pang of sadness and recalled past days when the country had been happy. The message generated a resolve in her to convince Felix to take a more active role in rising to power. His medical treatments were now complete and Rosita felt well enough to accompany him in addressing political rallies. She was determined that they would win an election and be in power.

It was dusk when Rosita turned into the driveway of the Villa. Already the lights on the lower floor had been switched on. She felt relief and comfort on entering the grounds. This was now her home.

Upon entering, she found Felix and Caesar sitting in the large living area. They had the maps and papers from the nurse's room spread out on the floor in front of them.

"Felix. What are you doing?"

"Rosita, this is interesting. These notes, and this map, document the discussions we had held about conducting a series of rallies in villages and the other cities. It seems Nurse Juliana had more than one purpose here. She was spying on us. Did you return her to the hospital?"

"No. She wanted me to leave her in the city. I left her at the Plaza del Toro. She claimed she would need some clothing and supplies. I was glad to see the end of her. Tonight I would like for us to dine out. Caesar must join us. There are things I want to discuss. It is important."

Felix looked at Caesar who shrugged and accepted her wish. Felix agreed and excused himself as he wished to change into a more casual outfit for the evening.

An hour later, they were seated in the upscale La Pegaso restaurant. Many of the wealthy patrons recognized Rosita and Felix as they had entered.

Felix ordered a fine Chilean wine which they shared before ordering.

"Rosita you must tell us why you wanted to dine out this evening. Our chef at the Villa could have prepared us an exquisite meal."

"I am concerned that some of the staff may be listening too closely to our plans and betraying us. I have decided that it is time for us to commence our campaign. General Perez and his group have been weakened. If you read the protest graffiti and listen to the radio, you will hear the voice of the people. It is now we must move. Are you prepared to do this?"

"I am more than ready. I will call a meeting of our supporters and we will start the process."

Caesar smiled. It was now his chance to settle some scores with old enemies. He was silently looking forward to the days ahead.

The waiter fussed over them and made some recommendations for the specialties. Rosita ordered the roast pheasant and both Caesar and Felix ordered Filet Mignons with fresh vegetables.

Over dinner, they laid out the plans for the days ahead. Caesar insisted on a publicity campaign that would tell the people that Felix and Rosita had heard them and were taking up the cause. He wanted to advertise locations of future rallies.

They left the restaurant with an agreed plan. Their spirits were high. Rosita felt the inner spirit of her evil relax in quiet satisfaction. Her plans were unfolding in the way she had plotted.

It was early when they returned to the Villa. Felix decided to call several of the key supporters of his campaign and arranged a meeting for the following day. He had started a journey from which there would be no turning back.

Chapter 65

Felix busied himself the following week with meetings, press interviews, and local appearances. At each event, the attendance increased and more of the attendees called for a speech from Rosita. Finally, Felix and his advisers decided to make Rosita available. Speeches were written and rehearsed.

When they were alone, Felix took her into his confidence. "Rosita, this Saturday afternoon we will be speaking at Xavier Fuentes sports arena. I am concerned. Will you be alright? I am worried that the bombing we experienced may cause you to relapse. I will go and speak. If the crowds call for you, I'll explain that you are still suffering from the attempted assassination."

"No, I will be fine. I have always believed you will become the leader of our country. I will be there by your side and help you. The time is right for us. The people of the country are with us and want this change."

"To me, you are more important than my political aspirations. I will abandon all for you. My love of you has grown since that attack. Our lives together are more important. We have money and can live a good life here. I don't want to create a situation where we are in danger again."

"Felix, I have ideas and the people will not allow any efforts to hurt us. I will win their hearts and souls."

He looked at her and observed the quiet strength he had first detected when he had met here at the barrio Nos Grande.

Felix walked over to her and wrapped his arms around her. It was the first time he had felt any intimacy since the attempted assassination. He was embarrassed and pulled his prosthetic arm back from the embrace. This seemed to excite her and she reached up and ripped open his shirt. She sank her hands into the thick black hair on his chest and swooned as she felt his private member stiffen as she stroked him. Panting like an animal she fell back onto the old chaise lounge and dragged him down. There was unbridled passion and after some length of time, they both lay exhausted.

"My dear Felix that is the passion I will bring to your efforts to be elected the leader of our country. You will not regret my involvement."

Felix attempted to ease himself from the chaise but found his head swimming. He was experiencing a strange form of tiredness. Slowly he lay back down and within minutes was in a heavy sleep. As he snored loudly, Rosita arose and crossed over the room and removed the scotch glass she had spiked and offered him. She wanted no intruders as she moved to arrange her next conquest.

In her room, she picked up the phone and dialed the number to connect with the organizers of the campaign.

"Hello, Sergio. I have just spoken with Felix and he agrees that I should provide an interview with the people and especially the women. Felix is not here this evening, he had some personal family business to attend to. Is it possible to do the interview tonight?"

"Madam Rosita. This is very short notice. I will contact the paper and TV newsgroups who are friendly to our efforts. I will call you back."

Twenty minutes later, the phone shrilled. Rosita answered it calmly.

"Rosita they can do a short interview. The paper is interested and hopes to be able to print the interview in the morning paper. Readers of *'The Golden Dawn'* will be in for a surprise and treat. Is it possible for you to come here to our headquarters? It will make the logistics of the interviews easier to manage."

"I will be there within thirty minutes."

Rosita went to her room and applied makeup and dressed in plain clothing. She did not want to create an image of privilege or wealth. Afterall her appeal was to the masses and the common woman who would never possess the luxurious clothing she owned. She decided that image and humility were essential in presenting herself for their acceptance.

She called Enzo to drive her and before leaving the house she checked on Felix. He was in a deep sleep. The drugs would likely keep him sleeping until mid-morning.

Rosita met Enzo at the base of the front stairs. He was dressed casually and seemed to be ill at ease.

"Miss Rosita, I have a personal favor to ask. I have a lady friend who lives close to the office you will be in. I would like to visit her while you are being interviewed. She is an old family friend and may be able to help you and Felix. Her husband died serving our country. She has no love of General Perez."

"That is fine. I expect the interview to only take an hour. Please do not be longer than that. I am concerned about Felix and wish to return as soon as the interview is over."

"I will be no more than one hour."

They drove the rest of the trip in silence. Enzo found it suspicious that Felix was sleeping and had allowed Rosita to take the interviews in his absence. He glanced in the rear vision mirror and examined her. She had an expression on her face that portrayed someone whose mind was far away. Enzo drove on in silence, leaving Rosita to her private thoughts.

When they arrived at the rented campaign offices, Enzo noticed three TV reporting vans and several press cars. He was surprised. This was going to be a larger event that he had envisaged. He turned to Rosita.

"I think I will stay with you. I will see my friend another time. I wish to stay with you as it seems this press conference is going to be much larger than you initially thought. I will be here in case we need to leave quickly."

Enzo jumped from the driver's seat and ran to open the rear door for Rosita. Reporters swarmed the car. Cameras flashed and questions were shouted. Rosita stopped and turned to face them. She held up her hand.

"Gentlemen. I will give you an interview after the TV session. Please be patient."

Rosita turned and walked in the entrance to the old office building. The reporters followed her in a tight bunch like bees in pursuit of the queen bee.

Chapter 66

Inside the offices, a makeshift TV studio had been hastily erected. Two chairs were arranged behind a low table with a vase of flowers and a pitcher of water and glasses. Rosita glanced at the setup. It was not ostentatious.

A young TV journalist came forward to meet her.

"Good evening. My name is Claudio Sanchez. I am the host of *"Our Daily Lives"*, the daily program of events that shape our lives. I have heard so much about you. It is indeed my pleasure to meet and interview you."

Rosita politely replied and took her chair behind the table. She watched as the cameramen gave the signals for the countdown before the live cameras were rolling.

"Good evening, Rosita Valquez. It is a pleasure to have you here this evening. I was hoping that your partner, Felix de Santos would be joining us for this interview."

"I am sorry but Felix is resting. As many of your viewers know, Felix suffered significant injuries during the recent attempt to assassinate us. Besides, my address tonight is for the women of our country, whether they are in the countryside or those who work in our bustling cities. We are all women and deserve the same respect and assistance from our government. It is time for the Generals and their puppets to move away and allow women to be represented and a voice in running our country. For too long we have been quiet. I say 'No More'. It is now we have the opportunity to make a change. My partner, Felix de Santos will ensure that women are treated

fairly in the new government he will form very soon………..”
Rosita continued on the interview for another thirty minutes. At the
end of the interview, she provided the viewers with the dates and
locations of the rallies that she and Felix would attend.

Claudio, the host approached Rosita.

“That speech you gave was amazing and has aroused a lot of
support. My studio reports they have been overwhelmed with calls.
I am requesting another interview with you soon.”

“It will be my pleasure, but I must go now as I had promised the
reporters another interview.”

Rosita left the makeshift studio and stoped beside the car to answer
the reporter's questions. The mood was friendly. Rosita described in
detail her ideas for improved social programs for the poor. She took
the time to think before answering any of the questions. She was
fair with the reporters. They loved her. She made a deliberate effort
to remember each reporter's name, recognizing she would need their
support for her plans.

Back at the Villa, Felix was still in a deep drugged sleep. Rosita
went to the bar and poured herself a brandy before settling down to
watch the evening news.

The screen burst into colorful graphics before fading into the
background. Sitting at the newsdesk was Claudio Sanchez and to
his right a woman that Rosita despised. It was the TV reporter from
VTV, Carmilla Vesco. Rosita scowled. She immediately realized
that she had been set up.

Claudio welcomed Carmilla to the program, before asking the

opening question.

"Good evening, Carmilla. You have heard the interview with Rosita Valquez. I understand that the two of you have very different opinions. What is your reaction to the interview Rosita gave this evening?"

"Claudio, that woman is delusional. There is no possibility that the women of this country will fall for her false words. She is Felix de Santos' little whore. She came from the barrio where the residents say she was involved in many questionable acts, including seducing the barrio's priest. There are reports of confrontations with other women and girls in the barrio. I visited Nos Grande to verify the claims. I spoke with men in the barrio and visited the hard-working men at the local mine. They all were reluctant to discuss her, but those that did had stories of a very corrupt and evil person. I implore the women of our country to be careful. Do not accept the lies of Rosita Valquez."

"That is some statement. Are you sure that you were not misled?"

"Claudio, that bombing at the stadium is an indication of the deep hatred that exists amongst people who are frustrated with Rosita and Felix de Santos and want them silenced."

"Carmilla, she has a huge following of supporters. That many can't be fooled by her."

"Claudio, look at who those 'followers' are. They are poor uneducated souls. They cling to her in the hope that they will receive some kind of handout. They are not intelligent people who will contribute to the development of our country. Felix de Santos and the de Santos family and businesses have succeeded on the backs of the people for years. Felix de Santos is a fraud."

"I must disagree with you there. I have spoken with officers and soldiers in our military. They have the highest regard for Felix. The family has supported shelters and has financed programs to help the less fortunate."

Rosita fumed as she watched the show, but relaxed and felt relief when Claudio Sanchez confronted the comments that Carmilla Vesco was making. Carmilla had set out to influence the direction of the program, but Claudio had taken firm control. The frustration showed in Carmilla's actions and comments. Her doll-like face slipped to that of a scowling and vengeful woman.

The program format changed to the part where viewers called in their comments. There was no shortage of callers to tonight's program. All were overwhelmingly in support of Rosita.

The show reached its conclusion.

"Carmilla, I must thank you for appearing tonight and sharing a different view."

"You are welcome, but again I advise the viewers to reject Rosita Valquez and Felix de Santos in their bid for leadership of our country."

The screen flashed the logos of the station, before the filling with advertisements for cat food.

Rosita flipped off the TV. She looked over at the sleeping Felix before pouring another scotch.

Chapter 67

In the morning, Rosita returned to find Felix still asleep. She shook him awake. He barely awoke and had difficulty sitting up.

"Good morning. You have been asleep for hours. A lot has happened while you were sleeping."

Felix seemed to be having trouble focusing on the conversation. Rosita wondered whether the amount of Zolpidem she had given him had caused permanent damage. She had stolen the Zolpidem from the nurse's room before she had killed her. It had been prescribed for her while she was in the hospital to help her sleep and erase her memory of the trauma she had experienced with the bomb blast. She had been warned that a side effect was a loss of memory. It was the ideal drug for her to use on Felix and maneuver her way into power as he weakened.

Felix blinked himself awake. He felt ill and disoriented.

"Rosita I am not feeling well. I think I may have the flu. I need to lie down for a while."

"I will get you something to drink. I am sure it is just a minor bug you have caught."

Rosita watched nervously as Felix shook violently. The dose she had mixed into his drink was too high. The packaging for the drug had cautioned not to take the drug when consuming alcohol, but she had not expected such an intense reaction. She was worried.

"Should I call a doctor?"

"No. I will just lie here for a while."

Rosita went to the windows and pulled the shades closed. She decided to learn more about Zolpidem. She called the hospital where she had been treated and asked to speak to a doctor.

After a short wait, a doctor who had treated her came to the phone. She asked questions and was afraid after he explained the serious side effects and consequences of an overdose. She thanked him and wondered how to get Felix treated. She had chosen the right drug but administered it incorrectly. She decided to do nothing.

Rosita was sitting in the living room watching Felix when the phone rang. She heard one of the servants answer the phone, then there was a light knock at the door.

"Madam, it is a doctor from the hospital. He needs to speak with you."

Rosita suppressed a desire to panic. She took the phone and after announcing herself, she listened in relief.

"Rosita, it is Dr. Estevan. I have some good news for you. We have received an acknowledgment that Dr. Steven Blake in New York is prepared to operate on you to remove that remaining shrapnel that is lodged partially in your brain. He is to be assisted by two of the top neurosurgeons from Switzerland. They are world-renowned research scientists. The surgery is to take place in New York City. No dates have been established yet. It is excellent news."

"Doctor, I am so pleased to hear this. Can you answer a question for me, please? I took some Zolpidem and am feeling strange. What can I do? Is there something I can drink or eat?"

"No. If it's a minor reaction just stay calm. Make sure nothing is obstructing your breathing and under no circumstances drink anything alcoholic for a day or two."

"Thank you, doctor. If I don't feel well in a few hours I will come to the hospital."

"I will be back in contact when we hear more about the planned surgery. Goodbye."

She hung up and sat thinking. How could she get treatment for Felix and not expose what she had done?

She heard a car pull up in the driveway and shortly after. Caesar arrived at the door of the living room.

"Good morning, Rosita. Is everything fine? Why is Felix lying there? Is he ill?"

"It is a problem. I think he was overtired and took some sleeping medicine. I don't want to take him to a doctor as the news will be circulated that he has a problem and it could hurt his election chances."

Caesar thought for a few moments. He touched Felix's forehead.

"He is not running a temperature. I agree we need to treat this quietly. I have a good friend at the military base who is a doctor. If I tell him to be discreet he will. Can you give me the meds he took?"

Rosita handed him the empty pill bottle. Caesar pocketed it and left.

Chapter 68

Caesar returned with the young doctor who had a serious expression on his face. There were no introductions. He went directly to Felix and took his pulse. He removed some medicine from his bag and forced some into Felix's mouth.

"Do you have any idea how this happened?"

"He was tired and was having a drink. He had been having trouble sleeping and I saw him take some pills. I was later called out for a press interview. He was in a deep sleep when I returned."

"I saw that interview you gave. It was very powerful. Now we need to get Felix sorted out. It can be fatal to mix alcohol and that drug. I will need to administer some drugs and procedures. I would appreciate some privacy."

Rosita and Caesar left the doctor and went to the kitchen area. Rosita asked the staff to leave. She wanted to speak to Caesar privately.

"Caesar, I received a call from the hospital. They are preparing to perform a surgery to remove that shrapnel that is in my head. It is time for us to get our campaign underway. I want to see Felix win before I have that surgery. There is a big risk associated with it. If I should die, I want Felix to be the leader of our country. I am worried he may give up if I was to die and he had not yet been elected. Will you help?"

"Rosita, we already have a schedule drawn up. I will meet with our other supporters and we will start. I am concerned about Felix.

Some days he seems fine and others he is withdrawn. That bomb attack has affected him in many ways. He is not the same man. Carmine and I spent hours talking about it. I think you will need to take some of the load from him during the campaign.

I have brought you today's newspapers. You will be happy. The editorials and journalistic comments on your impromptu press conference have been flattering. You have helped tremendously and you are correct. Now is the time to launch our campaign. I will convince Felix that the time is right. Will you tell him about your surgery in New York?"

"No, not at this time. Now show me those papers."

Rosita scanned through the various papers. She was pleased with the photos. In her conservative dress, she represented authority and not a former peasant girl from a barrio.

Rosita made them coffee and toasted bagels and they sat talking about the campaign. Their conversation was interrupted by loud shouting outside. Rosita arose and went to the front door. There outside the gates to the property was a huge crowd carrying posters in support of her and Felix. They demanded that Felix assume leadership. Other posters were in support of Rosita and the rights of women. The crowd, while well behaved, was boisterous and noisy.

The mood turned ugly when heavily armed police arrived and started beating the participants. Rosita ran down the driveway in an attempt to stop the police. Her pleas were met with laughter and jeers. She did not doubt that the attack on the crowd had been arranged by General Perez and his supporters who were now scared of a loss of the election. Their high paying jobs and perks would be gone. They were becoming more desperate to control the people and the election process.

The crowd of people ran from the front of the property down towards some office buildings. Within minutes the crowd had dispersed.

Rosita returned to the house and found the doctor standing with a very weak Felix at the door.

"Is he all right? Will he be able to get out of bed and join us? He looks so tired."

"You are lucky that Caesar came to get me. Had he not been treated, he may well have died. I have spoken to him about using medication with alcohol. He claims to have no recollection of doing so. That does not surprise me. Many who use that drug suffer a loss of short term memory. I am leaving a prescription for him. Please be sure to make him take the pills for the next two days. Now I need Caesar to drive me back to the base before my absence is noticed."

Rosita thanked the doctor and offered money, which he refused.

"Come, Felix, I will take you back inside. We have a lot to talk about if you are well enough."

Inside the living room, Rosita told Felix of the TV interview the previous evening and showed him the articles in the various newspapers. Initially, he was angry but calmed when he saw how Rosita had been portrayed and the acceptance she had received.

"Rosita, General Perez is going to be furious about this. He will react."

"Felix, I had a long discussion with Caesar today. He agrees with me that we should start the campaign now."

Felix sat in silence thinking of the situation.

"I agree. I hope I will feel better and then we can start. Our schedule is already prepared. Since you are now a favorite with the press, I'm asking you to announce it."

Inside, Rosita's feelings jumped. She resolved not to let her feelings be evident. This was the moment she had hoped for.

"I will contact Caesar and ask him to alert all our supporters. We will need a meeting to coordinate activities."

Felix watched her in amazement. He wondered how the young girl he had met in that barrio at Nos Grande could be so intelligent and motivated.

"It is important we select our team carefully. There are some I noticed who I believe are not your true friends. We must be careful in who we decide to assist us."

"I agree. Caesar will carefully check each person. We cannot have anything go wrong."

"Felix my love, I want you to win. Please agree to allow me to appear with you. I know I can win people over for you."

"Yes, Rosita. You will be my partner. I have been thinking about us. I think we should marry."

"I am so happy you feel like that. Let us plan after the election."

Chapter 69

Felix and his advisers quickly assembled the team to operate the campaign. Funds were raised, promotional materials were printed and local candidates selected. Felix and Rosita recorded TV and radio commercials. Interviews with newspapers were hastily arranged. Details of upcoming rallies and the locations were broadcast throughout the days.

At the end of two weeks, Felix was ready for the first rally. The attendance was huge. Caesar had assembled a security detail that shielded the platform from which Felix and Rosita spoke. The security was tight. Caesar was determined there would be no problems. The image of the bombing still flashed through his mind.

"Good citizens. It is truly time for a change. Ten years ago, our country was wealthy. We were wealthier than any other South American country and ranked stronger than China and some Middle East countries. It's time for us to enjoy those days again……………"

Felix spoke with passion for the next twenty minutes. The assembled crowd called for Rosita to speak. Finally, Felix beckoned her to the microphone.

"My friends, you all know my devotion to this country of ours. I will fight for both you as individuals and the country. I will protect the poor and ensure justice is done. I will change how women and the less fortunate are treated. These are not just words, they represent my commitment. I am asking all of you to help Felix de Santos in this election. Do not believe the lies and tricks of General Perez. He does not have your interests in his heart."

Rosita stepped back from the microphone. As she did the crowd roared its approval.

Caesar assisted them down from the speaker's stand and to the waiting security car. Rosita noticed the Felix was moving slower and his balance was disoriented. The effects of the Zolpidem, that she was slipping into his morning coffee, were accumulating. She had noticed Felix's memory was also suffering. He was starting to forget things. She needed to be careful now. The prize she yearned for was in reach.

On the drive back to the Villa, Rosita sat in deep thought preparing the next step in her plan. She smiled as she devised the next action she would take.

It was a long drive to the Villa. Felix rested his head against the car's window and fell into asleep. Caesar watched him from the front seat and thought to himself that this was not the Felix he had known for years. He was worried.

They arrived back at the Villa after an hour's drive. Caesar went to the rear door and gently opened it. Felix stumbled awake.

"Where are we? Are we at the offices?"

"No, darling. We are at home." Rosita purred in his ear.

"Come now. Let's go inside. Its been a long day and I think a relaxing drink and a light meal will do you a lot of good, and then you can retire early."

"Yes, that sounds good. Caesar, take the rest of the night off. I will see you in the morning."

Rosita and Felix climbed the stairs and entered the house. They went directly to the living room and found Carmine buried in a pile of magazines. She was pleased to see them and peppered them with questions about the rally.

"It went well, Carmine. I am concerned that my man here is overdoing it. He has been forgetting things recently, and after today's rally in the heat he seemed to be lacking energy and tired."

Carmine put down the magazines.

"Felix, you must take better care of yourself. It would hurt me greatly should something happen. You haven't fully recovered from that assassination attempt. You need to take time away. Go to the Riviera for a month. We can afford it."

Rosita jumped at the opportunity to put her plan into action.

"Carmine, that is a great idea, but first let me suggest something. Felix, you asked me to marry you, and I will with much happiness. We will announce it in a day or so. People will love it. It will make them happy and see us as the most romantic couple. Carmine, we will marry after the election and take a month's honeymoon on the Riviera."

"Oh, such good news. I will be able to assist and plan the wedding. I am speechless. I will have my precious daughter-in-law."

Carmine took a tissue and wiped away the tears that streamed down her cheeks.

"Come here, my boy. Let me hug you. You are so lucky to be getting a wife like Rosita. Let me summon the servants and together we will all toast with the finest of our champagnes."

"Perfect", thought Rosita, as she went to hug Carmine before Felix. "My plan is foolproof. Now for the next step."

The staff was summoned and as a group, they all celebrated the 'good' news. When they left, Rosita spoke.

"Carmine and Felix. I think that after we announce that we will be a married couple. I should be made an equal political partner. People love me. There is nothing to lose. I will strengthen your chances of winning."

"Felix, I think Rosita has a brilliant idea. Do it. She is clever."

Chapter 70

The announcement of the engagement of Rosita to Felix de Santos polarized the country. Newspapers clamored for interviews, fashion magazines lobbied for access to Rosita. It seemed everyone was happy and eagerly awaited the day. No one was more excited than Carmine. She was busy planning parties and perusing wedding magazines for ideas of the dress for Rosita. It was as if a breath of fresh air had blown through the Villa.

The attendance at the rallies grew steadily. Crowds pushed and jostled to get close to the couple to shake hands or request autographs. Rosita and Felix had become stars.

The violence in the streets diminished when Rosita called for calm and promised the population improved living conditions and wealth. She appealed for an end to the riots. The results were almost immediate. General Perez and his regime observed this and a real worry developed. It seemed inevitable that they would be defeated.

It was time for the General to act. He had prepared plans for the possibility that Felix would gain the emotions of the people, now it was his turn to sabotage Rosita and Felix's game. He picked up the phone and called Carmilla Vesco and contacted the disgraced Father Lopez. He needed their help to turn public opinion against them. He was unaware of the plot they had hatched against him.

The phone rang briefly before a chirpy receptionist answered.

"Good morning. VTV studios. To whom can I connect you?"

"Get me Carmilla Vesco, please."

"This is Carmilla. Can I assist you?"

"This is Perez. Get Lopez and be at my office as soon as possible. things are getting out of control."

"I will try. I haven't seen him in days. He was going out of the city."

"Find him and be here, or you won't be a reporter much longer you won't be much of anything."

Carmilla Vesco knew of Perez's temper and brutality. She was shaking as she hung up. A threat from Perez was not something to ignore. She instinctively knew that to be summoned in that manner meant serious business. She took out a notebook and started dialing numbers to locate Lopez. For thirty minutes she called around the others who wished to overthrows the government, whether it was Perez or a new government formed by de Santos. The rebels were well-financed and determined in their purpose. Carmilla wondered if she had chosen the correct side to align with. Either side would kill her if a wisp of her deception leaked.

Hours went by until she received a call from Lopez. He was angry and did not wish to be disturbed. Carmilla told him of Perez's fury and immediately he agreed to meet her at his office within an hour. She called the reception desk and announced she had a lead on a story and needed to leave immediately and alone. No cameramen or other reporters could be involved. It was a fragile situation.

She met Lopez at a small coffee shop before proceeding to Perez's office.

"What does he want? He was abrupt and in a surly mood when he called me. I suspect we have a problem."

"I have informed our other comrades of this meeting. They are prepared to strike at any moment, should anything happen to us."

"How will they know?"

"I have arranged a call in an hour to the commander of our rebel group."

They entered the drab military complex and were immediately escorted to Perez's office. He was in a foul mood.

"I called you here because certain information has reached me. You are both traitors. You did not visit Nos Grande and gather the damning information I had asked for. I also have been told of a shadowy group you are both members of. I understand you are directing a possible strike against me and that it was your group who was responsible for the bombing that injured de Santos and Rosita Valquez. I am not happy. You will not be leaving here today. I shall see to that. Do you have an explanation?"

"I am not sure who has provided this false information. As a reporter, I do meet many people and yes, some are not happy with either you or de Santos."

Before she could finish her sentence Perez thundered his response while drawing a pistol and aiming it at Carmilla.

"You lying little bitch. To think that I have trusted you for years and paid you handsomely to spread incorrect news. How could you?"

He had barely finished when Lopez pulled a pistol and shot Perez in the head. Moments later the door burst open and armed guards opened fire with their automatic weapons. The noise was deafening. Blood sprayed into the air. Parts of Carmilla's head and hair flew across the room and splattered against the drab olive wall. The machine guns sliced Lopez's body in half. The top of his torso fell against the corpse of Perez. The office was a scene of carnage.

More armed soldiers rushed into the room. Several vomited at the gruesome sight. Panic and pandemonium set in. A senior officer attempted unsuccessfully to take control. The soldiers refused his orders and the majority ran from the room.

News of the attack on Perez circulated with lightning speed.

Rosita and Felix were meeting with other of his campaign staff when they were informed.

Felix was stunned and sat silent for minutes before he spoke.

"This changes everything. Who will succeed Perez? Will our constitution allow us to proceed with an election earlier than planned. We have a lot to learn and quickly."

As the group was discussing the situation, Caesar burst into the room.

"There is trouble. The rebel insurgents have started fighting on the northern and eastern borders. They are attacking with significant force. Felix, you are militarily active. We must go to the base and meet with other officers and decode how to proceed."

"With Perez gone and most of his regime in retreat, I propose that we immediately establish contact with their leaders. Their disagreements were not with us, but rather Perez. We should be able to stop this quickly."

"Felix, remember that many of these rebels are former prisoners and thugs. I'm not sure you will be able to reason with them."

"I will try. Many of them were falsely arrested and incarcerated by Perez for standing up to him. I can understand that. Some men had their livestock taken or lost their land and houses. They were treated poorly. I will arrange a trip to the borders and speak to these rebels. I am sure they will cooperate with us and end the insurrection. I will present our plan for rural areas."

"Felix, as your Head of Security, I advise you not to make that trip. The country is too unstable. Besides, you have that complete communications installation downstairs. I suggest you contact the base and have the communications personnel establish a video link with the rebels. Anything you need to say can be done from here. There is no need for you to go to either the base or to the borders at the moment. I think you and Rosita need to go on TV and radio and explain what you are doing to bring calm to those areas. Rosita is loved by women throughout the country."

"Yes, Caesar. I agree, also I am still having moments of great tiredness and forgetting things. My memory is strange. I never forgot anything before."

"It seems that the injuries you sustained in that attack are more serious than the doctors realized. I will arrange for Rosita to address the nation. You must rest."

Caesar left to speak to Rosita.

Chapter 71

Rosita made several speeches to the nation via radio, TV, and newspaper. The public was infatuated with her. Each interview she gave was examined and the source of conversation at homes or in the numerous bars and cafes in La Luminada. The deeply religious country believed that Rosita had been sent by God to lead them out of the horrible situation in which they found themselves. Even the rebels accepted her request to stop fighting and give them a chance.

To many, she had become a de facto benevolent leader.

Weeks elapsed until the elections. Without General Perez, the results were hardly surprising. Felix de Santos was elected to lead the country, assisted by Rosita.

Felix selected his team to lead the country. An uneasy peace settled throughout the country. Rosita decided it was time for her to exert control. Her constant drugging of Felix allowed her to easily manipulate him. She had increased the dosage, allowing her greater control. Caesar had watched Felix,s behavior with concern. He discussed his observations with his doctor friend. It was not making sense.

It was mid-afternoon and Rosita was about to leave for yet another interview and speech. As she entered the living room to say goodbye to Felix, the private phone rang. She waited while Felix answered it. He listened in silence to whoever was calling and finally spoke after several minutes.

"We will be there for the appointment tomorrow morning. Thank you."

He hung up and looked up at Rosita.

"That was the hospital. They have a meeting arranged for tomorrow to discuss sending you to New York for that operation to remove the metal fragment in your brain. The operation is scheduled for next week. We will need to plan this carefully. I will accompany you and we will fly to New York on one of our military jets. I will have Caesar make the arrangements."

Rosita was quiet and worried.

"Felix, I am scared. What will happen if the operation is not a success?"

"You must not worry. The hospital will explain everything in the morning. If the possibility of failure existed, I am sure they would not operate. Now, go to your interview. Tell the people that you will be gone for a while for surgery. They will understand and pray for you."

Rosita left for her interview, which was carried live on both radio and TV. She spoke of the changes she and Felix had initiated and how the country was responding. Towards the end of the interview, she played out her best acting and told of her upcoming surgery in New York. She seized the opportunity to deliver the most dramatic account of the surgery and the fact that the doctors were coming from Switzerland. Her performance was brilliant and the female interviewer was reduced to tears as the interview closed.

When she arrived back at the Villa, Rosita was thrilled to see crowds assembled with handwritten placards wishing her well and supporting her. She knew she had won over the public. Now she was in control.

The next morning, Caesar drove Felix and Rosita t the hospital. The hospital's head surgeon met them.

"Good morning. I will advise you of the plans and the procedures. The surgery will be lead by Doctor Steven Blake and he will be assisted by Doctor Rosenbusch from Israel and Doctor van den Breckell from Holland. These are the top three neurosurgeons in the world. Together they have pioneered many life-saving procedures.

You are lucky to have them as a team working for you. After you arrive in New York, you will need to attend the New York Neurology Center. There they will perform several tests which will include blood tests, X-Rays, an MRI and others. The tests will be done over a two or three day period. They will provide you with more details about the preparations that will need to be made the day of surgery."

The doctor provided more mundane details of dates, locations, and items Rosita should take with her. It was two hours later that they left the hospital to return home.

On the way back to the villa, Rosita was quiet. She finally spoke to Felix in a worried voice.

"Felix, I would like Carmine to be there. She has been a mother to me since I arrived here. I need her to be with me."

"I doubt that will be a problem. I am sure she will want to be there."

Part 4

Unseen

Chapter 72

New York City

Overhead the blazing noonday sun baked the narrow street that was lined and shadowed by tall skyscrapers. Exhaust fumes from cars, trucks, and buses added to the oppressive atmosphere by creating a stifling hazy blue pollution. Discarded fast food containers rolled along the sidewalk as the rush of air from passing cars caught them and chased them to the street. Sheets of newspapers twirled and eddied in the air as an occasional gust of wind tumbled down the face of one of the buildings.

Dr.Steven Blake quietly cursed under his breath as he drove toward Saint Marys Neurological Hospital. He wondered why he had returned to New York from the paradise he had enjoyed during his sabbatical in Sydney, Australia. At least there he could escape the city to one of the many beaches that lined the harbor. Here he felt smothered.

In the one hundred twenty-degree heat, there seemed to be no escape. Stepping from his car at the hospital's private parking area, he experienced a blast of hot air that punched into his chest and arms. The contrast between his air-conditioned car and the air outside was extreme.

As he slowly walked away from the parking area, he twisted and sidestepped to miss colliding with other pedestrians, all of whom seemed to be aggravated by the heat. He did not want a confrontation. The task ahead would be difficult enough and he didn't need his adrenaline pumped any higher than it already was.

He pondered the task ahead. As Chief Surgeon of Neurology, he always fretted the prospect of cutting into a patient's brain and the possibility of an inevitable mistake.

Suddenly he remembered that he had not eaten since early that morning. He looked in through the grimy glass window of the small delicatessen he was passing. Beaten up Formica tables with chrome and red leather chairs lined a wall. Two rotund men in dirty white outfits stood behind a huge glass counter taking orders and bantering with the customers. Dr. Steven Blake decided to stop and eat.

 His surgical skills would not be required for another four hours. He had ample time for a sandwich and he knew this particular surgery would take more than four hours and would not commence before the preoperative procedures were completed. He wondered why the hell the hospital had been chosen for such a high profile surgery. He was aware that there was already an intense security presence both outside and within the hospital.

He threw the door open and stepped into the refreshingly cool deli and ambled over to the glass counter. One of the men serving glanced up at him and called to him.

"Be with ya in a minute. Gotta get this fellas plate finished."

Dr. Blake enjoyed the no-frills atmosphere that these hard-working people created. There were times when he despised the high and mighty attitude of the other surgeons and hospital administrators. He thought back to a saying that his Aussie counterparts used.

"Everyone's shit sinks in the same amount of time."

He smiled recalling the saying and right then decided he would return to Sydney, Australia. Life had been good there. He already missed the many friends he had made there.

"What'll it be fella?"

Doctor Steven Blake ordered a jumbo pastrami on rye, with latkes and a cabbage roll smothered in a rich tomato sauce. He knew he would not be eating again for maybe twelve or fourteen hours. He sat at one of the chipped tables and waited for his order to be prepared. He loved this deli and the continual bustle and the constant barrage of New York accents trying to outdo each other. The window-mounted air conditioner vibrated and rattled as it tried in vain to cool the interior of the deli. As a result of his walk from the parking area, he was perspiring heavily. Beads of perspiration trickled down his nose and neck from his mop of thick curly brown hair. He didn't notice as his mind drifted and he thought of the intricacies of the surgery he would need to perform.

His patient had arrived yesterday and had been transported by military helicopter to the rooftop landing pad of the hospital. She had undergone a battery of tests and the results had been examined by other doctors. From the briefing he had received it seemed the patient was in excellent health and fine physical condition.

He was still deep in thought when the waiter slapped down an ancient enamel plate loaded with his food. He grunted his thanks and reached out to the waiter's greasy hand to tip him a five-dollar bill.

Rich aromas arose from the plate. The unique spicy scent of the pastrami filled his nostrils causing him to salivate. At age thirty-eight, Doctor Steven Blake was in excellent shape and had an appetite to match his strong physique.

He finished his late lunch and continued his walk to the hospital through the sweltering heat. While only four blocks, the heat made it seem much further.

He arrived at the nondescript entrance to the hospital and climbed the dirty grey stairs up to the entrance doors. Upon entering, he showed his security credentials and was buzzed into the wide corridor behind the security desk. He had watched a grieving family as he waited for the security check. The family was distraught and weeping. He wondered to himself which member had passed and what had happened. He hated death.

He proceeded to walk through the hospital until he reached the doctor's offices adjacent to the operating theaters. The temperature inside the offices was stifling.

"Nurse Johnston. Are the operating theaters as hot? Have the hospital maintenance people been able to reduce the temperatures at all?"

"No. I assisted at surgery this morning. It was difficult. The surgeons were perspiring and we were constantly mopping their brows. It distracted from the work they were concentrating on. I will contact maintenance again. I understand the surgery you will be performing is delicate and will require all your attention. The other surgeons are already here. I will let them know you have arrived."

Doctor Blake removed the patient medical record and charts. He scanned through and checked off the procedures that had been done. He paused at a couple and examined the attached results. He was finishing reading when the other two doctors were brought in to meet him.

"Good afternoon, I am Sam Rosenbusch. I'm pleased to meet you. I have heard a lot about the work you have performed over the years. I look forward to assisting with this complicated surgery. As you may know, I had developed a technique that has been used successfully in Israel for several years now. I am sure it will work here."

"I'm Richard van den Brekel, the chief neurologist at Rotterdam's neurological research center. I supervised an operation the same as the one we will be doing here. Hopefully, my experience and techniques will be of value."

The doctors continued to talk and finally looked at the procedures that had been completed. An IV drip with saline had been started. Radiological-X ray, MRI or CT, blood tests, cardiac monitoring, vital sign monitoring, pulse, oximeter, BP cuff, had all been completed. They were ready to meet the patient.

Chapter 73

Rosita nervously glanced across the room as the three doctors entered. They introduced themselves. A nurse was busy with last-minute preparations, checking her name, date of birth, and other particulars. Felix and Carmine sat quietly beside her bed.

Doctor Blake took her wrist and attempted to reassure her that she would be fine. He felt her pulse racing.

"Nurse, please call the anesthesiologist. Tell him that we will need a sedative to be administered ahead of any other anesthetic."

Sensing that she would experience pain and lose control, Rosita's evil streak arose. She wanted to strike out at the doctors, but due to the straps the nurse had placed on her arms, she was unable to move.

After a quick consultation with the doctors, the anesthesiologist inserted two small needles into the back of her hand and attached a drip. Rosita found herself fading into a deep sleep. Within minutes she was unconscious.

"Mr. de Santos, we are now taking her for surgery. Please provide your contact information to the nurses. We do not expect that you will be able to see Rosita for at least eight to ten hours. I suggest you check in the morning."

Felix met Caesar in the hospital lobby and they left to drive back to the hotel. Felix was in a subdued and distant mood. Caesar decided to leave him to his thoughts.

At the hospital, Doctor Blake was hot and uncomfortable. Ahead of changing into his scrubs, he decided to take a cool shower. In the shower, he aggressively soaped his body and lathered his private shampoo through his thick hair. The scent of the shampoo was strong and reminded him of the bush smells of Australia. He was missing Australia more then he realized.

He rinsed off and toweled himself dry, before pulling on his scrubs. Even though the shower had been cool, the oppressive heat and associated humidity had him perspiring again within minutes.

He entered the operating room to find the other surgeons waiting. Nurses moved back and forth organizing equipment and pulling mobile trays containing various instruments to the operating table. The anesthesiologist stood at the head of the table and monitored the breathing and read other details from the devices attached to Rosita, who lay completely motionless with her head held in a fixation device to keep it perfectly still during the procedure.

The nurse who was in charge of the room looked at the anesthesiologist, who nodded his approval and verbally assured her it was fine to start the procedure. The doctors moved in to start the craniotomy. Doctor Blake took the scalpel and was soon cutting open the bone flap to access Rosita's brain. He removed the bony flap and set it aside for reattachment upon completion of the surgery.

The doctors examined the exposed brain and consulted X-Ray images to accurately locate the piece of metal, but were initially unable to identify it. A nurse passed the infrared camera to the doctors to scan her head and match it to the MRI image.

"Doctors Rosenbusch and van den Breckel, it seems that the foreign object may have moved slightly since the MRI was done. It is not in the same location. Should we continue? This is a strange occurrence."

The doctors huddled to discuss the matter. The anesthesiologist continued to check his instruments and make adjustments.

"Nurse, we are going to have to cut into part of the skull. Please pass me the craniotome saw so we can cut a small part open."

Doctor Blake was sweating profusely. A young surgical nurse was constantly wiping his forehead. The room was becoming hotter with the overhead lights and the heat from the equipment.

He took the craniotome and placed it close to the area in which the infrared camera had shown the object. The saw whined and bone fragments, flesh, and blood sprayed. Using a pair of retractors, he separated the brain and the skull. He pulled down his magnification glasses and examined the nerves and vessels. There was a minuscule piece of metal. Doctors Rosenbusch and van den Brekel craned to see the open brain and advised they stop and discuss the best process to remove it without causing injury to Rosita.

They spoke for a long while. It was impossible to use many of the standard instruments. Doctor Rosenbusch made a suggestion, which was to use an ultrasonic aspirator. Doctor Blake wondered. This was an instrument that was generally used to break up tumors. Doctor Rosenbusch explained that it could dislodge the metal piece and the suction function of the aspirator would act as a vacuum cleaner. The doctors agreed. Blake gave over the operation to Doctor Rosenbusch. Minutes passed and the metal worked loose and was sucked away. The doctors were happy.

As Doctor Blake bent over Rosita to start the reattachment of the bone flap, a bead of perspiration trickled from his hair and dropped into the open cranium. He thought of alerting the other doctors but decided that it was harmless. It was not observed by the doctors or the nurses. Unknown to them, the shampoo Blake had used contained the chemical Methylisothiazolinone, which in laboratory test had caused the death of animals when brains were exposed to it.

The operation was completed and Rosita was returned to her hospital room. The doctors congratulated each other on the result.

The scrubs of Doctor Blake were saturated with perspiration, bloodstains, and other matter.

"Doctors, please excuse me. I need to shower and change. I will meet you for a coffee, or something stronger in a few minutes."

Chapter 74

It was morning and Felix was sitting with Carmine in the hotel garden with his after-breakfast coffee when a hotel employee ran up to him.

"Sir, the hospital is on the phone asking for you. I hope Miss Rosita is fine."

"Thank you. Where can I take the call?"

"Please follow me, sir. There is a private room off the lobby. You can take the call in there."

"Felix, I will wait here. Please hurry. I am most concerned about Rosita. I hope my 'soon to be' daughter in law's surgery was a success."

"I will be back immediately after I get an update. Please relax."

Felix followed the girl to the lobby. She showed him into a small office and picked up the phone and contacted the hotel operator to put the call to the office.

The phone jangled and Felix snatched up the receiver.

"This is Felix de Santos. How is Rosita?"

He listened intently before thanking the caller and returning an anxious Carmine in the garden.

"There is good news. Rosita has gone through the operation. There were no complications. She is still heavily drugged and the hospital recommends that we only visit tomorrow. They say she will be in a coma for the day. Now, we are in New York. What would you like to do today?"

"I would firstly like to visit a couple of bridal salons to get some ideas for the upcoming wedding. Afterward, you can buy me a delightful lunch at The Russian Tea Room. I have heard so much about it and I am dying to try it."

Felix groaned at the prospect of visiting the bridal salons, as he had hoped for a more interesting visit to some of New York's landmarks.

"Mother, I am not sure that traveling around is a good idea. The heatwave here is brutal. I don't think it will be good for you. I suggest you choose one bridal salon only. I am sure the girls here at the hotel can advise you on the best."

"An excellent idea. Let me go and ask them."

Felix watched as Carmine strode across the manicured lawn on her mission to extract recommendations and information from the poor unsuspecting girls who worked in the hotel. He smiled as he thought of her age and determination.

"Excuse me, sir. I am Joseph the waiter for the garden. It is now time for our bar to open. Can I get you an early morning drink? I suggest the Campari and soda for a hot morning like this."

"Certainly, Joseph. That sounds delicious."

He watched the white-jacketed waiter return inside the hotel. He looked around. No others were sitting in the garden. Felix was feeling special and refreshed. His memory seemed fine and he did not have the lethargic feeling he had been experiencing home at the Villa. He felt ten years younger and wondered if New York had that effect on everyone.

Felix was sipping his Campari when he noticed Carmine returning. She was accompanied by a tall young woman. He watched them as they approached.

"Felix, Meet Juliette. Juliette comes from the area of Nos Grande. A remarkable coincidence. She knows Rosita."

He examined the young woman. She was beautiful. Her long dark hair hung over her shoulder and shone in the sunlight. Her complexion was light olive and her figure made Felix gasp. Unlike other girls he knew in his country, her eyes were a violet color. He was struck by her beauty.

"Senor Felix, it is my honor to meet our newly elected leader. I know you and Rosita will create good things in our country. I was forced to leave with my family as it was no longer safe for my father. He had opposed the government of General Perez. I have been working here in New York for almost six months. Your mother told us that you will marry Rosita soon. She is a lucky woman."

"Yes, Rosita and I will marry soon. I hope that we can build our country back up. It is sad so many had to leave to escape Perez or find work. Will you return?"

"I do not know yet. I have two jobs here and the money is good. I will wait and see what happens at home. I will not return to the illnesses and violence of Nos Grande though. That Canadian mine brought many problems with it."

"I understand. Hopefully, we can restore things to a happier life there."

"Your mother has asked the other girls to suggest shops to visit for bridal clothing. It will be very expensive here, but there are some amazing shops. We have given her some names. Now, I must return to my duties. Goodbye."

Felix looked after her as she gracefully walked to return to the hotel. Carmine had watched the interchange with curiosity.

"She seems a nice girl. I wonder if Rosita remembers her?"

Before Felix could respond, the waiter returned.

"May I get the lady a drink? Sir, would you like another?"

Carmine eyed the waiter and put her hand to her cheek as she pondered her choice.

"Yes, I will have a glass of Moet Chandon, and yes, my son will have another."

Carmine chatted about visiting the bridal stores and how she hoped that Rosita would recover in time to visit with her before they left New York to go home. As they talked, Felix noticed Juliette approaching them. Her employee uniform was gone and she was dressed in a light and airy lemon sundress. Juliette stopped and spoke to Carmine.

"The manager and I spoke. He is aware of Felix de Santos and his plans. He admires Felix. I told him of the planned wedding and that you wished to visit some of the bridal salons. He gave me the day off to go with you."

Carmine was ecstatic.

"That is excellent. After we visit the stores you must join Felix and me for lunch at The Russian Tea Room. My expense."

"No. I cannot do that. I would be taking advantage."

"You will. I insist, and I know Felix agrees, don't you Felix."

"Of course. It will be our pleasure, besides we can discuss your time at Nos Grande. I am curious. Please excuse me, as I need to call the hospital and check on Rosita's progress."

As he spoke he noticed a flicker in her eyes that could have been a disappointment.

"Mother, You will have to excuse me. I have some calls to make and there are matters I need to deal with now. That I have been elected. I will have one of Caesar's security men drive and accompany you. I will meet you both for lunch at one this afternoon at The Russian Tea Room."

Felix noticed an obvious look of disappointment on Juliette's face. He wondered why she was acting this way when she knew he was about to marry Rosita.

Felix called Doctor **B**lake to enquire about Rosita and her recovery.

"Good morning, Felix. I checked on Rosita's progress this morning. She has recovered from the anesthetic but is very tired and in some pain. All of her vital signs are strong. She seems to have some sort of strange force that is fighting for her to recover. We have never seen such determination with any other patient. She seems quite remarkable."

"Yes, Doctor. She can be a very strong-willed woman at times. How long do you expect her to remain in the hospital?"

"Normally for our patients who have had this type of surgery it is ten days. It depends. There are several factors. Even if Rosita was to be released earlier, she should not travel by plane for at least another week. We will, of course, monitor her frequently as I understand your need to return home since you are the newly elected leader."

"Thank you for the information. When can we visit her?"

"I suggest you check tomorrow morning. Tomorrow should be fine."

Felix hung up and immersed himself in his work. He checked his watch and was surprised to see it was to meet Carmine and Juliette for lunch.
When he arrived at The Russian Tea Room, it was bustling. He

spied Carmine and Juliette sitting at a table near the front and joined them.

"Felix, we had a great morning. We found several ideal wedding gowns. I think Rosita will be thrilled. I have never seen anything like these before. They are truly unique."

Carmine continued chatting until a waiter appeared to take their lunch order. The menu selection offered many appetizing items.

"Let me order for all of us

Carmine ordered the Caviar and Vodka for three, which included

Wild American Hackleback 10g.
American Paddlefish Roe 10g.
Wild Alaskan Salmon Roe 10g.
And a Flight of Vodka of 3/4 oz. tastes.

 The vodkas were - Jewel of Russia Wild Berry, Voda, and Ruskova.

And then she ordered the Khinkali Georgian beef and pork dumplings for them to share, along with a bottle of the finest Sancerre.

Felix always enjoyed dining out with Carmine. She always selected something different and delicious.

Carmine continued chatting throughout the lunch. Felix watched Juliette who remained very quiet. He wondered why she was not joining in the conversation. Back at the hotel, she had seemed much more talkative. He caught her watching him on several occasions and was tempted to ask her if something was bothering her. He decided against that as he did not want to embarrass her.

When the lunch was over, Felix summoned the security man to
drive them back to the hotel.

Chapter 75

Felix spent the balance of the afternoon reading and telephoning back to his political associates. By the end of the day he was exhausted. He called Carmine and told her he was too tired to dine out and was going to order in his room. Carmine decided to join him.

Felix dressed casually in jeans and a polo shirt. The impact of the trip, Rosita's surgery, the election, and the oppressive heat of New York had hit him. He was pleased that Carmine was agreeable to a casual dinner.

By the end of dinner, Felix was falling asleep. Carmine saw his tiredness and excused herself.

"Felix, get some sleep. We will meet for breakfast and then go to see Rosita."

Felix said goodnight and then lay on the bed. He was drifting off to sleep when there was a soft knock at the door. He swung off the bed and found Juliette standing there.

"Felix, I need to speak with you. Do you have time?"

"Yes, come on in."

"No, I cannot do that. It is forbidden for us to be in a guest's room with them. There is a small coffee shop close by. Can we go there to speak? What I have to say is important."

"If that is the case, then yes I will join you."

The heat in the coffee shop was almost unbearable. A noisy airconditioner slave in an attempt to provide the patrons some relief. Felix found a corner table that was in the path of the blown air. He held back a chair for Juliette then slid himself onto the chair across the table. A large black woman took their coffee orders. Sweat was streaming from her forehead.

"Juliette, what is so important that you have brought me out here?"

"Sir, I was not sure I should meet you and discuss these things. I spoke to my friends who encouraged me to meet you.

I know that I am going to speak of some things that you will find disturbing. Please do not be offended.

I am the same age as Rosita. I too grew up in Nos Grande but left the barrio years after you took Rosita to La Iluminada. While growing up in Nos Grande, Rosita was seen as a charming and helpful little girl by the adults. My friends and I knew a different Rosita. Felix, Rosita has an evil streak in her. We experienced some of the things she did that hurt us and our families. We were too scared to speak out against her. Several of the boys were injured by her, some seriously. They told their parents that they fell or made up other stories. As she grew older her outbursts became more violent. She had men from the cantina do certain tasks for her in return for sex. At the time you arrived in Nos Grande she had established herself as someone to avoid. While you were there, the dancer from the cantina disappeared. The villagers believe that Rosita killed her, but no one knows for sure. You may not know that Rosita has made return visits to the barrio. She was seen with one of the men from the cantina. She was discussing something with him that night. Several of the men observed her with him. He was drunk and seemed happy with whatever she was telling him. The next day he disappeared. Again, the villagers believe that she killed him. Her neighbor, a man named Fernando followed her one morning. She met the man from the cantina. After this, he was never seen again.

As kids, we used to tease her a little to make her go crazy. As we grew older we knew she was different. Now I believe she has multiple personalities and is schizophrenic.

Felix, be careful. She is dangerous. Carefully consider this before you marry."

Felix sat back and digested the information. He thought back and remembered times when Rosita had been angry. He recalled her attack on Carmilla Vesco at the Villa. He tried to recall other events. Slowly a pattern of Rosita's loss of temper emerged in his mind, but none were as severe as the events described by Juliette.

"Juliette, I appreciate your concern. Can you provide me the names of some others who witnessed these outbursts? What you have told me is most serious and I wish to check further."

"Yes, I can give you the names of some friends who have experienced Rosita's wild behavior. I will give you a list."

"Juliette, why are you telling me this? Why do you care?"

Juliette blushed and looked down at the table and started fidgeting with a packet of sugar. Her hands were trembling.

"Please don't ask me any more questions. If you check what I have told you, the truth will emerge."

Her discomfort was extremely evident. Felix decided not to probe further. He intended to find out from her friends and contacts why she felt obligated to tell him of Rosita's past.

They changed the subject and spoke of the foods, music, and times they had enjoyed years before General Perez had destroyed the country.

It was late when they left the coffee shop. Felix offered to escort Juliette to her home, but she firmly declined. Felix then walked back to the hotel with questions flooding his mind.

Chapter 76

The morning arrived quickly for Felix. He showered and dressed before calling the hospital. The nurse to whom he spoke gave an account of Rosita's recovery and informed him she was alert and doing well. Felix was advised he could visit.

Felix enjoyed a slow and relaxed breakfast with Carmine. He was still thinking of the previous evening's discussion with Juliette. For the first time in their relationship, he was bothered. He recalled moments when Rosita had been aggressive and argumentative with people she had taken a dislike to. He decided to speak with Rosita and ask her about Juliette's allegations.

"Mother, I will go and visit Rosita alone this morning. She is still recovering. This afternoon we will go together. Maybe you can spend time with your new friend Juliette."

"Yes. I'm tired after visiting those bridal boutiques yesterday in that heat. I will stay here and rest a little."

Felix excused himself and left to hail a cab to the hospital. Already in the early morning, the heat had soared to an uncomfortable level. The city's pollution and humidity added to the oppressive atmosphere.

Horns blared and tempers flared as commuters attempted to navigate the crowded streets. The heat was not helping.

Upon arrival at the hospital, Felix was welcomed by the security officer, who now recognized him. He asked Felix to wait until a nurse could accompany him up to Rosita's room.

Felix walked into the darkened room. Rosita slowly turned her head to him and gave a small smile. He crossed to her and took her wrist and gave a gentle squeeze. He tried not to stare at her head and the area where the operation had been performed. The hair surrounding the area was matted. A large shaved area had some dressings and small sutures showed. Felix felt a pang of sorrow for her. He looked at her and her eyes blazed with a determination. He instinctively knew she was fighting back.

"Rosita, how are you feeling after this big ordeal?"

"I feel tired and my vision is strange. I will fight to be well enough to get out of here. When can I go home?"

"That is not for me to guess. The doctors will decide. You must accept their advice."

For the next five minutes they engaged in talks about Carmine and her shopping trip, then Felix decided to mention Juliette. At the mention of her name, Rosita became a screaming writhing animal. The evil force within her activated stronger than she had ever experienced before.

 Felix was shocked. Rosita's screams brought nurses and a doctor running. The doctor immediately plunged a syringe with a sedative into her arm. Within minutes Rosita slumped down in the bed with a dazed expression.

Felix pulled up a chair and sat with her. When she was calm the doctor and nurse left.

Although drugged, Rosita turned her head to Felix and spoke.

"What did that lying little bitch want? Where did you meet her?"

"Rosita, she came to introduce herself. She works at the hotel Carmine and I are staying at. She seems nice and said she grew up near Nos Grande and knew you."

"Don't you go near her. Do not listen to her lies."

"Rosita, what is the problem? Why are you so disturbed?"

"It is a long story. She did a lot of bad things with me when we were growing up. Before I met you something happened between us. Juliette is a lesbian and wanted to do things with me. I refused and she swore to get even with me. Stay away. She will cause trouble. Promise me."

"I will be careful."

"Felix, she used to follow me around after I refused to be friends. She spread rumors, some of which were horrible. Did she try and make you doubt me?"

Felix had watched Rosita and knew she was not telling the truth. He waited before answering.

"No, we talked about the changes we want to make in the country and about her job here in New York. It was just small talk. Nothing of any importance. She did not mention her family in Nos Grande. I don't know if they are still there or here in New York. Maybe after all the years that have passed, you might feel different about her if you were to meet."

"I will never meet her. She deliberately tried to hurt me. I will never forgive her. I must ask you to leave now. I am feeling very tired. I need to sleep."

Felix stood to leave. Before he did he turned and looked at her. Again he knew she was not being honest.

"I will return with Carmine this afternoon. Get some rest."

Felix left the hospital with considerable doubt. He thought about Rosita's outburst and the events Juliette claimed happened at Nos Grande. It was troubling him, and he decided to investigate.

Back at the hotel, Felix placed a phone call to Caesar and told him of the claims that Juliette had made.

"Caesar, if any of this is true and is exposed, it will be the end of my career. I need you to send your best men to Nos Grande to investigate. They must not be obvious. Try to select them to fit in at the barrio. Have them as laborers looking for work or similar. I am disturbed by what Juliette has told me and how Rosita reacted."

"Felix, we have been friends for many years. It is not my place to speak badly of Rosita, but recently, I have had some concerns. I have watched you closely and your behavior has changed. You seem dazed and lacking the focus and drive I have known you to have over the years. I have watched Rosita inserting herself into a more powerful role. I am surprised you have not spoken to her. It is as if she was the leader now. I am sorry, but I would have talked about this when you returned, so it is good that you are asking for the claims to be investigated. If you wish, I will personally go to Nos Grande with my men. I am sure I can disguise myself and have a good story for anyone who gets too inquisitive."

"No. I want you to stay in La Iluminada. If Rosita is playing some game, I will need you there."

" I will select the men this afternoon. By tonight they will be on their way to Nos Grande."

"Good. I will be with Carmine this afternoon, visiting the hospital. I am going to find Juliette and ask her for more details. I believe she has other friends here in New York from Nos Grande. Maybe she will arrange for me to meet them individually."

"Be careful. If what Juliette says is true then we don't want to do anything to let them know we are investigating. I am sorry Felix. I did not see her true intent at the beginning either. I thought she would be the ideal partner for you. Now, it seems she may have had a plan all along. I advise you to be careful with Carmine. If Rosita has killed before, then she may hurt Carmine if she detects anything. Will you tell Carmine of these developments?"

"No, not at this time. I will later when we know more. I must go now, Carmine will be waiting for me to join her for lunch."

Felix met Carmine in the hotel lobby. Initially Carmine wished to lunch on the outside patio, but the heat drove them back inside. The waiter who had served them previously hurried over to them to take their orders. Felix was impressed by the waiter's attitude and friendliness.

Carmine was full of gossip and small talk as they ate. Felix looked up and across the restaurant to see Juliette standing and watching them. He waved her to join them. Carmine was happy to see her and wanted Juliette to sit with them, but was told it was against the hotel's rules.

As she was leaving, Felix excused himself and asked her for directions to the men's washroom. Juliette guided him through the tables and pointed to the doorway to the toilets. Felix spoke to her rapidly.

"I must speak further with you. It is now a matter of national interest. Can we meet again this evening at that coffee shop? It is important."

Juliette hesitated before quietly answering him. She twisted her hair and smiled at him.

"I don't see what more I can tell you or add. Why would I know anything that is of national importance?"

"I ask you to trust me. I will explain."

"I don't want to find myself in trouble. The country can be very dangerous. How can you assure me that I will not be making a mistake and endangering my family and me?"

"I, Felix de Santos swear to God Almighty that you will not be harmed."

"I will meet you at eight this evening. Please do not be late or I will be forced to leave."

"I will be there before eight."

Felix returned to Carmine, who was looking directly at him with a knowing look. It was obvious he liked Juliette. Carmine considered the intrigue of another woman in his life at this time. It gave her excitement.

"Come now, Felix. It is time to finish and go see that future bride of yours."

As Carmine spoke those words she examined Felix for any sign of unease.

Chapter 77

The taxi ride to the hospital was chaotic. The incessant heat brought out the worst in human nature. Bicycle couriers wove through the crawling cars shouting obscenities. Horns blared. Taxi drivers shook fists out of windows. Felix was appreciating La Iluminada more and more.

At the hospital, a steady stream of visitors, nurses, doctors, and others continuously entered and left the building.

Felix stopped at the security desk and requested an escort up to the secure floor where Rosita was convalescing. As they entered the room, Rosita sat up and seemed truly pleased to see them. Felix thought her mannerisms were different from what he had observed that morning.

He did not lean to kiss her but placed a chair close beside the bed for Carmine to sit and talk with her.

"I will be back in a few minutes. I need to speak to the doctors. They have asked to see me," he lied.

He walked to the nurse's station and inquired whether Doctor Blake was and available. The nurse checked and called someone to announce that Felix was at the hospital and wished to speak to the doctor. When the nurse hung up she wrote a room number and directions out for Felix.

Felix made his way to the floor below and found the room. Doctor Blake was standing and thumbing through a patient's file. He recognized Felix.

"Sir. Come into my office. How can I help you?"

"When I visited Rosita this morning she became very agitated and angry. One of your fellow doctors had to sedate her. Is that normal after the type of operation Rosita has had?"

"No, not at all. Generally, the patient is in a lethargic state for several days. That has not been the case with her. The nurses have had a terrible time with her. She has been demanding and her foul temper has reduced a couple of the nurses to tears. She has thrown things. Those nurses work hard for long hours. If her behavior continues this way she will need to be moved. She may be placed in restraints and a room in the psychiatric ward. Her behavior is unexplainable, and quite frankly, we are not prepared to tolerate it."

Felix's mind immediately raced to the descriptions of her temper outbursts at Nos Grande.

"Thank you. I will go and speak to her. I will explain the consequences of her actions to her. Hopefully, that will calm her down. I apologize. It hasn't been an easy time for a few months now."

"I need to ask. Was she like this before the operation?"

"No. She would get annoyed, but not like the way you describe."

"I am wondering if something we did during the operation has triggered this. I will examine the procedure and drugs used to see if there is any possible cause."

Felix left to return to Rosita's room. She appeared to be dozing off to sleep. He signaled Carmine for them to leave.

"I had a meeting with the doctor who performed the surgery. He tells me that her post-operation behavior is really bad. She is causing significant problems. They are very concerned. Something has gone wrong."

"I do hope she recovers well. We need her to be well in time for your wedding. Have you set a date for the wedding yet?"

"No. I don't think I will until she is settled and we are back home and getting our country settled. It may take a while." He did not want to tell Carmine the truth about delaying the wedding.

"When Rosita is better and fully recovered, I intend to return to New York with her to select a wedding dress. I assume she will need to return for a medical check-up after that serious operation."

"Yes. The doctors have not given any dates yet. I am eager to return home. There are lots of matters that require my attention."

"You are a good man Felix. Just like your father was. He would have been proud of you."

It was late in the afternoon when they returned to the hotel.

"Felix, I am going to take a brief sleep, and then we will go for dinner. I will call you."

Felix used the time to call Caesar.

"Caesar, I am meeting Juliette tonight. What information do you need? I will ask her many questions."

"I have already sent two of our best men to Nos Grande. I hope to speak with them in the morning. Please ask for names of people they should try to question there, and any events that she recalls where Rosita may have been involved. Can you ask about whether she had any relationships before you? I know this is unpleasant, but there is a lot that depends on what we find out."

Caesar and Felix spoke for a long while and dealt with several administrative issues. He was surprised when the phone rang, and Carmine told him of the time and the need to leave for their dinner reservation.

Felix's mind was preoccupied and he barely spoke during dinner. He was mentally preparing for his meeting with Juliette.

"Felix, are you not feeling well? You are very quiet."

"No. I am fine. I am just thinking through some things that Caesar mentioned when I called. He needs advice and I need to give it to him. Some of the matters are complicated."

"I am sure you will give him the best advice."

With the dinner finished, Felix looked at his watch. It was seven-thirty.

"Mother, I am going to take a long walk. I need to make some very difficult decisions. It may be late when I return. I will see you in the morning."

He excused himself and headed for the exit door and out onto the street.

It was seven-forty five when he entered the coffee shop. There were fewer people than the previous evening. He sat at the same table and impatiently awaited Juliette. At eight he ordered another coffee and sat enjoying it until eight-fifteen. He was rising to leave when Juliette arrived. She was accompanied by a tall blonde man with striking blue eyes. Juliette went straight to Felix.

"I am sorry we are late. I wish to introduce you to Marco. He grew up in the barrio and spent considerable time with Rosita Valquez. He can tell you many things. We are late because he was reluctant to meet you."

Felix extended his hand to Marco.

"Marco, relax. I am trying to understand what happened in the Nos Grande barrio when Rosita was growing up. Recently, many rumors have reached me. I am trying to determine which are real and which are lies borne out of jealousy."

"I am pleased to meet you and sincerely hope you can implement the promises you made during the election campaign. Yes, I did grow up at the same time as Rosita. We were in the barrio together. She was my first romantic encounter and my first experience with a woman. After she got what she wanted from me she turned against me in the most hurtful way, both mentally and physically. I was surprised. She did things to me and others that we could never speak of. All the adults thought she was an angel. She was far from an angel."

For the next hour, Felix sat and listened to Marco's story. He was shocked and angry. How could she have hidden her past from him so effectively? Why had no others come forward during the election campaign, as she had been visible and easily accessible?

"Marco, is there anything else you can tell me?"

Marco shifted uneasily and looked at Juliette.

"Please, Marco. You must tell Felix everything. Eventually, he will find out."

Marco looked down at the surface of the table and while buried deep in thought, stirred the spoon around in his almost empty coffee cup. Felix sensed that there was something significant that Marco was holding back.

"Marco, I have sent investigators to the barrio. They are in disguise and will find out what there is to know. I will ensure you are protected if you can assist in the investigation."

Marco looked at Juliette, who nodded her head in agreement with Felix.

"Marco, please go ahead. If you don't, I will tell Felix the little I know."

Marco raised his head and looked directly into Felix's eyes and held the stare for some time before he spoke.

"The deception of you goes far deeper. There is a hidden truth. Unknown to you, but known to Rosita, her father, Jorge Valquez is alive. He was not killed during that roadblock. He was taken back to the mining camp and given medical treatment. When he recovered he was imprisoned and used as slave labor. He is still alive and knows of the evil that was exposed after you took Rosita from Nos Grande to La Iluminada.

Jorge has a neighbor, Fernando who was suspicious of Rosita after she made a return trip to the barrio. He followed her one morning. She met a man from the cantina. He was a man with a bad reputation as a thief and had raped other men's wives, yet no one would confront him. He was feared. Rosita met him one morning and they were seen walking into the thick tropical forest. Fernando waited and hours later he saw Rosita emerge from the forest wearing completely different clothes and alone. After that morning, the man was never seen again. Months later some native fishermen found clothing and some tools at a bend in the river. It was rumored that Rosita killed the man. No one in the barrio wanted to look for his body. He was not liked and most were silently pleased he had disappeared."

Felix sat in disbelief. He was shocked and angry that he had been deceived.

"Can you tell me how my men can contact Jorge Valquez?"

"He is no longer known as Jorge Valquez. He never returned to his adobe in the barrio. He left the barrio and works on a farm outside the barrio as a laborer. He is old and may not cooperate."

Marco fell silent. He looked at Felix with obvious apprehension. Felix knew there was more that he wanted to tell him."

"Marco, there is something else you want to tell me? Please go ahead. I will not be angry. I need to know everything."

"I do not wish to hurt you. Rosita has been back in the barrio. When you were traveling, she would return. She has a lover in the barrio. Like her, he is an evil person. He is a leader of a gang who grows and transports drugs through that mine. His name is Frederico (The Bird) Pelicanos. He is much feared."

"I have never heard of him. Who is he?"

"He came here from Mexico. It is rumored that he received special favors from General Perez as he arranged for drugs to be transported through one of Perez's companies. He is brutal and has murdered those who opposed him. I don't want to get hurt. I have already said too much."

"I give you my word. You will be protected. I will not disclose the source of the information you have provided. If there is anything I can help you or your family with back home in our country, please tell me. You have been of great help.

That night Felix called Caesar to his room.

"Caesar, this is what I learned this evening. If this is true then I have a huge problem to contain. Have you any reports yet from Nos Grande?"

"Yes. The men are settling themselves in and spreading rumors of their need for work."

"I have names of the people in Nos Grande who witnessed or experienced Rosita's actions. You will need to get the names to them. There was one big shock in what I was told tonight. Rosita's father is still alive and she has visited him. She also has a lover in the barrio. A Mexican drug gangster called Frederico Pelicanos. See what you can find out. This is turning into something far more serious than I expected."

Chapter 78

Three weeks passed before Rosita was discharged from the hospital. Her stay in the hospital was disruptive to the staff. They grew to immensely dislike her and her tantrums. On the day of her discharge, several of the nurses stood along the walls of the corridor and cheered.

Doctor Blake had never seen that behavior on any other of his patients. He thought long and hard about the surgery. He recalled the bead of perspiration that had dropped into her open cranium. He wondered whether any chemical element from the shampoo he had used before the operation could have contaminated her brain. He decided to call the Center for Disease Control and request an analysis of the chemical ingredients.

His request took a week. The chemical makeup along with a description of known reactions to certain of the chemicals in the shampoo arrived at his private practice. He did not want to draw attention to the incident that had happened during surgery.

The doctor studied each chemical. He was shocked when he read the impact that one chemical, Methylisothiazolinone. He read of the research that had been done, and the impact the chemical had on the neurons of rats and how it had, in a controlled test on a human fetus, caused severe unbalanced growth of the brain. In some tests, exposure to the brains of rats to Methylisothiazolinone had resulted in their death or behavioral change. Doctor Blake now knew the 'harmless' drop of perspiration had caused damage to Rosita's brain. He worried. He did not wish to disclose this to his peers.

Relatively sure he had identified the cause of Rosita's bizarre behavior, he contacted the research professors at MIT, who listened with great interest to his observations and concerns. They offered to review his assessment and provide feedback.

Felix and Rosita were settling back into life at the Villa. Carmine was fussing over Rosita but often received sharp rebukes for her efforts in trying to assist. Felix watched Rosita with new skepticism. His trust was shattered, but he remained unsure of her loyalty. When they were alone she was sweet and kind. It seemed when their privacy was disturbed that Rosita became aggressive.

Rosita recovered and soon was attending meetings with various women's groups whom she had promised major reforms and benefits during the election. They looked to her for leadership.

Initially, Rosita was kind and assisted the women. She helped establish health clinics for women in the country areas. Medical supplies and treatments were made possible. For the hungry and poor she arranged food and assistance.

Throughout her recovery, Caesar had kept a trained eye on her. When she left the Villa alone he had his men shadow her. Weeks went by and there was no report of any issues that needed to be reported to Felix. All seemed well.

The change came slowly and unexpectantly. One of the leaders of a women's group leveled criticism at Rosita and her handling of a situation. The woman was found strangled in her bed. The death was decided as a foiled break-in at her house. Nothing more was said, though Caesar expressed his doubts to Felix.

A series of misfortunes visited many of the other women in the groups. Babies died from unexplainable circumstances, children of mothers in the groups were beaten on the way to or from school. The frequency and horror of these mishaps increased.

Caesar decided it was time to act. It was late one evening when he found Felix sitting alone. Felix was not feeling well. Without his knowledge, Rosita was drugging him again, only she had increased the dosage and explained his tiredness as a permanent result from the bombing. She told him he was aging and tiring and offered to take on more responsibility. Felix told her he would consider it.

Caesar decided the time had come for Felix to take steps to control Rosita.

"Felix, it is time we both have a meeting with Rosita and tell her of what has been uncovered. I imagine it will be a difficult and possibly dangerous meeting. I will ask my men to wait outside the door. Before we meet, there is one other serious matter that my men have discovered.

I had expressed my concerns about your well being, tiredness, and loss of memory. One of my men decided to investigate. He found these drug containers in the garbage. We checked all the staff. No one is taking these pills. I suspect that Rosita has been drugging you to get more control. There is no other explanation. I am truly sorry for you. I know that you initially loved Rosita, and probably still have feelings for her, but she has to go."

There was a gentle knocking at the door and one of the maids entered.

Sir, there is Doctor Blake on the phone from New York. He wishes to speak with you."

Felix looked at Caesar.

"I wonder what he wants. Maybe he is following up on Rosita?"

Felix took the phone and listened as the doctor explained the possible contamination of Rosita's brain and how that was a probable cause of her erratic behavior. When he was finished Felix advised him of the problems they had discovered existed before the surgery.

Upon hearing this, the doctor was excited.

"I would like to visit you. I can be on a flight tomorrow. Please don't say or do anything that could change Rosita's normal daily pattern. There is an experimental treatment that may help her, but she must not be stressed or know of what it will do to her. I will explain to you in person."

"I will have Caesar meet you. Please call with your flight info. You met Caesar in New York."

"I am excited to explain all this to you. I will call with my flights."

Felix hung up the phone and returned to the living room to tell Caesar of the call.

"I suggest we do nothing at present. I will keep an eye on Rosita and I will not be drinking or eating anything she passes me. I suspect you are right and I have been drugged. I cannot explain it any other way."

"I am not confident, Felix. It seems that Rosita has been deceiving us all for a long time. You and Carmine must both be careful. I don't believe there is anything that the doctor can do to solve all the problems that my men have uncovered and what you found out through Juliette."

Chapter 79

Caesar met Doctor Blake and drove him to the Villa. Along the way, they made small talk. It was obvious to Caesar that no amount of probing would get the doctor to discuss why he needed to make the trip.

At the Villa, Felix was waiting to greet the doctor. He introduced him to Carmine and suggested the doctor take some time to freshen up after the long trip.

Doctor Blake joined Carmine, Caesar, and Felix on the garden patio. He looked unsure of having others present while he discussed the purpose of his trip.

"Doctor, it is all right. Anything you have to say to me can be openly discussed in front of my mother and Caesar."

"Since the operation, I have been researching Rosita's actions and trying to determine whether the operation caused this pattern of behavior."

"Stop there, doctor. We have undertaken some checking of Rosita's background and it seems there have been problems for years. Some of the findings are very disturbing."

Felix provided a lengthy description of the information he had gathered. Carmine was in shock as she had never been told of the investigation. When he was complete the doctor smiled.

"Well, what I have to propose may address some of those issues. After consulting with the scientists at MIT, I was placed in contact with a research group in England. Their work is fascinating. I am sure you are all aware of 'magic mushrooms' that are a favorite of some who use drugs for recreation. There has been research done into a hallucinogenic chemical found in 'magic mushrooms' and the findings are astounding. The chemical is called psilocybin and has properties akin to performing a reset of the brain. The way that the chemical interacts with the brain's neurons is complex and I will save you the need to understand the mechanics. The chemical can create a psychedelic effect similar to serotonin. The effects will be to impact the feelings of happiness and love. This medicine is being researched to intervene and reduce human suffering due to neuropsychiatric disorders. I believe that Rosita suffers from these disorders. The use of this medicine has the effect of resetting the mind. I have spoken in detail with the research doctors and all agree that with the patient's permission we should conduct a trial. All the research doctors are convinced."

Felix looked at Carmine and Caesar before speaking.

"Has this been tried before? Is more surgery required?"

"No, no more surgery is needed. It is administered as a medicine. It is, however, necessary to monitor the patient throughout the treatment."

"How long does the treatment take and where will it be performed?"

"It will only take around two weeks and the treatment can be done here."

"I do not believe that Rosita will agree. She is not thinking correctly. I will authorize this treatment. I am responsible for her."

The doctor was thrilled.

"I need to let others know. I can stay and start treatment within a few days. I will need to receive medicines from New York. I will also need to meet with local physicians at the hospital here before proceeding. Can you arrange that?"

"Yes, we have a very good relationship with the hospital. I will arrange a meeting in the morning. I suggest we have Rosita join us now. I will explain that you will be performing some followup work that will help her grow stronger."

Felix left and within minutes, returned with Rosita. She was not pleased to see Doctor Blake.

"Hello, Rosita. I have come here with some good news. I have explained to Felix that there is a new treatment that will help you to recover much faster. It is a simple process. There is no surgery involved. It is an oral treatment but it must be monitored closely. Felix has agreed that we could start the procedure here if you wish."

"What will it do to me?"

"You will enjoy a calm feeling and not be anxious. The medicine can cause you to feel happy and relaxed."

"If that is all then I agree that I should receive the treatment. It will help me in speaking to my people. They are enraptured with me since the election. If I am more relaxed I will be able to understand their problems and assist them more."

Felix and Caesar exchanged looks. Felix's plan for Rosita was very different.

"Good. I will need to first consult with the doctors at the local hospital before we can proceed. I will need their support in case of any unforeseen issues arising. I will contact New York to arrange shipment of the medicines."

Felix and Caesar sat and spoke with the doctor. Rosita left with Carmine to walk in the gardens.

"Doctor, how quickly will the effects of the treatment be evident?"

"Felix, there will be no reaction after the first treatment. By the third treatment, you will see a tremendous difference in her personality. She will be placid and less focused."

"I hope that is the case as we have some news she will find devastating. I assume that we will be able to give her this news?"

"I cannot predict how she will react. If the medication works correctly and her mind is 'reset', then yes, she should be able to accept anything you need to discuss with her. I will get an indication of her mental state and advise you when it would be appropriate. I suggest you do nothing to trigger her temper at this time if you can avoid it. There is something I would like to talk to you about.

Rosita seems to possess some type of deep spirit within her. At the hospital, she was able to function and the heavy sedations we gave her were ineffective. In the past, we have seen these reactions. It seems the mind can counter the sedatives. We do not see this reaction very often. I have only seen it twice in my fifteen years as a doctor."

"Thank you, doctor. We will wait to hear from you, but please make your plans. I will contact the hospital tomorrow and arrange for you to meet the senior doctors there. I am sure you will be well received and get the assistance you need. Goodbye."

Chapter 80

Treatments were performed at the hospital. Several neurological doctors observed and recorded information. Rosita responded well. She was able to remain at the Villa during the treatments.

Felix, Carmine, and Caesar were shocked at the transformation. Rosita was calm and charming. The staff was no longer afraid to approach her.

Caesar had watched the changes and remained skeptical. He did not trust Rosita, especially after receiving the reports from his men of their findings in Nos Grande.

"Felix, do not be swayed by her. She is a bad person. How do you know that the treatment will not wear off over a while? You will be back in the same situation. If the information I have about her past leaks out, you and your political career are finished. I suspect your family and business will also suffer. You must do what is right. Rosita must go."

Felix nodded his agreement.

He was feeling energetic and his old self, now that he was no longer under the influence of the drugs that Rosita had been surreptitiously giving to him. He threw himself into matters of governing the country.

Weeks passed before he received the call from Doctor Blake. He advised Felix that all tests showed that Rosita had reached a level where no further improvement was possible and assured Felix that it would be possible to discuss difficult things without the previous mental instability flaring.

The next day, Felix asked Carmine to sit in on a meeting with him Caesar, and Rosita. He warned Carmine it would not be an easy meeting. Carmine knew what would be discussed but reluctantly agreed to attend.

Felix called Rosita and the others to join him in the salon. He asked all the staff to leave for the rest of the day. Caesar was first to arrive, then Carmine.

The chairs were arranged in a circular pattern. Felix had left the chair nearest the door for Rosita.

Rosita arrived dressed casually and confused.

"What is so important that we are meeting like this?"

"Rosita, this is not going to be an easy meeting. Many things have surfaced about you and your past in Nos Grande. I had Caesar send his best men there to check out what I had been told. I needed to know the truth. What I have found out is horrible. I want to say first, that I will not be marrying you."

Before he could continue, Rosita was screaming.

"That fucking Juliette set this up, didn't she?"

"No, Rosita. Many spoke of the evil deeds you have performed. I was hurt and shocked to learn that your father was still alive and you had seen him. You knew he was a prisoner of the men who run the mine. He was forced into labor. Your neighbor in Nos Grande, Fernando followed you one morning after you had lied to him about the farming tools you had taken on the trip back there with him. He saw you leave with the old man from the cantina. He has never been found. He saw you change your clothes. You should know that local fishermen have found tools and the dress you were wearing when you entered the forest with him that morning. We have sworn statements from many. I also found out of your ongoing affair with Frederico Pelicanos. There is much more."

Rosita launched herself at Felix.

". We almost had all the power to own this country. How could you?"

Before she could reach Felix, Caesar used his best rugby tackle and brought her crashing to the floor.

Felix looked at her in disdain

"I will give you one hour to go to your room and pack and be out of here. I never want to hear from you again. You will be accompanied by two of the security staff. There are a woman and a male officer. They will check everything you try to take. Don't give them a reason to have you arrested."

Rosita was dragged to her feet and stood with a smoldering look on her face.

"Just tell me Felix, who could ever be a better wife for you. Our marriage would have been great."

"Rosita, the truth is that I never intended to marry you. My lifelong partner has been with me for years."

Carmine was confused.

"Felix, you have never told me this. Do I know this person?"

"Oh yes, mother. He is here now. My lover is Caesar. We will marry soon.

It was too much for Carmine. She fainted and slumped down in the chair. Rosita stood looking at Felix with her mouth open.

"But what about all those times. The trip to Australia. All the times we made love?"

"You were a pleasant distraction and covered up my true intentions. Now, leave."

Caesar grinned and roughly pulled her by the arm from the room to the waiting security offices.

"I will kill you, Caesar. You won't win."

Chapter 81

Rosita's life back in the barrio was difficult. Many who had known her, now shunned her. She was not welcomed at the stores. The women of the barrio gossiped about her and Frederico Pelicanos.

Her life became impossible to live in the barrio. Eventually, she pleaded with Frederico to move them out to the countryside or another barrio. Frederico refused to move too far from the barrio. He had his crime ring firmly established and Rosita was second to his interests. Every time that Rosita would cry and complain about her life, he would beat her. Each time she felt the evil spirit that lived within her rise. She knew that one day he would go too far and the evil would overtake.

Her life was dismal. She reflected on the nastiness of her past, but she had no real regrets.

She had never fully recovered her strength after the operations. Months of pregnancy had tired her. She thought back to the days when she had accompanied Felix to political rallies and of the overseas trips she had made. She drifted off into a dream of the past.

Rosita was woken by the piercing cry of her newborn baby. Slowly, she raised herself from the chair and walked to the bedroom that she had decorated for the baby. The room was darkened and Rosita crossed to the window and raised the brown roller blind. Sunlight streamed into the room. She looked over to the crib. The baby was kicking and screaming. She wondered what was wrong. The baby seemed restless and aggravated.

Carefully, Rosita reached into the crib and lifted the baby. The moment her hand made contact she calmed. The screaming and kicking stopped. She took the baby and carried her out onto the shady porch. She sat in the rocking chair and shielded her from the light wind that was blowing up from the river. The temperature was pleasant and Rosita felt content to sit with her there and take in the late afternoon sun. She expected the child's father, Frederico, to arrive in the next hour. He would be full of tales of the events she missed so much now.

As they sat and she rocked the chair, the baby grunted a deep and troubling sound. She quickly turned the child toward her, concerned she was suffering some problem breathing. She looked at her angelic face and was shocked as it stared back at her in a menacing manner.

It was then that Rosita realized that her demon was still with her, but no longer in her body. Her problems were not over.

The baby smiled at her. It was the smile of an old person and the traces of evil were etched on her face.

Rosita wondered if she should kill the child, no matter how hard that would be. She did not want a reoccurrence of the upheaval and problems that she had created.

She made her decision and was going back into the house when the car carrying Frederico turned into the driveway. Her business remained unfinished.

______________________________FIN______________________________

www.ingramcontent.com/pod-product-compliance
Lightning Source LLC
Chambersburg PA
CBHW032134110726
47902CB00003B/582